Binge-worthy reads keep the world turning... one page at a time...

In this omnibus of steamy shifter romances, wild desires are unleashed as the inhabitants of small-town Gray Vale learn valuable life lessons and find their fated mates!

When these alphas fall in love, they'll do whatever it takes to protect their mates from any dangers on the horizon...

GRAY VALE PACK

OMNIBUS

BOOKS 1-3

EVIE RILEY

Gray Vale Pack Omnibus

Books 1-3

Copyright © 2021-2023

Evie Riley

Second Edition

ISBN: 978-1-77357-702-9

Naughty Nights Press LLC

Cover Art By Willsin Rowe

HIS FATED MATE

GRAY VALE PACK

BOOK ONE

EVIE RILEY

The truth of the heart is written in the stars...

Conall Blair is the son of Gray Vale's Alpha, but he'd rather be a thorn in the side of the neighboring Stoke Ridge pack. For him, peace and harmony are little better than death—in all aspects of life, even relationships.

Zoltan Valenta, heir of Stoke Ridge, is a man of duty who's suddenly having doubts. Though his father has arranged his marriage to Fiona Blair, Zoltan can't shake his fascination with her twin brother, Conall.

When the two men find themselves unwittingly pushed together, there's no denying the heat between them. Against all rules, expectations and commitments, can they really just yield to the hand fate deals them?

His Fated Mate
Gray Vale Pack
Book One

Copyright © 2021 Evie Riley
ISBN: 978-1-77357-341-0
978-1-77357-340-3

Naughty Nights Press LLC
Cover Art By Willsin Rowe

CHAPTER ONE

CONALL

THE FOREST AROUND us radiated life. I drank it in through nose and ears, but there was so more to it than that. My wolf growled inside me, sensing prey.

The feeling was so strong that even my human side itched for action. Any excuse to shift would be fine by me. Patrolling this disputed region between our lands and Stoke Ridge only tossed me a little excitement once in a while, but today felt rich with potential.

Glen came up beside me. The prickling of energy coming off him only got me even more keyed up.

"Deer," I murmured.

"Duh," Glen replied. "You're not the only one with a fuckin' nose, Connie."

I reached out and slapped the back of his head without even looking. "What've I told you about calling me that?"

Glen let out a low growl. "Used to let me."

"That was when I was also fucking you. You see the connection there, dude?"

Immediately, our attention flew across to the clearing, and the big buck that crept into sight.

Glen slid his rifle down off his shoulder, but I stopped him.

"Uh-uh. We do it like nature intended."

"Ugh, seriously? That's one thing I definitely don't miss about you."

I stripped off in seconds, fending away Glen's lustful glare as I did. We'd had our chance, and it didn't work out. If he couldn't get over it then he was no good as a member of my patrol.

He kept his voice low and deep. "Why do you even come out with us lowly shit-kickers, anyway, Conall? You have options guys like me could never even dream of."

"You call going to fancy-pants shindigs and week-long meetings *options*? That's not me, bro. Besides, in three days, my sister is taking the fall for all of us."

That was the biggest downside to being what amounted to pack royalty. Marriages and matings that were all about strategy. Thankfully, that shit didn't apply to me. Only hetero pairings were recognized, still.

Because of all that, my twin, Fiona, was gonna be all hitched up to the pristine, primped and puckered heir of the Stoke Ridge Pack, Zoltan Valenta. And all for the lamest of reasons.

Peace.

More like death, as I saw it. If we couldn't get into harmless little pissing contests with our snobbish neighbors, then what the hell was the good of being wolves? Life is conflict, and vice versa.

I glanced across at Glen. "You're still dressed."

"C'mon, Con. You know how your father is."

Yeah, I knew. He treated shifting like

it was a religious ceremony. Just like the ancient ones had. Tradition was everything in wolf packs.

"Dude, if my father's fancy notions mattered to me, I wouldn't be out here with you lowly shit-kickers, now. Would I? I'd be lying back on a fucking velvet sofa with servant boys feeding me grapes."

Glen made a quiet scoffing sound and worked his clothes off. "Let's just fucking get this done, so I don't have to hear any more shit."

I shook my head with a wry smile. "Do you even shift, bro?"

Before he'd finished rolling his eyes, I opened myself up to the wolf, letting it ignite within me. Shifting was like sex. No matter how many times I did it, I always wanted more.

My body jolted, my muscles and bones danced around each other, and then it was done. I didn't even wait for Glen. The scent of that buck was too fucking delicious.

I crept forward, keeping low. The buck was spooked already. It was a buzz in the air that brought his scent with it. Twenty feet. Fifteen. His big body quivered and he cast his head around. No need to run this guy down. He was so close I could almost taste him.

As I tensed to spring at my prey, a rifle shot rang out. The assault of noise had me flinching away, and a second later the buck dropped dead.

I'd been so close. Glen was gonna pay for that. Robbing my wolf of his succor. In my rage, I shifted back, ready to tear my cohort a new one.

Before I could turn around, three men in Stoke Ridge uniforms moved into the clearing from the far side. One of them carrying a rifle, all of them pleased with themselves. Obviously new recruits, or they'd be treading a lot more carefully.

I marched forward, more than ready to turn my anger on them. I sensed, rather than saw, Glen moving into position behind me.

"Hey! You fuckin' Stoke Ridge assholes."

All three of the other side's patrolmen tensed as we moved closer. "Back down, Gray Vale. It's our trophy."

"Not when you bag it on our land."

Rifle dude sneered at me. "Well, when

we bag one on your land, pal, we'll be sure to let you know. But this here is Stoke Ridge land."

I took a cleansing breath. As much as I'd been looking forward to taking down that buck, that would have been little more than an appetizer. This here was main course and dessert, all rolled into one. There was nothing I liked quite so much as tussling with these hoity-toity Ridgers.

"Is that right?"

"You know it is, grunt. Now, run off back to your kennels." He flicked his eyes down for a split second and then back up. "And tuck that tail of yours between your legs."

I gave the guy a flash of teeth. "Or maybe you want that... *tail*... right between *your* legs, Ridgy. I see how you look at me."

For me, that was just a throwaway comment. But for a Ridgy, it was the ultimate slur. Stoke Ridge society was stuck in the fucking nineteenth century when it came to sexuality.

Okay, a taunt like that one was low-hanging fruit, but all I wanted was for them to make the first move. The fact it worked so well every single time only meant I'd keep using it again and again.

Rifle dude snarled and handed his weapon to his right hand man. I went into a crouch, arms out, waiting.

The guy burst forward, charging straight for me. Like a fucking amateur. I let him slam into me, chest to chest, before spinning on the spot and throwing him halfway across the clearing. He landed in a sprawling mess of limbs.

"Now, you guys stand down," I said, letting all my menace and breeding come bubbling out in my voice. It did no good, though. These guys were young, dumb and full of... themselves.

The rifle guy sprang up to a squat, baring his teeth, which were growing longer.

I raised one eyebrow. "You gonna take this down to wolf level, kid?" That was the other thing with Stoke Ridge. They were even more stuffy about shifting than my father was. "'Cause I spend half my life there. Do you?"

That gentle little reminder seemed to do the trick, and he came back up onto his feet. When he approached me this time, he showed a ton more caution. Still not enough, though.

He threw a wild punch that couldn't have been more telegraphed. It was like a movie punch. He spent so much time pulling his arm back I could have made a coffee while I waited for him to throw it.

I pulled my head back and let his fist fly past, then wrapped my hands around the back of his head and neck, throwing him into the scrub and dirt face first.

No other man had even moved yet. Glen leaned back on a tree, stifling a yawn. The Stoke Ridge guys looked wide eyed and shell shocked. I already knew they were green, but I wouldn't mind betting this was their first ever patrol. That'd explain why they were so cavalier about taking down the buck on disputed lands.

As the main Ridgy came back up onto his feet, I held my hands up for calm. "Give it up, dude. Take your lumps and head back home."

"I'll take my lumps. And my trophy."

"No, you'll be leaving the buck." I crossed my arms and narrowed my eyes. "Understood?"

I could see a thousand different words bubbling up in his head. Some of them were punching so hard at his pride he almost said them.

"All right," he ground out. "But you understand *this*... I'm not backing down."

"No? It kinda looks like you are."

"Well, unlike you peasants, we here in Stoke Ridge value tradition. So, I'm allowing this to pass, for the sake of the upcoming wedding." He took his rifle back from his cohort and curled his lip. "You... do know about the wedding, right?"

"Of course he does," Glen interrupted. "He's—"

"I'm not interested in it. Perky prince Zoltan is lucky we're letting him into our pack at all."

The other guy tensed all over. I wasn't even sure he realized he'd tightened his grip on the weapon. "Let's be clear, you ass. It's your woman who's being elevated here. You and your caretaker Alpha should get on your knees and thank—"

That was as far as he got before my fist hit the side of his face. As much as I loved being wolf, sometimes hands worked better than paws.

The guy dropped like a sack of dirt, and I landed on him just as heavily. My weight on his chest, my hand on his throat.

His two patrolmen froze, their fear filling my nostrils. I'm sure they could sense the battle experience and silent aggression radiating off me, and made the sensible decision to stand down.

"Now it's your turn to listen, sunshine," I growled. "Yeah, Patrick Blair is only a second generation Alpha. If you think that weakens our pack in any way, you're welcome to test your claims."

"Get the hell off me. And for God's sake, cover yourself up."

"You Ridgies are so damn uptight. Never met a bunch of shifters so fuckin' scared of being naked." I rolled my hips just a little. "Or maybe you're scared of how much you're enjoying the view."

"Get off."

As much as I enjoyed roughing up Ridgies, this little scene had passed its sell-by date. There was nothing to be gained anymore. I stood, and offered the guy my hand. He slapped it away and got to his feet at his own speed.

"Lord Valenta will hear of this."

"Lord? You guys are so into this hierarchy shit it's... well, it's fucking embarrassing."

"Whether you accept it or not, every pack is a hierarchy, grunt. And the wrath of your Alpha will come down on you for this."

"It won't be the first time."

They turned and headed back into their territory with a last, narrow-eyed glare at the buck they'd taken down.

As they disappeared into the brush, another of my patrol team came running up from behind.

"Alec," I said. "What's up?"

"Better get dressed, dude. I'm taking your duties from here on. Daddy wants a word with you."

Glen chuckled without any real humor. "Wrath of the Alpha, indeed. News travels fast."

CHAPTER TWO

ZOLTAN

MY FATHER STRUTTED around the grand hall, chest swollen and stride long. Barking orders to staff and craftsmen, deciding on the menu, the decorations, the... I don't know. The ideal temperature for vows to be taken, or something.

It seemed he dedicated his every waking moment to nothing less than my upcoming wedding. He was worse than the most caricatured bridezilla.

"Ah, son," he blustered. "I only wish your mother was still with us. She'd be so proud."

I'd only been four when she drowned, taking my unborn brother with her. Over twenty years had passed, and still the pain sliced me as though it was new.

Father, on the other hand, had simply rolled on with life. That's what generations of Alphas had always done.

I'd watched in disappointed awe, the way he kept on keeping on, barging on with life as though the loss of half one's family was nothing more than a hiccup. But it had planted deep doubts in my own heart.

If he coped so well with their loss, then would it hurt him any deeper were I to die? Over the years, I let that thought drive a deeper and wider wedge between us.

Now here we were, at another tipping point. Three days. That was all I had left before I'd be absorbed by the great machine. In marrying this Fiona Blair, I would cease to exist, in a sense. Forgo my identity in order to be one more puzzle piece in the vast history of the Stoke Ridge pack, and the two dozen generations of Valenta ancestors who'd led before me. Nothing more than the latest portrait in the great hall.

Tradition. That's what mattered. I knew, because for as long as I could remember, father made sure to hammer that home with me.

In all honesty, I couldn't tell if I agreed with him or not. In the jumble of teachings, dogma and lectures that had been drilled into my head all my life, finding an independent thought—a part of myself that was truly mine—was near impossible.

For a thousand years, Valenta men— and *only* men—had presided over this pack. Back in Europe to begin with, and for over two hundred years here in Stoke Ridge. Time moved on, rendering this place little more than an anachronism, yet I truly had no idea how to change things, or what they should change to.

More telling, I had even less idea what was in my own heart. All I knew was what I *didn't* want. Deep down, I didn't want to disappoint my father. Even deeper down, I did *not* want to marry this woman. Or *any* woman. I couldn't yet discern the reason. I simply had no interest in the idea.

Being the Alpha of a wolf pack was, to

me, the antithesis of freedom. We were more bound by customs, rules and *thou-shalt-nots* than any of our pack members. Even those in the military.

The Blairs were new to leadership, but I'd encountered the Alpha many times over the years. His presence was as commanding as my father's, yet in a whole different way.

Father balanced precariously at the top of an ancient tree. He was born to be an Alpha, but had to grow into the role.

Patrick Blair, on the other hand, filled rooms with just his charisma. His face and body bore the kinds of scars my father let others to take in his stead.

I'm sure Blair's daughter would be a formidable and honorable woman, but I'd never met my bride-to-be. As was customary, it was the first born son who'd accompanied Patrick Blair to any joint functions.

Though technically, I'd never met Conall Blair, either. Nor had I even seen him in close to ten years. He'd stopped attending functions in his mid-teens, which had robbed all the light from the experiences from then on. He'd been the one part of the whole rigmarole I'd enjoyed.

With his midnight black hair and his sharp, blue eyes, he'd had me mesmerized from the first instant I'd seen him. It took all my will power to keep from staring at him every time we were sat across from each other.

He'd radiated such intensity that I'd never been game to initiate a conversation. How could I, the latest in an immeasurable line of sheltered nobles, measure up to men like these? Men of action.

Most of my pack looked down their noses at the Blairs, simply because they were so new to leading. But that boy—man, now—possessed the magnetism and charisma an Alpha needed. Perhaps too *much* of it, if that were possible. I knew I'd have done just about anything he told me to... had he ever spoken to me.

That in and of itself was damn troubling. How was I meant to be the Alpha my pack—and father—expected, if I was so ready to kneel before another man?

The arrival of a messenger brought me back into the here and now.

"Lord Valenta."

"What is it? Can't you see we're in the middle of preparations?"

"There has been another skirmish in the disputed lands, lord. By the description, it's the same troublemaker from Gray Vale as always. Shall we send men to exact reparations?"

"Of course not. We're days from reaching a resolution. I'll deal with it."

"My lord."

The messenger bowed, and I bit into my tongue to keep from laughing. I understood my father's desire for order and hierarchy, but in truth, he'd turned pack leadership into a parody. As if he'd watched too many movies about King Arthur and thought they were documentaries.

The messenger marched out, and my father went back to strutting around and making plans. Plans that felt like a thick blanket wrapping around me, and suddenly I found breathing difficult.

I slipped away unnoticed, desperate for an escape of some kind. I knew my place, and what was expected of me. Yet, there was an aching inside me that could not be assuaged by duty alone.

I made my way down from the main hall and out into the open air. As I came out to the courtyard, I spotted the messenger and called out to him.

He waited obediently as I approached. "Your name?"

"Rogers, sir."

"Tell me, Rogers. This troublemaker..."

"Yes, sir. They say he's as strong as three men, and as ugly as a bear. And he has... unnatural desires." He said the last part with a sour sneer.

"What kind of desires?"

"Sir, they say he—forgive me, sir—he *consorts* only with other men."

I bit down on my tongue. As sinful as the thought of that was, somehow it called my wolf out of his torpor. I'm sure all my beastly half wanted was to bite out the throat of such a wrongdoer. That was the *only* explanation.

"You've encountered him?"

"Thankfully not, sir. He may be just a patrolman, but he has a real hard-on for fucking up our guys." The man gasped as he suddenly remembered who I was. "My deepest apologies for my language, sir."

I waved off his embarrassment. "And this latest encounter? Where was it?"

"In the Bark Gully area, sir."

"Hm. All right then, Rogers. Thank you."

He seemed relieved as I dismissed him without any comment about his harsh words. My father has always been strict on public decency—as defined by his own standards—and no doubt everybody expected me to react the same way.

I simply couldn't shake the image of this troublemaker from my mind. Though I'd never met him, he'd become an obsession for me through reputation alone.

I closed my eyes and let my mind picture him. My breath became short and sharp again, only this time it was from exhilaration. I couldn't have explained it if I'd been asked to. He was little more than a brigand, yet he seemed to represent all that I'd never experienced. And all that I wondered about.

That was a man who was truly free. No rules, no quarter, no fucks given. Just the thought of him excited me in ways my unseen fiancée never had.

Of course, that was a whole other problem. While there were no laws in place, my pack had always frowned upon anything other than strict one man, one woman partnerships. Married, de facto, whatever.

And the fact was, no woman had ever excited me like this anonymous scoundrel did. If I was to be trapped in a marriage for the rest of my life, I vowed I wouldn't go down without a fight.

I needed to understand what it meant to be truly free before I allowed myself to be locked in to the prison of leadership. My entire pack had sticks up their butts all the damn time. Even our lowest-ranked military guys were all about the rules and propriety.

What little I knew of Gray Vale led me to believe they were essentially the same.

All except one man. I needed to meet him before I gave up everything that was truly me. And I needed to do it now, before common sense intervened.

CHAPTER THREE

CONALL

THE MEETING WITH my father went pretty much as I'd expected. He hadn't heard about our little squabble with the Ridgies when he summoned me, so the first half was all about how I had to step up and represent at an official level.

Then, he hit me with the news that I'd be acting as best man for Fiona's husband-to-be.

"What the fuck? He doesn't have any brothers or friends?"

"No brothers. No friends of what Anton Valenta calls the *right status.*"

Father leaned back in his chair. "Besides, I know you, son. This is pretty much the only way I can be sure you'll even attend."

The phone rang just at that moment, and father took the call immediately, while I seethed quietly at his crafty maneuvering.

Glen was right, as it turned out. News really did travel fast. The call was from Anton Valenta, and my father's expression left no doubt the discussion was all about my hijinks out on patrol.

Father made all the usual assurances, and then ended the call, only to give me his standard lecture about winning meaning nothing when the fight was pointless. That it wasn't a requirement of leadership to beat your chest. It was the same speech he always hit me with.

"You could learn a thing or two from your sister, Con."

There was no doubt in my mind he was right about that. Fiona was six minutes younger than I was, but she was all calm, measured control. Though I knew I had to get my shit together, for the sake of the pack, I couldn't escape the truth; that my entire life was still driven by my balls, all day and night.

Still, it felt as if father was ashamed of everything that had brought us to power. With the ending of the previous Alpha's bloodline, the traditional challenge took place, and my grandfather won out. Through strength, resilience, and sheer bloody-minded will. The mark of an Alpha, in my opinion.

Patrick Blair clearly thought that was an idea whose time had passed. I swear, every day, he wanted to be more like those fucking Ridgies, and the way they geek out over rigmarole and ceremony.

Finally, I managed to work my way out of the meeting, after giving him all the assurances that I'd behave myself, and would attend the wedding. He even went down to the nuts and bolts of having me promise to wear a fucking tux.

I ran into Fiona as I left the main hall. As always, the first thing she did was pull me into a hug.

"I heard you've been defending our honor, big brother."

"Is that what I was doing? Dad says I'm making life difficult for everyone."

"Yeah, well, that *is* kind of your special skill. You even used to elbow me when we were in the womb."

"You were putting your feet on *my* side. I'd clearly drawn a line across the middle."

"Doofus." She eased out of my arms. "But have you ever thought about... oh, I don't know. Acting your age? Playing the part of Alpha's understudy?"

"Ugh. That would require a whole set of special skills I don't even want to think about."

"You mean like *my* kind?"

"I don't know. You claim you can sense mate bonds. Sounds kinda dubious to me."

"That's *one* of my skills. There's a range of others. Importantly, none of them involve poking at the bruises of another pack."

"What fun is there in that?"

She gave me a light punch my shoulder. "So, what's the damage, Con? Bread and water for two weeks?"

"I wish. That I could handle. No, he's taken me off patrol. Says I can't be trusted. You believe that?"

"You want the truth?"

"Of course not."

"Then, uh... let's see. Oh, holy fuck, bro! That's so crazy—"

"Knock it off, asshole."

"You won't be able to call me that when I'm a queen, buddy boy."

I gave her hair a brotherly yank. "Still can't believe you're going through with it. I could never do that."

"Yes, well, you know my thoughts about the different ways men and women make sacrifices for their packs."

I put my hands up in mock surrender. "Please, no more."

"Jerk. But really, I guess I don't mind. All in all, things could be worse. I mean, I've never met him, but I've heard he's crazy good-looking, and a calm and considerate man."

"You got the first part right. Can't really say about the second. But how do *you* know all this?"

"I have a few contacts over there."

"Stoke Ridge?"

"Of course. You throw fists, I throw parties. There's more than one way to be enemies with people, y'know."

Once again, my sister both surprised and inspired me.

We walked in silence for a few seconds, before she spoke again. "Look, the guys tell me you've been targeting the Ridgies pretty hard the last couple months. What's your problem with them?"

I made a short scoffing sound, hoping that would speak volumes. Of course, it didn't work with Fi. It never had.

"Spill it, bro."

I sighed once for show, then put my arm over Fi's shoulders. "It's a lot of things. But mostly, it boils down to their attitude. They have the high ground and all the game. We have the fertile valley and all the crops. They treat us like peasants."

"It works out in the end. We do a lot of trade with them."

"We're fucking *wolves*, Fi. *Hunters*. We take, we don't trade."

"God, for someone who claims to hate tradition..."

Glen came running up to us before she could finish. "Con, you better come with me."

"Now what?"

"Something to show you."

"I've seen it, bud. It's very nice, but

it's not for me anymore."

"Ha ha. C'mon, man."

"Fine." I kissed Fi's forehead. "I'm gonna miss the fuck outta you when you become a Stoke Ridge geek, y'know."

"Oh, but I'll have no problem looking down on you, bro. All the other peasants, too, but *especially* you." She flashed me a wink and fled before I could get another word in.

"Cheeky little shit," I murmured. Fi was always the one who could make me smile, no matter what. I turned my attention back to Glen. "So, what is it that's so important?"

"Just come with. It's in your apartment."

"About time you gave me back my key, bro."

"Yeah, yeah. What, you worried I'll bust in on you and whoever you've replaced me with?"

That was exactly my worry, but I wasn't going to say it to Glen. The guy was basically a straight shooter, so to speak, but I'd seen his jealous side when we were lovers, and it wasn't anything I had time for.

We got to my door and he knocked

four times. I was about to point out that it was my place so I was fine to just go in, when an identical knock sounded from the inside.

"What the fuck, dude?"

"It's Alec."

I pulled out my key and unlocked the apartment. These two seemed to think they were secret agents all of a sudden.

When I pushed the door open, Alec stood in the entrance. He had his hands up, making a calm down motion. "Now, take it easy, Con."

"What the hell are you two up to?"

"Come on through."

"Giving me the grand tour? Can I just remind you I fucking live here? I know my way…"

My voice faded to nothing when I entered the living room and finally saw what these two knuckleheads had done. Bound to one of the kitchen chairs, with one of my old ties as a gag, was a Stoke Ridge man.

I didn't need the nose or the senses of a wolf to tell that, either. It was all over him. The scents of the forest, and expensive soap, and good, rich living. Same as it was on every Ridgie, except it was much stronger on this one.

Because this one was Zoltan Valenta.

I turned to Glen first. "What the fuck is this, you idiots?"

"We found him creeping around in Bark Gully."

"Creeping?"

"Yep. Figured he was some kind of spy, probably come to sabotage the wedding."

I almost laughed at the idea of that. Alec and Glen obviously had no idea who they'd grabbed. Why would they? Neither of them had ever been to an official function in their lives.

"You guys realize I'm gonna get the blame for this. Don't you?"

"Blame?" Glen said. "Don't you mean *credit*? This'll get you back in the good books with your father."

"Wait... you haven't told anybody about this, have you?"

"Just a couple of the guys. We made sure to say it was all your idea. Y'know, so your dad—"

"Sure, whatever. Now listen, you two. Not a word about this to anyone else, okay?"

"Of course, Con."

"All right. We're done here, guys. Leave us."

"But we—"

"I said leave." It was a struggle to keep my voice—and my wolf—under control. It wasn't just my anger at what my guys had done here. It was also that heady mix of scents coming from Valenta.

The guy was nothing like any man I'd ever been with. I had a type—or so I thought. Rough trade. Poor but hungry. Rugged, frayed around the edges, big enough to push back against me if I wanted them to.

Zoltan was the absolute opposite. Smooth and beautiful, his scent somehow both familiar and exotic at the same time. Even seated and bound, he had that regal bearing I remembered from years ago.

He was everything I believed I despised about pack leaders... and yet my heart was punching at me, and my belly was squirming. And my cock... holy fuck, my cock was as hard as hell.

Back when father still had me attending official functions, I'd seen this man—youth, back then—from across the room, or across the table, dozens of times. I hadn't truly understood my own sexuality at the time, but he was the only part of those gatherings that I could remember with any clarity.

For all I knew, it was the sheer irresistible beauty of Zoltan Valenta that had confirmed my orientation for me.

I hadn't seen him in years, and I'd never been quite so close to him before. Now here he was, with his crisp sandy hair and his pale, unmarked skin, and I had to admit he'd always inspired feelings in me. And the feeling he mostly inspired was the desire to mess him the fuck up.

The guy had probably never done a lick of work in his life. Right here and now, as I stood over him, I suddenly had ideas for all kinds of work he could do for me.

And licking would definitely be a part of it.

CHAPTER FOUR

ZOLTAN

WHEN THOSE TWO oafs grabbed me in the forest, I almost capitulated and told them who I am. Whether they would have believed me, I'm unsure, but even if they did, it would have been almost impossible to explain why I'd been there.

Fate works in strange ways, though. All I'd wanted was to see, in person, the man who'd been terrorizing my troops, and now here he was. And of all people, it turned out to be the son of Patrick Blair.

He fit the description to a T. I had no

doubt now that he was the troublemaker.

My senses told me he recognized me, too, so I'd felt sure that the moment he sent his underlings away, he'd release me. Still, he showed no sign of doing so. Just towered over me, with his thick arms crossed, and his steely eyes slicing through me. He hadn't even taken this damn gag off, yet.

He was everything I'd heard and imagined, and so much more. All except the part about being ugly as a bear. I couldn't imagine a single way the man could be any more attractive.

The years had been kind to Conall Blair; though perhaps it was a cruel type of kindness.

The handsome and intense young man had grown taller, broader, and more powerful. With his shoulder length hair as black as night, and the range of scars on his arms, and smaller marks on his face, he looked more like a pirate than the son of the Alpha.

Finally, he reached over and worked the tie out of my mouth and off over my head. Every move he made was definite. Abrupt, yet smooth, like flames dancing.

"You're early," he said.

"Excuse me?"

"Wedding's not for a couple days, yet. Are you that eager to get your paws on my sister?"

In the heat of Conall's aura I'd almost forgotten everything else in the world. I would say especially his sister, but it's impossible to forget someone you've never even seen.

He came around behind me and released the ropes securing my wrists. Then, he prowled back to the front of me. Even if I hadn't already known he was wolf, his fluid, predatory motion would have tipped me off.

When he knelt before me to untie my ankles, I barely contained my gasp of surprise. And it was at that moment I could finally admit to myself exactly why I had no interest in marrying this man's sister.

I'd never wanted anybody like I wanted Conall Blair. As frowned upon as it was in my pack, I couldn't deny the sweet tension in my core.

The howling of my wolf.

The blistering hardness of my cock.

"Oh, the wedding. No, that's not...

um..."

Why was it so damn hard to think, or speak? I was the next in line to lead my pack. I'd been groomed from birth to handle... *situations*.

Yet, my heart beat against my ribs so hard I thought it might burst through.

The flash in Conall's eyes told me he sensed it, too, and my belly tightened in fear. I knew little of the ins and outs of Gray Vale, or their feelings about... *non-standard desires*, shall we say.

As he released the final knot, he showed concern on his gorgeous face for the first time. "You *are* planning to go ahead with the wedding?"

"I'm... confused, to be honest. I know what's riding on it, and I don't want to disappoint my father, or yours."

"Believe me, buddy, Fiona's the one you don't want to disappoint. However shit-scared you are of your father, you should be doubly scared of my sister."

"Because that really makes me keen to go ahead with it."

A low growl sounded in Conall's throat, and my hackles stood up instinctively. Valenta men so rarely shifted. We had people to do that for us.

But this man's intensity had my wolf pacing within me. Searching for a reason to come out.

Conall clearly sensed that turmoil instantly, as he gripped my shirt and hauled me up off the chair. Off my feet.

"You watch what you say about my sister, asshole."

Oh, holy hell. I was close to drowning in sensations. Not once in my life had I been threatened with anything more than sanctions, or the temporary denial of liberties. And only ever by my father.

No man or woman in Stoke Ridge would ever dare to treat me this way. Conall's aura grew bitter with threat and anger, and though I knew he could harm me as easily as breaking a twig, that couldn't divert the heady wash of desires pouring through me.

Still, that didn't mean I could simply push aside a lifetime of command training.

"It's not about your sister, Blair. Put me down."

"I'll fucking *knock* you down if you so much as breathe half a word against Fiona."

He dropped me to my feet, but kept a

hold of my shirt. He never once turned the cold heat of his gaze away from me, though the hard ridge of his brow gradually softened.

His frown grew deeper again the moment he drew in a long breath. No doubt my own scents were telling him exactly what was running through my head.

"Wait," he said, his voice suddenly lower, and much darker. "You're telling me..."

I slid my hands up onto his wrists. "I'm saying I don't have any problem with your sister. At least, apart from the whole deal wherein she is, in fact, a woman."

"And you're... not into women?"

I tightened my grip, but struggled to find my voice. To say it out loud was such a big deal for a Stoke Ridge man. "I've never done anything. Never truly understood it until right now. But... as it turns out, no. I'm not."

"You're fucking kidding me." He tightened his mouth, and I couldn't help fearing I'd completely misjudged the situation, and the man.

Maybe Gray Vale was just as old-fashioned as my own pack. I probably shouldn't have relied simply on hearsay regarding Conall's sexuality. Especially hearsay from the men he bested in every fracas between the packs.

"You have a problem with that kind of thing, Blair?"

"With your sexuality? Not a single one." He shoved me back down into the chair, and turned on the spot, walking across the room shaking his head. "What I do have a problem with is you letting things get so far with this marriage."

"I never said I wanted it. But the needs of our packs dictate I still go ahead—"

He whirled and jabbed his finger toward me like he wished it was a spear. "You will do no such thing. My sister is not a toy to be... uh... toyed with."

Conall's eyes lit up, turning almost white with the heat of his twinned emotions. I could feel them as much as I could smell them. Anger weaving itself through arousal. His beast coursing through his blood, and pumping through his breath.

My own pulse quickened in reaction,

my teeth tingling as they fantasized about becoming fangs. I sensed the sweet pain in Conall's mind as the same need pumped through him.

The room filled with the essence of this wild and beautiful man. My skin crackled with electricity, as his desire to shift reached out to my own wolf.

I'd heard fairytales in my childhood about this kind of thing. Wolves who were fated to be paired. But never had anybody said that it could happen between wolves of the same gender.

Was that just the old so-called morals coming through? Or was this, what was happening now between Conall and me... was this something completely new?

CHAPTER FIVE

CONALL

EVERYTHING I KNEW of this man, every way I'd ever experienced him, told me he was wrong for me. The beliefs he'd grown up with, the sheltered way he'd been raised, the sneering superiority that all Ridgies adopted when dealing with us.

Yet, I had to be honest to myself and say I'd never *actually* experienced this man. For a half dozen years, I'd glared across a table at him once every three months. Everything else I supposedly knew had come from second hand news, and my own assumptions.

Even now, as he stood with such lithe grace, and closed the distance between us, he was both everything I expected, and a complete surprise.

How could it be that he was hauling my wolf to the fore with nothing but his presence? He was locked up tight with the stupid pack peacemaking marriage situation that both our fathers still believed in. In other words, he was off limits to me in every fucking way.

Yet, the rich golden glow in his eyes drew me in, and made promises to every part of me. Both sides of me—man and wolf.

"So," Zoltan said, the soft music of his voice doing nothing to soothe my savage beast. If anything, it only made me wilder, and hungrier. "What happens now, big guy?"

"What happens now is that I take you..." I was trying to say I'd take him back home, but my wolf clamped around my throat before I could finish.

"Oh? Rather presumptuous, don't you think? Perhaps we could get dinner first."

There was that teasing little smile again, winding my brain into fuzz. My wolf had the fucking zoomies inside me, and it was all I could do to keep my human side in charge.

Zoltan's heat and scent clouded me, sending my breath into overdrive and short-circuiting my mind.

Finally, he let that delicious smile fade as he frowned with genuine concern. I couldn't imagine how I must look to him. Up close to him, my fists tight, my anger at my own confusion radiating like a physical force.

I thought at first he was scared. He wouldn't be the first man—or wolf—to react that way. But when he pressed his hand to the center of my chest, it was as if he'd hit me with a battering ram.

"Did you feel that?" he said, his voice low and ragged.

I clamped my hand over his and squeezed, searching for a path. A way out of this utter fucking mess. But all that skin to skin contact did was set off flares in my already smoldering head.

"Of course I felt it. I'd have to be dead not to."

Zoltan slid his hand free and moved it higher, not stopping until he had his palm pressed to my cheek. Our faces were mere inches apart, a distance that was slowly but inevitably closing. I'm sure the sweet mix of confusion and hunger I saw in his eyes was reflected in my own.

"So, I guess I have to ask again," he murmured. "What happens now?"

In my whole life, I'd never been lost for words the way I was right then. So, I answered him the only way I could. By grasping his shirt and pulling him to me, taking his mouth in a kiss that seemed to transcend time and space.

I swore there were sparks literally flying from us as he opened for me, as I drove my tongue in to meet his. His soft moans played against my deep grunts, like a stream washing over rough rocks. Filling the gaps between them, slowly wearing them smooth.

I threw my arm around his taut, slender frame, gripping his firm ass and pulling him against me. The hard, raging heat of his cock ground against mine, and again the fireworks lit up inside my mind.

Though we'd only just officially met, and it defied any kind of rational explanation, Zoltan's body promised the kind of delights I'd sought, but never found, within the men of my own pack.

I slid my mouth down to his neck and bit into his flesh, hard enough to bruise him. But not nearly as hard as I wanted to. Wolves are hungry beasts.

Zoltan reached down between us, working at my jeans with an urgency that seemed almost life threatening.

The instant he got them open, a heavy pounding sounded on my apartment door, the noise hitting me like a fist made of cold water.

"Conall. You in there?"

Holy fuck. Of all the people it could have been.

"Uh... yes, father. Just a minute."

"Now, son. We have a shit storm brewing."

No prizes for guessing that particular shit storm involved my boneheaded buddies and my new boner-buddy.

I stepped backward and closed up my jeans again. There was no way I could risk speaking out loud to Zoltan, nor could I let father in to my room. He'd hear me, and no matter how well I hid the heir of Stoke Ridge, my father would scent him.

So, I put my finger to my lips, and hurried through to my closet, changing my shirt as quickly as I could. Whatever I could do to mask the heady aroma of this beautiful man.

"Son, come on."

"I'm here." I made a quick frowny face at Zoltan, who thankfully took the hint and scooted through to my bedroom. I took a half-second's pause as I pictured what I could get up to with him in there, and then slipped out of my apartment and into the line of fire.

"What's happening, father?"

"Can I come in?"

"No! Uh... it's a real mess in there. Fuckin' embarrassing, really. You'd think I'd grow up, huh?"

"It's my greatest hope, son. Then, if we can't go in, you'll walk with me." He marched off down the hallway and I followed along, feeling all of ten years old. "Your future brother-in-law is missing. Anton Valenta is accusing us of foul play."

"That's, uh, a mighty big call. What's his proof?" Besides the man himself being in my apartment, of course.

"Nothing concrete, or we'd already be

at war. But with all your recent antagonism along the border, can you blame them for thinking the worst of us?"

I began to protest my innocence when my father stopped short and silenced me with a big hand on my shoulder.

"Tell me you had nothing to do with Valenta's disappearance, son."

His *disappearance?* That was easy.

"I promise you, father. I had nothing to do with it."

"Good." He nodded as his grin grew predatory. "Then, we have the higher ground."

"We do?"

"Oh, undoubtedly. We're not to blame."

"Wait. Have you asked anybody else?" My hackles rose, just from suddenly learning how my father saw me. That he believed I—and only I—would be reckless enough to interfere with the merging of the packs.

"Oh, you think I should ask Fiona? Has she ever struck you as impetuous?" He let out a quick, booming laugh. "Son, don't get your snout out of joint. You have a well known history. But now, it's his milksop son who's insulted *us* by fleeing."

How dare he insult Zoltan! My wolf growled so hard and deep inside me that the sound formed in my throat. I managed to cover it with a cough. How could I be so attached to the younger Valenta so quickly? To be so protective of his honor?

"Where do we go from here, father?"

"We're still formulating our strategy. But I need you confined to quarters for the time being." He clearly anticipated my reaction, holding up his hand for silence. And like I'd been trained to, I obeyed instantly.

"Son, this is your own doing. It's like the story of the boy who cried wolf, but in reverse. You're the boy who *was* wolf. You've bitten the Stoke Ridge pack too many times for them to allow you even the slightest benefit of the doubt."

I clenched my fists as my teeth tingled. Just because father was right, didn't make the bitter pill of truth any easier to swallow.

Still, being confined to quarters right now wasn't the punishment my father might believe it to be. I wouldn't be in solitary, after all.

CHAPTER SIX

ZOLTAN

I'D BEEN TRAINED in the art of patience all my life. Yet, waiting alone in Conall's apartment was a torture I was ill prepared to handle. To have had that brief taste of pure ecstasy, only to have it torn away just as quickly; to then sit idle and unaware, wondering at my fate... it would test any man.

Of course, this heat I felt for Conall had to be nothing but a naïve infatuation. Something that took root before I was old enough to understand it, and which only grew over the years because in his absence, I'd cultivated an idealized version of him.

Now, it had become a flare. One that would burn too hot and brightly for either of us to handle, only to die out as quickly as it ignited.

That *had* to be the truth.

For the good of both packs.

So why did that flare feel more like a raging firestorm?

Why was my wolf suddenly prowling, and bristling, where he'd always been content to doze?

One way or another, I would be found and returned to Stoke Ridge. To the life I'd been born into, and the consequences of it. That was the way of things, and the way they should be.

But...

But what if that *wasn't* the way of things?

Or at least, not the *only* way?

For hours after being captured—right up until Conall appeared—I'd desperately hoped to be released and sent home. Suddenly, the instant the apartment door re-opened, I *dreaded* the idea that it was about to actually happen.

And then his scent came to me.

A moment later, Conall appeared in the doorway, as though my desire had pulled him all the way back.

"This is fucked up," he growled. "Seems everyone thinks I kidnapped you."

"Oh?"

He let out a cold laugh. "Yeah. Apparently running around picking fights with people makes them think you're some kind of hothead."

"Hothead? I'd have said barbarian."

Conall smiled lightly as he ran his hands back through his thick hair and shook his head. He looked more of a lion than a wolf with that dark mane flying around him. My bones tingled as I studied him; the power in his movements, the confidence in his stance.

I was more like my own father than I cared to admit, most times. My power, my bearing—such as it might be—was entirely learned. *Cultivated*. I wore it like a ceremonial robe.

Conall's leadership qualities pulsed through his body, and glowed from his pores. The man simply owned any room, any space, he entered.

"So," he said, more of a growl than a word. "I'm under house arrest. Apparently father needs plausible deniability or some shit, and me running around out there isn't it."

"Does this count as irony, you think?"

"Yeah, maybe. But in any case, I can't go out there, and needless to say, neither can you, just yet." He sighed and leaned against the wall, all languid strength and graceful power. "You drink?"

"Not usually. I had plans to step up my game on my wedding night."

The exquisite torture of being so close to him, yet not touching him, became a physical pain. My wolf had always been well behaved, but he was truly flexing his power now. In ways I was entirely unprepared for.

As Conall turned and headed toward his kitchen, I stood and followed along in his wake, though I'd had no conscious thought to do so. It was merely the feeling—the absolute certainty—that I needed to be exactly where he was.

My feet became independent, speeding me up until I was right behind him just as he reached the doorway. Conall spun instantaneously and reversed his momentum, slamming bodily into me and driving me back against the wall, as though he thought he was under attack. As though I had any ability to inflict the slightest pain on his impressive body.

I'd made no sound pursuing him, my inner beast exerting its influence on the outer me in ways I'd never experienced. His beast, on the other hand, was battle-hardened, and that was clearly one of the biggest differences between us.

"What the fuck are you doing, Valenta?"

"I honestly don't know. I'm... drawn to you."

"Well, fuckin' stop it." His heart punched at me through our chests, and mine punched back. Like neighbors complaining about the noise.

"I didn't start this, Conall. It has a momentum of its own."

His expression darkened as he tightened his grip on my shirt. "This can't happen, Zoltan."

"What can't?"

His broad shoulders swelled for a

moment, as his wolf rearranged itself beneath his skin. His eyes flashed at me. It was probably meant to be a warning, but it felt so much more like a promise.

"This."

He drove his mouth against mine, hard enough to slam my head back into the wall. I speared my hands into his hair and made fists, my every move governed by pure instinct. The same instinct that got me following him in the first place.

Conall's deep, sonorous voice filled my head and my heart and my lungs as he snarled out his base and brutal desires. He conquered my mouth, pure and simple, as he tore my shirt from my body.

His nails grew sharper as they thickened and lengthened, and he dragged them down my chest, drawing blood. Where I knew I should feel pain, I felt only release.

Bliss.

The big man hauled me up off my feet and swung around, slamming himself back against the wall without ever looking like breaking our kiss.

I threw my legs around him, climbing

him like a tree and finding a level of brute strength within me that had never shown itself before. The harder I squeezed him, the deeper his growling voice fell.

He had the power to conquer me. Of that, there was no doubt. I was born to lead, yet was beyond ready to bow to Conall and his potent carnality.

I suckled on his thick tongue as he gripped my ass, pulling me against himself and grinding. Every way he touched me, in every place, burned like fire. We fell to the floor hard enough to break plain old human bones.

Only then did he take his mouth off mine, and only so he could bury his teeth into the flesh of my neck. I fisted his shirt and he let his wolf free just enough to swell his body and shred the fabric. The tattered garment came away in my hands as he dug his teeth into my chest, right where he'd already scratched me.

Conall swamped my nipple in his mouth and gripped my jeans, working them open in seconds. When he opened them and yanked down my underwear, my cock leapt free for a split second before his big, rough hand came down to capture it.

He made a fist so tight around me that I saw galaxies. I slammed my head back onto the floor as I arched my back. No hand had ever made me feel such blistering pleasure.

Not even my own.

With my hands still in his hair I clamped down, fisting that thick magnificence as he slid off my chest and headed south, stroking his hand up and down my length like he was starting an engine.

It took him an embarrassingly small amount of effort to shake himself loose of my grip and come up onto his knees, with one hand on the floor. As broad and attractive as his body was in a shirt, it was frighteningly magnificent bare. Scars peppered his arms and torso, beneath a neat coating of hair.

Still grinding my cock like he was beating a confession from it, he turned his face to the sky and arched his back, his breath coming in waves so thick they became sound. Grunts, moans, and the beginnings of howls.

Then, he dropped like he'd been shot,

slamming his head into the center of my chest and I slapped my hands onto his shoulders, digging in my nails. Only when they pierced his skin did I realize I was as close to shifting as he was.

Conall swept down and pulled my whole cock into his mouth, down to the root. He made a tight fist around my balls as he pumped up and down, igniting fists of electricity up the length of my spine.

He yanked at my jeans and I writhed my way out of them, all without him releasing my cock from his mouth. When he reached up and jammed his finger into my mouth, I sucked like it was his cock until he dragged it back out.

Conall came up off me for a second, letting my cock slap against my belly. He growled out a *holy fuck* and then fell on me again, grinding his tongue up and down the length of me, then swamping my balls with the heaven of his mouth.

He gripped my ass and spread it, his wolf making deep snarling sounds in his throat. I grasped my knees and pulled, truly baring myself for the first time, and he drove his tongue against my rippled hole.

I finally knew exactly what had been missing from my few clumsy and abortive encounters with the women of my pack. It would have been the same problem even with the men there. No matter who I might have fucked from Stoke Ridge, I would *always* be the one in charge.

With Conall, that wasn't an option. His power was inseparable from his being, and at that moment I was his willing serf. I was in his thrall, and had been for far longer than I realized.

While he gripped my cock and stroked it, he used his tongue to perfection. I simply opened to him, riding waves of bliss so unfamiliar to me, yet exactly what I'd always needed.

He replaced his tongue with his still wet finger, driving the tip inside me as he hauled my cock into his mouth again.

I threw my hands down and clawed at the carpet, shredding it as I fought the waves of pleasure buffeting my body. Conall had me so worked up I was teetering on the edge of a deep, narrow chasm. My wolf was on the other side, so close I could stroke him.

"Conall," I moaned, my throat

tightening before I finished, drying up the sound. He snarled back at me, the sound more of a geyser, all heat and power. His wolf wrestled with his human side, his back rippling and his arms flexing. Still he hauled on my cock, the fiery heat of his mouth dealing the final blow to my resistance.

This magnificent man hunkered before me on all fours with his shoulders hunched. My fangs tingled as they grew, and the sensitive flesh of my cock told me his did, too. Our wolves met in the middle as I dived into the abyss.

My climax pierced me like a million silver bullets, and I filled Conall's mouth with my essence. He clamped around me, savoring every drop as his breath coursed across my belly.

When the waves of pleasure finally abated, he rose on his haunches, his form still human but his aura pure lupine.

He glared down at me, his wolf pacing just behind his glowing, ice blue eyes. Eyes I couldn't turn away from, revealing a soul I couldn't resist.

CHAPTER SEVEN

CONALL

ALL MY LIFE, I'd felt alive. It sounds obvious, of course. But I had *never* felt as complete, as entirely *vital*, as I did at that moment. The heat of Zoltan's fluid still in my mouth, the rich musky flavor of him existing more as a concept even than as a reality.

My own wolf roared at me to take what I was owed. What I'd earned. Well, it was either my wolf or my balls, and not for the first time I couldn't separate one from the other.

Whichever part of me it was, the rest

my body obeyed instinctively. No need for any interference from my mind.

I grasped Zoltan by the legs and flipped him onto his belly, diving down to swathe the crease of his ass with my tongue, still coated in his juice.

He arched his back and moaned, propping himself up to me. I let his come gush from my mouth as I worked my tongue inside him, and it was the perfect blend of my two halves. Human and beast working hand in paw.

Harder and deeper I stroked and prodded him with my come-covered tongue, getting him all greased up and ready. My wolf was impatient at the best of times. And this moment was absolutely the best of times, so his lupine patience was absolutely nonexistent.

"Please, Conall..." Zoltan's need was a physical presence in the room.

I pumped two fingers deep into him as I came up on my knees. In seconds, I had my jeans open and my cock practically cheered.

"You have a fuckin' beautiful ass, man."

Before he could reply, I fisted my cock

and nudged it in place. I had to keep reminding myself this was his first time. The guy was just so fucking into it he seemed like a veteran.

I sank my half-claw nails into his hips, drawing blood, as I punched my cock forward.

Zoltan hissed as he stretched around me, but he bounced forward and back to get me deeper inside as quickly as possible.

Shifters run hotter than regular humans, and that was never more obvious than when I had my cock buried inside one. But nobody had ever burned into me the way Zoltan did. It went beyond pure heat, expanding into the crackling of electricity, the viscous bubbling of lava.

"Oh, fuck... Conall..."

I took his sandy hair in my fist and dragged on it, pulling him up until his hands left the floor. Yanking backward in harmony with every forward punch of my hips, admiring the ballet of his body as it reverberated with the hard impacts.

His creamy skin glowed under the coating of sweat I'd put there. His taut muscles danced along with the writhing of his wolf, until it wasn't clear which side of him I was watching.

I'd been a player for more years than I'd care to admit. Always searching for more than I found, forever hungry for deeper connection.

Turns out, all along I'd been searching for exactly what I'd found here. A man equal but different, whose strengths bolstered my weaknesses, whose needs embraced my gifts.

And whose ass was as tight as a fucking vise.

I sat back on my haunches, dragging him with me. Zoltan slammed back against my body, his skin gliding across my chest as sweat met sweat. The delicious savory scents of his sweat, his cock, his armpits, his every fucking pore, filled my nose and my head and my heart.

Every harsh, driving pump of my hips, he let out a sweet, whining moan, and slammed himself down on my length, working me just as hard as I worked him.

"Fuck me, Zee... I'm going..." Forming the words was the hardest thing I'd ever done. My jaw was the wrong shape, already narrowing and stretching as every muscle and bone in my body twitched, anticipating a shift.

My wolf hunkered down, feet spread, and took a deep breath. I closed my eyes, and threw my arms around Zoltan's body, bending him forward as I clamped my teeth into the flesh of his neck.

And as my climax erupted, my beast arched, taking me with it. I curled back on myself, dragging Zoltan with me, every hot, frenzied jet of fluid from my cock accompanied by a howl from the beast inside me, and a gush of blood across my tongue.

My muscles rolled and rippled, my bones shuddered, as I pumped my climax deep into this beautiful man. The world flashed perfect ice blue behind my closed eyes, pulsing in rhythm with my cock.

Time meant nothing. We stayed there, locked together, for as long as it took. Two men and two wolves, somehow becoming a single entity for a window of time.

All the stories I'd ever heard about fated mates had been like fairytales.

Even to the point they'd only ever described it happening between males and females.

Suddenly, here we were. This was the final confirmation for me, of all my suspicions. Never had I experienced a totality like the one that still had me wrapped up in its warmth.

A fated mate, who was a fucking Stoke Ridge man. All my life I'd ruled them out as anything but snobbish and soft, and now I was fucking lost inside one. Metaphorically as well as physically.

After who knows how long, I eased my teeth out of his delicious flesh, and Zoltan raised himself off me. My eyes spun as I searched for a way back into the real world.

My lover fell forward, landing on the floor of the hallway in complete exhaustion. Blackness swelled inside my head, and it took all my effort to control my own descent.

I landed on Zoltan's back and slid to the floor, one arm and one leg tossed over his body in possession. His invigorating scent was the last thing I comprehended before I lost myself to the darkness.

CHAPTER EIGHT

ZOLTAN

I RARELY DREAM. Or at least, I barely ever remember anything by the time I wake. This time, I absolutely inhabited my dream world, because I was not alone. I had Conall with me. A bristling black wolf with eyes of perfect ice blue.

Time had no meaning as we ran together, and wrestled, and play-hunted. He kept leaping over objects—boulders, fallen trees—and disappearing for minutes at a time. Whenever he did, my whole body went cold, and the entire world was a dark abyss. Only when he came back out of hiding did the color and light return.

After a time, I realized I wasn't entirely dreaming. That I was partway between sleeping and waking, and that Conall himself was leaving me where I lay, for minutes at a time, only to come back and wrap himself around me.

All I wanted right then was for him to roll me down onto my back and make love to me again.

Wait a minute.

Make love?

Could we even call it that?

When it was so carnal, so impetuous.

So... *lupine.*

A heavy pounding noise hauled me all the way up to full consciousness. For the briefest instant, I luxuriated in the heat of Conall's body, curled around mine once more. I brushed my fingers over the sweet ache on my neck, where he'd marked me.

Made me his own.

The pounding at his door sounded again, and we both sprang to a crouching position. Wolf instincts always came through in a crisis.

The booming voice of Patrick Blair

came through the closed door. "Son, you'd better be in there. If I find out you're sniping at those fucking Ridgies again..."

Conall let a low growl rumble in his chest, and I felt his fear and anger as if they were my own. The power of his bite at work.

He shot me a fierce look, though it didn't take any sensing between us for me to understand what was at stake here. It didn't matter how things *were*, it only mattered how things *looked*. And this made Conall look guilty as hell.

Together we stood, prowling silently away from his front door. He led me through to the back of his apartment, and the small balcony that came off his spare bedroom. We were still naked, we were thirty feet up, and there was nothing but wide fields behind the building.

In any case, we were out of options. Conall pulled me to him and planted a deep, lingering kiss on my lips that had a real tang of regret to it. Then, he climbed over the railing and swung himself down to the balcony below.

It took me a few seconds to get my

brain working again after that kiss. I wasn't sure I had the agility to follow Conall, but my decision was again made for me when the front door of the apartment burst open.

"Conall! Son, don't you fucking test me."

I clambered over the railing and hung down from the edge. Conall grabbed my legs and pulled me to safety beside him.

"Gonna have to jump from here, Zee."

"It's twenty feet."

"Then let's do it the easy way," he murmured.

"Easy way? What do you mean?"

He shot me a lighting fast wink. "Do you even shift, bro?"

"Um... no, not really."

His surprise flashed on his face for a moment. "Might be time to refresh your memory, then."

He crouched and let his shift take over. In seconds, he was wolf, and exactly as he'd appeared in my dream. Fur as black as midnight with eyes like glowing ice. He did it so easily, so naturally. Like he was changing a shirt.

He licked my leg, urging me again to shift as well. It was my only option, but I was so out of practice. Only by once again grinding my fingertips into the sweet bruise on my neck did I gain the confidence I needed.

I dropped to my knees and closed my eyes, letting my wolf free—*truly free*—for the first time. Every other time I'd shifted had been for ceremonial reasons.

The sharp-winged butterflies in my belly flew through my limbs, cutting away everything human and leaving only wolf behind in their wake. The world became uncomfortably bright and impossibly fragrant.

There was no time to savor the moment. Patrick Blair's swearing from the floor above got me raising my hackles, and the instant Conall leapt over the balcony and dropped the two stories to the ground, I once again followed him.

Together, we fled across the fields, heading for the distant forested hills. The world hit me like a slap in the face, and I realized I'd never been wolf out here. Out in nature, where it really mattered. I'd only ever shifted in halls and rooms.

My body pulsed with energy as I ran

and leapt, and I couldn't keep my head still. The wash of scents poured into me until I overflowed with sensations. I had no idea where we were headed, but all I knew was I had to follow my mate.

Holy hell that sounded weird.

My mate.

I knew it beyond any doubt, though. Conall was mine and I was his. The ideas and the concepts were too hard to fathom with wolf thoughts, but the truth was so basic and perfect it needed nothing but instinct to understand it.

As we ran, I sensed the utter joy radiating off Conall's wolf as well, though it was tinged with something else. Something murky and vague, reminiscent of that tinge in his kiss just before. All I could tell was that, again, I'd need my human side to understand it. But it was such a weak trace that I doubted my human would detect it.

We ran on, chasing after rabbits and birds, with no real intent. The thrill came from the pursuit, from the rush of fear we instilled. From impacting on the world around us, even in only a tiny way.

This wasn't leadership. This wasn't

the destiny I was born to. This was pure, wonderful freedom. And I could get used to it so easily.

Only when we'd gone deep into the forested hills did we come to a halt. We stopped at a stream and jumped in, the icy water as sharp and refreshing as Conall's bite was only hours before.

When my mate shifted back, I followed along. The process was so much easier already.

He climbed out and sat on a flat rock, dangling his feet in the water, and I swam over to him, standing on the bed of the stream, my body between his knees, my face level with his thick chest.

Conall cupped my head in his palm and I leaned into his touch. All I could scent on him now was the joy from earlier. Anything else had been washed off in the water.

But even as he bent to kiss me, his eyes held a sadness I couldn't yet read. He was still too new to me.

The touch of his lips to mine eased my worries instantly. Even in the cold water, this man had me hotter than hell. I opened to him, dancing my tongue around his as he gripped my hair and claimed my mouth.

I knew then that this man was my food, my drink, my soul. There was no longer any reason for me to return to Stoke Ridge. Maybe we couldn't stay here in Gray Vale, but my place was beside Conall, for eternity.

He snarled and broke our kiss, pushing me back far enough to glare down into my eyes. I could almost see words dancing behind his lips, though I couldn't read their intent.

"Zee, please..." That was all he said before I had my fist around his cock, and his balls in my other hand.

"You have nice manners for a barbarian," I murmured. And that was all I said before I drove my mouth down the length of his incredible cock.

CHAPTER NINE

CONALL

NO. HE HAD to stop.

Oh, fuck...

Zoltan had me deep in his mouth, and the sensation went so far beyond pleasure it was almost unrecognizable. He'd been working me for under a minute and I was close to finishing already.

I never should have given him my mark. That was fucking stupid, but I'd had no control of myself at that moment. He'd spoken to a deep part of me that I'd never explored, in either form.

But this definitely *had* to stop. I'd already made too many mistakes, and this was one I couldn't let continue. This had to be the line I drew in the sand.

For too long, I'd enjoyed my privilege without taking the responsibilities that went with it. As difficult as it was, I had to put my own wants—needs—last this time. The packs needed this man to marry my sister.

"Please, Zee... you gotta... oh, fuck..."

He climbed out of the stream and slammed his hand into my chest, knocking me flat on my back. He never once let my cock slip from his mouth as he prowled up beside me, spinning around so we could both fit on the rock.

My climax simmered just below boiling point, but I couldn't just let things go on like this. If he wouldn't end it, then I had to.

But that line I drew just a moment ago... I wasn't so much toeing it as struggling not to leap across it.

Until finally, I let out a long moan that became a ragged snarl, and gripped Zoltan's leg. I rolled onto my side and pulled him over to me, hauling his cock down my throat.

Again, my mark was a blessing and a curse. Every stroke of his mouth down my length, and my mouth down his, only bound us tighter. And the tighter our bond, the harder the impact, the farther the fragments would fly, when I had to break it.

But holy fuck. This moment was sheer perfection, as his body completed mine.

I gripped his thighs and dragged him closer to me, driving my own hips toward his beautiful face until there was nothing between us but sweat and water.

My climax hovered, closer than ever, and Zoltan's kept pace. We circled each other, connected in every way that mattered.

My spine fizzed as it buckled, stretching and thickening as my wolf flexed his muscles. Zoltan's strength grew as he plunged his length deep into my throat, and we rolled as we wrestled.

The bliss when my climax hit was matched only by the musky heat of Zoltan bursting in my mouth at the exact same instant. We formed a complete circle, each drinking the other's essence as we buried our half-shifted claws into the flesh we desired so much.

Still, we rolled, until we came free of the rock and plunged into the icy water again. Only then did we separate, each of us finding his way to the surface through the now fading red mist of arousal.

I clambered up onto the bank on one side of the stream. Zoltan ended up on the other, and though my mate couldn't realize it, it was the perfect sign for what was about to happen.

A sign that made itself clear an instant later, when heavy footsteps came thudding through the brush on the far side of the stream. No Gray Vale man would make such a fucking noise, so I knew exactly what was about to happen.

Zoltan fired a worried look at me, and I looked away in shame. His puzzlement pulsed through my veins and my anger at myself grew beyond belief. When Zoltan pressed his fingers to the mark on his shoulder, we both groaned in pleasurable pain. And it was clear just how strong our bond was.

A figure stepped out from behind a

tree, on Zoltan's side of the stream. A man wearing the patrol uniform of a Ridgie. Exactly as I'd asked for when I contacted Anton Valenta while Zee slept in my hallway.

The patrolman stopped short the moment he saw us, a puzzled expression on his face. "What the hell is happening here?"

Typical Ridgie reaction to nudity, as always. I shook my head as I stood. "Man, we had to shift to get away. You guys really need to lighten up."

I finally summoned up the guts to look at Zoltan again. And I instantly regretted it. The pain of betrayal was written all over him. "You... called them? You planned this?"

"*Planned* is way too fancy a word. I took the only available moment, and did what had to be done." I took a ragged breath and fought down the red hot waves of loathing I had for myself. "It's time I stepped up. For the future."

"What the hell are you talking about? This is not stepping up. It's turning tail."

"You have a prior commitment, Zee." I barely whispered it, yet I knew he heard.

"But what about..." His throat

tightened, and our bond told me it was a toxic cocktail of hopes smashed and beliefs betrayed.

This was the future of longing and torture I'd made for us both. I'd marked him, made him my own, and no matter where he was and who he was with, I'd feel him.

And he'd feel me.

He stood abruptly, glaring across the divide between us. "I thought we'd—"

"Remember where you are, Zee," I murmured. The return of the heir would be a most welcome event for the Ridgies. I doubted they'd celebrate the combination of coming back and coming out.

He growled out his anger. "I know where I am. More importantly, I know where I *should be*, Con." He took the shirt his patrolman offered, and tied it around his waist. His voice turned soft and smooth, almost boyish. "Tell me honestly this is what you truly want. Make me believe it really is for the best."

There was no way I could do that. I'd made a habit over the years of lying to lovers, with the express goal of making them ex-lovers. But even if I wanted to lie now, it simply wasn't possible.

I rubbed my fingers over my own neck, in exactly the place where my mark was on Zoltan.

"I had to do it, Zee. It was for the good... of the packs." My chest tightened so hard I could barely breathe, let alone speak. The pain of the moment was so great, I might as well be cutting my own leg off. The difference being that I could still live without my leg.

Zoltan spoke no more. He just turned and walked out of my sight.

Out of my life.

CHAPTER TEN

ZOLTAN

IT WAS MY wedding day, and I was nothing but a shell. I'd dodged the barrage of questions when I arrived home, and had barricaded myself away to let my soul bleed out.

Since Conall cut my heart to ribbons, I'd barely spoken at all. Not even to my father, though I couldn't be sure whether he noticed. At this point, I was little more than a chess piece to him, in any case.

Worst of all, my wolf paced and howled and nipped at my conscience. I should probably call the ASPCA on myself, the way I'd neglected him since my return.

He—*I*—could still sense everything about Conall. Not as a memory, not as a dream, but as a part of my own mind and body, in the here and now.

His ongoing irritability coursed through my blood, though it carried resounding echoes of rage.

There was no way to reconcile his betrayal with his current state of mind. His anger stemmed from hunger. Hunger for me, even though he'd deceived and dismissed me as effortlessly as he'd seduced me.

Why the hell had he given me his mark if he'd never intended to keep me?

I was in limbo, though it felt more like purgatory.

This impending marriage had already been on shaky ground, and now Conall had completely doomed it. I could never be anyone else's mate but his. It was the same for him. That was the nature of the mark. Nothing but death could end the bond.

Yet, here I was, minutes away from marrying his sister.

How could I even look at my bride without picturing her brother?

Worse still, how could I ever make whole our union when I clearly had no sexual interest in her entire gender?

After all, the purpose of these marriages was to give the packs a common heir. To unite our people, for peace. So folks had always said, especially my father over the past few months.

There was no way that was ever happening. Not between Fiona and me, at least. She'd have to hire in a stunt double to put a bun in *her* oven. Without my mate, I honestly believed I would never get hard again.

Of course, every time I closed my eyes and opened my heart, Conall came rushing back in and proved that belief entirely wrong. Though I strove to hate the man, just the sense of him was enough to get me hard.

What good was a hard cock, though, when your mate was off limits?

What good was *anything*?

Father pounded on the door, breaking through my near catatonia. All that did was take me straight back to the stolen night in Conall's apartment. The morning that was torn apart by *his* father knocking. And though I didn't know at the time, by my lover's deception.

"Son? It's starting."

I winced and shook my head, searching for a way out of this mess. But I'm a man of duty; born into it, and bred to embrace it.

There was no room anymore for me to question my place. I'd long ago accepted exactly which cog I was in the big machine. For what felt like a single heartbeat, I'd outrun it. That brief window of time with Conall, where I'd experienced pure joy and belonging, was over.

Dead.

The problem was, he'd be my brother-in-law. I couldn't put him out of my mind, or out of my life. He was up there, right now. Not just in the congregation, but right up in my face. An integral member of the wedding party.

As an only child, and the Alpha in waiting, I'd had nobody to act as the equivalent of a best man. So, of course, my father organized a suitable stand-in.

The only man with the status befitting such an honor.

Conall *fucking* Blair.

How the hell would I get through this without confessing my feelings for him, either accidentally or willingly, through words or actions?

That was the real trouble. My hatred for what he did could barely surface through my desire for who he truly was. I already knew him as well as I knew myself. It was impossible not to, thanks to his fucking mark.

"Son? If you've disappeared again—"

"I'm here, father."

"Well? Don't keep the packs waiting."

I opened the door and father blessed me with the only genuine smile I could remember seeing from him in months.

Maybe even years.

"Son, I'd begun to think this day would never come."

"Yes, father."

He softened visually. "I'm sorry I rode you so hard, son. You're doing the right thing, though. You know how the tradition works."

I sure did. As if I hadn't felt enough pressure already. With no surviving brothers, I was the only one who could be the next unopposed Alpha of Stoke Ridge. And the only one who could then supply a Valenta heir.

Should I step aside, it would mean anybody could challenge for pack leadership. So, in addition to being railroaded into marrying someone other than my fated mate, I also had twenty generations sitting on my shoulders.

"Come on, son. Time to take your place in history."

This was it. I was to pledge my life to someone I didn't, and couldn't, love. Three days ago, I was fully prepared to accept that as my lot in life. How quickly everything changed.

I simply had to put Conall out of my mind.

The moment I walked into the hall, it was clear to me that *I* was the one who was out of my mind. To ever think I could suppress my feelings for Conall Blair.

With father beside me, I trudged up to the altar, missing my mother more than I had in many a year.

My body tensed before my mind even gave the order. I'd believed I could handle this moment. I was wrong.

My mate stood in place, looking somehow as if he could simultaneously host an award ceremony, and commandeer a scurvy crew of buccaneers. And searing my damn soul with those crystalline eyes.

My mark pulsed, heavy with his emotions. Those emotions manifested words in my head. Disbelief that I was still going through with the wedding. Shame at his own actions.

And desire.

Pure, ravenous and scorching.

The sheer power of his hunger had my knees buckling and my wolf bristling. Even my father, standing the other side, sensed a change in me, and put his hand around my arm, holding me up.

"What is it *now*, son?"

The blend of distaste and disapproval in his tone was exactly what I needed to get through this. His cold disappointment was the perfect shield for Conall's lust.

"Nothing, father. I'm just soaking up the gravity of the moment."

"Well, do it privately. Show no

weakness. You're the next Alpha. Of both packs."

"What?" This wedding was supposed to settle the petty arguments between packs. Join them in spirit, not in law. In short, it was meant to be a marriage, not a coup. "What have you put in place, father?"

"Don't concern yourself, son. Just stand there and marry that... *woman*."

It didn't take a lot of imagination to realize he'd said *woman*, but meant a whole other five-letter word. One that was even worse for wolves than for humans, since it leveled totally different insults at both halves.

Bitch.

Music began, and the bride-to-be appeared at the end of the aisle, with her father. Though she was dressed in a white strapless dress, at least she'd managed to eschew the wearing of a veil.

Fiona Blair shared her brother's intense beauty, though her features were of course much finer and more delicate. The lack of scarring on her face and shoulders suggested she didn't share her brother's reckless nature, at least.

They came toward me, but though I

watched them, my entire focus was off to the side. I swore I was getting a sunburn from the heat of Conall's glare.

Patrick Blair released his daughter's arm, and she let out a small sigh that sounded for all the world like resignation.

I was supposed to do something at that point, but my mind was a sizzling pan, and every thought bit into me like spitting oil.

Fiona stepped right up beside me, then reached over and took her brother's hand with a smile.

Conall pulled her to him and the siblings shared a tight hug. I couldn't help but envy their closeness, and it re-awoke my sadness at losing my mother and unborn brother when I was so young.

Over his sister's shoulder, Conall speared me again on those hard but heavenly eyes of his. My mark pulsed harder than ever and I gasped with the ecstatic agony of it.

And between us, the slender figure of Fiona jolted. She pushed out of her brother's embrace and held him at arm's length.

He dragged his steely gaze away from me and met his sister's eyes. Not a word passed between them, but she tilted her head, raising it as though scenting prey.

Slowly, she turned toward me, a frown creasing her forehead.

When the celebrant began speaking, Fiona held up her hand to silence him. She stepped up closer to me, drawing in a deep breath.

"What the hell is going on?" my father growled. "You damn Valentas are making a mockery of—"

"Quiet!" Fiona's voice sliced through the moment, and for the first time I'd ever known, my father—the Alpha of Stoke Ridge—was silenced.

My bride-to-be took my hands in hers, and looked me over, from head to toe and back again. "Oh, this is too bad. You're absolutely lovely."

"I, uh..."

"Where is it?"

"W–what do you mean?"

"His mark."

What the hell? How did she know?

I glared at Conall. "You told her?"

Conall shook his head, but never even looked like breaking eye contact.

"He didn't have to, Zoltan," Fiona murmured. "I have a gift. Dubious as it might be." This last part she said over her shoulder, and it was clearly directed to her twin brother.

"Sis—"

"You shut up, too, Con."

Fiona turned and addressed the congregation. "I'm sorry, everyone. I'm afraid the wedding is off."

Fiona walked back down the aisle, her head still held high, her gait easy and relaxed, as if she did this kind of thing every day.

And though I took comfort that, for the moment, all eyes were on her, I knew it wouldn't last. The instant she walked out of here, it would be my head on the chopping block.

CHAPTER ELEVEN

CONALL

LIKE EVERYBODY ELSE, I simply watched in awe as Fiona sauntered back out, apparently unruffled by what she'd just learned about her ex-fiancé and me.

Despite the fact I knew her better than anyone, I couldn't be certain she wasn't in pain. That she didn't hate me.

Not to mention Zoltan would be right in the firing line here, and despite everything I'd done, every mistake I'd made, and every barrier I'd put between us... he was my mate. He, more than anyone, was my responsibility here. To protect, and to nurture. And the only way I could do that would be to get him the fuck away from this farce.

I leaned over and murmured to him to follow me, and though he pulled away like I'd cut him, he did as I asked.

My father blocked our path for a moment. "Son, what the hell happened?"

"I promise I'll tell you, just as soon as we have a handle on it, father. Right now, we need to check on Fiona."

I definitely knew father well enough to manipulate him. As patriarchal and condescending as it was, he'd always been overprotective of Fiona. She was his biggest blind spot, and his greatest weakness. If only he could recognize she was truly his greatest asset.

Zoltan followed me out of the hall and around the corner, where we found Fiona gazing out over the scenery. The hills and mountains of Stoke Ridge and out to the plains and valleys of Gray Vale.

"Fi," I said. "Talk to me."

She whirled on the spot, jabbing me right in the chest. "Why the hell didn't you tell me?"

"Fi, this wasn't something we

planned. It was... fuck, it was about as far from planned as anything could be."

"No excuse, bro. You were going to let this go ahead, anyway? And you?" She turned her irritation to Zoltan. "How exactly did you think this was going to work between us, when we already have *this* asshole between us?" She indicated me with a casual toss of her thumb over her shoulder.

Zoltan's beautiful features hardened, and he turned to me while speaking to Fiona.

"Because that asshole betrayed me and tossed me aside."

"That's not what I did," I muttered, though of course it was *exactly* what I did. "You know why I had to send you home, Zee."

He laughed, a cold, hard burst of sound, and spread his arms to encompass the whole situation around us. "For this? You shouldn't have. You *really* shouldn't have."

It didn't matter he was exactly right. It didn't matter that I'd absolutely fucked things up, and maybe risked my relationship with my sister along with it.

I'd fought battles against man and

beast, any one of which could have ended me. Never once had I panicked or lost my head.

As much as I tried to tell myself I'd been working for the greater good, I knew in my heart I'd been nothing more than a scared little boy.

The threat of death had never paralyzed me. No, it took the threat of love to do that. Pure, shameful panic in the face of my own stupid fucking feelings.

That was why I'd called Anton Valenta. That was why I betrayed all that mattered to me.

Now, all that mattered to me was undoing the damage. Earning my mate back.

Fiona reached out to us both, one hand on my shoulder, one on Zoltan's. "You boys will be the death of me. And of our packs."

"Zee," I said. "I know it can't erase anything, but I'm so fucking sorry. It was pure cowardice on my part to send you home."

"That part was your duty, Conall," he replied. "I could accept that—maybe even respect it—if that was what really drove your actions. What hurt was that you hid your intentions. That you lied straight to my face."

He tore open his shirt, pointing at my mark, and my wolf hunkered down, hungrier than ever for this man, and ready to pounce. "Your cowardice was in giving me this, with no thought to the ramifications."

"For fuck's sake, you two." Fiona landed a light slap on each of our cheeks. "This is why our packs are damned. We've been led by men for too long without any balance."

Zoltan straightened his back as if he'd been personally insulted. "Tradition dictates—"

"Screw tradition," my sister countered. "You boys have such a warped sense of duty, and no understanding of self-sacrifice."

"Sis, how can you say that? I gave up my life's happiness so this wedding could go ahead."

"Yes. That's exactly the problem. It's what I've tried to tell you basically forever, bro. Men don't self-sacrifice right. For you guys, it's always a blaze of glory, all or nothing, liberty-or-death kind of situation. Either through nature or nurture, we women self-sacrifice daily. We step around an obstacle, rather than blasting it apart. We take the small hits so nobody has to jump on a damn grenade. Metaphorically speaking."

I couldn't tell if she was right in a global sense. But holy fuck, she was absolutely right about me. My behavior compared to hers.

Zoltan chuckled at my obvious discomfort, but Fiona thudded the heel of her hand into his chest. "You don't get off lightly here, mister. I was prepared to take my lumps and marry you, sight unseen, because it was for the greater good. But that was when I believed it would be a... well, let's say a *fruitful* marriage."

"I apologize, Fiona. But as the daughter of the Alpha, you must understand the pressures on me, to some degree."

"The pressures, yes. Your actions, no. You're still a man, capable of independent thought and decision. Were you *ever* planning to tell me you're gay?"

"Gay? He's not *gay*." The booming

voice of Anton Valenta sounded behind me, where he and my father had come to check on us. "While I hear that kind of sin is all the rage in Gray Vale, it simply doesn't happen in higher packs like Stoke Ridge."

I made fists as I turned to face the man. "The only way your pack is higher than mine is simple geography."

Anton raised one eyebrow. "The savage speaks." He glanced at my hands and rolled his eyes. "And I see you're already regressing to your barbarous ways. You are aware that you'd be excommunicated for striking an Alpha, boy?"

"Conall," my father said. "Stand down."

The punishment would just about be worth it. The seams of my tux whined in pain as my wolf asserted himself. I spread my feet as the shift threatened to take over me.

"Oh, put it away, son," Anton said, sneering at me.

"Not your son," I growled.

"Fi?" father said.

"Enough."

Fiona's tone was all business, and

sliced through the moment effortlessly. She even managed to get my wolf to stand down.

"Look at you all," she continued. "Con, I love you to death, bro, but you need to calm the fuck down. There's a wide and bountiful middle ground between wolf and human, but you only ever leap from one side to the other. And you—"

She stabbed the air in front of Anton Valenta's face. Where my rage had only made him annoyed, her disappointment had him flinching.

"Don't you have more important things to do than baiting my brother?"

"I was planning to preside over this wedding, but clearly you have cold feet now, girl. Why else would you make such fanciful claims about my son."

My wolf snarled again, as he always did whenever someone spoke against my sister.

And once again, she cut through the moment. "Conall. Get your shit together, bro." Her strong tone worked on me so much better than shouting would.

Anton continued, as though oblivious to my wolf and the threat it posed. "It's of no concern, in the end. I never thought you worthy to be elevated to Stoke Ridge."

The honor of my pack, of my family, of my sister, had been called into question once too often. My wolf could simply take no more. He sank his teeth into my mind, and I fell into a crouch to let the shift take over.

CHAPTER TWELVE

ZOLTAN

I WAS STILL in awe of the way Fiona Blair simply took control of the situation. As much as it could be controlled, anyway, with Conall ready to shift at the drop of an insult.

When it was clear my mate had succumbed to his basest instincts, I felt a burst of heat in my chest, and a charge of panic in my mind.

My mark burned and jolted, like it was going to leap free of my body.

"Zoltan?" Fiona said. "Your move."

"What?"

"He's only going to respond to you, now. Step up, buddy."

Conall grunted as if in pain, resisting the shift his wolf demanded. His agony called me through our bond, through his mark, and everything became clear to me in an instant.

His sister was right. Only *I* could reach him now, and break through his rage. And the consequences of failure could be fatal. Perhaps even cause a proper pack war.

But to soothe my mate now would mean admitting my relationship with him. I'd be confessing my orientation— my so-called *sins*—to my father. Coming out, when I'd barely even come to realize I'd been *in*.

In the end, that was a small price to pay. Either he'd accept me as I am, or I'd be the one excommunicated. Whichever way it went, there was one thing I knew about myself, and it was that I was never meant to be Alpha. I would rather be happy than in command, and for me, the two were mutually exclusive.

And despite everything, the only way I could be happy was with this man before me. I needed him the way he needed me.

The way we both needed water and food.

I crouched before Conall's tortured form, and pressed my palm to his fevered cheek. He jerked his head up and glared deep into me, his eyes burning like sunlight on snow.

My mate's features contorted as his wolf flexed beneath the surface.

"Conall," I murmured, barely more than a whisper. "Breathe for me. Slowly."

He gripped my forearm, sinking his half-formed claws through my skin. I hissed with pleasure as much as with pain, and slid my hand down to his neck.

He mirrored me, pressing his other hand onto my neck and finding his mark. The instant he made contact, it was as if we'd completed a circuit, and his anger flowed into me. My wolf jolted, hackles rising, but as always, a burden shared is a burden halved.

With the two of us riding the wave of rage, quelling it became so much simpler. It was another blessing—and sometimes curse—of the mate bond.

Gradually, his claws retracted, and the heat of his rage cooled. Finally, we were both back under control of our human sides, and we stood.

Unfortunately, the skin to skin contact had other consequences. Big, hard ones, which were obvious to all around us.

"Zoltan?" my father said, through clenched teeth. "What the hell is going on here? This was to be the culmination of years of work."

"I thought it was to be my wedding, father."

"Let's not split hairs." He shot his harsh Alpha glare at the Blair pack. First Patrick, then Fiona, neither of whom flinched.

Before he turned his rage on Conall, I slipped my hand into my mate's grip. Letting him know I was there for him. Hoping to convey with just a touch that I understood what he'd tried to do—for me as well as himself—and that I could even forgive him. And to encourage him to keep his wolf tethered. At least until we could get some time together.

Father's searing gaze threatened to slice right through both of us. The instant he saw our hands clasped, his own wolf seemed to awaken.

"Zoltan? What is the meaning of

this?"

I raised my hand, bringing Conall's along for the ride.

"Yes, well... about that, father. I'm sorry you had to find out this way."

"Find out? Zoltan, this... thing you think is happening? It's a lie. No Alpha of Stoke Ridge has ever had this kind of... perversion. More to the point, no son of mine would even entertain the possibility."

"Perhaps I'm adopted."

The growl that burst from father's throat was three-quarters wolf. So soon after him sneering at what he saw as my mate's hair trigger for shifting.

"I'm serious, boy. Be careful with your choice of lifestyle. You end these shenanigans now, or you're no longer welcome. Not just in my home, but in my pack."

"Choice of lifestyle? Father... this is who I am. Who I've always been. It's where destiny has put me. This goes far beyond choice. You know how the mate bond works, after all."

"Mate? You're already mated?"

I faced him straight on, and opened my shirt, revealing the mark on my neck.

"Whose is that?"

Conall stepped forward. "It's mine."

My father rolled his eyes and sneered. "Marking only happens between a man and a woman. That's not a true mark. We can still fix this."

This time it was Fiona who stepped in. "There is nothing here to *be* fixed, sir. Time moves on. Things change. Why, one day we might even end up with a female Alpha."

"And that's no doubt been your plan all along, hasn't it, you little bitch?"

My wolf came fully alive, as did Conall's. But if Fiona was bothered by father's insult, she never let on.

"My plan was to marry your son, and ease tensions between the packs. Circumstances changed. It's always been my belief that adaptability is not just a strength, but an absolutely vital survival mechanism."

Anton Valenta crossed his arms. "Last chance, boy. Think what you're throwing away."

I turned to Conall, finding strength and hope in nothing more than the light in his eyes. "I'm not throwing anything away, father. I'm just leaving it behind."

For a few more seconds, my father stood there, bristling. His voice was cold and quiet when he finally spoke again. "Then you will serve as an example to the rest of *my* people."

I heard, rather than saw, him leave. I only had eyes for Conall by that point.

This wasn't the way I'd wanted to tell him. There was still a huge part of me that insisted I should go to him, and fulfill the duty I was born into. That he'd drilled into me every day of my life.

But that would mean turning away from my future. The only future I had, or could want.

Life with Conall.

EPILOGUE

TWO YEARS LATER
CONALL

I WOULD NEVER tire of this. Waking up with Zoltan's hot, tight body snuggled up to mine was as important as the air I breathed.

From that aborted wedding day onward, he'd been an out and proud member of the Gray Vale pack, and neither of us had ever been happier.

His father turned out to be absolutely right when he said Zoltan would serve as an example to his people. But he could never have predicted exactly how.

When Anton went public with the details of Zoltan's excommunication, he'd unwittingly launched a revolution in Stoke Ridge. Dozens of previously secret same-sex couples were inspired to come out in support of the deposed son of their Alpha.

The shift was seismic, and in a last ditch effort to shore up his position, Anton Valenta had taken the clichéd old *if you're not with me you're against me* stand. Turned out, the majority was against him, and he vacated. Even Zee doesn't know where he's gone.

Though my mate was within his rights to stand for the position, he'd shot that idea down in flames. That suited me just fine, since I'd come to feel exactly the same way about pack leadership. Now, we lived a life of blissful happiness and comfort, without the pressures and hassles that we were clearly unsuitable for.

In fact, we were only a week or so away from moving to a quiet cabin we'd had built right in the heart of the formerly disputed lands. A small place where we could hunt and garden, and raise some kids sometime in the future.

A place we could grow old together.

The perfection of that idea hadn't waned one bit since Zee first suggested it. In the bliss of his warmth and his scent, I took a few seconds to gaze at his smooth and chiseled features, studying them as if they were new to me. As if I hadn't done exactly this, every morning for the past two years.

A few moments later he stirred, so I rolled him down onto his back and came up over the top of him. He opened his sweet, golden eyes to me, and I had to catch my breath.

The man was just so fucking beautiful.

He reached up and pressed his fingers to the side of my neck, right where he'd marked me. The exact same location as where I'd marked him first. I gasped when he pressed harder, and then let my body fall, taking his mouth in a deep kiss.

A light knocking on my apartment door cut through the moment. It seemed visitors were always interrupting us.

"Go away unless you have pizza," I yelled.

"I know you're a lazy ass, brother

dear, but you haven't slept *that* long. It's not dinner time yet."

"Shit. It's the boss!"

Zee rolled his eyes at me, which only made me want to tackle him to the floor and make wild, lupine love to him. Of course, we were still sleeping off last night's crazy sex. That was the whole reason we were still in bed at... I glanced at the clock...holy fuck. 10:30?

I slid out of bed, fending off Zee's grabby hands as I pulled on a pair of track pants. I went through and opened the front door, firing my best cheeky grin at my sister.

"Why did you let me sleep so late, Fi?"

"You want the truth?"

"Of course not."

"Then, uh... let's see. Well, now that you're just a layabout loser with zero responsibilities—"

"Woah. That's the sugarcoated version? I mean, you're not wrong and all, but still..."

"Is my *other* brother in?"

I couldn't contain my broad grin. "Why do you think I'm sleeping so late?"

"Ugh. Keep it in your pants, bro." She called out to Zee, over my shoulder.

"Other bro, time to dress up in your fancy duds."

"Oh, yeah," I murmured. "Today's the big day. The handing over of the royal staff and shit."

"I thought you'd already taken care of the *royal staff.* But we'll wake you when it's over, if you wanna grab your blankie and go back for a little nap time."

"Uh-uh. I'll be there, front and center. You think I'm gonna miss out on seeing my little sister being anointed as the united packs' custodian? You'll even get to boss dad around."

"It's not that kind of situation, bro. You know that."

"Yeah. But you could come up with some way to make him squirm, surely."

"If I was gonna make anybody squirm, bro, you know it'd be you. But thank you for your support."

"No problem. And since it's a formal event, I'll bring my *black* whoopie cushion."

She shook her head. "Thanks again for reminding me of the bullet we all dodged when you stepped away, bro."

I pulled her into a tight hug. "Wrong, Fi. I didn't need to step away. You're the true Alpha, even if we're not calling it that anymore. You always were."

Zee came up behind and wrapped himself around my back, making sure to ruffle Fi's hair.

"God, you really *are* an extra brother now, aren't you?"

"Definitely. And I have a lot of years of annoying to catch up on."

She pushed away from us and tidied herself up again. "Well, you clearly have the best teacher."

I took a theatrical bow. "Thank you, oh Grand Poobah. I live to serve."

"Well, to dish it out, at least." My sister sighed heavily, a tiny grin forming on her lips. "You were bad enough when you had authority. Now... I think you're gonna put your back out from bucking the system."

"It'll be fine, sis."

"Oh?"

"Yeah." I put my arm over Zee's shoulder. "I have help."

Thank you for reading!

For book 2 in the Gray Wolf Pack series,
His Wounded Warrior, all you need to do
is turn the page. *grin*

Don't forget, for more of the steamy mm
goodness you love so much, follow me on
all my social media channels and watch
for all the delicious new books to come
in the future. The ideas I have are
endless... or so it seems.

Love, Evie

HIS WOUNDED WARRIOR

GRAY VALE PACK

BOOK TWO

EVIE RILEY

**One man has to break the rules...
the other must discover who he truly is.**

Braden Craig is a popular schoolteacher in Gray Vale, and unlike most wolf shifters, he's one of life's peacemakers. When old tensions rise in the newly merged pack, he's quick to douse the flames. But nothing can cool the heat inside him when he locks eyes with the giant blond stranger who has become the target of some less than welcoming packmates' aggression.

Tragedy pushed Marius Voss out of his so-called comfort zone in Stoke Ridge. After being forced to move to Gray Vale with his young son, and still recovering from life-altering injuries, he just wants to keep to himself and figure out his new life. He never expected to find an ally at all, let alone a man like Braden.

When fate plays a hand, and the two men find their lives intertwined, will they find a way to be together?

CHAPTER ONE

Braden

STANDING BEFORE THE bright and shiny faces of my 2nd Grade students, I savored that bittersweet and beautiful pain that always came at the end of the last day of school.

Even I sometimes found it strange how much at home I felt in the company of kids. Especially for a man with no real chance of ever being a father. I can only put it down to my own family's strong support. The fact they never insisted I take any predetermined path was, in the end, what led me to teaching.

EVIE RILEY

One of the things I loved most about teaching these early grades was that I got to know the kids long before any of them had experienced shifting. There was such a sweetness to them at these ages, and I'd never tire of it. They had some of the senses, of course, since we're all born with them. But they were such perfect little creatures, all singular of mind and being.

With all the eager little faces shining up at me, we performed my own little classroom ritual of gazing at the clock, counting down the last ten seconds until the final bell rang.

Right on cue, it sounded, and we all cheered. The kids, their parents, me... even Kayleigh, the school principal.

I'd still see these wonderful kids around, of course—in town over the summer break, and around the school in years to come—but there was always that sense of something wonderful coming to an end when school finished for the year.

This had been my best year of teaching, though it wasn't as if I had a huge history to compare with. I was six years into it, but every year still felt as fresh as my first.

Now that Gray Vale had completed the long process of amalgamation with Stoke Ridge, there was an even greater sense of anticipation for the coming school year.

Nothing much had changed, in a day-in, day-out sense, in the two years since the great upheaval. We all just had to remember that Fiona Blair bore the lumpy and cumbersome title of *United Clans Custodian*, rather than the more traditional *Alpha*.

In a couple months' time, though, we'd be welcoming a new intake of people none of us knew. That was such a rarity in wolf clans. Everyone knew everyone, with only rare exceptions. Exceptions like Kayleigh, one of the few humans living in Gray Vale.

I stood by the classroom door, saying goodbye to all the kids in turn, and their parents. Mostly moms, a lot of whom were regulars at my weekly life drawing classes.

Little Tommy Welsh held up his hand for a high five as he passed, and I returned it. His mom, Lillian, touched my arm as she came to a stop in front of me. She was one of the most persistent flirts I'd ever known, even though she was fully aware of my sexuality.

"Braden, will we see you tomorrow night?"

"Um... sorry?"

"Life drawing? We have to *submit* our final piece, right?"

There was no missing the emphasis she put on the word *submit*, but I glossed over it. Lillian lost her mate not long after Tommy was born. She'd found solace in my art classes, and I was certain she'd blurred the lines I'd always drawn between myself and my students. She'd even gone so far as to offer to pose for me.

In private.

"That's right, Lillian. I look forward to seeing yours."

"Hey, at least buy me a drink first, handsome." She delivered the come on with just enough smirk and wink to let it exist as nothing more than a joke. But enough sincerity to let me know the offer was well and truly on the table, if I was down for it.

Which I wasn't.

I felt for her, of course. It was a huge

part of who I was, after all, to empathize with others. But I'd known since childhood I was gay, even before I knew what being gay meant.

I caught Kayleigh's eye, and made my *come and fucking rescue me* face. To her credit, she hustled right over and stood with me, defusing the flirtations immediately. None of the moms ever risked it when my protector was around.

"Y'know, Braden," she murmured. "All this would stop if you'd mate up."

"Mate up? You're seriously going with *mate up?* Like being alone is a fashion choice?"

"With guys your age, it usually is." She helped me see out the last of the parents, and then closed the door and leaned back against it. It was almost as if she was blocking anybody coming back in.

"So, next year," she said, bugging her big brown eyes and making them stand out against her rich, dark skin. That's how I knew she had bad news. "I have to switch you to kindergarten."

"I was really hoping to stick with 2nd Grade."

"We have at least a half-dozen new

kids coming in from the other mob."

"Stoke Ridge was a clan, like ours. Not a mob. Anyway, you're human. You shouldn't have any of the baggage." Normally, I'd tell a human they didn't have the right, but Kayleigh had earned it. She was as much a part of the old Gray Vale as anybody born here.

She flipped her hand in dismissal. "Anyway. I think it's important to these kids to have a positive male role model in their first year."

"And the fact I'm a *gay* positive male role model?"

"Well, that's more for the parents. They need to get the hang of things in these parts."

"Great. I get to be a token."

She threw her hands onto her broad hips as quickly as a gunfighter. "Is that sass?"

I hung my head to hide my grin. "No, ma'am."

"Sounded like sass. You know there's only one place I'll let you sass me, Braden Craig."

"Which reminds me, your final piece is due this week."

She put on the most amazing pout.

"Aw, teach... can't I have an extension?" She even made her voice into the most annoying teenage whining sound I'd ever heard.

"Sorry, Ms Powell. No can do."

"But teeeach..."

"Do I have to have a word with your parents, young lady?"

She chuckled along with me, then poked me in the chest. "So listen, when the hell are you getting us a *male* model to draw? It's been nothing but T and A. Very beautiful T and A, but a girl got *needs*, y'know?"

"A boy has 'em, too, lemme tell ya. And if you can find me a guy in the whole of this jambalaya of clans who'll do it, you let me know, huh?"

"You telling me you can't even get one of your exes? I never met anyone before who could stay friends with every single person they got jiggy with."

"My exes? Not a good idea. It sends the wrong message, don't you think?"

She shrugged in defeat. "Shit, it shouldn't be that hard. I never met a shifter could keep his pants on more than ten minutes at a time. This place is junk city." She gave me a hefty hip-check. "Why you think I never left?"

"It's not the nudity that bothers them. It's the standing still."

"Oh, yeah. Not exactly a strong point among your kind. There's always a new sound or scent wafting around."

I hip-checked her back again. "And with all you thirsty females gazing on them, there'd be scents a-plenty, for sure."

"Now why you gotta call me out like that, boy?"

"Because you gave me kindergarten next year." I heard the self-doubt in my own voice, and there was no doubt Kayleigh heard it, too. She never would have lasted among shifters if she didn't have such good instincts.

"B, you're gonna ace it. I've seen you in action."

I still had my doubts. But having the support of my principal helped, at least.

CHAPTER TWO

Marius

THE ESTATE AGENT worked the key into the apartment door and jiggled it.

"It's got a real personality, this one," he said, and though his back was to me, I could hear in his voice the foolish grin he wore. A disturbingly brittle crack sounded, and then he drew open the door and stood aside.

"There we go."

I raised one eyebrow as I glanced inside. My son leaned into my leg and I reached down, ready to put my hand on his shoulder, then held back.

"It smells funny, dad," Noah murmured.

The estate agent—Carl—put on his showiest chuckle. "Oh, it's just the cleaning agents, kiddo. You guys are Ridgies, right?"

"There's no Stoke Ridge anymore," I growled out, not meaning to sound quite so bitter about it.

Carl's canned grin slipped a little, but he recovered quickly enough. "Well, not in name, of course. But we have our own brands we use here in Gray... well, in what we used to call Gray Vale."

That sounded like nothing so much as complete bullshit to me.

Did this guy really think he could fool a fellow shifter when it came to smells?

"C'mon, let me show you inside."

I just about had to drag Noah with me to get him in. Couldn't blame the kid. I was still a stranger to him. A stranger who happened to be his biological father.

Inside, the place was everything I'd expected. Bland, worn, tattered. But fuck, it was all I could afford. Couldn't serve in the guards anymore, but hadn't served long enough for a decent pension.

At least there were two bedrooms, so

Noah could hide his tears from me if he wanted to.

"Why can't we live in mom's house?"

"C'mon, Noah. We've been through that."

Carl coughed, to edge himself back into the conversation. "Uh, I was told it was just the two of you? If there's a Mrs. Voss...?"

"There's not," I said, more of a snarl than a statement.

"Mom's dead." The antiseptic way Noah said that, every single time, hurt me much more than it would if he showed the slightest sadness. It was like he'd had an emotional bypass.

The apartment went silent for a moment. Carl was so neutral, his façade so false, I couldn't even tell for certain whether he truly was a shifter, or just a human. Especially, when I factored in that cleaning agents crap he tried to spin.

Carl seemed unsure how to proceed at the news of Kellie's death. The look on his face told me he was wondering if I'd killed her. I saw that look all the time. My size, and the way I radiated such clear and obvious *fuck you* vibes, worked well in the guards. Now I couldn't wear the uniform. I was just a huge, messed up guy with some real angry injuries.

"Car accident," I said. "She died in a car accident."

"Oh. And is that where you, um..." He nodded toward my left arm. What there was of it, anyway. I raised it and looked at the short stump below my elbow. I did an exaggerated double take.

"What the hell? It was there a minute ago."

"Um..."

Noah let out a little giggle. It was the only way that I'd ever made the kid laugh, but it was definitely a dad joke. It probably had about two more weeks before he was sick of hearing it. It'd been two months since I got sick of saying it.

I picked up a vibe from Carl that he'd rather be anywhere else, so I held out my good hand, palm up. "We'll take it."

The guy handed over the keys. "Great. And let me know if you ever need a hand with... uh... I mean..." He licked his lips and checked his watch. "If you need any help."

I walked Carl back outside, then brought the bags in one by one. By the time I was done, Noah had claimed his bedroom.

I stood at his door, gazing in on him for a moment. He was small for his age anyway, but in this strange room, in a place we'd never been before, he was hunched over into himself so much it was like he'd shrunk.

"Hey, uh..." I'd been going to call him *son*, but that word still caught in my throat. Truth was, I'd planned never to have kids. Last thing I wanted was to dump all my baggage on a child.

But a child happened anyway, and out of fear and uncertainty, I'd let Noah get away from me for years. In the guards, there'd always been another clan to fight, another training session. The fact I'd never been with his mom in any formal way—just physically—hadn't helped me bond with my son.

"Noah? How about we head out and see what's what?"

"'kay."

"I saw something going on in the town square. Big crowd. Maybe we can get to know a few people."

"'kay."

Truthfully, I'd be happy to stay a

stranger to them all. It wouldn't be so different to where I'd been living back in the old Stoke Ridge. Weird that a guy as big as me could be as good as invisible. Then again, I'd done all I could to keep things that way.

But I had to face the truth. Without contacts, I'd be lucky to get any work. And rent wouldn't pay itself.

Noah slid off his bed and came over to me. He took my hand freely enough but there was no real strength or feeling in his grip. I thought about picking him up and putting him on my shoulders, but it felt like too big a move.

Too soon.

Thing is, I loved the kid like crazy. Always had, from the moment he was born. I'd just never known how to show it, let alone how to say it. But when his mom was taken so suddenly, I swore I wouldn't let anybody else write Noah's story, the way mine got written.

The foster system had been tough enough for me, and I'd always been a big motherfucker, even at Noah's age. Of course, that painted a target on my forehead for all the little dogs who wanted to fight the big dog. A kid like

Noah would have been chewed up and spat out within a week.

I'd had to fight Kellie's parents for custody, which was a shock to them. They'd never even known of my existence until their daughter's funeral. Apparently she'd told them Noah was from a one night stand and she never actually knew the guy.

Which was a whole lot closer to the truth than I liked to think about. Couldn't blame Kellie for that, either. I was never mean to her, but that didn't mean I was good to her.

Or *for* her.

But in this beautiful little boy, I saw a chance for redemption. Right my own wrongs, and heal the hurts life had already piled on him.

I was probably the least qualified man on earth to raise a kid... but I was his only hope.

CHAPTER THREE

Braden

EVEN THOUGH WE weren't officially a single clan anymore, Gray Vale still existed as a concept. And as a town, we'd decided to keep things running as smoothly as we could.

In this first week of summer break, that always meant it was time for the Country Fair. And for me, that meant setting up my tent and scrawling caricatures of anyone who wanted them.

My skills were far more suited to fine art than cartooning, so my caricatures were only fair to middling. People didn't seem to mind, though. Especially, when all the earnings were being pumped back into the school arts program.

It was the only time I could actually get a male shifter to pose for me, simply because it wasn't serious, and it never took long. It also played into our kind's natural egotistical tendencies. Even when I made fun of a feature, or a personality trait, all that did was let the subject feel more seen. Maybe even understood.

I was halfway through a portrait of Conall Blair, brother of our Alpha-who's-not-an-Alpha, when I caught the scent of trouble. Conall obviously noticed it as well, and he stood immediately. It was clear his guard instincts still ran strongly through his veins.

We glanced across to where the low but urgent voices were coming from. Conall looked ready to shift, but his partner, Zoltan, placed a hand on his shoulder.

"Con, you're a civilian now. Remember?"

"I can't just sit back and let shit go down."

"We have guards for that."

I moved up beside them and tried to work out what was happening. All I could see was a circle of our guys—off duty guards, all of them—and an untamed head of mid-blond hair protruding above all of them. Big guy, obviously, but outnumbered four to one.

I turned to Conall and Zoltan. "I'll get this one, guys."

"Seriously, Braden," Conall growled. "You don't have any guard training."

"I don't have any scars, either."

"So?"

I gave him my calmest, most disarming smile. "So obviously, nobody's ever seen reason to smack the shit out of *me*."

Before he could reply, I strolled over, easing myself through the crowd. It was an ambitious move on my part, sure, but I'd known Conall for years. I'd trust the guy with my life, and choose him to fight on my behalf any time.

The problem was, this was the Country Fair, and fighting was the exact opposite of what we needed. This thing, whatever was happening, was just a little... spot fire.

And Conall Blair was gasoline on legs.

As I reached the small mob, I realized the guy in the center was a stranger.

But holy hell, what a man.

A little older than me, taller even than Conall, and broader in the shoulders. There was no missing the trauma on his left arm, since the lower half was, itself, missing. His square, rugged face bore scars of battle, but his aura was even more scuffed up and broken.

"Come on, then," he growled, looking from one man to the next. I found it impossible to look away from him. It was more than just how goddamn sexy the guy was. He radiated all the isolation and brittle aggression of a stray dog.

And I'd always had a thing for strays.

"Fuckin' Ridgie," one of our guys said, and spat on the grass. "Yeah, I recognize you. There can't possibly be two fuckers as big and ugly as you. Only last time, you were better... *armed.*"

The speaker took a step forward, and the big guy's entire bearing changed. The Gray Vale guys were too invested in hating him to see clearly, but from my place as an observer, it was plain as day.

If this thing played out, then I had no doubt there'd be only one man standing by the end of it. This damaged but determined giant.

The other off-duty guards moved in as well, and the stranger glanced down toward the ground. Only then did I see the kid with his eyes wide with fear, clinging to the man's tree trunk leg.

That was all I needed to get stung into motion.

"Fellas," I said, grabbing a couple of our guys on their shoulders as I glided between them. "What seems to be the trouble here?"

"Fuck off, Braden. This isn't your concern."

"Oh, come on. Just think about what you're saying. And the young, impressionable ears you're saying it in front of. Yeah?"

"They've heard worse."

"But you know better." I put myself between the guardsmen and their quarry, facing our guys. Which of course, meant turning my back to the most dangerous man in the situation. "Seriously, guys. This is all kinds of messed up."

"What do you care? This asshole—" He jabbed his finger at the guy behind me. "Fought against us for years."

"Us?"

"Gray Vale."

"Then it's a good thing we're all one big happy family now, isn't it?"

"What would you even fucking know about it, Braidy-Cat? You ever done anything real with your life?"

"Everything I do is real, Simon."

"What, drawing your stupid cartoons? Playing dress-ups with children?"

I knew he was just trying to get under my skin. Thing was, I was beyond used to it. I'd taught *their* kids, for fuck's sake.

"Your boy Billy loved dress-ups. Always wanted to play at being a Gray Vale guard. *I'm gonna be just like my daddy,* he'd say." I leaned a little closer. "You think he'd be saying that right now?"

Simon visibly relaxed at the mention of his kid. I guess that counted as my biggest talent. Defusing bombs.

As a last shot across the bows, he pointed at the big beast of a man behind me. "You just keep out of my way, you hear?"

"Wasn't in your way to begin with,

sunshine."

God, even the guy's voice was sex on legs. Deep and sonorous, with more than a hint of sharpness in there. The sound of it so close behind me took my mind to all kinds of places. Places I really shouldn't be going in public, even when it was only inside my head.

The guardsmen dispersed and all ambled away, making sure to stare menacingly back at the big man. I let myself relax a little, right up until the guy spoke again.

"Didn't need your help, y'know."

I turned to face him, and bit down on my tongue. I mean, *damn*. Every single part of him sang to me, in ways that really never happened. In my experience, anyway. His scent filled my nose like his profile filled my eyes, like he would no doubt fill me in every other way.

Except, there was also no doubt that kid was his, and that, of course, meant the big, beautiful guy wasn't even playing for my team.

I let my mouth venture into a tiny grin. "You did, y'know? Need my help. Not in the way you meant it, but you sure did."

He stood a little straighter, his whole aura galvanizing. "What? You think I couldn't have taken those old guys down? There were only four of them."

Still with my peacemaking smile, I shook my head. "That's not what I meant. I'm talking about first impressions here. Just 'cause we're all shifters doesn't mean we have to be animals about it."

"You sure about that? Comes with the territory."

I shrugged off his comment. "For some, maybe. Those who are all about the strength and not the senses. They hide the tongue behind the teeth."

We stood in silence for a few seconds while he put in some work on deciding whether I was any kind of threat to him. Or just some hippy-dippy nobody.

"Well," I said, and held out my hand to him. "Since we're currently human, I should observe the customs. My name's Braden Craig."

He raised his eyebrows just the tiniest amount. To the eye alone, it probably looked like surprise. With the added depth of shifter senses, I could see it was more confusion than anything. I was more used to that reaction than I cared to admit.

He finally reached out and took my hand. "Marius Voss. And this is my son, Noah."

I dropped to one knee and held my hand out to the kid. "How are you, Noah?"

The kid flashed a smile at me, made brighter by being so brief. He took my hand and I feigned agony.

"Hey, hey, don't squeeze so tight, man."

That drew a proper chuckle from the kid, and his whole face came to life.

Of more interest to me was his father's reaction. Marius drew his head back ever so slightly. It was almost certainly nothing more than surprise, but the motion had all the appearance and feel of a flinch.

I stood again, and reached out slowly toward Noah. Giving him, and his sex-on-legs father, all the chances in the world to stop me. When neither of them did, I ruffled his blond mop, eliciting another small laugh.

"So," I began. "You're from the *enemy*, huh?" I made sure to say it with a smile.

To my relief, Marius smiled back. A genuine, though tiny, grin. And fuck me if the man didn't just light up, in exactly the same way as his kid had.

This was not good.

He was far from the first straight man I'd fallen instantly in lust with, but all the others had at least been single and childless.

"Yeah," he said, his voice deep and soft. "Stoke Ridge, born and bred. As far as I'm aware."

Noah jiggled around from foot to foot. "Dad, I'm bored."

"Hey, young man," I said. "How'd you like me to draw a caricature of you?"

He stared at me like I'd spoken a whole other language, so I bent to his level again. "It's sort of like a cartoon. You like cartoons?"

Noah looked up to his father for reassurance. I did the same, looking for permission. Marius lightly patted the kid's shoulder and nodded at me.

"Y–yes," Noah said, barely more than a whisper.

"Come on over, then."

CHAPTER FOUR

Marius

I'D BEEN READY to take on all four of those assholes. Being outnumbered was par for the course in my life. From the moment way, way back when my father was killed, it'd been me against the world.

Moving here to Gray Vale, where we'd so long been the enemy, I'd expected to be the odd one out. And for as long as it took.

What I hadn't expected was to find an ally. And not a brother-in-arms, like I'd have expected, but a damn peacemaker.

I got the feeling this Braden guy could be a whole lot more.

Maybe even a friend.

My first impression was that he had a broad smile that was always right there below the surface. It was as if his mouth could shapeshift, too. He could draw that smile out as quick as an old-time gunfighter with his pistol. Only in his case, it seemed to disarm everyone around him.

Including me.

As soon as Braden stepped into the mix, he cooled the entire situation. That was a kind of talent I couldn't remember ever seeing before.

He led us over to his stall. It was little more than a tent with the sides rolled up. A picnic blanket on the grass below it, an easel at one corner, and a stool at the opposite.

"Why don't you sit there, Noah?" he said.

My son looked at me again, and all that did was remind me how little I knew the kid. We'd been in forced proximity now for a few weeks. Intense, inescapable togetherness, which still hadn't managed to break down any barriers.

"Go, son. It's fine."

Noah got onto the stool, and it was just like it had been in the apartment, when he sat on his new bed. With his back bent and his head bowed, it was as if he was trying to take up the absolute minimum of space.

It showed up most when he was in a position like this. Out in the open, the focus of attention. Even when that attention was only from me, and this Braden guy.

"Sit up straight, son," I said, trying to keep my voice neutral.

Noah jolted upright so quickly he almost fell back off the stool. I hated the way that looked. The way I imagined it would look to Braden. Like the kid was scared shitless by his own father.

Fuck, that probably wasn't too far from the truth, if I was honest. But when it was out on display like that, for anyone to see, it cut me deep. Because no matter the truth, it would be easy for people to think the worst of me. That I spoke with my hands.

Well, *hand*.

Finding the right balance was the

hardest part of parenting for me. All my examples were at the extreme ends. A father killed in the line of duty, a mother who lost her shit and abandoned me, and foster parents who either ignored me or smothered me—in one case, literally.

All I really had was my training in the guards, and the only thing that had going for it was consistency. It served its purpose, and helped mold me, but it was also what led to me being the physical and mental wreck I now was. No way I could use that shit for raising my son.

If Braden thought anything negative, he kept it well hidden. Standing at his easel, he flashed that incredible smile again, and it had the exact same effect on Noah that it had on those assholes before. My son's posture, his whole bearing, relaxed.

"So, Noah," Braden said. "What do you like doing?"

"Um..." My son looked at me again, as if I had an answer. I wished I did, and I knew I should, but recreation just hadn't been a feature in our lives, yet. Too busy just trying to keep ourselves one step ahead of chaos.

Again, Braden didn't seem flustered. The guy clearly had some skills with kids, and I couldn't help envying him. But at the same time I was more than grateful. He put out an aura that my wolf responded to in ways that... well, frankly, ways that confused me. Like he could become even more than just a friend.

A confidante.

A brother.

Braden rubbed his chin as he made a big show of studying my son. "So, too many things you like doing, and you can't nail it down. I see that a lot. You like riding bikes?"

Noah lowered his head again. I'd never been there so far to teach the kid how to ride. I doubted his mother ever did, either.

Kellie had never been into the outdoors. In some bizarre way, I think that's what drew me to her in the first place. She was the opposite of what most shifters were like. And suddenly, I realized that Braden had some of that same energy about him. He gave off a real vibe of being an indoorsman all the way. Which was another factor that made me wonder why I felt an instant kinship with him.

"Well, maybe I can draw you on a bike anyway. Whaddya say, kiddo?"

Noah raised his head again, his face all lit up with excitement, like I'd never seen it before. "Yes, please."

"Awesome." Braden disappeared behind his huge sketchbook, popping out every few seconds to take another look at Noah. The scratching of his pencil against the paper seemed like the only sound, despite the bustling fair going on around us.

"And what about music, Noah? You like music?"

My son nodded unconvincingly, reminding me of the bare bones nature of our shared life. Music was yet another pleasure that had escaped us as we scrabbled desperately just to find a foothold.

Right here and now, though, there was a great sense of belonging. I wondered if we might have found our forever home. Not that shitty apartment, of course, but the town of Gray Vale.

Braden continued to toss easy and lighthearted questions at my son, and I made sure not to get in the way of it. Noah opened up to this man in ways I could barely believe. I was learning almost as much about the kid as Braden was.

It only took a few more minutes, and then Braden pulled the page off his sketchbook and turned it around to face us.

"Damn," I said, keeping my voice soft. "That's good, man."

"I might not be much of a fighter, but I *see* people. Y'know?" He put his hand on Noah's shoulder. "This young fella likes to hide himself, but I have ways of uncovering a man's true nature."

I looked over the picture again. As promised, he drew Noah on a bike. He captured my son's furtive smile perfectly.

Braden rolled up the picture and handed it to me. I took it, and tucked it under my arm so I could reach out and shake the guy's hand.

"Thanks, Braden. It's been... tough to find my way in over here." I released the handshake and rested my hand on Noah's head. "Until today."

He flashed that megawatt smile of his again. "Don't think you're getting out of it that easy, big guy."

"What are you talking about?"

He pulled the pencil back out from behind his ear and used it to point to the stool. "Your turn, sunshine." He even used the name I called that guard.

I could feel the look on my face. It was my classic *you gotta be fucking kidding* me expression. To his credit, Braden didn't give an inch. He just took his place at the easel.

"Dad?" Noah said, looking up at me. "I did it. You can do it."

"See?" Braden said with a victory smile. "Noah, you are wise beyond your years, young man."

Between the two of them, they'd sucker punched me. No way I could refuse now. It'd seem rude to the only guy who'd been on my side. And it would be a fresh new way to disappoint my son.

So, I took my place on the stool, feeling more conspicuous than I did when I stood. That, despite being a good three inches taller than almost everyone around me, was all the time.

"Just get comfortable, big guy," Braden said, once again disarming me with that brilliant smile.

I couldn't even get it straight in my head what *comfortable* would be. I tried leaning forward, then sitting back. I went to cross my arms, momentarily forgetting I was missing half of one of them.

"Hey, Marius?"

"Huh?"

He held up his pencil. "It isn't really mightier than the sword, you know."

It was a pretty lame joke, but as with everything else he'd done so far, it worked.

And for the first time in a long time, I not only felt relaxed... I felt at peace.

CHAPTER FIVE

Braden

FOR A HUGE and sexy guy, Marius looked adorably uncomfortable as he tried to strike a pose. I had no doubt he could wrestle alligators and lift rolled-over cars. It was sitting still and being looked at that made the guy nervous.

"Seriously, man," I said. "Just relax. Nobody's looking. It's just Noah and me here with you."

He frowned as he clenched and opened his fist. "I'm just... I'm used to being invisible."

"Dude, you could be seen from

space.”

He let out a quiet, humorless chuckle and raised his damaged arm. “This, though. This makes people look away. Or stare right through me.”

I let a breath pass before I asked my next question. “So, you want me to draw it back in? Or go more true to life?”

“You’re the artist.”

That was too vague for me to decide yet, so I started with his face.

His rugged, beautiful face.

As I sketched his strong features, I tried to engage him in conversation. “So, what about you, Marius?” he asked. “What do you like?”

“Huh?”

“Are you a football fan? You like needlepoint? Rollerblading?” I just hoped he understood I was teasing.

He looked completely blank for a moment. “Y’know, I don’t think I have a *thing*. Been so wrapped up in adjusting to all the changes in my life.”

“You must have had something before all that.” Even with shifter senses, I couldn’t quite get a read on him. He presented straight as fuck, but there were all kinds of doubts running through him as well. I couldn't be sure none of them were sexual.

"Nothing that matters anymore."

The dull tone of his voice had me feeling the topic was closed for discussion, so I changed tack. Even though I could tell it was a sensitive area, I hoped he'd open up about his injury.

"So, your arm," I said. Yeah, okay... subtlety wasn't my strong point.

Marius raised one eyebrow, but otherwise remained still.

"You miss it?"

He lifted the damaged limb and looked the scarred stump over. It almost looked like he was seeing it for the first time. "I, uh... well, I've learned how to get along without it, but I wish I'd never lost it. I guess that might count as missing it."

I kept drawing as I absorbed his words, rolling them around in my head to see if I could pick up any of the unspoken ones. Marius seemed used to presenting himself as a vault. Impregnable and unreadable. Like his heart and soul were both more scarred than his arm.

So, again, I tried a disarming side step in the conversation. "What are your plans, now you've upgraded to Gray Vale?" I made sure to let him see me smiling. What good was a generations-long rivalry if you couldn't poke fun at people about it?

"No plans, yet," he murmured, low enough that humans wouldn't have heard him. "Looking for work, and... well, I guess I should try and get a few, uh..."

I waited for the last word, but it never came. "Friends?"

"Mm. Those." He let out a long, low sigh that took on a little gravel as it rolled along.

I had to clamp my mouth closed to stop myself asking about people who'd be more than friends.

Or friends with benefits.

There was no chance of a future with Marius, despite how hard I already crushed on him.

He took another breath, and then opened up a little more. "Truth is, this is the most conversation I've had with an adult in... probably, six months."

"Well, I'm honored. And..." I signed

my name at the bottom of the caricature. "I'm done."

Noah scurried around to get a look at my work. Marius was a whole lot more circumspect, but when he stood, there was no doubt he'd relaxed a little more. He moved with a cautious grace now, which seemed at odds with his height and bulk.

"Look, dad," Noah said, pointing at the drawing. "It's you."

I stepped back and let Marius see it properly. His expression stayed stony as he looked it over. I was more interested in watching him than studying my work.

One thing I'd picked up as soon as I saw him was that Marius might as well be covered in spikes. He was clearly so hard to get close to. I didn't know his past yet, but I was fully invested in finding it out.

Only thing I felt certain of was that he hadn't let anybody see him—*really* see him—in many years. And it was probably because of however people saw him before that.

Right back into childhood.

So with my caricature, I'd accentuated his size, of course, and the strength of his handsome features.

He raised an eyebrow and looked at me. "What's going on here?" He poked at the illustration, where I had his damaged arm lifted.

"Oh, that," I said, flashing him a tiny smile. "That's just you flipping us all the bird."

"You didn't draw the arm in."

"Didn't think I needed to."

His heavy brows drew together in a deep frown. I suddenly feared for my safety, wondering if I'd misread him. My wolf raised his hackles deep inside, but with a man as fearsome as Marius, I was definitely preparing for flight, and not fight.

He surprised me by simply grunting, and then kneeling beside his son. "What do you think, Noah?"

"It's really good. You look silly but still scary."

I caught the look of pain on the big man's face, though it only lasted a fraction of a second. Marius nodded, then stood again, turning toward me.

"How much do I owe you?"

I waved him away. "No charge." I'd cover it from my own pocket. Strange as it might be to anyone else, I actually felt that I got more out of this whole thing than he did.

"You work for free? Your wife must be very understanding."

That one little sentence gave me a clearer picture of the guy. And especially his experiences with women.

"No wife." I had the choice to leave it at that. Of course, I didn't. "Never was, and never will be."

The fold between his brows deepened. "You don't strike me as a loner, Braden. I see how you are with, uh... y'know."

"People?"

"Mm."

"Well, I'm not. A loner, that is. I'm very popular, even with the ladies. But, uh... the ladies aren't popular with me, if you catch my drift."

He raised both brows instantly as he processed what I'd just told him.

"Huh. Well. Uh..." His whole body language changed instantly. He reverted to that uneasy confusion he'd had when he first sat to pose. As if my confession somehow exposed him.

I couldn't help but take the tiniest bit of hope from that. Maybe there was a chance, however slim, that he'd be open to trying something new.

"But either way," I said, trying to change the subject to stop him thinking too hard, or in the wrong direction. "The drawing is yours."

For a few seconds, he looked determined to argue. The guy clearly wasn't used to any kind of charity. Maybe he thought it looked weak. Eventually, he nodded his thanks, rolled up the picture and handed it to Noah.

He reached out and I shook his hand, and then he turned to leave. My wolf whined deep inside me, like he hadn't in many a moon. It was more of a warning to my human side than anything else.

"Listen," I started, and Marius turned back. "If you need, uh... y'know, anything? I'm pretty well connected."

Ugh.

That sounded like the lamest pickup line that had ever been tossed out there. And to no avail, of course. After all, widowers did tend to be dudes of the old hetero persuasion. While he didn't run screaming or threaten violence, it was clear my coming out to him also hadn't landed the way I'd dreamed it might.

Marius kinked his head to the side, growled out a quick thanks, and then left.

Without my number, my address, my details, or any way to contact me.

Message received.

CHAPTER SIX

Marius

IT WAS HARD as hell to make sense of this place. When Stoke Ridge was a separate entity, we'd all been taught to sneer at Gray Vale. And one of the chief reasons was their open and accepting culture. Especially when it came to gay folk.

I'd taken that school of thought on easy enough in the guards. Fuck, it was practically mandatory to hate on anyone who wasn't part of Stoke Ridge. Doubly so for what our rulers determined to be *perverts and sinners.*

EVIE RILEY

Now that I was actually living in Gray Vale, the truth was much simpler. People are people, whoever, wherever, and whatever the fuck they are.

On the other hand, unlike back up on the ridge, at least down here there was *one* person in my corner. I couldn't work out Braden's deal, but my wolf didn't give me any danger signals.

I felt like the world's rudest prick when I left. All the guy did was to offer help, and listen to me. Fuck, he just about yanked some little home truths out of me, without me quite understanding how.

Like a magic show.

He had me concentrating on one thing and suckered me into opening up.

Noah dragged behind me, and I took hold of his hand to keep him with me. I realized I'd been striding at my own speed. Still thinking about Braden. Wishing I'd been brave enough to ask his number, wondering if I should go back and get it. Tail between my legs and whining.

Was I seriously that fucking desperate?

I'd take the first bone anyone tossed

me and call it a friendship?

The guy radiated charm, in a way I'd never seen in anybody before. He'd be friends with every fucker in town. Last thing he needs is for the new guy—the big, wounded oaf—to crowd him.

"Dad, you're hurting me."

I glanced down to where Noah's tiny fist disappeared inside mine, and let go like I'd been burned.

Fuck.

That was exactly how I did everything.

Over the top, or not at all.

"Sorry, son."

He looked close to tears, and I held my breath as I tried to figure out what to do.

What had Braden done?

Whatever it was, Noah relaxed around him.

I dropped to one knee, like Braden had. And I reached out for my son, moving my hand slowly. His big eyes bugged in confusion, but he relaxed when I stroked my fingers back through his hair.

"I mean it, Noah. I'm sorry. I got distracted."

"It's okay, dad."

No, son.

It isn't.

I'm your world, and I'm just not big enough or strong enough for the role.

Thank fuck I managed not to spill my thoughts out all over the kid.

"Come up here," I said instead, picking the boy up and sitting him over the back of my neck. "Let's go home."

"To our old house?"

I winced in reaction. Poor kid didn't seem to get how permanent this situation was. "To the new place, son."

"Okay. I like your new friend."

"Who, Braden?"

"Uh-huh."

I gave a brief nod and kept walking. "Yeah. Me, too."

Was *like* a strong enough word, though?

The guy made me feel stuff. Stuff I didn't feel. Ever. Not with any of the guards, not with any of my foster parents.

In only a matter of minutes, Braden had my head whirling with the kind of thoughts that would get a man whipped back in the old Stoke Ridge. Because whatever it was that Braden awoke inside me, it was closest to how I'd felt right at the start with Kellie.

Except much stronger.

And honestly, that scared the shit out of me. I knew Gray Vale folks had been cool with that kind of thing for generations, now, but I still had my baggage.

***

It was probably for the best that I didn't get anything more than Braden's name. No address or number, no idea where he worked.

Okay, yeah, so I'd barely stopped thinking about him in the weeks since we met. And sure, I could ask around and find out more about him. Track him down and just see where things might go.

But the fact was, things might go way beyond anything I was prepared for. I'd never been a fearful man. Even against the bear shifter who took my arm, I never backed down.

So why did this one guy have me all torn up inside?

Why couldn't I shake him?

Why the hell hadn't I even entertained the idea of being with any of the women around here?

More than a few had thrown themselves right into my path, after all.

I kept telling myself my continued celibacy was for Noah's sake. I didn't want to bring any more instability into his life. But the truth was much simpler than that.

Lack of interest.

In the women, in a relationship, in the chaos that always, *always* came with sex. Even casual sex had loud echoes in a place where everyone knew everyone. And Noah was living proof that the most casual encounters still had lifelong consequences.

So I kept rolling through life, putting one foot in front of the other. Making sure Noah at least had all he needed, even if I couldn't give him much of what he wanted. I knew the kid was hurting for some friends but I just didn't have the contacts yet.

But it was finally his first day of school, and surely that would make things better. At least, it'd give me a chance to really look for some work.

Something casual to start with, so I could work around Noah's school day.

Our apartment was close enough to the school that we could walk it. When my son's nerves got the better of him, I suppressed my ingrained instinct to bark at him. Tell him to man up, or some equally awful shit. The kind of so-called parenting I'd always had.

Instead, I picked him up, and carried him. Said nothing, just held him close. He snuggled against my neck in a way I couldn't remember him doing before, and it felt as if my heart suddenly woke up.

At the entrance to the school, I put him back down and walked him in. We followed the crowd through to the hall.

The teaching staff were all lined up on the stage, and all the kids and parents had arranged seating. I stayed up near the back out of habit. Just to stop anyone behind complaining they couldn't see past me.

Once I took my seat, Noah clambered up into my lap. Again, my first instinct was to push him off, onto his own seat. Didn't want people to think he was a mama's boy, or anything.

I managed to push that feeling down. Something I'd grown better and better at in the last few weeks. And all because of Braden, and his natural way of just letting people be their best fucking version of themselves.

Nobody had ever influenced me so much, in so little time. It dawned on me then that I was an idiot for not looking him up. Trying to connect with him. Maybe now that I'd have more time on my hands, I could try to make a genuine friendship with the guy.

Noah wriggled on my lap and leaned against my chest. The kid was getting closer to me every day, and I had to be honest... I fucking loved it. Even though I was constantly shitting myself that I'd screw him up through inexperience or simply by being myself.

Then my son made a little *ooh* sound, and I glanced down at him in case he was in pain.

"What is it, son?"

"Look. Braden."

"Huh?" I looked around the parents but couldn't see the guy. "Noah, come on. You gotta stop doing this."

Since that day when we met Braden,

Noah had kept insisting he saw the guy everywhere. And he'd never been right. Not once. I thought it must have been wishful thinking, since the two of them hit it off so well.

"I saw him, dad."

I took a breath rather than shoot him down. Another little thing I'd been trying which seemed to work. "Okay, son. I can't see him, though."

Any further discussion was knocked aside by the principal standing up and beginning her welcome speech. We sat through it all, and I paid as much attention as I could.

Honestly, since Noah said the guy's name, all I could think of was Braden.

What the hell was going on with me?

I never got like this over anybody before. Hell, even my wolf was pacing around inside me, licking his lips and whining.

Over a *guy*.

What gives?

Then the school principal cut through my confused inner monologue, by saying the very name I couldn't shift from my head.

"And teaching kindergarten this year,

Mister Braden Craig."

Ah, fuck.

He not only worked at my kid's new school, but he was Noah's classroom teacher?

That felt like it really threw a spanner in the works. Sure, we could still be friendly, but somehow that made it seem like we couldn't be *friends*.

Or... anything.

I turned my attention back to the stage and held my breath as the man himself stepped up to the lectern. He was dressed a little more formally than when I saw him at the Country Fair, but he still had that same aura of calm certainty.

Which was the complete opposite of everything that was whirling around inside my mind and my body. A sensation something like a fucking maelstrom of confusion, with a light dusting of—weirdly—happiness.

CHAPTER SEVEN

Braden

I ALMOST HOSED up my welcome speech, and for one reason only.

Marius.

Even when he was seated, and even way up the back, the guy stood out like a hard-on in church.

Or in my case, a hard-on at the lectern. Because just catching a glimpse of him had my cock tingling as it filled and stiffened. I was a damn lost cause.

Why did I so often fall for straight guys?

I seriously thought I had a better

brain than that. I probably did, actually. It was just that I was thinking with a whole other part of my anatomy, yet again.

At least I did manage to get through the welcome, and back to my seat, and I didn't think anybody noticed the boner I was sporting.

Of course, I'd known that Noah would be in my class this year. I got the list from Kayleigh a couple weeks back. So, I shouldn't have been surprised to see Marius. He'd be one of "my" parents all year, and we'd no doubt have some time to chat.

Unfortunately, that would be all we could do.

There weren't exactly rules about this stuff, but there was at least a strong expectation. And that was that we keep our hands off our students' parents.

Even the big, rough diamonds of pure sexiness.

Dammit.

If Noah was in someone else's class, then I could be more friendly with Marius. But the way things were, it was too easy to cross lines that couldn't then be uncrossed. I'd rather look forward to a lifelong friendship with him, starting next year, than to never see him.

Stupid me, I still held out hope that he'd be open to a little one-on-one time with me, sometime down the track. If I had to wait a year, until Noah was in another teacher's class, I could do it. It'd be hard as hell—and so would I—but I'd manage.

Finally, the welcome session was over, and we made our way to our classrooms. I welcomed all the kids into my room, one by one. I noticed that Marius hovered right at the back of the line, and Noah was clutching at his father's muscular leg like he had back at the Country Fair.

It sure seemed I'd have some work to do with that sweet kid. I'd only met him for a short time, but my impression was that he was smart, polite and kind, but that there were some real trust and self-esteem issues whirling around inside him as well.

The pair of them reached the doorway last of all, and though I didn't want to single Noah out for special treatment, I kinda couldn't help myself. For him, I dropped to one knee again and held out my fist.

"Noah. Good to see you again, my man."

The kid looked at my bunched up hand in confusion, then up at his father. Marius made his own fist and pumped it gently forward, and Noah's understanding showed on his sweet face.

He followed his father's example and moved his little hand forward, his fingers barely even curled back. The feather-light touch when his knuckles met mine only seemed to confirm what I'd thought.

Now I really couldn't help myself. I was here for it, whatever *it* was. I wanted to know the back story for what made this adorable kid disappear into himself like he had. The dynamic between son and father wasn't smooth, but there were no warning signs at all.

This man clearly loved his son, but it was kind of like how I love the French language. It takes my breath away with how beautiful it is, and yet I barely understand a word of it.

That was how it looked with Marius. I could see it on his worn but handsome face how much he adored his little man. But it was as if he was constantly searching for the subtitles so he could work out what was going on with the kid.

"Come on in, my man," I said to Noah, and held out my hand to shake with Marius. "Good to see you again, too."

He shook back readily enough.

"Braden. I should have guessed you'd be a teacher."

His voice was just as I remembered it. Volume and pitch low, like he was doing everything possible to be invisible. I swore there were harmonics there that only my wolf could hear. And damn if it didn't just confuse the hell out of both sides of me.

Marius seemed a little easier to get a handle on than his son was. There was a reclusive nature about the man that I was certain had nearly everything to do with his size. After all, that day I'd met him, he'd been the center of attention mostly because he stood out so much.

He must get that kind of shit all the time. Factor in his crunched up arm and it was no wonder he wanted to move through life in the shadows.

Well... not on my watch. Just

because I couldn't be with him didn't mean I couldn't hang around him. Force him into some quiet socializing. Not big groups or loud events. Hell, if I had my way they'd be just the two of us.

Sittin' in a tree.

Whether he knew it or not, Marius needed me. Maybe as much as his son did, but in a different way.

***

I knew Noah would need some help easing his way into school life. Not only was it his first year, but he was the only kid in the class who wasn't born and raised in Gray Vale.

To begin with, I cherry-picked a few of the kids whose parents I knew well, and gave Noah some time paired up with them. The kids who were naturally quiet but strong, and whose families had strong bonds.

Within a few days, the gentle and involved attention of the kids—and me— had Noah coming at least partway out of his shell. It helped that he'd not only shown a great interest in art... he also had some ability. That gave me something to work with outside of regular school stuff.

Over the past couple of weeks, he'd been staying back after school, waiting for his dad to pick him up. Marius always arrived later than most. I never minded since it meant I could get a little time to actually talk to that big, sexy man without interruption. Plus I knew it was one of his coping mechanisms.

There was so much less chance of him having to talk to strangers—the other parents—if he got here after they'd all left. Especially, all those desperately thirsty single moms. Even the married ones were too handsy for my liking. And damn if I hadn't had to run interference on Kayleigh more than once.

Not that I could blame them.

Marius really was something else.

And as much of a thrill as it was to watch Noah begin to blossom, it hit me even harder to see his father opening up to me. Of course, I wasn't naïve enough to think things would ever go beyond friendship. Straight guys are pretty hard to score with, after all.

By the end of the second week, Noah had almost become a brand new boy. He'd settled in beautifully and had a couple of kids he clearly thought of as friends.

He seemed to really appreciate the extra time I took with him, too. As we waited for Marius to arrive, I looked over Noah's latest artwork.

"I love what you're doing here, my man," I said, and the boy practically wriggled in reaction. Praise still worked magic on him.

"Thank you, Mister Craig."

As usual, he'd drawn a house. A standalone house with a wide pathway. Perhaps a symbol of welcoming, although he rarely actually drew any people in or around the houses. The only times he did, the figures were clearly his father and himself. Nobody else.

The kid still radiated a sense of loss, and a feeling of solitude. I could pick those up almost as well in my human senses as my wolf. Despite how he was becoming more gregarious, he still awoke in me a desire to protect. I lost myself in the moment, and before I thought about it, I rested my hand on Noah's shoulder.

I gave him the lightest little squeeze of solidarity before taking my hand away. I had to really watch myself there, of course. I'd grown fond of the boy beyond the level a teacher should, and there was no doubt it was in part because of how I felt about his father.

"Are you ready for tonight, Noah?" He'd been invited for a sleepover, and he clearly was beyond keen to go. Still, he shrugged as if it was nothing.

"I have to ask my dad."

I had great hope that Marius would okay the deal. Surely, he could do with a night off as well. I'd learned enough to know that active and involved fatherhood was still relatively new to him.

At that moment, I spotted the man walking in to my classroom to pick up his son. Prowling toward us, moving with natural stealth, radiating peril, and as always, I simply couldn't look away from him.

Once again, I had to push my wolf down. The hunger my inner beast had for this tall, rough man was beyond anything I'd ever known. And it got sharper whenever Marius smiled at me. Like he was doing right at that moment.

"Braden," he said, more of a growl

than a word. Then he turned to his son. "Ready to go, Noah?"

"Noah has something he needs to ask you," I blurted, desperate to keep Marius near me for a little longer.

Marius glided down to a crouch to bring himself eye to eye with Noah. "What's up, son?"

The boy didn't look away from his drawing as he spoke. "There's a sleepover tonight. I got invited."

Marius frowned, and looked up at me. "Sleepover. Already?"

"Noah's really getting popular." Marius still looked a little confused, so I pushed a little harder. "I do think it'd be good for him to go."

That seemed to be all Marius needed to make his decision. "Then let's get you home and packed," he said, sounding more playful than I could ever recall.

Noah packed up his drawing and picked up his bag while I gave Marius the details for the sleepover. The big man shook my hand and I soaked up the feel of his skin, his heat, for a moment.

Just as they were about to leave the classroom, he turned back. "Listen, Braden..."

My wolf leapt up inside me, ears pricked, tail poised. On the surface I tried to remain calm. "Yes?"

"I wanted to thank you for... helping us both."

"That's no problem. It's what I do."

He nodded and scratched his jaw. "Yeah, but... it's not something anyone's done for me, before. I was thinking..."

"Hmm?"

"This might be breaking some kind of rule, I guess. But since Noah's gonna be out, maybe you'd like to get together?"

Oh man.

There was nothing I wanted more.

"It's not against any rules," I said, though I wasn't completely sure I was right about that. "But like... beers at the tavern kind of thing?"

He screwed his face up at that idea. "I was more thinking of dinner. I have a couple steaks thawed, and maybe we can... y'know. Talk about Noah's progress."

That wasn't quite what I wanted, but fuck it.

I'd take it.

"I'd love to."

CHAPTER EIGHT

Marius

I KNEW WHEN I invited Braden in that I was overstepping. Moving outside my comfort zone. But he'd been so good with Noah, helping my son adjust to the new town, to the daunting experience of starting school.

The guy had been pretty much the perfect blend of teacher, father, and even mother to my son. I still didn't really get how socialization worked, but when it came to Braden, I wanted to make a real effort. Even if all I could do to start with was mimic what I saw others doing.

That was why I'd extended the invitation. That was why he was sitting here at the dining table, across from me, savoring the basic-ass dinner I made for him.

Or so I told myself.

"This is really good, Marius."

"It's four ingredients."

"Well, I like it. It's nice not to have to cook, for once."

Thing was, even if he was only pretending to enjoy it, that was more than most people had ever done for me. Hiding the truth to spare my feelings.

He poured us both another glass of wine, and I couldn't help eyeing mine off. I'd tried not to drink more than a couple glasses a week since Noah came into my life full time, but my son wasn't here tonight. Besides, it was so rare for me to have company. It felt rude to refuse.

Almost the instant we both finished eating, Braden stood and began picking up plates.

"Hey," I said, a lame protest.

"I got this, big guy."

"No, you're my guest." I flinched for a second as my wounded arm gave off one of its annoying little hot twinges. I didn't quite manage to mask my reaction, and there was no doubt Braden noticed it.

Fucking wolf senses.

"See? Even your arm insists I should wash up."

It was tough to let him take over like that. Pride still had a strong hold over me most times, but cooking had been hard enough with only one hand. The amount and kind of dishes I'd dirtied were pretty much impossible.

"Thanks, man," I said. Even that felt odd, since I rarely call people anything but their given names. Or some title. A pet name was really off kilter for me.

Wait.

Not a *pet* name.

What the fuck was I doing here?

A *nickname*.

Like between buddies.

I shook my head to try and clear it. All it seemed to do was filter the confusion down into my soul. Somehow it didn't really feel like confusion, though.

More like... friendship.

And was there really anything wrong with being friends with Braden?

I followed him into the kitchen and

grabbed a dishtowel.

"Uh-uh," he said, shaking his head. "I got this, I told you. Stay and chat, sure, but don't you lift a finger." He turned and winked. "And don't think for a second I don't know this is bugging the hell out of you, dude."

Finally, I relented, and I sat on the edge of the kitchen table and watched him work. My wolf raised his hackles out of uncertainty. Whether as a man or a beast, I'd always had the same instant reaction to an unfamiliar feeling.

Hackles up, teeth bared and growling. Attack before any shit hits my particular fan. My wolf paced inside me, trying to help me make sense of what this feeling was.

When Braden finished the dishes and turned to face me, it made me catch my breath. Realization hit me like a damn bear shifter.

I was attracted to the guy.

As if in protest at the truth, my damaged arm stung me again, and that time so sharply that I grunted with the pain.

Braden came straight across, his handsome face creased with concern, and he took hold of my upper arm and elbow. Tingles ran through my entire body, and rained down on my wolf.

"What do you need, Marius?"

"A fucking miracle."

He looked up at me, gliding his hand gently over the mangled skin of my stump. He slid the other hand down and pressed both his thumbs up against the old wound, gently at first. Then, he ground at the area like he was giving it a massage.

When it was clear he wasn't hurting me, he lifted the arm and took a much closer look at it.

He stroked his fingers over the damaged flesh, his face reflecting some mix of sadness and admiration.

It was the first time anybody had paid any kind of attention to the injury since the doctors did. Outside of stares and sneers by strangers, at least. Everyone who encountered me seemed to feel either revulsion or pity.

But my wolf could tell Braden, true to form, had nothing but empathy. The sadness was genuinely on my behalf, not from imagining the same injury on his own body.

And then, to my surprise, he kissed it. He pressed his mouth to my scarred and ugly flesh as if it was just a normal thing.

The wolf deep inside me whined, and pure need flooded through me. I couldn't remember the last time I'd had any kind of closeness with another being, apart from my son. And Noah still wasn't completely open with me.

Even though shifters are capable of secrets, it took a lot more effort. Too many senses in play. That was how I knew Braden was being as open with me as anybody ever had.

Without either of us speaking a word, I could taste his honesty.

Fuck, I could just about taste his heart.

And a moment later, when I grabbed him around the back of the neck and pulled him to me, I could taste his lips.

The guy responded immediately, opening up to me and drawing my tongue inside. He speared his fingers up into my hair and held on, his moans shifting into whimpers and then to growls.

Just like mine.

Every hair on my body bristled with pure desire.

To be held, to be touched.

To be *wanted*, not needed.

My wolf howled, and the sound came up through my body. I sang that note into Braden's hot mouth, and his wolf joined in as well. All the aggression I'd kept suppressed, just to help me fit in as a member of this new community, and as a father as well... it all came bubbling up.

I bit down on Braden's tongue, hard enough to hurt him. Hard enough that I drew blood. It didn't slow him down one bit. If anything, it just drove him harder.

Kellie had been wolf, too, but she'd never responded to me like that. Fuck, maybe I'd never responded to her the way I was to Braden. It was too hard to remember myself clearly from back then.

The only certainty in my body right then was that I wanted this man. In the most base and carnal ways. After a lifetime of obliviousness and assumptions about myself, it was all too much, and I shoved Braden away.

He stumbled back, his eyes quivering, caught somewhere between man and wolf. Fear overtook me like a tornado, but it wasn't fear for myself. I couldn't be sure I wouldn't hurt this man in some way.

I had a history, for fuck's sake.

Before Braden even spoke, I turned and fled. Straight out the front door of my apartment, and on down toward the thickest part of the forest.

The shift overtook me before I reached the halfway mark. My limbs prickled and my bones creaked. Fur erupted from the skin of my arms and spread over my face. I hadn't shifted once since my injury, but the sensations were still so fucking clear.

I shed my clothing as best I could without breaking stride. Anything still on me just tore or dropped away. By the time I reached the tree line, I was fully shifted.

And I landed flat on my fucking snout, thanks to my missing front leg.

All that did was slice into my rage, which stemmed straight from my confusion and embarrassment anyway.

I scrabbled up onto my paws again and loped into the forest, learning quickly how to balance myself on only three feet.

This part of the forest was new to me, but it wasn't too far different from what I knew up on Stoke Ridge. The trees were the same, the birdsong, too. But the ground was smoother, which I welcomed.

The scents and sounds of the place embraced me like an old friend. Only by shifting this time did I realize how much I'd missed being wolf. How hard I'd been working to stop myself from doing it, for the sake of my son.

Once again, I knew I had Braden to thank for that. He awoke something ancient inside me. Not just my wolf, but my instincts.

And I'd turned away from him. Ran like he was the bear who took my arm. Simply because I was confused, and confusion made me a scared little kid.

Or at least, that confusion was the fuse that ignited the tightly bound powder keg inside me. The shitstorm of life that had rained down on me over the past couple of years.

I should have been strong enough to handle it all, but I suddenly realized all I'd done was to push it down, compress it. Wall myself off from every other fucker in the world. Even, to a certain degree, my son.

And then Braden came along, and with what looked like no effort at all, he simply scaled that fucking wall. Or more like he found a door.

And he opened me the fuck up.

Since my son lost his mother and came to me, I'd done everything required of me, and hopefully, a little more above and beyond. I'd provided, and I'd cared, and protected.

But who'd been there for me?

The short answer was Braden.

Only Braden.

And tonight he'd been there for me again, in a way I hadn't ever expected any man to be.

CHAPTER NINE

Braden

AS MARIUS TOOK flight away from me, I cursed myself.

Too much.

Too fast.

Everything I'd suspected about the man, everything my wolf had sensed, turned out to be true. Including the fragile and confused nature of his attraction to me.

As soon as I'd pushed my emerging wolf back down, I hurried out to follow him. The last thing I wanted was to leave him to process such a huge shift—no pun intended—on his own. Whether as man or wolf.

I'd barely taken a dozen steps before I found his shredded shirt, and realized he actually *had* shifted. I wasn't surprised. It was the way many of us dealt with a complex or challenging situation.

My best chance of finding him, and easing his turmoil, was to follow suit. I closed my eyes and let the tingling heat wash over me. The sweet pain and harsh sounds of bones breaking and reforming, the stretching and swelling of my jaw into a snout, the ragged tearing of fabric as arms and hands morphed into fur-covered paws.

Once I was wolf, I ripped away whatever clothing was left, and bounded into the forest, following the scent of that beautiful but troubled man.

Even with only three legs, he'd had a good head start and if not for my nose, I would have had no chance to follow. But I was so attuned to Marius that I could just about *see* his scent, even with all the other smells of the forest arguing for attention.

In mere minutes, I found him in

Burton's Clearing, standing by the stream. He was facing me, all coiled up and ready for fight or flight. Even with his one front paw planted beneath his head to balance him, he was formidable.

Just like when he was human, he was ruggedly beautiful, and so damn huge. I paused for a moment at the edge of the clearing, crouching to keep my head low.

On the surface, it was an act of submission. In reality, it was more about reminding him that I was no threat to him. Not in any way.

He slackened his stance enough to give me hope, and I took a few cautious steps forward. The low growl he let rumble from his lips was clearly not a true warning. More a way to tell me to slow the hell down.

I licked my muzzle and let my tail swing lightly. Every step I took, he watched like I was prey. In under a minute, I was right there with him. I ducked my head under his and nudged forward, leaving the back of my neck open to him.

Marius huffed and leaned his head on my back. He was so big, and so heavy, but it felt better than heaven to have him accept me like that.

His damaged leg was right before me, and this time, I gave it a quick lick. The wolf equivalent of kissing it, the way I did it just before, when we were human.

Marius made another huffing sound and dug his fangs into the skin of my back. I felt no threat from him. If anything, all it felt like was a connection. A show of possessiveness. As if he was grabbing hold of me, to stop me from getting away.

If only he knew just how crazy into him I was. The biggest trouble with being in wolf form was the narrow corridors of communication. Using scents, sounds, and body language was all well and good for the basics. Emotional state, territorial boundaries, even hunting tactics.

There were nuances to it all, and sometimes the absence of words made it purer and more meaningful. But wolf Marius was new to me. Not from the same clan. It was so easy to get signals wrong, especially with a shifter who was so out of touch with his inner beast.

But to try and tell Marius how I felt

about him, I'd need the advantages of human speech. To help him work through the complicated nature of whatever he was going through, I'd need words, and so would he.

I stepped away from him and once again closed my eyes, letting the shift overtake me. In moments, I was back in human form, and I stood slowly, keeping my hands held out from my sides. I was not a threat to him and I wanted to make sure that fact made it through the wolf's consciousness to the man underneath.

Holy hell.

Even as wolf, Marius still reached up almost to my chest. With his head raised, his breath washed all the way up to my neck.

He watched my hands as I reached out toward him, and when I threaded my fingers into his thick fur, his skin quivered at the touch.

I was anything but certain about that moment, and where he'd go from there, emotionally. Physically. But he closed his eyes and huffed out a hot breath against my chest.

I snaked my fingers up and scratched

behind his ears, moving myself forward and to my right, so he could lean on me a little more. To counterbalance for his missing leg.

Marius angled forward, pressing the top of his head to my belly. His breath was now coursing downward, and flowing over my cock. This big wolf could obviously pick up my scent, since his nose was only inches from my stiffening member.

We both stood frozen for a moment. Then the coarse fur in my hands gradually shrank away, as this brutish wolf shifted back into the delicious, huge man I'd first met.

Marius jumped instantly to his feet, towering over me. For one brief instant, the wild wolf remained still there behind his eyes, before he coiled his hand around the back of my neck and pulled me forward.

The impact of his mouth against mine was as brutal and as painful as it was beautiful. I tasted blood and couldn't tell whose it was.

Probably both of ours.

Marius drove his tongue inside me and I gripped his hair, and stroked his scalp, just as I'd done when he was wolf. He growled deep into my throat like he still hadn't quite shifted all the way back.

I absolutely leaned hard into the kiss, doing all I could to own the moment. Marius made a tight fist in my hair, and stroked his damaged arm up and down my side.

I slid one hand down and caressed that arm, gliding around to the scarred end of it, and dragging my palm over the rough skin. Almost like I was stroking a massive cock.

Then, I eased my other hand out of his hair and scratched down over the thatch of blonde curls on his chest, flicking a fingernail over his pebbled nipple. Then on down through the thick bush below his belly.

The instant my fingers met the skin of his cock, I whimpered, overwhelmed by his heat, his hardness, and his pure fucking size. I snaked my fist around him and squeezed tight, and Marius threw his head back with a deep, groaning howl.

"Christ, you're fucking beautiful," I moaned as I fell to my knees in worship.

I buried my face in the curls of his bush, and drew in the musky scent of him. My wolf and human merged for a moment as both halves wrestled for dominance. For possession of this man's scent.

I stroked him, squeezing hard as I licked at his hip. Marius rested his big paw on the top of my head and let out a deep, breathy moan, and I lost a little bit more of my sanity.

As I drifted back inward, I hauled his huge thick cock downward. I glanced my lips across the shaft of him and once again soaked up the crazy heat of this man.

I stroked the long length of his gorgeous cock with my tongue, up one side and back down the other. I squeezed the fat blunt head in my hand as I dragged the face of my tongue slowly up the belly of his thick beast.

Marius tightened his grip on my hair, pulling hard enough to hurt me—just how I needed it. Desperation overtook me and I slid my fist back down his length and hauled his cock into my mouth, humming my appreciation as the flavor of him burst across my tongue from the pearl that had formed at his slit.

This immense, sexy beast of a man huffed out a deep-throated grunt that sounded as much like surprise as pleasure. His weighty cock filled my mouth so fucking beautifully it was like destiny.

The natural salty taste of him, seasoned by traces of his wolf, seemed to hook into my mind, and my soul. I drove myself forward and back, groaning with the pure bliss of pleasuring him. Showing him a tenderness that I felt certain he hadn't known for many, many years.

Maybe not ever.

Marius pumped his hips and drove himself deeper inside my mouth. He nudged at the back of my throat and I relaxed myself to give over control to him. If there was one thing I was sure of, it was that control was exactly what he needed right at that moment.

Then, he released a long breath, sliced through clenched teeth, as his legs quivered, and his belly tightened. He groaned with pleasure and released my hair from his iron grip.

I glided him in and out, growling from

pure hunger as I drew him closer and closer to his inevitable climax.

Marius leaned his good hand on my shoulder, and his whole body trembled. Then, he swore like he truly meant it, and a moment later, he flooded my mouth with his musky fluid.

Bursts of heat washed over my tongue, and I drank him down without a second's hesitation. His flavor filled my senses, all masculine and beastly.

The essence of nature and of life.

His last drops trickled out, and I let his hot, swollen length glide free of my mouth. Still kneeling, still gazing up at him, I stroked my hands up and down his tree trunk thighs, coarse hair tickling at my palms.

Marius seemed unable to look at me, though it was impossible to tell if he was ashamed, regretful, or overwhelmed. That was a moment of pure fucking perfection to me, but I knew he had to process it in his own way.

Still, he didn't resist, or pull away, when I pressed my mouth to his lower belly. Or when I gradually stood, licking the salt from his skin as I rose to my feet.

And even more promising, he didn't turn away as I tilted my head and kissed him again.

CHAPTER TEN

Marius

WHAT THE HELL just happened?

I mean, of course I knew.

But how the fuck had I lived this long and never understood myself?

Never realized what it was I was missing.

Braden's mouth worked around mine, his lips soft but his stubble harsh. My own flavor flooded my senses as he danced his tongue inside my mouth, running the appendage over my tongue and behind my teeth.

I took hold of his short, lush hair and

dragged on it, harder than I'd meant to, but he just moaned with pleasure. When I wrapped my damaged arm around him, he leaned back into my embrace, baring his throat, his soft underbelly, to me.

More importantly, he put his trust in the strength of my biggest weakness, and despite everything else we'd just shared, that one moment made my heart soar like nothing ever had.

I was lost to this man. He was all I could think about, all I could see, the only scent I could find.

Until something new washed over me.

Bear.

My heart jolted with adrenaline as I raised my head, standing Braden back up on his feet.

Somewhere near.

Bear shifter.

Fuck.

Braden clearly sensed it as well. "What the fuck is a bear shifter doing in Burton's Clearing? Or anywhere in Gray Vale?"

Realization must have hit him at that moment. Either that, or he sensed my own turmoil. He pushed on my chest, hard enough to get me stepping backward.

"Come on, Marius. Don't even think about it, please."

Even though he knew the story of my mangled arm, that didn't mean he understood what I was thinking. Maybe he guessed I wanted some kind of vengeance, or that I simply wanted to see if it was the same guy.

Honestly, I had no idea what I was thinking, either. Just that a tornado of troublesome feelings had suddenly blown into my mind and were in danger of laying waste to the incredible warm sensations that Braden had awoken within me.

"Marius," he said, in a low, quiet voice that reached me through the funk of bear shifter, better than a roar would have. "Come home with me."

The undiluted need in Braden's voice cut through the danger, and the last of my lingering doubts.

With him was exactly where I wanted to be.

And somehow, the word *home* had never seemed more fitting.

"Let's go," I said, the words barely audible to human ears.

Braden reached up and tugged on my hair, and took my mouth in a far too brief kiss. That one touch eased the last of my tension and I kissed him back. Then, he eased out of my embrace and started running away toward the town, slowing down only long enough to shift back into wolf form. For speed, no doubt.

I couldn't say I blamed him. Having finally uncovered who I truly was, I needed to explore it fully.

As soon as fucking possible.

Still out of practice, it took me a moment longer to shift. But even on only three legs, I caught up with Braden again by the time we crested the tree line. I couldn't remember ever feeling so free, so light-hearted, and I took a playful nip at my man's hindquarters.

Fuck.

My man.

How the fuck did I so instantly come to think of him that way?

Even weirder, how the fuck did it feel like the absolute truth?

Outside his place, we shifted back. I wondered for a moment how we'd get in, since he had nowhere to keep any keys.

But his door simply opened when he turned the handle, which was a sweet reminder of the trusting life here in Gray Vale.

Once inside, Braden turned and closed the door behind him. Then, he did the unthinkable and actually locked it.

I could wait no longer, and I gripped him around the throat, pushing him back against it. He closed his eyes and parted his lips, and the only thing I could do was dash my mouth against his, like the ocean slamming into the shore.

He hummed with a beautiful blend of relief and need as I plundered his sweet mouth. He fisted my hair with one hand and reached down for my cock with the other.

I switched hands, slamming my damaged forearm against Braden's chest to snare him against the door as I took his hot, hard cock in my one good hand.

He hissed as I tightened my fist around his shaft, and he growled as I stroked him, his beautiful voice growing harsher and more beastly with every fierce pump of my hand.

Braden slipped his mouth free of

mine and pulled me down into the crook of his neck. His scent filled my head as his flesh filled my mouth. I sank my teeth into his skin as he clambered up onto me, throwing his legs around my waist and wrapping his arms around my neck.

"End of the hall. On the right."

My eyes spun as I tried to work out what he meant. My wolf was too close to the surface and he clouded my understanding.

But I spun on the spot and marched to where Braden indicated, finding his bedroom and snarling with a fresh burst of hunger for this man as I cleared the doorway.

We fell in a solid tangle of limbs and mouths, Braden's hot, firm body feeling utterly perfect beneath me. My cock ground against his, and they hooked together as we devoured each other's mouth in a ravenous kiss.

I had to make him feel as magical as he made me feel. Give him the pleasure he deserved. I hungered for this man in so many ways, and one of them absolutely required me taking him into my mouth.

It was too urgent to even work up to it. No more foreplay or teasing. I simply took my mouth off his and slid down his tight, hard body.

I kissed his rippled sack for a moment and drew in the deep woody essence of him. The blast of pheromones and musky sweat made me hunger for him even more than I already had been.

I slipped my hand behind his hard length and raised it so I could glide the face of my tongue right up the underside. He moaned so sweetly it just made me wilder.

Up and down I licked him, wetting every fucking inch of his perfect cock. He fired his hands down into my thick hair and held on, tightening his grip when I flicked his head, loosening when I slid down to his balls.

Finally, I could wait no longer and I lifted his cock upright, and plunged my mouth down his length. All the fucking way down, surprising myself as much as Braden.

"Fuck," he moaned, gripping my hair so tightly it set my scalp on fire. I pumped up and down, soaking up the music of his moans as much as the symphony of his scents.

"Please, Marius..."

I glanced up at him, and the sweet, glistening need in his eyes made me weak for him. His wolf was so close to the surface, as was mine, and together they let me understand exactly what this man needed.

I slipped up off the end of him and raised one eyebrow. "Are you sure?"

"I need you, big guy. Please, fuck me."

"Jesus..." It came out as all breath and no voice.

Braden rolled over and reached to his bedside cabinet. He came back with a tube and popped the lid. He squeezed a load of clear gel out into his palm and reached toward me. When he touched my cock, I swore the bitterly cold lube turned to steam against my scorching skin.

Braden coated me, stroking up and down gently at first before tightening, and speeding up.

"Fuck," I whispered, almost losing myself in the intense pleasure. Then suddenly, he stopped, and rolled over, propping his smooth, perfect ass in the air.

"I fucking need you, Marius."

Nobody had ever sounded like that with me. So into the moment, so desperate to have me inside them.

Only now did I realize that the few women I'd been with had all been low level terrified. Even though they'd all been wolf, I must just have radiated such a violent energy.

I'd never once raised a hand to a lover. Not in anger or defense. Still, they'd all quivered and submitted as if I'd been about to snap at any moment.

There was such a level of trust between Braden and me that it made my cock pulse and grow inconceivably harder. Thicker.

"Jesus, you're beautiful," I growled out, the words barely passing through my mind before gushing through my lips. I pressed my one good hand into the small of Braden's back and he arched a little deeper, opening his tight little ass up a little more.

I moved in close behind him, stroking my hand down his body until I could grip my own cock. Braden gripped his cheeks and pulled them apart, and I nudged myself home against his pretty, puckered hole.

"Yesss..." His need had transcended words and actions. It was an actual scent in the air, and my wolf took turns snarling and howling and rubbing against my skin. Licking his lips and crouching, ready for action.

The kiss of his ass hole against my tip sent a sharp, sensual thud through my body, like an electric shock. It took all my will power to keep from punching forward. Maybe Braden would be okay with it, but I knew my own size and power. And I already cared too much about this man to risk hurting him like that.

"Do it, Marius. Fuck me. As hard as you like."

"Fuck..."

I lost it at that moment. Beast and man merged inside me, and I thrust hard, driving half my thickness into Braden's tight, blistering hot ass. He threw his head back and let out a long moan that moved closer and closer to a howl with every passing second.

Harder, faster, deeper, I thrust myself into him, driving farther inside until the blissful moment I was completely connected. That instant when the hardness of my hips slammed against the smooth heat of his ass. My whole long, steely cock was inside him, and I was fucking *home*.

Braden grunted with pain and pleasure, and arched his back like a drawn bow. I rested my damaged arm on his lower back and threw my good hand around his throat from behind.

With every hard, ragged thrust of my hips, I squeezed tight around Braden's neck. He whimpered with undiluted need, bouncing himself back at me, drawing more pleasure from inside my core than I could ever have imagined.

This beautiful man writhed before me, tightened around me. The sharpness I felt on first contact had doubled.

Tripled.

My wolf snarled inside me, as I instinctively knew somehow that Braden's did the same within him.

As my climax crouched and readied to pounce, my teeth lengthened, my nails grew into claws. Braden's skin rippled as his muscles danced beneath it. His whole body darkened as the hint of a shift overtook him, and his fur threatened to appear.

And then I swore I was struck by lightning.

My orgasm hit me with all the power of a shift, and all the sharpness of a blade. I clawed my hand, and the scent of blood coursed its way into my head. The hunger of a predator bit heartily into my very human ball of bliss, taking my climax to a level that I'd never known could exist.

I unleashed bolts of heat deep inside Braden, punching against him like a sledgehammer as the most intense release flowed through me. This went beyond just the physical.

This was an affirmation of my own life.

My being.

My entire self.

Braden howled in harmony with me, a dark wall of sound that would reach every fucking inch of this town. Even human ears could hear us as we claimed each other.

When my climax finally eased, my wolf panted as hard as I did, and together we softened and released our hold on this incredible man.

I glided out of Braden, and he swung right around and dived at me, mashing his lips into mine, and falling back, hauling me down on top of him.

We landed with a thud, our kisses turning slower but deeper. His breath, his heat, his scent merged with mine until it was impossible to separate one man from the other.

"That was incredible, Marius."

"I've never... known it could be like that."

His handsome face lit up with a smile, and held my head in his two good hands. He gave me one last light kiss and then rolled over and backed into me. He pulled my mangled arm over him like a blanket and nestled in against my body.

Like *he* was home.

CHAPTER ELEVEN

Braden

I CAME AWAKE gradually, to the feeling of hot breath washing over the back of my neck. Marius's thick arm was still draped over me, his hard body still nestled in behind me. As if we hadn't moved at all through the night.

The morning light was just beginning to beat away the darkness of night, and I soaked up that moment of quiet bliss as the luminous beams split the curtains.

Who knew what the day had in store?

I had never slept better, deeper, or longer than I did in the arms of this big, damaged man. His heat, his size, and his aura conspired to make me feel safer than I ever had. Something I'd never known was even missing from my life.

Marius stirred, and I slowly spun to face him. I honestly didn't know how he'd feel, in the light of day, after the night we had. There was plenty of chance he'd regret the whole thing. Not just because he'd never been with a man before, but because I was his son's teacher.

So many layers.

When he opened his beautiful crystal blue eyes, though, he opened my heart as well. The smile on his rugged face told me everything I needed to know.

I leaned over and slanted my mouth over his, and thankfully, he kissed me back. Deeply. It was too soon to believe any kind of fairytale, but that kiss, and the connection between us, slammed into me at a level way deeper than just the physical.

My wolf and his were in harmony. Marius felt the same way I did. I didn't need to ask him anything to know that. Everything I felt in my heart was also drifting through the air between us, as a rich range of scents.

As our kiss deepened, Marius growled with need. His thick, hard cock pressed into my thigh, and holy fuck but I wanted him again.

Immediately.

The big brute rolled me onto my back and bumped my legs apart with his knee. I spread them willingly, begging him to do to me whatever the fuck he wanted.

He held himself up on his battered arm, and reached down to squeeze my cock, all the while plunging his tongue into my mouth. But where last night had been savage and harsh, this morning his kisses were like the tide.

Slower, smoother, but utterly relentless.

I threw my arms around his neck and held him to me, returning his passion with a hunger I'd never felt with any other lover.

Marius released his grip on my hardness and came down, resting his entire wonderful weight on top of me. Holding me down as if I'd ever try to escape his embrace.

He ground his wonderful, swollen

cock against mine and sent deep, subterranean shocks of pleasure running through my body.

Even though every move he made was softer, slower than it had been last night, it was the same as his kiss.

Deeper.

More intense.

This time, it meant something more to him than just scratching an itch he'd never known was there.

He knew, I knew, and our wolves knew... this time it meant everything.

I broke our kiss for only long enough to reach over for the lube. I had him greased up in seconds, and even on only one arm, he held himself up easily. Towering over me in the most delicious way.

He rested his injured arm against my chest as I notched his thick cock in place. I pulled my legs right up to my chest and made myself as open to him physically as I already was emotionally.

Marius let loose with a low, rumbling moan, then drove himself deep into me. The sweet, stretching pain of the invasion was beyond perfect. Everything about this man made me whole.

"Fuck..." he snarled. "You feel so fucking good, Braden."

I couldn't talk. I could barely breathe as he glided in and out, slower and more measured than I expected. Last night was raw and ravenous, and such an incredible release. It had been a wonderful, gluttonous night of hedonism.

This morning, Marius seemed more like a connoisseur. Savoring every moment, every sensation. His eyes never left mine, and he watched intensely as every thrust of his magnificent cock played itself out through my body and across my face.

His gaze sliced through me, cutting so deep I swore he was opening me up, down to my soul. Letting out the wolf within. Taking me back to my most elemental form, and meeting me there the same way, through the connection we shared.

The way he rocked against me, driving in and out, went beyond pleasure and into some new realm I'd never imagined. I threw my hands around the back of his neck and hauled him down, desperate for his mouth.

Marius opened up and plundered me, with tongue and cock, as if drinking my essence. We formed a circle, connected top and bottom, and my heart soared as much as my cock did.

When Marius sat up, I held on so tight that he hauled me up with him. I straddled his lap, still riding his thick cock, still drinking from his sweet mouth.

He kept his hurt arm as far around me as he could, and reached his good hand down, gripping my cock and squeezing so tight. He stroked me hard and fast as he punched his hips up at me.

My wolf and his both paced in circles, snarling at their cages of bone and flesh. Desperate to come out and take their share of sensations.

Marius leaned back, his mighty fist pounding my cock into sweet oblivion as he took his own pleasure from my ass.

My whole body ignited with electrical prickling, as if I was about to be struck by lightning, as the head of his cock brushed over my prostate and I clamped my muscles around him.

Marius's growls became grunts,

became ragged breaths, as he surfed the same wave of pleasure I did.

Then, I swore I truly had been electrocuted as my climax hit me. It came at me as if from outside my body, in a rush, like a pack of wolves sinking their fangs into my flesh all at once.

Marius shot his heat deep inside me, searing my walls as I pumped mine out over our chests and bellies.

The pleasure hit me, harder than pain and hotter than fire. It radiated through me, centered bizarrely on the side of my neck.

For a few seconds—that felt like hours—of bliss, I rocked my hips forward and back, letting my body drink in the majesty of Marius.

Only when the haze of climax cleared, did I finally come back to my senses. To find I had this big, wonderful man's teeth embedded in my flesh.

Right at the side of my neck.

***

We held still for a short while longer, before we both realized exactly what had just happened. Not just that we'd made the most incredible love I'd ever experienced. But Marius had given me his mark. Claimed me.

As we came apart, it was clear he was as surprised as I was. His rugged face somehow looked boyish. Confused, yet beneath that, deeply understanding of exactly what he'd done.

"I, uh…"

He shook his head, but not in denial. Just to clear it. Already our bond had grown well enough that I could sense his emotions and thoughts more clearly than before.

"It's okay, Marius."

"But I… we didn't talk about it. We've hardly even…"

He backed away a little. Distancing himself from the moment as much as from me. Giving himself space to think.

Well, fuck that.

I didn't need time or space. I already knew how I felt. About him, about us, even about Noah. This little pack of three was the family I'd longed for. And I would do anything to be the home that Marius needed.

I crawled toward him and he watched my every move. That prickly exterior he'd worn since the moment he'd arrived in

Gray Vale, that he'd only let slip when we were together... it was coming back.

His natural reaction to confusion.

The instant I touched my lips to his, he calmed. He sighed, and opened up to me, and I eased him onto his back.

"I promise, Marius. It's okay. It's more than okay."

I picked up his hand and pressed his fingers to the still raw wound on my neck. His touch awoke the same kind of pleasurable agony that his cock did in my ass, and I sighed as fresh tingles poured through my blood.

"It's perfect," I whispered.

When he spoke, it was barely audible, even to wolf ears. But now that we were mated, it didn't need to be.

"I wasn't even thinking. It was pure instinct."

"It was the right instinct. Can't you feel it?"

He said nothing, but he stroked that mark he gave me and made a low humming sound.

My belly interrupted the moment by loudly growling.

Marius finally cracked a smile, and sat up. "You got a wolf in your belly, or you just hungry?"

"A little of both. Plus, don't forget horny."

He put his huge paw in my face and pushed me down onto my back. "Little whore," he said with a chuckle. "No time for that. I have to go and pick Noah up this morning."

My belly tightened in anticipation of the question I had to ask. "You want me to... uh... come with?"

I knew the answer would be no before he said it. Maybe before he even knew. But the fact he had to think about it was, to me, a victory. A week ago it would have been an immediate and automatic rejection.

"Might be a little too confronting," Marius said. "For Noah."

I nodded in understanding. Understanding that Noah likely wasn't the one who'd feel confronted, but also that Marius would still need time to adjust to this.

"Well," I said. "I need a shower. Someone made a damn mess of me."

That at least brought a smile. "I take it you have food in your kitchen?"

"Pretty sure. Maybe even enough for a

big lug like you. Help yourself, man."

"If you're lucky I might just whip something up for you." He shoved me back down again, with a broad grin covering his features. "But don't count on it."

I made sure to take a little extra time in the shower to let the water ease the wonderful aches and pains of the previous night. The rapid shifting and running, and of course, the incredible sex. Oh, and the even more intense morning fuck, as well.

All cleaned up and warmed up, I threw a towel around my waist and headed out to the kitchen.

And stopped short in my tracks, confronted by the sight of Noah standing there, gazing at me. Confused, surprised. But I couldn't help noticing the little flash of genuine pleasure in his eyes at seeing me, either.

I opened and shut my mouth a couple times as I tried to work out what the hell was going on.

Why on earth was Noah here?

He was still supposed to be at his sleepover.

"Good morning, Braden."

I glanced at the front door, where Pauline herself was standing, just about to leave.

Pauline, the mom of Vincent.

The boy Noah had a sleepover with.

One of *my* moms.

"Oh, uh... hey, Pauline."

"I came here to ask if you knew Marius's address, since Noah couldn't remember it." She kinked one eyebrow upward. "Imagine my surprise when I found the man himself here."

Fuck.

This was gonna be awkward. Not for me, exactly. I mean, I'm out as out can be and there are very few people who don't know that.

But for Marius?

Fuck, this whole situation had come out of nowhere. The guy hadn't had a moment to steel himself in private for acceptance, let alone in public.

I glanced across at the big man, who was pale and evasive. And I improvised the first lie I could think of.

"So, uh... thanks for trying to fix my sink, buddy. I guess I'll have to call a plumber."

"Uh..." Marius straightened a little.

"No problem. I was glad to... lend a hand."

One glance across at Pauline told me she wasn't buying it. Not even close. But that wasn't really my concern.

"Well," she said, cocking an eyebrow. Her gaze wandered just south of my eyes, and I realized she must be looking at my neck. At the mark Marius had given me. "I'll leave you guys to it."

"Wait," I blurted. "Just let me get dressed and I'll walk with you."

"Guys, it's fine," Pauline said, her mouth curling up at the corners.

"No, I wanted to discuss... uh... Vincent's progress."

Which was absolute bullshit, of course, but I had to speak to her away from Noah. At least my bullshit worked, as I knew it would. No mom could resist talking about their own kids.

Once I was dressed, I strolled back out to the kitchen. I told Marius to make himself at home, making sure I said it loudly enough for Pauline to hear. I ruffled Noah's hair with a smile, which he thankfully returned, and then headed out the door.

I made sure Pauline and I were a

good distance from my place before I sucked in a breath to speak. She managed to get in just before me.

"Braden Craig, you devil."

"Huh?"

"Oh, come on, now. It doesn't take a genius to work out what's going on."

Okay, so that confirmed that she was not even slightly fooled.

"Okay... Pauline, I know what it looks like, but—"

"Hey, it isn't really my business, y'know? I mean, I'm pissed, of course, because it's completely unfair."

"Hey, I treat all my students the same."

"What? Oh no, fuck that noise. I know you wouldn't let it change your teaching. It's just... I had visions of sinking *my* teeth into that big, rough hunk of a man."

It was my turn to give her the side-eye. She fired back with a smirk.

"What? Why the hell do you think I went out of my way to try and drop his boy home?" She sighed theatrically. "Oh, well. Another one bites the cock."

"Well, anyway," I said. "Obviously I'm not so bothered about... being discovered. It might be a little wrong given the whole teacher and parent situation, but I can wear that. It's Noah I'm worried about."

"You know Gray Vale has never been bothered about homosexuality. None of the kids will say anything."

"It's not even that. I don't think Noah would have a problem with his father being gay."

If he truly is.

"But the kid's been through a shit-ton of stuff already. He lost his mom and hasn't recovered yet. I don't know that he's ready to accept me as anything more than his teacher."

Pauline nudged me with her elbow. "You'd make a great mom."

I laughed along with her, but it wasn't without worry. Because I knew I couldn't truly fill that mom-sized gap in Noah's life. But if I was lucky, I'd at least get the chance to be part of his pack.

CHAPTER TWELVE

Marius

WHEN PAULINE TURNED up with Noah, I lost the power of speech. Of thought. Everything I'd shared with Braden last night, and in the morning, suddenly felt like a betrayal.

And why?

I had nothing to feel guilty about. No partner to cheat on, nobody I'd made promises or pledges to. But I still hadn't wrapped my head around the massive shift in my perception of who I was, and suddenly I felt I was facing judgment from a relative stranger.

More importantly, the moment Noah saw me at his teacher's place, with Braden coming out of the bathroom wearing nothing but a towel, I could sense the confusion radiating off my son.

As lame as it was, Braden offered me up an excuse and I ran with it. But we were all fucking shifters in this town. There was no way Pauline didn't figure out exactly what happened. My only hope was that Noah believed the ridiculous half-assed story.

I mean, why the fuck was this woman even trying to take my son home?

The arrangement was I would pick Noah up at ten. And now everything was fucked.

There was no way I could keep seeing Braden. Noah wasn't even ready for a new *woman* in his life.

How the hell was he meant to adjust to his father being with a man?

It was all so far out of my comfort zone I couldn't process it.

But holy fuck.

There was no denying the pull of that mark I gave Braden. I could feel him, even now. Across the distance, across time, whatever. I was in Braden's blood, now, and his blood was in me. And all because I lost my stupid fucking head while we made love.

It surprised me to realize that's what it had been.

Making love.

When we started last night, I thought we were just fucking. I tried to convince myself I was simply taking something that was offered, just for some kind of relief.

Braden blew that out of the water almost instantly with his passion, his empathy and his sheer voracious appetite. He opened up rooms in my head and in my heart that hadn't just been locked away.

They were fucking secret.

I hadn't even known I had such a deep well of emotion to draw on.

To feel with.

I had to at least discuss the situation with Noah, though. Once Braden and Pauline left, I wasn't entirely sure what to do. But remembering that the door was unlocked when we arrived last night, I figured it was fine to just leave it that way.

We headed out, and as I struggled to

think up the words I needed to use, I put my hand on Noah's shoulder.

"Did you... have a good time last night, Noah?"

"It was fine." He walked beside me but made no attempt to get close to me, or hold my hand. "Why did Mister Craig leave like that?"

Was that a trick question?

Had he worked out what happened?

"Oh, he has stuff to do today." I didn't want to actively lie to my son, and I hoped that he didn't ask questions that would drag me down to those depths.

"It was nice to see him."

You don't know the half of it, son. "You like him, huh?"

Noah nodded, keeping his words to himself like he used to back at the start. When we first got essentially forced together.

Every time I thought I'd made a little inroad with the kid, he shut himself off again. I got the feeling he'd sensed that hail-Mary lie that Braden tossed out there, and it bothered him.

All that did was reinforce it to me. He wasn't ready for me to move on with anyone, yet.

And the fucked up mixed messages that would come from me being with his classroom teacher?

That was out of the damn question.

***

My determination to end things with Braden lasted all of two hours. That was when he called me, and I swooped on my cell and answered it like I was a fucking teenage girl.

"Marius." That was all he said, but it had me closing my eyes in ecstasy. My tongue buzzed like I was touching it to a battery, from the connection between us. Where I'd lapped at his neck as I marked him.

"Hey," I replied, which was more than I thought I'd be able to come up with. There wasn't any way to put into words what I knew I had to say. That we had to stop, even as we'd barely started.

That no matter what, I had to protect Noah.

"Can we meet up?"

There was nothing I wanted more in the here and now than to see that man. To touch him. Explore whatever the hell it was going on between us, both at human and wolf level.

"I have Noah."

"I know. But there's the park. He can play and we can watch him while we talk."

The guy didn't have any kids of his own but he still seemed like a more organized parent than I ever would be. That feeling scared the fuck out of me more than anything. I could see myself diving head first into Braden. In truth, it was too late to think of doing anything else, now that I'd sunk my teeth into his beautiful neck.

"Okay. Sounds good." I wished I could say the same about myself. That I sounded good. In truth, I sounded like a fucking meathead.

We met up an hour later, and when he saw his teacher, Noah's little face lit up. At least, by his standards. He smiled and held his head a little higher than usual.

"Hey, my man," Braden said, dropping to one knee and holding out his fist. This time around, my son landed his punch properly. With some real weight. It looked like something that had become a regular thing between the two of them.

"Hey, son," I said. "Why don't you go play on the swings? Braden and I have a couple things to talk about."

Noah looked from me to Braden as if needing permission from both of us. A moment later, he strolled over and stood off to the side of the other kids, probably waiting for them to invite him to play.

Braden sat on a bench and I took the seat beside him. "So, that was fucking unexpected this morning," he said. I wasn't really sure it was something we could make light of. Not yet, at least.

"She really caught me by surprise, man."

"It's all good. I've known Pauline a long time. You want us to be secret, she'll do her part. It's just..." He sighed and scratched his hand back through his hair. "I don't know how we'd even hope to keep everyone from knowing. There's, like, three people in the whole town who aren't wolf."

There it was. My chance to give this thing a mercy killing. "Braden..."

"Fuck," he hissed, clearly reading me like a picture book. "Don't do this to me, Marius. Please?"

"I have to, man. Noah's not ready for... other people."

"He's not? Or you're not?"

How could I explain it properly?

That my son not being ready, and me not, were two sides of the same coin.

Maybe that made me weak.

Maybe selfish.

Maybe—probably—a fucking coward.

"This is not how I want it to be, Braden. I want... fuck, I want you."

"Then have me. Take me." He grabbed my arm and pulled it upward, and I knew exactly why. He wanted me to touch my hand to the mark I left on him.

Only, he'd grabbed my damaged arm.

He didn't let that stop him. It was as if he meant to get that one. He simply leaned forward and pressed my roughened stump to his fresh and beautiful wound.

"You *know* what that mark means, dude."

Even through the muffling of scar tissue, I still felt it.

Braden's heart pounding in time with mine.

My spine tingling as it searched for his.

My wolf leaning heavily against his.

Two sides of the same coin.

"Braden, please... I can't."

"You can. This isn't Stoke Ridge. We can be as open as you fucking like."

Christ, I wanted it like food.

Like air.

Braden could read that on me, of course, just as I could read it on him. But he could obviously sense my fear, and the reasons for it.

This beautiful man swallowed, his eyes reflecting mine. Both of us glistening with a raw emotion that I was too chickenshit to give a name to.

Because what if it was *love?*

This was so new. We'd met a few months back, and been in each other's company a couple weeks, but we'd only been *together* for one fucking night. One sweet, passionate night that I would remember for the rest of my life.

But that would be all I could take from it.

The memories.

"I'm sorry, Braden. I can't choose anyone else over Noah."

"You don't have to. I'm in for it. All of it."

"He's a scared little kid."

A flash of anger ignited in Braden's eyes. "I wonder where he gets that from."

The fire in his words cut me bone deep, and had my wolf crouching and snarling. "Watch it, man."

"Noah is far more resilient than you give him credit for, Marius."

That was the final straw. Nobody lectured me on my own fucking son. I lashed out with my good hand and snared Braden around the throat. The red mist and tingles of a shift hovered right around the edges, waiting for me to give in to it.

Instead, I squeezed, and Braden closed his eyes in what looked like bliss. Only after a moment did I realize I was pressing my fingers into the mark I gave him.

A fresh wave of panic hit me and I pulled my hand back like Braden was a snake, coiled and ready to strike. I stood and marched away, collecting Noah and heading for home.

Feeling more like a coward than I ever had. Emptier than I ever knew I could.

Because I left my heart back there on that bench, with the man I loved.

CHAPTER THIRTEEN

Braden

THE NEXT COUPLE of days were a fucking living hell for me. Catching short glimpses of Marius only when he dropped Noah off at school or picked him up. Tiny moments of eye contact that made my mate mark throb with need.

There was no doubt Marius sensed it as well. The clench in his jaw, the heavy creasing of his brow, every time he saw me, confessed the depth of feeling in the man.

True to his usual form, he somehow

managed to honor his word and keep his distance, despite the fact it was hurting him at least as much as it hurt me. To see each other mostly from across the classroom, to exchange only the occasional word in crisp, cool tones. And never anything personal between him and me. Only ever discussing Noah and his progress.

By the Thursday afternoon, I was a damn mess. Marius keeping aloof like that had me aching inside. I rolled through every day, every lesson, half in a trance, constantly distracted by the pulsing heat of my mate mark reaching out for my other half. My body crying for him. My wolf switching on a dime between whining and sulking, snarling and clawing at my skin.

Even through all that, I felt I'd been doing my job well, and keeping things on track. It was only when the students went for an outing on Friday afternoon that I knew something was up. When Kayleigh came in to my classroom as I cleaned up, ready for the next week.

"Braden. Got a moment?"

"For you? Always."

The kink of one eyebrow told me she

was not in the mood for lame-ass charm. "Take a seat."

All the tension inside me from the situation with Marius threatened to harden into diamond. There was definitely something wrong, and it was clearly important. Just what I needed when I was barely keeping a lid on my pain and frustration.

Once I sat, Kayleigh crossed her arms and stared into me. She had the most intense focus I'd ever seen in a human. It made me wonder if she'd once been nipped by a shifter, just in passing. Not enough to make her become, just enough to give her heightened senses.

"I've had complaints," she said, not without some warmth in her voice. "Some of the parents think you're... playing favorites. With Noah."

"Let me guess. Pauline especially?"

"I'm not at liberty to say," she replied, but confirming my suspicion with a nod.

"She's just saying that because—"

"She's saying it because it's true, Braden." Kayleigh sighed and relaxed her body language, sitting on the edge of my desk. "Honey, I get it. I saw your neck the Monday after he marked you.

Just because I don't literally feel what a mate mark does to you, doesn't mean I don't understand that it happens. That you gotta answer to your wolf just as much as to your human side."

Even without mentioning his name, she managed to bring me low. I leaned my elbows on my knees and closed my eyes.

"It doesn't take shifter senses to see how he's pulled away from you."

"He doesn't think Noah is ready. That's what he says."

"You don't agree?"

I stood and thrust my hands back through my hair in frustration. "I don't agree, no. It's Marius who's not ready. Except he only worked that out *after* he wrecked me for anyone else."

"Honey, what happened to the guy who's stayed friends with every ex he's ever had?"

I stopped short of howling in pain and frustration. "That's different. It was easy with them because none of them mattered like Marius does. As much as I thought they meant at the time, there was nothing between us that could touch what I have with Marius. What he *had* with me."

"Braden. Honey."

I could hear the words she hadn't yet said, as surely as if she really had said them. That I should give it time. That either he'd come around, or I'd get over him. But that was human thinking. That didn't take into account the depth and irrevocability of this fucking bite on my neck.

"I... I think I'm gonna have to leave town."

"Honey, no."

"Not forever. I hope. But for a while. I don't see any other answer."

Kayleigh came forward and swept me into a hug. "I won't let you."

I leaned into her embrace, and rested my forehead on her shoulder. "Sorry, human girl. You don't have the strength to stop me."

"Maybe I don't, but the kids will. You can't turn away from them."

"The kids aren't here right now, Kayleigh. I can turn away from people who aren't here."

She tensed against me. "You're... not thinking of leaving right away? You can't."

"I have to. It's eating me up, inside and out, that I'm so close to the man and can't be with him. I need to at least put some distance between us."

I was closer than I'd ever been to swearing at work. Even though it was just Kayleigh and me, and it'd be okay, the teacher side of me still held the balance over the man. And the wolf.

"Braden, at least wait until they're back from Burton's Clearing in a couple hours. Would you give me that much?"

"Wait... they're at Burton's Clearing?"

"Of course. You didn't read the memo?"

Jesus.

The bear shifter.

What if he was still there?

"We have to get them back, Kayleigh."

Normally, she knew better than to argue with wolf senses, but this time it obviously seemed to come out of the blue. With all my talk of leaving, she probably thought I was simply off my damn rocker.

"What are you talking about, B?"

"We caught the scent of a bear shifter there. It wasn't just in passing. It was heavy, like the guy had been living there for weeks, or even longer."

"Holy hell. And you didn't say anything?"

I winced in reaction. "I meant to, but..."

In the moment I'd scented the guy back then, I'd had every intention of telling the authorities. I'd just gotten distracted by the majesty of Marius, and the intense, soul-searing sex we'd had.

My mind had obviously been running pretty much on empty since Marius pushed me away.

If I'd even so much as caught the memo about the school outing, I'd have mentioned it then. More proof how badly I'd dropped the ball in my messed up state.

Kayleigh pulled out her cell phone to make some calls.

"Can I?" I asked her, holding out my hand. "He won't pick up when I call from my phone."

She sighed and handed it over. "Be quick. We have to tell the guards."

I fired my finger at the screen, tapping out the numbers for Marius's phone.

"Marius Voss."

"Marius. It's Braden. Please listen."

Even through the phone I picked it up. Relief, concern, and something much deeper. I wouldn't risk giving that emotion a name. Not while he still had the power to eviscerate my soul a second time.

"What's wrong?"

"We have to get to Burton's Clearing."

"I don't know where that is."

"Where we smelled the bear shifter. Noah's there."

"What the fuck?"

"School outing. I didn't know."

He said nothing more. Just disconnected the call. I handed the phone back to Kayleigh and ran for the door. By the time I hit the outside, I'd stripped off completely, and a moment later I was wolf.

I'd never run so fast. Not even when I chased down Marius that first night. Greyhounds had nothing on me.

I hit the edge of the forest and steamed ahead along the paths, the trees and shrubs whipping past me in a blur. My only focus was Burton's Clearing.

The funk of bear hit me when I was

still a few hundred feet away. Then, the sound reached me. The fearful whimpering of children, the trembling false calm of adult voices alternately soothing their charges and reasoning with their foe.

And the snuffling, grumbling noises of a bear. It sounded irritated more than anything. Like it just wanted everyone to leave. Thank fuck for small mercies.

I stopped at the edge of the clearing, rather than bursting in and startling the big guy. He had to have known I was coming, of course. I'd made no effort to keep quiet.

Still, charging out of the scrub at breakneck speed could only have made things worse, so I made sure to slow down to a walk before making an entrance.

Immediately, I knew I'd made the right decision. This guy was beyond big, even by bear standards. Even more than that, he was clearly wired on something. Standing on his back legs and towering over us all, he kept shaking his massive head, and blinking. Mouthing at nothing, pulling back his lips to bare his teeth at phantoms flying around him that only he could see. What teeth he had, anyway.

When he swung my way, he pawed at his mouth, even going so far as to draw blood from his own tongue.

Normally, we lived in a tense harmony with bear shifters. It wasn't like wolves and bears were natural enemies or anything, but we were competitors at the very least.

Even though I knew I stood a better chance of defending the kids and teachers when I was in wolf form, I had to take a chance. This situation needed the human touch.

I let my shift come on slowly, taking almost a minute to get back into human form, hoping to inspire the bear to do the same.

It seemed it was working, too. The bear's fur gradually paled and shrank, and he dropped to all fours as he began shrinking back to human size.

"Mister Craig!"

I didn't have to turn around to know it was Noah. A second later the boy slammed into me, his little arms gripping my leg like two tiny pythons.

Whatever this bear was on, it had

him highly spooked. Noah's sudden cry and movement got the big guy all keyed up again, and he rose on his back legs and raised his head in panic as he fled back into his beastly shape.

I still thought maybe things could be okay. He'd been bear when I arrived, and hadn't done anything. A quick glance across at the kids and teachers told me they were all terrified, but ready to move.

I signaled with my eyes and a nod of my head for them to start making their way backward through the brush, and I waved my arms to keep big bear boy's attention on me.

"Noah," I murmured. "Can you go back with your classmates?"

"No. I want to stay with you."

"Please, son," I said, and suddenly I realized that was exactly how he felt to me. Like my own son. He was that important to me, and I'd been missing him almost as much as I'd been missing his father.

A moment later, it was all academic. The bear dropped to all fours and swayed his massive head side to side. He sprang forward, heading straight for us, just as Marius, in his massive wolf form, came charging into the clearing.

CHAPTER FOURTEEN

Marius

I'D NEVER KNOWN a rage like the one that overtook me as I burst into the clearing. The two people who meant more to me than life itself, facing down a motherfuckin' enormous bear.

As big as my wolf was, that furry black bastard dwarfed me. None of that mattered, though. I only had one duty and that was to throw myself in his path. Whatever shit he was planning, it was my responsibility to take it to protect my son.

And my mate.

I launched myself into the ever-narrowing gap, landing in front of Braden and Noah and facing the oncoming danger. I crouched as best I could on three legs, snarling like my life depended on it.

Because it very well might.

The bear cocked his head and—thank fuck—slowed to a stop only inches from me. I gathered my strength, bunching up on my hind legs, ready to pounce. This guy threatened my family. No way I was taking that lying down. I wouldn't stand a chance, wolf against bear, but the only thing I was certain of was that I was going down swinging.

"Marius."

Braden's voice behind me pulled my attention for a second.

Why the fuck was he still standing there?

Why hadn't he taken my son to safety with all the others?

I couldn't even spare a second to look back at him. Instead, I concentrated on our connection and begged him to get away while he could. While the bear was still confused by me challenging him.

"Marius," he said again, this time

resting his hand on my back. "Please. Don't take him on. He's just... confused."

Confused?

If Braden wanted to see confused, he only had to look into my mind.

What the hell was he talking about?

A second later, I felt it. My mate actually *was* looking inside me. Tingling tendrils of sensation coursed through my blood as Braden connected his thoughts with mine.

There were no words. It was just senses. Images, memories, emotions. Despite my instinct to stay wolf, to stand and fight—and die, without a doubt—Braden had some other idea in mind.

Could I truly listen to his advice?

His wishes?

I knew combat. Sometimes, I thought it was all I knew. In that moment, faced by an insurmountable threat, it was the only reaction that came to me.

"Daddy," Noah said. "Please, listen."

Every inch of my skin quivered in reaction. My son had never called me that before. It was always *dad*, or *father*, or he'd find some way not to call me anything at all.

The bear still hadn't moved off the

place he'd stopped. Just swayed his head side to side, worked his gap-toothed mouth in weird ways. It was suddenly clear that something wasn't right with him. That was what Braden and Noah were trying to tell me. The guy wasn't angry, probably wasn't even vicious. Just fucking messed up.

I closed my eyes and welcomed the shift. Let it wash through me. Let it calm me, which had never happened from a shift before. There was no doubt in my head that Braden was the stabilizing factor for me.

Back in human form, I stood slowly, holding out my hand, palm forward, toward our big bear intruder. He leaned to the side and scratched at the side of his head with one paw, and it looked to me like he was chasing invisible insects.

I risked a glance back over my shoulder, and the sight of both my guys there, fit and uninjured, gave me strength. Braden reached through our mate connection to help keep me cool and balanced, and it was exactly what I needed.

"Hey, buddy," I said to the bear. "You seem to be outta place here."

He snuffled and jumped with just his front paws, like he was testing me. To see if I'd turn and run, see if I'd shift. Just see what was what, maybe.

"You wanna shift back, that'd be cool," I continued. "If not, that's cool, too."

He let out a low, rumbling noise, and I sent a message through to Braden to get my son out of the clearing. Thankfully, he was already way ahead of me on that, and had handed Noah over to one of the other teachers who'd come back for him.

I paused for a little while, until their footsteps faded and I knew they were likely all the way back out of the forest. Assuming I survived this, I'd pick Noah up later.

Thing was, I needed Braden to leave as well, but the damn fool stayed.

How the fuck was I supposed to protect him if he stayed in the danger zone?

My mate clearly picked up on my fears. He came over and put his hand on my shoulder, the way he'd touched my back when I was wolf. "You're not alone. You never have to be alone."

He also must have sensed the whirling dilemma inside me. How to best handle the danger when all I'd ever known was fight or flight. I was more grateful than ever when he stepped back to the edge of the clearing. Letting me work out what the fuck I had to do without having to worry about the man I loved.

I decided to just go with what amounted to common ground.

I raised my damaged arm and leaned slowly toward our big, brutish companion.

"Maybe you can see, I've had my run-ins with your kind before, brother." I didn't feel any real kind of fraternity with this guy, of course. But somehow it seemed to be the right way to address him. Show some solidarity. Make it so we're all on the same side, working toward a common goal.

"I lived with hate for a while after this." I gave the scarred stump a light slap with my hand, and our bear buddy kinked his head to the side. I pointed smoothly across to where Braden stood.

"That guy there," I said. "He's the one who pulled me back from the edge."

Bear-boy turned and looked at Braden.

My mate.

My family.

I tensed up, ready to step between them if anything went wrong, but all that happened was the guy seemed to relax.

His fur gradually receded, and he shrank down into human form. When he stood, he was still twitching and scratching. A real loose cannon, but at least he was a more manageable size.

"What is it you need, brother?" I asked him.

"Uh..." He flinched from something only he could see. "Just wanna be... be left alone."

"You know where you are?"

"Of course!"

I tensed, ready to shift in an instant, banking on the chance I could become wolf faster than he could become bear.

"I mean..." the guy continued. "I'm... I think this is..."

I took a long, slow breath as I channeled Braden. I couldn't even tell now if my mate was connecting with me again, or if I'd just absorbed the man's nature enough to mimic him. All I did was think back to that first time we met, when he defused a situation that threatened to explode. And he did it with nothing but well-chosen words.

"This is Gray Vale, brother. Does that help?"

"Gray Vale?"

"And that was a school outing you just scared the hell out of." He looked just as confused then as he had in bear form, so I pushed it a little. "You really worried about what a bunch of little kids can do? They haven't even become, yet."

"Didn't mean... they were on my turf."

There was no point arguing whose turf we were standing on. Instead, I stepped in closer, until I was just about eye to eye with him. "What is it you need, big guy?"

He scratched at his arms, his neck, his face. He flicked his head like he was shooing flies. I was no expert but I figured he was probably a meth head. Why the hell he'd ended up in Burton's Clearing, or in Gray Vale at all, I couldn't even begin to guess.

What mattered most was getting him to stay calm, and taken care of. And it felt as if I'd got that mostly done.

Right up until a half dozen guards came plowing out of the scrub, armed and shouting.

And our big buddy reacted pretty much the same way I always had when confronted by danger, uncertainty or confusion.

He shifted.

CHAPTER FIFTEEN

Braden

IT WASN'T MY place to say it, or my right to feel it, but I was so damn proud of Marius. The way he'd suppressed his natural aggression and looked for a peaceful solution had my heart aching with love for the guy, despite the fact he'd made it clear we couldn't be together.

Not now.

Probably not ever.

The fact he'd also faced down a bear shifter without even looking for vengeance by proxy was even more inspiring. Even when he was still hurting after losing his arm, and by extension the career he'd hoped would last forever. I wouldn't have been surprised if Marius had just said fuck it and gone rogue himself on the massive guy's ass.

Then, when the guards came charging in, and the stranger shifted back into bear form, suddenly it seemed it had all been for nothing. As enormous as Marius was, the immense furry form of the addled shifter dwarfed him.

If my mate had chosen to shift as well, I would have understood it completely. There were six adult wolves here, all males, and together we could at least see this guy off, if not subdue him.

But Marius held out his hand and his damaged arm toward the guards.

"Wait."

"Get out of the way, Ridgie."

Marius shook his head and looked with scorn at Simon, the guard. "Really? You're still holding on to that?"

Simon nodded toward the scarred stump of Marius's left arm. "We can see how well you handle bear shifters, asshole. Let the professionals take over."

A low snarling sound filled the

clearing, catching us all by surprise. Most of all me, even though—or really, *because*—I was the one making it.

"Oh, what, Braidy-cat? You're gonna be a fuckin' hero now?"

"You don't know what I'm capable of, Simon, when the people I love are under attack."

The guardsman just shrugged and turned back to the main event. The bear shifter who was on his hind legs, casting his head side to side. Whether he was looking for escape, looking for drugs, or just seeing pixies, I couldn't tell.

The only two things I was certain of were that he was dangerous... and that my mate was right there in the firing line.

"Hey," Marius said, waving his hand to get the bear's attention. "Brutus. Down here."

Somehow, he got through to the guy. Bear-boy glanced down at my man, who still had his hand held up.

"Yeah... remember me? I'm still here. Let's just take a breath, huh?" He nodded toward the two pairs of guards, either side of the clearing. "These guys are ready to fuck you up, man. We can't take any chances with you, y'understand? We all know what a bear can do. *I* sure do, anyway."

The bear snuffled and flinched away from a few more invisible specters. Marius stepped in even closer, making my heart ache and my breath freeze in my throat.

"Can we... can we bring it back down? As badass as you are, man, these guards are armed. They're trained, and they're ready. They're good men. Don't make 'em do bad shit."

The bear opened his mouth wide, and for a moment, I swore he was about to take Marius's head off, even with that scattered assortment of teeth he still had. Instead, he flapped his tongue a moment, and then came down onto all fours.

Marius reached forward, slow as molasses, and did to the guy exactly what I did that first night to calm my mate. He worked his hand over the bear's big, round head, and scratched him behind the ear.

"It's all cool, Brutus. There's no stranger danger here, buddy. We're all just friends you haven't met."

Christ, I almost burst out in laughter at that. It was absolutely the least *Marius* thing I'd ever heard the man say. Somehow, though, it worked.

Once again, the giant bear's fur receded, his claws and fangs shrank, and he came back down into human form.

He was clearly still scared and confused, but now he could add exhausted to the list. Shifting took a ton of effort every time. To do it so many times in such a short period was bound to have an effect.

The guards came in closer, ready to use their weapons, but the guy gradually came up to his feet. "Don't want trouble."

Marius put his hand around the back of the guy's neck and pulled forward, until their foreheads met with a dull thud. I thought at first he was trying to head butt the guy, until I realized he was connecting with him.

"I've been where you are, buddy. Alone. Scared. Fucking lost."

"Just need a hit."

"I get it." My mate stepped back and Simon and the guardsmen shifted in closer at a cautious pace. "These guys are gonna get you some help. They might need to restrain you. We cool?"

Bear boy nodded and repeated the words that seemed to be his mantra. "Don't want trouble."

The guardsmen clasped the heavy duty cuffs on him and led him away. Finally, I felt safe to move, and I rushed over to Marius, throwing my arms around him from behind.

Simon paused at the edge of the clearing, barely glancing back over his shoulder before talking.

"Y'did good, Ridgie."

Before either of us could reply, the man simply walked away.

I gripped Marius by the good arm and pulled, trying to turn him to face me. Of course, the big lug resisted like hell, so I moved around in front of him instead.

"What the fuck was that? Do you have a fucking death wish?" I wasn't truly angry, but all the tension inside me had to come out somehow. That was the path it chose.

Marius glared down at me, his eyes bright and intense. I tried to block out the emotion flooding through my mate mark, because it felt too much like fucking stupid fucking *love*. No way I was strong enough to resist that, and absolutely no fucking way I'd survive if he dangled it before me and then pulled it away again.

"Well?" I continued. "Got anything to say, you fucker?" I even slammed the heels of my hands into his bull chest, which pushed me backward, rather than him.

"Not a thing," he murmured. I was just about to swing at the guy when he pulled me in close and slammed his beautiful hard mouth into mine.

My entire body—both parts, the man and the wolf—turned to soft, hot liquid. All except my cock, which grew so hard, so fast, I thought it might burst.

Marius opened up and danced his tongue past my lips, and let our connection speak for him. My mate mark absorbed every thought, every feeling, every sensation, and pumped it through my body in a heated rush. Apology, loneliness, regret, need.

Destiny.

My mark tingled so hard it burned me, and so help me, it truly was love between the two of us. This big, beautiful bastard had gone and made me fall in love with him, and there wasn't a single damn thing I could do about it.

I pushed myself back out of his embrace, just to catch my breath. To give my soul a chance of surviving if he let fear get the better of him once again, and pulled away from me.

"Braden..."

"Don't start anything you can't—or won't—finish, Marius. So help me, I'll wolf up and I'll bite something else off you. And it won't be your damn hand."

To my surprise, he paused... and then he burst out with laughter. Maybe that was just his tension escaping, but it lit the man up like a firework, and my entire being ached for him.

"Fuck, I've missed you," he said, and it just about cut my legs out from under me.

"I mean it, man. Don't fucking... don't you..." My wolf had too much control to allow me to speak. It prowled and circled inside me, huffing and brushing under my skin, far closer to the surface than I'd have liked. My beast was ready to spring into action at a moment's notice.

"Braden, please. I'm sorry. Shit happened so fucking fast, and... Jesus, I still don't have a handle on simply being a good man, let alone a father. Now suddenly, I'm gay?"

My mark transmitted to him everything I was feeling. Doubt, fear, the beginning of scorn.

"No, no," he said, holding out his hand. "I am. I definitely *am* gay. It's just... it's a lot, y'know?"

It *was* a lot. Even when the two clans were separated, and Gray Vale was the more open and understanding place, it was hard at first to be open. I couldn't imagine how it must be for Marius, with all his background and baggage, to have his sexuality basically body slam him from out of the shadows.

"Yeah," I said. "I know. But our secret ain't all that secret, anymore. It's kinda well and truly out there now. So the question is more about how you deal with that."

He pulled me right in against his thick chest and kissed the top of my head. "Come home with me. Let me show you how I plan to deal with it."

CHAPTER SIXTEEN

Marius

I THOUGHT ALL the children and teachers would've gone back to the school, but they were waiting in the clearing between the forest and the town. The moment we stepped out of the tree cover, Noah broke away from his class and ran over to us.

And to my surprise and delight, he came straight to me. If I was honest, I'd expected him to run to Braden, instead. And it wouldn't have bothered me, since the man is my mate. Still, my heart swelled, and it was like a bear shifter in my chest. I swore it was too big, about to explode.

As I picked my beautiful son up and hugged him to me, and Braden put his arms around me from behind, I finally understood what it meant to be home.

To be loved.

Others tried to talk to me as we walked through town but I couldn't focus on them. Couldn't even hear them. I was too busy with my son and my mate.

My family.

The walk home passed in a blur as Noah snuggled against me and Braden used our connection to send me all kinds of warm and loving vibes. I managed to hold my son in my damaged arm, which meant I could put my other arm around my mate, and caress the mark I'd given him.

As we walked into my shitty little apartment, I realized it had never looked more like a home to me. And it was because of who was there with me, and nothing else.

Exhaustion overtook Noah in a rush, so we made a quick and simple dinner, and then together, my mate and I tucked the kid into bed.

After Braden kissed my son's forehead and left, I stroked my fingers back through the Noah's hair. Something I didn't remember ever doing before. The kind of casual affection that had been missing from my life, and as a consequence, from my kid's.

My boy went out like a light, and that bear shifter in my chest made it damn hard to breathe. Fuck... apparently unconditional love is both a killer, and also everything I'd ever wanted to live for.

I quietly closed Noah's bedroom door as I left the room. Something I usually didn't do, out of fear. So he could get to me, or I could get to him, with as little trouble as possible. In case he had nightmares, or called out for his mom. Or in case I needed to look in on him to reassure myself he was still actually there. That he wasn't some little angel who only existed in my dreams.

But this time, I knew I needed it closed. The things I was about to do to Braden... those needed to be done without interruption.

***

He was waiting for me in my bedroom. We'd been naked from when we shifted until we got back into the apartment, where we'd just put robes on. Somehow, his nakedness in that moment on my bed was different. Before, it was just the absence of clothing.

Now, it was a promise.

I strode over to him and shoved him straight down onto my bed, diving on over the top of him. He came up to meet me, plowing his mouth into mine and hauling on my tongue as he made hard fists in my hair.

Braden snapped his legs around my back and pulled down on my hips, driving us together, grinding his hard, swollen cock against mine. His rich scent poured into my entire being, filling me—mind, heart and soul—like nothing ever had.

I slid my mouth down to that mark I had given him. It had healed up into a scar, but it glowed red and burned as I traced it with my tongue. Braden kinked his head away to bare himself fully to me, and it took all my strength to stop myself from reopening that beautiful wound.

Still, Braden squeezed me in the sizzling embrace of his legs. My cock wrestled with his, driving lightning bolts of bliss racing through my body. His mate mark crackled as the sensations passed between us, until I couldn't tell what was his pleasure and what was mine.

My hunger for every part him, body and soul, had my wolf bristling, prowling, demanding succor. Braden's essence called to me, through my nose and through my mouth.

I slid lower, lapping at this beautiful man's chest, swamping his nipple with the wet heat of my tongue. His moans became growls as I bit down on his tight bud, and his whole body jerked when I curled my hand around his cock.

My ravenous need for him overtook me for a moment. It felt for all the world like I imagine madness would.

Wolf and man trying to coexist in a single space and time.

My skin prickled as if readying for a shift. Preparing me for thick fur to come bursting out.

I slid lower and drove my mouth

down the length of Braden's thick, engorged cock, growling with sweet contentment as his essence burst across my tongue and I finally tasted my mate again.

He tightened his grip on my hair and arched his back, pumping his hips at me as I swallowed every long, spicy inch of him.

Harder, faster, I stroked up and down his length, gripping his balls and squeezing lightly, wishing more than ever that I had my other hand so I could grind at his ass.

"Fuck... Marius..."

Jesus, the yearning in his voice nearly made me come. I needed to be inside him, as soon as fucking possible.

I released his balls and slid my hand up to his mouth. He sucked on my thumb for a moment, understanding exactly what I needed without me even asking.

With my thumb all slicked up, I brought it back down and pressed it to Braden's tight ass. He hauled his legs higher and wider, and I made hard circles around his rippled ring, then punched the tip of my digit inside him.

My mate hissed with sheer desire, and his cock pulsed hard in my mouth. I drank down his salty precum and worked more and more of my thumb inside his tight hole.

"Uhhh..." Braden was so close to coming, and though a part of me wanted to edge him, most of me—the wolf side of me—had no fucking patience. Both sides of me needed to finish him right now. Out of desire, out of apology... more than anything, out of love.

Braden hissed and slammed his hands down on my shoulders, hard enough to sting. He dug his lengthening nails into my flesh, and roared with his release as he arched his back and filled my mouth with his musky fluid. As tempting as it was to swallow, to take him into me like that, instead, I held his essence inside me for a moment.

God, it was fucking perfect.

He was still pulsing when I dragged my thumb out and sat up, letting my mate's cum drizzle out into my palm. I coated his ass and my cock with his slick juice, and notched myself in place.

There was no waiting. Nothing subtle. This was fucking beastly. As close as I'd ever been to my animal form without actually shifting.

Mentally, I was more wolf than man. Physically, I was teetering.

A different kind of edge play.

It would take so little for me to relax into a shift, and it was taking so fucking much willpower to stay human.

When I drove my hips forward, Braden cried out with the sweet stinging agony of my thick cock filling him. He whipped his hands up around the back of my head and hauled me down.

I slammed my mouth into his, tasting the fresh salty wonder of blood as I punched my cock in and out of him. My mate squeezed me deep inside his body, as if holding me tight, as if crying out for me to stay there, to never leave.

The heat in my mind cascaded down through my body, as the fire deep in my cock rose. They met in the middle and formed a solid force that punched against the inside of my chest, in the form of my wild fucking heart. Reaching out for Braden.

As I glided in and out of him, I snaked my one good hand down beneath his gorgeous body and held him close.

Mouth to mouth, chest to chest, soul to soul. His heart knocked against the wall of his ribs, like Morse code, and mine answered. It was a language neither of us had ever heard, but which both of us understood completely.

I slid my mouth down to Braden's neck, and clamped tight over his mark. An instant later, my mate completed the bond, embedding his partially-shifted fangs into my shoulder, sinking them so deep it was as if he was part of me physically. Like he already was, emotionally.

His sweet, spicy blood flooded my mouth, and mine his. A cycle of giving and receiving, of exchanging souls, pumped fiercely through both of us. I'd heard about those sensations and always thought they were fairytales. Only in the moment did I understand the stories didn't even come close to the truth.

With one long, ferocious pump of my hips, I reached a cyclonic climax, made stronger, hotter, wetter by the sharing of blood and souls as much as from the physical sensation of being so deeply embedded in, and connected with, my lover's body.

Braden snarled, his voice grinding against the skin of my neck, as he reached another climax, bursting between our bodies. The sweet heat of his release coated my belly and his, as my own juice erupted within him.

I gradually slowed to a halt, still inside him, still hard as fuck. Seated within his body as he was seated within my heart. I didn't want to pull out.

Not fucking ever.

"I don't want that, either," Braden murmured, his lips still pressed to my skin as our shared marks confessed all my thoughts to him, and his to me.

I had the feeling this would be one long, strenuous night. The first night of forever with this beautiful man.

EPILOGUE

One Year Later...
Braden

I HELD MARIUS close, emotional tears stinging the backs of my eyes as we both waved to Noah, heading in for his first day in first grade. As great as things had been in the last school year, I just knew it was going to get even better from that point on.

After that first night, way back, when Marius took my mark and reconnected us, life had bloomed into pure happiness.

We'd finally fallen asleep in the early

morning, after hours of blissful fucking, only to be awoken by Noah at sunrise. And as I'd hoped and believed, the boy had absolutely no trouble dealing with the whole thing. His father and his schoolteacher were sharing a bed. So what. It was time for breakfast. That was all that mattered to him at that point.

Turned out, Noah's wolf senses were a little precocious. He'd already scented me on his dad, and vice versa, long before he found us together.

Thankfully, they both agreed to move in with me, since my place was bigger and... well, frankly, Marius wouldn't know decor if it bit his other hand off.

Having two parents had suited Noah so well. Yeah, so, it was two dads where all his friends had moms. I'd always radiated a bit of mom-energy, anyway, despite being a dude.

The fact that nobody in all of Gray Vale blinked an eye at it was a bonus, but I knew Noah well enough now to realize he wouldn't have been bothered either way.

It had been almost impossible to separate my role as the school's kindergarten teacher from my role as a step dad to Noah. Days like this one were the hardest, since I had to leave him and go teach my own group of kids.

Even so, my heart swelled with pride, and reached out to Marius, who kissed the top of my head, the way he always did when I got all soppy.

"You're such a pussy, Bray."

"And you're just a big, horrible, smelly, ugly oaf," I said, digging my elbow into his ribs.

"Hey," he replied, tightening his arm around my neck. "I'm not ugly."

I turned in his embrace, and framed his face with my hands. "Hell no, you're not. But the rest is still true."

He smiled for a moment, before coming forward to kiss me, gliding his tongue into my mouth before I could even prepare.

Sparks ignited over every inch of my skin, like a shift beginning, and I almost lost myself in this huge, gorgeous man. Yet again.

"Dammit, man," I said, and shoved him in his chest. Of course, as always, the sheer size of the man meant all I managed was to push myself back from him. "Don't you fucking dare. I have a class to teach."

"Well, fine," he murmured. "I'll hold the rest of it for when you get home, handsome."

"I'll hold you to that," I said, flashing him a sultry grin as I smacked his ass cheek.

Turn the page to read His Healing Heart, Book 3 in the Gray Vale Pack series.

HIS HEALING HEART

GRAY VALE PACK

BOOK THREE

EVIE RILEY

Music *summons* the savage beast...

Skilled Chicago surgeon Ethan Roddick abandoned his wolf heritage—and elitist parents—when heartbreak tore his world apart. He swore never to let love sink its fangs into him again, but when a meaningful family commitment lures him home to Stoke Ridge, his determination is tested by Gabriel Mendoza, a sexy human with soulful dark eyes and the voice of a bourbon-soaked angel.

Pressured by his parents to mate—to a suitable shifter, of course, and preferably a female—Ethan is instead drawn to the sassy singer whose heat seems destined to heal the rift between his two halves. As passions rise, so too do tensions, and anyone who's not a predator becomes, by default, *prey*.

Can these fated mates fight old clan prejudices and find their future together?

His Healing Heart

Gray Vale Pack

Book Three

Copyright © 2023 Evie Riley

ISBN: 978-1-77357-519-3

978-1-77357-518-6

Naughty Nights Press LLC

Cover Art By Willsin Rowe

CHAPTER ONE

Ethan

I TIED OFF the final suture on Maureen Brady's chest. Hinchcliffe, the chief surgeon at Mercy Hospital, simply shook his head.

"You're some kind of freak, Roddick. I've never seen a surgeon work so fast."

"If I worked at top speed, you wouldn't see me."

The theater was always cool, but it suddenly went cold. I was accustomed to that, and more than fine with it. These people were my equals only on paper. Not a one of them—not even

Hinchcliffe—had one-tenth of my skill. It was one thing—perhaps the only thing—I could thank my wolf senses for.

"A little humility wouldn't go astray, Roddick."

I pulled off my gloves and pushed open the theater door. "Why, I'm simply following your own directive on efficiency, Doctor Hinchcliffe. What was the wording you used again? Oh, yes... if you don't need it, don't use it."

"And you know very well I'm specifically talking about surgery, Roddick. The faster we finish, the smaller the risk to the patient."

"I choose to apply it in life as well." I tossed the wadded-up latex into the bin behind me, without even a glance over my shoulder. "It keeps me from getting bored by conversations like this one."

As I shouldered through the theater door, I suppressed the smirk that tried to climb onto my mouth. I had a reputation as a cocky bastard, and I'd worked with all my usual attention to detail in order to cultivate it. Nobody ever got past that arrogant veneer unless I wanted them to.

Of course, mouthing off to the chief

like that was sure to come back and bite me. A risk, for sure, but a calculated one. In the end, it barely mattered. I could bite back just as hard.

Harder, even.

For a moment, I held my breath, centering myself. Bears might be the ones who hibernate, but I'd done my level best to send my wolf into permanent sleep. Even so, the beast stirred within me, baring its teeth, scenting the air. I leaned against the wall, working hard to think human thoughts, pulling my emotions into check.

For months now, even the slightest sense of passion had called to the animal. Today, it was the elation of a perfect surgery, blending with the buzz of rebellion.

Neither of those could compare to the rush of blood frenzy, or the scent of an available mate, of course. But I'd starved my beast for years now, and clearly it was prepared to take whatever crumbs it could get. In the past few months, my wolf had begun to lash out with a fierce hunger.

Hopefully, that activity was nothing

more than its death throes. Only when I'd finally closed down the fiend within could I think about opening my heart to another. Until then, I had to stand strong, and always on my own two feet. Never on four.

All scrubbed down again, I pushed my way into the corridor. Just as I reached the door to his office, Nurse Patrick came bustling up.

"Doctor Roddick."

"Tim."

"You had a phone call while you were in surgery. A Kiera Larson."

Tim held the note out to me, and I frowned but didn't take it. "It's been years. I'm sure it can wait. I have dinner reservations at Dominic's." A burst of guilt hit me for a moment. I'd never actively ignored my cousin Kiera. I'd just let life get in the way.

"She said it was urgent."

For my cousin to call me at all was a huge step, so I had no doubt it truly was urgent in her mind. But it was almost certainly about my parents, so as far as I was concerned, whatever the problem was could wait a while. And then it could go to hell.

Nurse Patrick pushed the note into my hand, cutting through my internal argument. I sighed and curled my top lip, as if the paper had come straight from the dump. "Okay. Thanks, Tim."

"Yes, Doctor Roddick." The man had already turned and headed back to the reception area. Such was my rapport with the staff.

I closed my office door and dropped heavily into the plush leather of my reclining chair, moaning with muted pleasure as the padding embraced my body. Soft and accommodating, and eager to both take on my heat and mold to my form. My interaction with my chair was as close as I'd allow myself to come to another relationship.

At least until I found a cure.

For a moment, I crushed my eyelids together.

How had I so easily led myself back down that path, to the singular seed of all my pain?

The chief trigger that had led to me pushing away everyone and everything before they could even begin to matter to me.

I tugged in a breath, filling myself

with cool air and holding it in for as long as I could. When I shot it back out, I let my pain go with it. The note felt inordinately heavy in my hand as I lifted it.

All it held was Kiera's name and phone number. If it had been anyone else from Stoke Ridge, I'd have tossed the note in the garbage. That place had scarred me like nothing else. Both in childhood and as an adult.

But Kiera had been like an older sister during my difficult early years. Her folks had shielded me from my own parents, and their unmasked shame at my... trouble. If not for the Larsons, I felt certain I'd never have made it out of adolescence.

With all that weighing on me, I pursed my lips and punched my cousin's number into my desk phone. She answered on the second ring.

"Kiera Larson Designs."

"Hey, Killa."

"Ethan! I seriously never thought you'd call back."

"Well, I didn't. I just put in the number for Dial-A-Ho and here we are."

"Har-de-har, scrotum-face."

"Answering your own phone these days?"

"My assistant is taking care of some, uh... urgent fact-finding research for me. At the patisserie."

"Uh-huh." I couldn't prevent the smile from curling its way over my mouth. I'd come to believe everything in my life was fine. That I didn't need anyone.

In only ten seconds, Kiera had undermined that very foundation. "I never thought I'd say this, Killa, but I actually miss you."

"Yeah, if that's meant to be sweet talk, then you probably should stick to insults."

"Noted. Now, what's so damn urgent that you're forcing me to be somewhat sociable?"

"This weekend. Back home."

"You must be joking. You know I swore I'd never go back."

"Things are different back there, now. You know we merged with Gray Vale?"

"Did you?" I no longer felt any sense of kinship with fucking Stoke Ridge. It did surprise me they'd blended with a pack that was supposed to be the enemy, though.

"We did. It's working really well. You'd be surprised."

"I'd be surprised if I ever saw the place again."

"Well, before you make any decisions, you need to know one thing. It's my parents' thirtieth anniversary. They specifically requested the presence of their favorite bun-from-another-oven."

I rested my head against my palm. "You know I'm one of those doctor thingies, right? That I can't just slice someone open and ask them to wait until Monday?"

"Oh, come on. Are you telling you're the only one in the whole hospital—in the whole city—who's allowed to play with cutty whatsits and stitchin' doohickeys?"

Using my work as a shield was such a clean—some might say surgical—way to avoid going back to hell. But the truth was, I had two weeks' leave organized, starting on Friday, and had no plans beyond holing up in my penthouse and glaring down at the city below me.

Chicago was about as far from Gray Vale as you could get. At least, in spirit. For me, it was the perfect antidote to the passions of nature.

I'd removed myself from the wilderness, yet the wilderness still had a hold on me. To go back would be to tempt my wolf out of its coma, and that was too much to contemplate.

Kiera interrupted my thoughts as if she could read them. "Please, Ethan. I know you have your issues with... y'know, everything there. But this is my parents. That has to mean something, even to someone like you."

"Like me?"

"Yeah. A bigshot asshole."

"Thanks for noticing. And yeah, it does matter. You know it does."

Her sigh came through the phone almost as a physical entity. "Honestly, buddy, it won't be nearly as bad as you think."

"You don't know how bad I think it'll be."

"I know you think all eyes will be on you. That everyone will talk about little Nimroddick and how he's become mister fancy-pants with his high-falutin' new life."

"I wouldn't have put it like that, but yes, that's how I think it will be."

Kiera scoffed down the line. "Please. Nobody will even notice you."

"Then what's the point of me going?"

"Because we built a fifteen-foot-tall rose gold throne with flashing neon lights on it for you. Duh."

"Yeah, you're right. Nobody will notice me at all."

Kiera's cackle hadn't changed in five years. "Well, of course, you're completely free to refuse this invitation. To spit in my face. To leave a burning paper bag of doody on the doorstep of my heart."

"Don't think I won't."

"But of course... there will be a follow up call."

"Do your worst."

"From my mom."

"Oh."

"Uh-huh."

I took a fortifying breath, then opened my diary and picked up my gold-plated fountain pen. "So, what time are you expecting me?"

CHAPTER TWO

Gabriel

I JUGGLED THE two coffees and the paper bag of sinful goodies as I walked back to my desk. I couldn't help but smile as I watched my boss hang up the phone and punch the air.

Passing Kiera one cup, I sipped at my own. "Good news, boss?"

"Great news, Gabes. Wonderful."

"New client? Big job?"

"Not actually anything to do with work, no."

"Oh, you're getting married! And you want me to sing at your wedding. This is so sudden."

Kiera crossed her arms and rolled her eyes. "That kind of nonsense would require a living, breathing, devastatingly sexy male person, wouldn't it? Have you seen any of those around here?"

"Apart from me, you mean?" I did a quick and—hopefully—graceful pirouette on the spot.

"Dude, if you batted for my team, I'd have fired you months ago so I could ride your fine ass into the sunset."

"Fair point," I said, and sighed heavily. "But to answer your question, no. I haven't seen a hot and available guy since... I dunno. The Bronze Age?"

"Damn. Because just talking about it has made me hungry for one right now."

I clapped my hands sharply. "Your news, loopy lady. Tell me."

"Oh, right. No, I mean it won't really mean anything to you. It's a family thing."

"I love family things." I bit into my tongue, trying to suppress thoughts of my late parents.

"Well, this is extended family. My cousin Ethan, the cardio-thoracic surgeon over in Chicago. He's been the, uh... black sheep of the family for a while, but I just talked him into attending my parents' anniversary party."

I guessed that was somehow significant, but it kind of flew over my head. I doodled on the pad in front of me, picturing her cousin as a distinguished but balding man. Maybe stocky, with a porn star mustache. "Oh. I guess that is good news. I'm happy for you."

"Oh, hey." Kiera walked over and sat on the corner of my desk. There was a twinkle in her eye that only ever showed when she had some evil plan running through her head. "You got me thinking, though, Gabes. How is your singing going?"

"What does that—"

"Stick with me here. I will, eventually, have a point. You still sing? You weren't just fooling?"

"Part time, yeah. Down at the Crazy Rabbit. Jazz and blues standards."

"How's that working out?"

"I love it. If I couldn't sing, I think I'd die."

"You're such a drama queen. And the

pay?"

I doodled a little more, adding extra randomness. "Well, let's just say it's lucky I do it for love. I sing for tips. And last week I only made enough to split a pack of cigarettes with my pianist."

"Cigarettes?" Kiera crossed her arms and kinked her head to the side.

"What? I barely smoke any. Only when I'm nervous."

"Any is still more than none, mister choirboy."

"Choirboy?" If she knew the things I'd done, and the guys I'd done them with... "I think you got your wires crossed there, loopy lady."

"Meh, it was the first singing related word I could come up with." Kiera slid back down to stand on the floor. "Anyway, I think it's crazy you're not making a fortune. You blow me away just singing around the office. I'm thinking I'll forget the hold music and get you serenading the clients. You're amazing."

"Thanks." I kept my focus on my random drawing rather than looking my boss—my bestie—in the eye. "It makes me feel alive like nothing else does. But

I'm not getting anywhere. Sometimes, I think maybe it's my sexuality working against me."

"Yeah... because who ever heard of a gay man in the arts? Am I right?" Kiera held her hand up, apparently for a high five.

I shook my head and crossed my arms, another sigh coursing out of me. "I think my real problem is that it's hard to sing love songs with any honesty when I'm chronically single. How long has it been since I had an awesome date? Or even a lousy one?"

Kiera glanced at her hand, still raised as if she was asking a question. Eventually, she spread her fingers and shook them, making a voice-over with a ridiculous French accent. "No, monsieur! You 'ave forsaken meee..." She mimed a time lapse of a dying flower until her hand was flat on the desk.

"You done?" I couldn't stop from smiling at Kiera's antics.

"Yep. Now, we sexy bitches gotta stick together." Suddenly, she stood up straight. "Which brings me back to my point."

"Um, sorry. You're not my type."

"Bitch-boy. My nickname at college was Peggy."

"Um."

"Y'know, because I could strap one on and—"

"Ew."

"Kidding, Gabes. But that's not what I meant, anyway."

"Whew."

"You should come."

"Ew again."

Kiera waved her hands, as if erasing the conversation from an invisible blackboard in front of her. "No, no. I mean, you should come with me on the weekend, to my parents' party. That little shindig is gonna need major distraction. Major." She coughed and turned her focus back to me. "Did I say major distraction? I, uh, meant light entertainment."

"Sounds peachy." I opened my day planner. "Oh, shoot. This weekend? I'm having my toenails ripped out by unicorns."

"Mock me not, olive-skinned demigod. You shall journey with me, and it shall be festive. And you never know what—or who—you might find there." She flashed me a grin.

I quirked my mouth. It wasn't like I'd had any plans outside of a sad movie and maybe a little me-time in the shower, but it still seemed sudden notice to prepare for an out of town gig. "Where are you from, again?"

"A little place called Gray Vale."

"Huh. Never heard of it."

"Nevertheless, you'll love it. It's a step back from the mad pace of the city. Even our airplanes are horse-drawn."

"Are you going to be like this all the time now?"

"Yeah, pretty much."

I tapped my fingers on the desk, searching for any reason not to go. "Will there be bugs?"

"All you can eat."

"Ew. What about wild animals? Lions and tigers and bears?"

Kiera screwed up her nose. "We don't let their sort in. Only wolves... oops."

"Wolves?" I arched my brows.

"Um... forget I said that." She fidgeted with her fingers.

I leaned across and tousled Kiera's russet hair. "Well, you better promise me one thing, curvy red riding hood. Don't let the big bad wolf eat me."

My boss paused, apparently searching for the right answer. "I won't let him do anything you don't want him to." She flashed another cocky smile my way.

"Why would I...? You're just a little weirder than I thought you were, loopy lady."

"Whatevs." Kiera pulled my day planner out of my grip and scrawled all over the Saturday and Sunday pages. "There. It's settled. We leave Friday night."

CHAPTER THREE

Ethan

GRAY VALE HAD barely changed since I'd left. A little bit more crowded, but I put that down to the merger with Stoke Ridge that Kiera had told me about.

The taxi ride from the tiny airport, going through the outskirts and into town, had been more confronting than I'd expected. My few happy memories were strangled by all the others: the teasing and spitting from my peers, and the emotional abandonment by my parents.

As a child, I'd been smaller than

most. An easy target, made easier by solitude. My parents were old school, and refused to offer me any protection or respite. Better I died on four feet than lived on two knees. Or some utter horseshit like that.

That had always been the way with the Roddick clan. And almost every other clan in town, if I was honest. It was the law of nature—of wolves—to sort the wheat from the chaff.

I'd retreated into books, and into my own intellect, as much for the refuge they offered as the pleasure they gave me. Bullying was my entire social life, right up until Kiera and her parents learned of my situation and formed a metaphorical wall around me. Protecting me where my immediate family wouldn't.

On one level, I couldn't really fault the system. It wasn't quite kill-or-be-killed, but it was close. And I was living proof that it worked, one way or the other. After all, those who treated me as weak were, in the end, the ones who made me so strong.

I stood in the shadows, at the outskirts of the gathering, casting a wary eye over faces that I'd never expected to see again. Faces that had more often worn monstrous sneers or vicious smiles than anything pleasant.

There was barely a single part of town that didn't hold some bitterness for me. And the less said about the surrounding woods, the better. Time and distance had allowed numbing scars to form on childhood traumas. Even now, as I poked at them, all they evoked were the recollections of pain. Ghosts of hell, and nothing more. But with Clinton, and all that happened...

I growled at myself as the more recent past slammed me in the chest, almost as a physical being. The sense of being truly alone sank deep claws into me, despite my being surrounded by so many others. A lot of the folks were family, though most of them were distant. And that was exactly how I felt.

Distant.

There was a reason I'd stayed away, turned my back on these people. After all, most of them had turned from me first. In the end, though, it had been my choice to leave, and to let this place fade. I'd turned Stoke Ridge into nothing more than a stranger's home movie.

When I first left the Ridge I'd thought of my journey as a simple regathering; a way to focus my energies on my career. But time and habit had numbed me to my heritage, to the point I'd let my city life become my only life.

After Clinton, there'd been nothing imaginable to keep me in the place. Not Kiera, not my uncle and aunt, and most especially not my damn parents, who were noticeably—and thankfully—absent from the gathered faces.

Just the thought of them had me reaching for a double scotch from a passing waiter's tray.

"Hi there, tall, dark stranger."

I turned to find my cousin Kiera smirking up at me. I was surprised to feel myself smiling back. Pleasantries over the phone were one thing, but now, face-to-face, everything was that much more real.

And incredibly confronting.

This woman had seen me at my lowest ebbs. Both of them. Though it bonded us deeper than the blood we shared, it was still a barrier. As unfair as it was, Kiera was a physical reminder of just how life could kick me.

I knew it would take my strongest effort not to turn away. To simply head back to the city and wrap myself up in that safe, new life I'd created.

But it was Kiera. Unlike the town, she'd barely changed since I last saw her, and as I released my tension, a tsunami of memories washed through me.

She and her parents had looked out for me constantly. It wasn't as if they'd been much more popular or accepted than I was, with their more liberal views. Gray Vale style of views, really. They must be loving the new merged pack.

The difference between them and me had been that the Larsons were fucking bulldozers. Nothing stopped them when the whiff of injustice was in the air. And nothing fun had happened in town without Kiera inviting herself, and by extension, me.

Now, years had passed, but the bond was still there, and it was like the bond between twins.

"Hello, Kiera."

"That's it? That's all you got for me after five years? Did your big-city surgeon buddies neuter you or something?"

I held her gaze for a moment before a small bubble of laughter erupted from my mouth. "Well, now I feel at home." I stepped forward and swept my arms around my much shorter cousin, lifting her in a hug that would rival a bear shifter's. "It's wonderful to see you, Killa."

"That's more like it. Now if you could just let me breathe again, that'd be super-great."

I gave her one more squeeze. She was wolf. She could take it. When I placed her back on the ground she gave me a light punch on the shoulder.

"But you're still not forgiven, you big lump. What, did the city lose power or something? All the phone lines were down? Someone broke the interwebs?"

"Yep, that's right. The city elders drafted a plan to get the Pony Express started up again. It probably would have worked, but I ate all the ponies." I took a healthy slug of my unhealthy drink.

"Ugh. Ponies. They taste okay, but they make me a little hoarse."

My expensive mouthful came straight out into the air, propelled by the laugh I couldn't suppress. "Dammit, Killa. How will I get through this if you won't let me swallow?"

"As the actress said to the shifter."

"Do you have to use that word?"

"What word? Actress? Said? The?"

I simply stared into her eyes.

Kiera stared straight back "You know that steely look doesn't actually work on me, right?"

"I know it never did. I thought perhaps my years of sharpening it might have made a difference."

Kiera hooked her arm through mine. "Cuz, it really is amazing to have you back here. And whether you acknowledge your... s-word status or not, well that's your choice. But hell, it was nice just to hear you joke about your wolf. Makes me think one day you might even embrace him again."

When she looked up at me with such hope in her eyes, it was my greatest temptation to simply lie. Tell her what she wanted to hear.

But in the end, though it would hurt her, I had to tell her the truth.

"I said it back then, and nothing will change my mind, Killa. I am no wolf. Not anymore."

Kiera rested her head on my upper arm and sighed. "All right then, mister serious. Be like that. But it just so happens I brought you a present."

"Me? But it's your mom and dad's special day."

"Well, you know me. I'm a giver."

"If memory serves, that so-called giving was restricted to purple nurples and wedgies, right up until I outgrew your ass."

"If you can't back it up with video evidence, then I'm afraid it never happened. And don't get off the point."

I bopped her forehead with the heel of my hand. "You actually have a point somewhere in all this?"

"Be nice or I'll take my present home with me."

I sighed and took another swig from my drink, making sure to swallow it quickly. "All right then. What could you possibly bring me that I don't already have?"

"Wait here and I'll show you."

"You know I have extremely particular tastes, don't you? In all things."

"Uh-huh. And I know exactly what they are." She shot me a quick wink. "In all things."

Kiera walked off across the clearing, glancing back over at me with that elfin grin that meant she was at her conniving best. In this case, I knew she was drawing out the moment as much as she could, trying to test my patience.

"Test away, Killa," I murmured to myself. "I can stand in one place for ten hours with someone's life in my hands."

I scanned around the gathered clan in a show of nonchalance. There were few other people I'd maybe even consider acknowledging. And only three people who I was certain I'd never met.

As if reading my mind, Kiera stopped right behind one of those strangers, catching my eye and nodding.

I glanced at my cousin, who flashed her eyes wide at me and nodded again at the man she stood behind. Kiera had clearly decided it was time to play matchmaker.

If only she knew what a pointless exercise that was. Hump 'em and dump 'em was absolutely the best I was capable of anymore. Life had given me all the lemons I was prepared to suck.

I raised the glass to my mouth to prevent myself scoffing at Kiera, and her wasted efforts.

The moment I shifted my gaze across, though, I froze in place. The hackles rose on the back of my neck as my blood simmered and surged, pumping through me more like a fist than like a river.

This was not just some random guy. This was a slick, graceful hunk of a man who'd absolutely been designed with the express purpose of tempting me back to the dark side. The side where ridiculous emotional and physical needs ruled. Where libidinous desires stole away a man's ability to think.

On the surface, his tux made him look overdressed, compared to the range of semi-formal attire the rest of us wore. The thing was, he filled it out so damn well, who could argue it was wrong?

The hormonal buzz around him was impossible to ignore, though. Not a woman here who wasn't lusting after the guy, which gave me some pause. I had no idea of his orientation, but the fact that Kiera claimed she brought him here for me had to at least hint he was into men.

As I scanned him from his head to his toes and then back up, my throat constricted. Everything about the man was utterly arresting. The way the light twinkled off his thick, glossy hair. The sweet fullness of his lips and the ready smile that seemed to appear at the slightest provocation. And the kohl of his eyes... dark enough they could match even my soul.

It took only a fraction of a second for waves of want to course through my chest. My lips tingled, sensing the vibrations of the man's own heart as it called across the distance between us.

Even worse, the lust in my belly howled for the succor I'd denied it these past five years.

The hunger of my wolf.

CHAPTER FOUR

Gabriel

AS I LOOKED around, I tried vainly to catch my breath. If I was into women at all, I'd still be a happy camper, but I swore my jaw was about to unhinge in the face of all the ridiculously handsome beefcake in this town. All tall, and broad, and so ruggedly handsome it almost hurt.

I'd long ago come to terms with being softer and prettier than most men. It sounded like a humblebrag, of course, but that was the way most people saw me.

I got it, too. Like, women across the world would kill for lips like mine. For skin this clear and moves this lithe. I sure leaned into that side of my nature, too, once I realized that owning it was the best defense.

Thing was, it wasn't like I was a small man. In this ridiculous place, though, it was like I was in a trench. Every man I could see, in addition to being hot enough to barbecue my buns on, was at least a half a head taller than me.

I suddenly noticed Kiera standing strangely close behind my back. "Hey, what are you doing back there?"

"My ex is here. I need you to hide me."

"Hide you? With those hips?"

"Oh, you little bitch." She slammed those mighty hips against me, and knocked me sideways. "Anyway, as big you are, you're still the closest to my size. If I hide behind any of these other guys we turn into a cello."

"What are you drinking, loopy lady?"

"Yeah, y'know... he's the fingerboard and the neck, and I'm the rounded body, and together we look... okay, never mind. My uncle's gone, anyway."

"I thought you said it was your ex."

"Why do you think I was hiding?"

"What? Ew."

Kiera shook her head, flashing me that cheeky grin. "Whatever. I was lying, obviously."

"Uh, whatever yourself." I pulled on a lock of Kiera's hair. "Speaking of uncles, you said this is an anniversary party. That means family. You mean to tell me all these human trees here are related to you?"

"For the most part."

I looked Kiera up and down. "So what... it skipped a generation?"

My boss and bestie poked out her tongue. "You be nice, now. Or I just might get one of these trees to fall on you."

"Promises, promises. Do I get to choose which one?"

"Nope. I've already chosen. That's why I was behind you. Marking you for him." Kiera flashed me a lightning fast grin and darted off again, in her usual flighty manner.

I took a quick swig of my champagne as I cast my gaze across the open area. Surely Kiera was joking. Really, what were the chances of finding a hot, handsome guy way out here in the middle of buttfuck? And one who's into guys, as well? Surely that was impossible.

And that was when I saw him.

The man was tall, even by the standard of the gathering. Lush, dark hair, framing a face carved to perfection, but deliciously roughed up by experience. And like me, he seemed frozen in the moment, his square tumbler of whiskey held in suspended animation just below his mouth.

But it was what I saw above the rim of the glass that had me all worked up. His eyes. Silvery gray and fierce as winter, he had those vicious orbs pointed straight at me. For a moment— one that seemed to stretch out through both space and time—the man drilled into my skull from across the clearing.

With three quick swishes, he moved those eyes down and across me, taking in every detail. It was as if he was wielding an invisible knife, slicing the tux straight from my body without even so much as nicking my skin.

I had to curl my fingers into the lapel

of my jacket just to be sure I wasn't actually naked. The blatant heat of his gaze left me feeling utterly uncovered. Not just skin deep, either. I swore that man was staring into my bones.

Into my soul.

With that man, I didn't even need my gaydar. I could practically hear his desire as a voice inside my head. As much as I wanted to believe in fate and astrology and all things woo-woo, in my heart I never had. So it was weird to have what felt like a true psychic moment.

I held my breath inside as if it was barbed, and to breathe out would tear me to pieces. Damn. No matter that I hadn't performed yet. No matter that I'd be letting my bestie down. The presence of that big, handsome hunk of pure temptation meant that, as far as I was concerned, this night was over.

Sure, I'd been alone for a while. And yeah, I'd been moaning for a couple of months now to Kiera about there being no good men around.

But that guy?

Hell, no.

That man was not just trouble. He

was peril. The kind I really couldn't deal with all the way out here in the sticks.

As if there wasn't danger enough from all the animal predators, now Kiera wanted to dangle me in front of a hungry, hungry hunk as well?

Still the guy stood there, pushing all my buttons from thirty feet away. Buttons I couldn't even reach on my own. Buttons I'd never even thought to look for.

The prickling flames of desire had already started in my cock, and begun to lick their way up my spine and into my head. I could feel the hot, syrupy trickle as my brain liquefied and drizzled all the way down until it took up residence in my balls.

I bit down hard on my tongue, hoping the pain would stem the flow of sinful, dirty thoughts in my fuzzy head. From only three seconds of eye contact, I already knew I was a goner. That I'd climb a tree just to get a taste of that man. Hell, a demigod like that, I'd climb an angry bear to reach him.

And that kind of desperate soul-sucking need simply didn't work with my busy schedule.

Thankfully, a small group of stupidly tall people walked across the clearing between us, breaking whatever spell it was that had me mesmerized. By the time they'd passed, Mister Eyeballs was nowhere to be seen.

For a moment, I entertained the idea that I'd simply imagined him.

A man that perfect?

It had to have been a mirage.

Exactly how many champagnes had I already downed?

As I always did when I drank and got nervous, I pulled out a cigarette from my pocket, noting ruefully that it was my last. As a singer, there was no doubt I should have kicked the habit before ever picking it up, but I was not exactly a man with a whole lot of self-control.

Holding the cigarette tight between my lips, I dug back into my pocket to grab my lighter. And then froze when a deep, smooth voice sounded from beside me.

"Please, allow me, friend."

I didn't even have to look up. Didn't need any confirmation beyond the sound of his voice. It was *him*. The guy who'd sent my thoughts and my morals flying south.

But when I did look up—way, way up—into his eyes, my knees almost failed me, turning to rubber in an instant.

It took more effort than I'd ever known, but I steadied my legs beneath me and leaned gently forward, presenting my cigarette for lighting.

Mister Eyeballs reached out, but instead of lighting it, he plucked the thing from between my lips and crushed it in his huge fist.

"What the hell?" That little cigarette was all that was left of my last gig's pay. And this asshole had destroyed it like it was nothing.

"This is strictly a no smoking affair, man. I'm surprised Kiera didn't tell you."

"But... I mean, you could've just told me. Didn't have to vandalize my property. And how did you know I was here with Kiera?"

"It's hardly an act of genius. She mentioned she had a plus one, and I saw you talking with her."

"Oh."

Every word, every syllable that came from the man's mouth hit like a slap.

Words issued so sharply and coldly they practically left marks on my skin.

If he'd just soften his tone, maybe thaw out that cold, dead heart of his, then that deep, sonorous voice would be like honey-cured sex.

"Look around you, man. It's been a dry year and this town is surrounded by forest. Already there are fires off in the distance. Not to mention there are plenty of sensitive noses here, as you must be aware."

"Well I'm sorry. Kiera never mentioned this was the annual Hayfever Anonymous meeting."

Okay, it had been a smart-ass remark, but you'd think I'd just scratched his Beemer the way he impaled me again with those steel gray eyes. "Are you serious?"

"I tried it once. It never took."

"Kiera didn't tell you about us? This town, these people?"

"Look, Kiera just said she was heading up here for the party, and asked me if I'd come along and sing. It was either this or hosting the Oscars, and who can take that kind of a risk, anymore?"

The big guy narrowed his bladed eyes and sliced through my soul again. "Well in that case, buddy, it would be better for you to simply toddle off to wherever you're staying tonight. This..." He waved his arm languidly around him, indicating the small crowd of nicely dressed people. "This is certainly not a gathering for a sheltered little city boy like yourself."

For a moment, my rage left me unable to form a sentence. All my words tumbled over each other like sweaty wrestlers, each jostling for the right to come streaming out of my mouth first.

"How dare... What the hell do you... I mean..."

"Oh, take a breath, buddy. Then hold it until you've turned around and walked away."

"I will not! Who the hell are you to tell me what to do?"

"Never mind who I am, man. Just trust me on this. It's for your own good." He made a condescending shoo motion with his hand. "Off you go."

Mostly, I was a pretty regular guy. It took a fuck-ton of provocation to get my inner bratty diva rising to the surface.

This guy had made it happen in under two minutes.

I stomped my foot and waved my empty champagne flute in the guy's face. "I will not. I'm here for a paid performance. You understand professionalism, mister? Or did you sleep through that lesson in life?"

He simply smirked, his sexy mouth both taunting and tempting me in equal measure. "Trust me. You're far better off being a long way away from us."

CHAPTER FIVE

Ethan

THE BEAST INSIDE me thrashed and howled, threatening to blow my carefully cultivated exterior. In the first days out of Gray Vale and in the big city, my wolf had come close to the surface, drawn out by anything that simply sent my heart racing. It had taken me years of self-control, and as much as possible, controlling my environment, to keep the beast subdued.

Being surrounded almost exclusively by humans had helped, but that didn't explain why everything was turning to shit at that moment. This guy was clearly human, but he had my soul blistering and my mind tingling.

And the creature... the fucking beast was practically bursting through my skin, making demands that were near impossible to suppress.

For me, the matter was beyond question, now. I needed to get this man out of my reach, before I sank my claws—or more likely my teeth—into him. And no way would I condemn this man to that bizarre lifestyle. Even if he knew what being a shifter was all about, and begged to be marked, I couldn't in good conscience do that to him.

He was beyond simply a temptation. His looks, his voice, his dark and sensual eyes, all woke a deep need within me. But it was his scent that had my wolf in a frenzy and scratching at my skin.

Not his cologne or his shampoo. His own natural spicy musk had grabbed a hold of my senses and made my hair stand on end in a way I'd never felt before.

Whoever he was, he held promises I couldn't afford to wish for. I'd sworn off any kind of relationship after Clinton. Even my idle dalliances had been few and far between, and always with men I knew I could never fall for.

While my intellect demanded I cut and run, and fast, my wolf had other ideas. This beautiful man had my senses all riled up in a cloud of red heat. I'd never warred so hard with my beast. My heart circled my mind, searching for a weakness to exploit.

Up close, he was even sexier than from afar. I'd pushed him pretty hard before, just to get him pissed enough to leave. Yet all I'd succeeded in doing was to ignite a robust and fiery anger inside him.

One that made him close to irresistible.

The fire in his eyes spread to the tanned skin of his chiseled face. That sensual peach of a mouth was practically begging for mine. To bite in, to suck the juice from him. To open him up, glide my tongue inside as he pressed his hard, young body against me. I lost myself in the moment, imagining the sweet and languid solidity of his body in my arms as I drove my cock home, deep inside him.

"Hey, you asshole." The fiery-hearted hottie pulled me back into the moment as he pushed at my shoulders, hard enough to have me stumbling back a step. "Who the hell do you think you are?"

The futility of him trying to use force simply made him even more attractive to me. It showed the fire inside him. A fire I suspected was near unquenchable, and one which my wolf was increasingly desperate to sample.

I quelled the landslide of erotic images coursing through me by downing the last of my scotch. There was no room in my life for the foolishness of a relationship. My efforts to fit in to the human world had been tough enough as a lone wolf. Bringing an actual human into my life was begging for trouble.

But the random, animalistic nonsense roiling within me at that moment was exactly the reason I wanted out of the shifter world. Only then, when I'd conquered my wolf, could I allow myself an indulgence like the one standing before me, eyes ablaze with indignation.

If I could kill the wolf but keep the nose, I'd do it in a heartbeat. If there were a single gland I could remove that would take the beast with it, I'd perform the damn surgery on myself.

But this sexy snack would bring me to my knees. The dark heat in his eyes called straight to my desires. And his scent was off the fucking chain. Part prey, part mate, part meal. Christ, he was just about impossible to resist.

His skin, his hair, and his breath were all rich and delicious. My real problem, though, was the other scent. The one only my wolf could detect.

His cock.

Living in the city, I'd learned early on how to ignore that scent from other people; to turn it into nothing more than a background noise, of sorts. No, this sexy man's scent hit me as a spicy cocktail of sweet and savory, of appetizer and dessert. More than anything, though, his scent was a revelation.

My parents had plenty to answer for in my life. Their passive-aggressive reaction to my sexuality had never surprised me. It was more their flat-out disgust at my choice to move into the human world that hit me harder. Above all that, it was their refusal to allow me a choice of mate, setting me up with one, instead.

And all because of one lie, told to me before I even reached puberty.

That I had no fated mate.

What better way to press me into the mating they wanted for me, than to convince me I had no other option?

I hadn't even learned this man's name yet, but the way he aroused my human senses—and devastated my wolf's—meant there was no doubt. He was mine.

"Hello?" He poked me again, much more softly. "You in there, butt-face?"

I searched for some way to deal with the moment. Scooping him into my arms and telling him that we were meant to be together forever probably wouldn't cut it. He clearly knew nothing of shifters, or their ways.

"Ethan!"

The familiar voice pulled me out of my internal struggle between wolf and man, lust and reason. I turned to see Abigail Larson beside me, arms outstretched.

"Come on now, handsome. Don't you leave me hanging."

I stepped into the waiting embrace and returned it with genuine warmth. She might be my aunt by marriage and not blood, but Abigail was more of a mother to me than Olga Roddick had ever been.

"It's so good to see you again, Aunt Abigail."

"Oh, hush now, darling. Since when do we have such a formal relationship?"

"Sorry. Abigail."

The older woman moved smoothly out of the hug, but kept her arm looped through mine. She held her hand out to my sexy sparring partner. "Hello, darling. Abigail Larson. And you are?"

"Ethan?"

"Don't be silly, darling. This is Ethan."

The guy shook his head. "Oh, sorry. I'm Gabriel Mendoza. Kiera brought me along to sing tonight." He turned his attention back to me. "You're Kiera's cousin?"

"Yes, but I don't see—"

"See, she told me you were a surgeon in Chicago and I just... uh, pictured you differently."

"You thought he'd be older?" Abigail rested her hand on Gabriel's arm, then drew in a quick breath, turning to Ethan.

"Older?" He coughed and licked his sensual lips, apparently in confusion. "Oh, yes. Older. That's right."

I glanced at the guy—Gabriel—and savored the fresh flush running through his cheeks. I looked at Abigail, whose expression hovered somewhere between surprise and bliss.

With one hand on me and the other on Gabriel, the truth was clear. Her face told me beyond a doubt she detected the same connection I did.

The rapid unfurling of emotion.

The swift heat of blood, pulsing out and in.

The bond between fated mates.

Until that moment, I hadn't trusted my own judgment.

Yet, even though I'd never experienced such an instant and powerful attraction to a man before, I'd been unwilling to truly trust my instincts. That's what I got from trying to deny them, suppress them, for so long.

I trusted Abigail beyond measure, though. If she felt the connection, then it must be real.

Damn it all.

CHAPTER SIX

Gabriel

WHY THE HELL hadn't Kiera warned me that Ethan was pure sex on legs?

Or more importantly, that he was a total jerk?

With all the chatter about him on the drive up to Stoke Ridge, the least my boss could've done was to introduce Ethan to me by name. If for nothing more than to let me know which of the tall, dark, and handsome men I was supposed to be the nicest to.

But instead, all Kiera had talked about was the guy's history. How something vaguely bad happened and he'd turned his back on the place. How this would be his first time back, and she hoped everyone would be nice to him. Or at least civil.

Which was more than he'd done for me. I'd been ready to take a swing at the guy for his rudeness. Hell, I was still bristling with irritation, made worse by that annoying feeling of desperate attraction. But knowing who he was meant I felt I should probably swallow my pride.

With casual violence off the menu, I instead tore a full flute of champagne off the next waiter's tray and took a long slug, letting Abigail keep the conversation going. With any luck, I could just ease quietly into the background and disappear.

Except, as much as I wanted to back away, there was an even greater force at work that kept me close. Not anything I understood, and nothing I'd ever felt before.

Ethan was so fucking gorgeous it physically hurt to look at him without touching. And he smelled just as good. Even though the smoky scent of the distant fires was ever-present, the animal musk of Ethan cut through it all. And hit me like an ocean wave. A body-wide slam of power that was impossible to ignore.

Despite that, I knew turning away was the smart move. Just to keep my distance until I could escape back to the city. That was the safest way to make sure I didn't put my foot in my mouth. Or into Ethan's ass, at speed.

I downed the rest of my drink and got ready to make my quiet exit. I had a gig to perform, after all. Surely, that gave me an excuse to leave.

Abigail interrupted my escape plan, though, hooking her arm through mine and holding me in place. Girl had some real surprising strength in her grip.

Then she rested her other hand on Ethan's shoulder. "A little heads up for you, darling... your parents arrived a few moments ago."

Rather than answer straight away, the big guy raised his glass tumbler and scowled at it when he noticed it was empty. "Thanks for letting me know, Abigail."

As if the mention of them had been

enough to conjure them, suddenly an older couple appeared from the small crowd and walked straight over to Ethan.

"Hello, son."

"Mother." He glanced over at his father's outstretched hand but otherwise didn't move. "Father."

"Come now, Ethan. We've not seen you in five years."

"Well, you know what they say. Time flies when you're shunning sons."

The older man scowled. "Who's been shunning who, boy?"

"Son," his mother interjected. "Please. What happened with Clinton was, of course, rather upsetting. For all of us."

Abigail made a clear move, sliding her hand down Ethan's forearm, which looked to me for all the world like she was marking her territory, which seemed bizarre. After all, these were the man's own parents. "You don't really think any of us can dilute or appropriate this young man's pain like that. Do you, Olga?"

The only answer was a stare with the same intensity as Ethan's. But this one was all ice and no fire.

Ethan's father stepped forward, his arms freshly crossed. "I certainly don't think this is anything for you to concern yourself with, Abigail. It is, after all, a family matter."

"Oh, I see. Now it's a family matter. Whereas five years ago you found his reactions disagreeable and embarrassing. I seem to recall you asserting he should simply grow a pair, as the rather unpleasant saying goes."

"We have certain expectations—"

"No, you have ridiculous prejudices from the Stone Age."

Ethan rested his hand on top of his aunt's and smiled down at her. "Thank you, Abigail. But I can take it from here."

The older woman patted Ethan's cheek, then tugged on my arm, gently drawing us both away from the tense moment. "I think we should get you ready for your performance. What do you say?"

I couldn't help glancing back at the trio as Abigail dragged me away. Okay, so Ethan had been a total asshole to me, but there was no denying how much he messed me up inside.

In the most exciting way.

The fire in his eyes held promise of a heat so powerful it could burn my skin off. Even while he'd been pushing me away with his words, the tone of his voice told a different story.

One of need.

Of desire.

And though I'd wanted more than anything to get myself out of range of his intoxicating scent, and his laser beam eyes, being separated by even a few dozen feet now meant the world suddenly felt cold.

Which was so ridiculous it was embarrassing. To cover myself, I tried to strike up a conversation with my new companion.

"So, Abigail..."

"He's quite a dish, isn't he?"

"What? Who?"

"Oh, come now, darling. Even a jaded city boy would have to be dead not to fall a little bit in love with Ethan."

Christ.

Was I just radiating gay vibes?

Had Kiera told everybody my orientation?

I tried scoffing to deflect how easily Abigail had read my desires. There was no doubt she saw through my charade, and another rush of heat filled my cheeks. "Okay, maybe to look at. But he's such an asshole."

Abigail wavered her head a little. "Oh, I don't know. I do think he was giving you a hard time, but I can't truly blame him for that."

"Well, there's nobody else to blame. You're not going to feed me that tired old boys-will-be-boys crap, are you? That might work for schoolgirls, but it's never worked on men. We were boys, once, remember?"

"Oh, I'm not saying that. He definitely behaved badly, but it was for a very understandable reason. Self-defense."

"What, that big brute was worried I'd scratch his eyes out?"

"Darling, there are far more effective ways to hurt a man than physically. It was just a confronting moment for him. After all, you're everything that boy needs and wants."

"What?"

"And he knows it, too."

"Um, Earth to crazy lady. He was desperately trying to make me leave."

Abigail's laugh was as soft and

measured as any other part of her speech. "Oh, darling. Believe me, if you knew his history, you'd know that simply proves my point."

We walked in silence until we reached the foot-high stage. As I stepped up, I glanced back down at Abigail. "So what, this place is totally full of crazy people?"

Abigail gave me a tiny smile back. "Always room for one more, darling."

CHAPTER SEVEN

Ethan

"ETHAN, AREN'T YOU going to shake your father's hand?"

I glared at my mother in a futile attempt to deter her with my eyes. For a moment, I'd forgotten where I inherited my steely stare from.

"Son?" Hugh Roddick had reached out again. "You're embarrassing me."

I switched my gaze to my father's outstretched hand. "Oh, yes. Embarrassment is a sin that greatly outweighs all others, isn't it?"

"What exactly is that supposed to

mean, boy?"

"It means you're both more concerned with how shit looks, than how shit is. Besides, you surrendered the right to tell me what to do when you..." My breath caught in my chest.

"When we what, son?"

I recognized the change in my mother's tone that told me she knew where I was heading. She could always read people far better than her husband.

"When you forced me into that mating."

"Clinton was a fine man, from an ancient clan. You couldn't have done any better for yourself."

"Right. Because who could possibly want me of their own accord?"

"Oh, son, you're mincing my words. I simply—"

"No." I stabbed the air in front of my mother's face. "Nothing you do has ever been done simply, mother. You are the most Machiavellian person I've ever experienced."

Olga glanced across at her husband and then back to me, sighing heavily. "Son, whether you understand or not, the truth is that Clinton was the best mate we could organize for you. The stocks are so much more limited for your kind. Not to mention your... issue, and all."

And there it was. Old time Stoke Ridge shit. I honestly believed they'd have coped with my other problem, if only I hadn't been born gay.

"I didn't need you to find me a mate. Hell, I was only twenty-five. I didn't need a mate at all."

Hugh clucked his tongue. "You were never going to get a quality one. Not while you insisted on slumming with those god awful humans."

"I like humans." I smiled to myself. "But I couldn't eat a whole one." Though with some humans, I'd certainly give it my best shot. I closed my eyes for a moment and pictured that succulent young man whose mouth-watering scent still hung in the air before me.

"Do keep your voice down, son."

I awoke from my reverie and whirled on my mother, speaking through gritted teeth. "Everyone has heard as much of our conversation as they've wanted to, mother. We're all wolves here."

The squeal of a microphone feeding

back cut through the clearing, and straight through the consciousness of every wolf in the area.

"Sorry, folks. Technical hitch."

Olga raised one eyebrow as she sneered at Gabriel up on the temporary stage. "Not all of us." She turned back to me with a small shake of her head. "I suppose you'll go chasing after him now, son? You'd do anything just to upset me."

"Mother, there is not a single decision I make, any day of my life, in which your feelings feature at all." I glanced across at my father. "Either of you. You couldn't let me be when I was young. You couldn't support me after Clinton. And you both actively strove to end my medical career before it began."

"Do you blame us? Son, you're putting your hands inside those things."

"Those things? You mean humans, mother?"

"Exactly."

"Oh, you are just too much."

I ran my hand back through my hair as though it could erase the last two minutes of my memory. With a small growl, I turned and marched away.

Olga and Hugh Roddick might be the people who'd spawned me, but they were not my family. And there was no way I'd let them work my anger up to the point where I'd make a scene. After all, though I never formally lived with them, Abigail and Bernard Larson were the ones who'd essentially raised me. And I'd rather miss their party than ruin it.

I'd just reached the road when the singing started. Up on stage, that delicious feast of a man poured all his worldly desires out into a microphone. Needs, wants, secrets... he'd turned them all into breath, and gushed them through his delectable throat, creating a sensual feast of music.

I froze in place, eyes closed, as the smoky blend of tenor and baritone washed over the clearing, bypassing my ears and spearing straight into my blood.

"No..." My voice was little more than a whisper, and a cracked one at that. As if that slick, handsome man wasn't already temptation enough, he had to go and slice me to pieces with nothing more than his singing voice.

As Gabriel crooned some classic Tony

Bennett numbers, I turned back, struggling to keep my hunger under control. It barely mattered that my mind still insisted I get away from him, that I free myself from the spell of that temptation. It seemed my body had overruled me.

Before I knew it, I'd walked to the side of the small stage, taking in every defined but graceful move of his hand as he caressed the vintage style microphone. Fuck, I was staring with the ravenous intent of a pure predator.

I shifted my focus, homing in on his mouth as he formed the words. Lips and tongue working with, and against, each other, like lovers in a perfect ballet.

I closed my eyes and let the man's music pour all over me. The rest of the world faded until all that existed was Gabriel's sexy voice and my fiery blood. And I couldn't tell where one finished and the other began.

All too soon, he sang the last note, thanked the audience and turned off his compact music machine. I took another flute of champagne from the table near the stage and prowled over to where he stood. It was impossible to take my gaze off him as he stepped back down to the ground. He moved like a dancer.

He moved like a wolf. And that should have been enough to make me pause. Instead, I held out the glass toward him.

"Champagne?"

Gabriel turned to me, a supremely bitable smile on his luscious lips. A smile that faded in an instant once he saw my face.

"What, as long as I take it to go?"

I nodded slowly, conceding that one to him. "Oh, come now. Surely we can be civil?"

"I know I can, but then I'm not a jerk." He crossed his arms and shot me right between the eyes with a fierce frown. "Not half an hour ago, you were doing everything you could to get rid of me. I half-expected you to set me on fire, just so you could tell me to go jump in the lake."

I held up a hand, a half surrender. "Please forgive my earlier, caddish, behavior. Is it all right if I call you Gabriel?"

"No. I won't forgive you. What kind of a dumb-ass tries to send someone into exile five seconds after meeting them?"

I nodded, but couldn't keep the smile from curling my lips. It was a struggle to remember the last time anyone but Kiera had spoken to him with such sass.

"I'm afraid that was a misunderstanding. On my part, by the way, I fully admit that."

"Oh, how big of you. Here, have my room key. Take me, big boy, take me."

The way his scent kept gnawing away at my composure was both heaven and purgatory. My wolf hadn't been so active in years. "I really would like to start fresh. And if I may, to call you by your name."

He frowned at me, but eventually took the offered champagne. "All right. I guess you can call me Gabriel. Anyone who gives me bubbly can't be all bad. And make it up to me how, exactly?"

"Well, I'm afraid I hadn't thought that far ahead. You've kind of made me dizzy with your voice."

The delicious frown on his forehead grew stronger for a moment. "You got some kind of disorder, buddy?"

"Ethan Roddick."

"Haven't heard of that one. Is it like Lou Gehrig's Disease?"

For a moment I paused, before I let a sharp bark of laughter erupt from deep within me. "Oh, you really are a sassy one, aren't you?"

"I have more sass than ass. But that's not so hard, when you have an ass as perky as mine."

I paused for a moment, as my wolf hunched up deep within me, ready to pounce. I'd never had to work so fucking hard to push the beast down. Nor had I felt so close to just giving up that fight. Not since I'd forsaken it, anyway.

In a desperate move to ease my wolf's claim on my mind, I tried a halfway measure. I reached out and stroked my fingers back over his cheek, then rested my hand on the side of his neck.

Though Gabriel watched my hand like it was a loaded gun, he remained still. The only change was in his breathing, which became quick and shallow. It was unlikely he even noticed the change himself, but to my highly attuned senses, it was everything.

"So, Gabriel. Where are you staying?"

"In what world is that any of your damn business?"

"I'm making polite conversation."

"Dude—"

"Ethan."

"Dude, you could punch me in the face and it would still be more polite than your conversation."

"Oh, come now. I'm playing nice."

He took a small step backward, shrugging my hand away. "Exactly. Playing nice. It's a wonder you don't have pneumonia, the way you keep running hot and cold."

I matched his movements, stepping forward into the small gap he'd made between us. "I've already apologized. I acted terribly, and for reasons I'm unable to explain. But I'd like to make it up to you, if you'll allow me. Perhaps I can show you around town."

"It's dark."

"In the morning."

"I'm sleeping in."

"After you wake up."

"I'm, uh... washing my hair."

"I'll help."

"The hair on my palms."

I burst out with genuine laughter, which felt much more freeing than it should have.

What the fuck had I been doing with

my life that a lame-ass joke like that felt like a holiday?

"Well, we'd be a good match, then."

Gabriel stared at me, his face like stone for a few seconds, before he too broke down in laughter. "All right then, butt-face. I suppose I could slum it and allow you to show me around town."

I bowed theatrically. "So, you didn't tell me where you're staying."

"With Kiera."

I nodded, raising my eyebrows. "Really? And how do you know her?"

Gabriel took a sip of champagne before answering. "She's my boss. And my best friend, really. God, that sounds pathetic."

"Hey!" The woman herself appeared, as if we'd conjured her by saying her name too many times. "What's so pathetic about me?"

Gabriel tousled Kiera's hair and smiled. "Not you. Me. That pretty much my only friend in the city is the woman I work for."

"It could be worse," I said.

"Oh. How so?"

I flicked Kiera's ear like I used to in childhood. "You could be related to her."

Kiera poked me in the arm. "Oh, I hope you brought your suture kit, Doc, 'cause my sides just split."

"Do you have insurance? My needle doesn't get out of bed for less than ten grand a day, you know."

"Har-de-har." Kiera leaned in a little closer. "Your mother is asking for you, scrotum-face. My mom and dad are running interference, but you probably should go take care of business."

"I already saw them. I couldn't possibly eat any more shit from them tonight."

"Ethan?" Kiera put her hand on my arm. "Look, I get it. I don't like it any more than you do. But it's been five years, and you really should clear the air with them."

"I'd rather clean the toilet with them."

She was right, of course. I knew my parents well enough to know they expected me to come back home eventually. And they surely assumed I'd take another mate of their choice. At the very least, I had to go and knock that ridiculous notion on the head.

CHAPTER EIGHT

Gabriel

IT WAS STILL nearly impossible to work out if Ethan was some kind of sexy godlike man, or just a complete jerk who happened to be physically perfect in every stupid way. I watched his lithe, muscular body—especially that tight, hard ass of his—as he glided across the clearing toward a small clutch of people.

"You okay, Gabes?" Kiera's warm voice pulled me back into the real world.

"Huh? Oh, yeah. He's just a doodoohead, is all."

"Oh, that. Yeah. He always has been."

"What's the deal with him and his parents? You all seem such a close family, but it's like he can't stand being anywhere near them."

"We Larsons are close, for sure. Sometimes waaay too close. The Roddicks, though, not so much. It's hard to believe my dad and Ethan's mom were raised in the same house. Uncle Hugh and Aunt Olga are real old-school Stoke Ridge assholes. They're all about social status, and Ethan never matched what they thought their son should be."

"What, because he's gay?" The fire of indignation rose inside me again, only this time it was for Ethan, not because of him.

"No, not that. I mean, they were dicks about it, but they came around eventually. I mean, he's their only cub."

"Ha. That's cute. Cub."

"Uh..." For the first time I could remember, my boss seemed actually flustered. She covered it a second later. "Yeah, anyway, like I say, he wasn't all they wanted, and for stupid reasons."

I tried for a moment to process that concept. "So, wait... he's tall, dark, and ridiculously sexy, in addition to which he's a rich, successful surgeon. Yes?"

"Uh-huh."

"My god, how do they stand the shame?"

Kiera squeezed her mouth into a rosebud shape and crinkled her nose. "Weird as it sounds, that truly wasn't their plan. When they arranged his mating with Clinton—"

"His what?"

Kiera gulped a quick breath down, and tapped her lips with her finger. "His marriage. What did I say?"

"You said mating."

"Huh. That's weird." She glanced off to the side, at nothing in particular as far as I could tell.

"So, he's married?" Why the hell did that knowledge feel like a cold lump in the middle of my chest? The guy had been ruder than rude to me from the moment I'd met him.

"No, not anymore."

Before I could say another word, a high sound filled the air. Somewhere between a siren and a roar. It wasn't exactly close, but it seemed to come from more than one direction.

"What's that?"

Kiera shrugged lightly. "That's just wolves."

"Wolves?" I tensed up and looked around myself again. "You have wolves here?"

"Like you wouldn't believe, honey."

"You didn't write that in my damn day planner. Head to Stoke Ridge for anniversary. Get throat torn out by overgrown pooches."

Kiera tensed up for a second, then relaxed. "Honey, we haven't had a fatality in years. And that wasn't by a wolf, it was... an accident." She checked her watch. "Well, most of the good stuff has already happened. You wanna blow this popsicle stand? Or would you rather stay around and blow Ethan's popsicle?"

"If you weren't my boss, I'd probably be telling you to go soak your head right about now."

"Is that all?"

"Oh, I guess something about you being a total bitch. Maybe not that wording exactly, but you'd definitely catch my drift."

"Hm. Probably just as well I am your boss then." She struck a cartoonish haughty pose. "Nobody talks to me that way."

"Uh-huh."

"So, which was it? Blow the joint, or blow the man? Want me to flip a coin?"

"How about you flip this?"

Kiera made a show of turning away from my raised finger. "Fine. I can take a hint."

"As long as it's delivered by a marching band, and packed in a luminescent box, with the word *hint* flashing in neon lights on the side of it."

"Yeah, well, whatever works." She turned back as she walked. "Coming?"

CHAPTER NINE

Ethan

WITH EVERY STEP I took, I could sense the tension growing within me, and around me. The gathered throng edged away as I passed by, clearing a path for my hotly radiating anger, until I stood once again before my parents.

Olga was the first to speak. "Hello again, son."

"Don't call me that. Your part-time commitment to me long ago rendered the word inoperable."

Hugh stepped in, his arm raised. "Ethan, some respect please."

"With me, Father, if you have to ask for respect then it's because you've not earned it."

"Come now, boy. It's time you let this Clinton thing go."

I crossed my arms. "Why do you two always assume it's about Clinton? My issue is with you, and predates him by twenty years."

"Oh, dear," Olga hissed. "This is about your darn childhood again. Do you need me to call a therapist, or will a silky-soft hankie do?"

Such cold words from my own mother should have had me firing up. I could feel my wolf within, pawing at my chest as if begging for attention. But knowing Olga's ultimate aim was to draw that very reaction from me helped keep my mind and body steadily human.

"It's a little late for all that, mother. And I'm successful, despite your best efforts. Despite my mate and all that happened."

"Oh, come now. You can't possibly blame us for Clinton."

"Why not?"

Olga took a sip of her white wine and sighed. "Son, you were the only one near him when—"

"I'm not talking about that. I'm saying he would never have been with me at all if not for you two and your damn lies."

Despite my determination, my wolf had his hackles up and was more than ready to pounce. Until this weekend, I hadn't felt so primal in nearly half a decade. But I was not going to let these two drag me back to the life—and lifestyle—I'd sworn off.

"What lies would those be, son?" Hugh crossed his arms and tilted his head in his classic you-have-no-idea stance. "We told the truth about that boy all the way. He was from an excellent family, he was pleasant looking, and he was of mating age. What more could you want?"

"What about love? What about my fated mate?"

Olga waved away my words as if they were meaningless. "Son, not everyone has a fated mate. You were, as you said, already twenty-five—"

"I said *only* twenty-five. Not *already* twenty-five. There's a world of difference in that one word."

"And, quite frankly, it was growing

rather tiresome watching you waste your time gallivanting around. Not to mention your distasteful choice in pastimes."

"By pastimes, you mean my surgical career?"

"You know how we feel about that. Surgery is a noble and admirable career."

"As long as I stay away from humans and stick only to shifters."

"That's not true, son," Hugh muttered.

"No?"

"It would be equally distasteful were you to be squelching around the innards of bears and cats, too." He screwed his mouth up. "Oh, don't get me wrong. Bears and cats have their uses, at least. But we wolves are the—"

"Stop it." I was thankful I didn't still have a glass of scotch in my hand, otherwise I would have crushed it. "I went through with it all, mating with Clinton, because of you two. To appease you. Because you had me convinced he was the best I could do."

"And he was. We're still very good friends with the Milfords. I won't have you speak ill of their son."

"Oh, I'm not. I'm speaking ill of you. What you say is true. Clinton was a fine man, a wonderful wolf. Clever, loyal, and mostly content to be around me." I leaned right in and hissed my anger straight into my mother's face. "But he knew as well as I did, we were not fated for each other."

"Your generation has such a fanciful notion about mating. What I said was true. Not everyone has a fated mate."

"But I do, mother. I just met him tonight."

For the first time I could recall, my mother's eyes flashed with true anger, and her voice sank into wolf register. "Boy, I know you don't mean that feral little human. I was joking about you chasing him."

"Oh, and you know as well as I do it is him, Mother. Or have your senses deserted you?"

Hugh stepped between the two of us, nudging me backward. "Ethan, you're not thinking straight."

"Ha."

"Sure, humans can be a fun little plaything for a wolf. Not to mention a snack, afterward. But there is no way—"

I held up my hands, halting all conversation for a moment. "Look, I'm not going through this with you two again. That man is my mate. If you don't like it, then you should make like good little wolves and fucking bite me."

CHAPTER TEN

Gabriel

THE SHORT WALK back to Kiera's family home got my blood pumping again. But more than the exercise, it was the memory of Ethan's eyes and ass that had me short of breath and breaking out in a light sheen of sweat.

As we walked up the hallway toward our rooms, Kiera tapped me on the shoulder.

"Unzip me?" She turned her back, lifting her hair out of the way. As I pulled down on the zipper, I sighed at my own internal conflict.

There was no denying how that man got me all fired up, despite his shitty attitude, but who the hell goes gaga for someone they've only just met?

Kiera turned around and grabbed my bow tie, undoing it for me, and opening my top shirt button as well.

"Oh, mama, that's a relief."

"Penny for your thoughts, honey?"

"The kind of thoughts I'm having will cost you more like $2.99 a minute."

"I knew it, you dirty man-whore."

I poked my tongue out at her. "I thought I told you that was a state secret."

"Not around here, honey."

"What?"

"Well, I don't mean about you being a man-whore. That secret's safe with me and the track team. I just mean about you and Ethan."

"What the hell are you talking about?"

Kiera shrugged as she pushed open the door to her childhood bedroom. "What can I say? People around here are very perceptive. We don't miss much. And it's clear you're super warm for his super form. Taking a class to study his ass. Ready to rock his big ol'—"

"Okay, okay." I shook my head, feeling the frown creasing my brow. "Well, you missed the mark this time. There's nothing between that doofus and me. Got it?"

"Oh, sure. If you say so, Gabes."

I pushed my way into the guest bedroom and stripped off that ridiculous, but still somehow awesome, tuxedo. It was the biggest relief to get out of that thing, despite how sexy I'd felt in it. How sexy Ethan made me feel when he scanned me from head to toe, up and down, over and over, like I was his next meal.

My grey sweatpants and coffee-stained T-shirt might look like they came from a new range of homeless chic, but holy hell they were comfortable. Any time I pulled them on it felt like coming home.

I wandered out to the kitchen where Kiera was making cheese on toast.

"Hey, honey. Want some chow?"

"Nah. Thanks anyway, but I have to hit the hay."

"Lightweight."

I rolled my eyes and grabbed my

crotch. "You wouldn't say that if you had to lug around a beast like this."

"Oh, please."

"Hey, you started it."

"No, I mean, please. As in, yes, please, give me a closer look at the goodies, man."

I crossed my arms again and put on my fiercest frown. "The only thing stopping you from being a fellow man-whore is the fact you're not a man."

Kiera mimicked me, crossing her arms and making her big breasts pop halfway out of her loose T. "Who told?"

"Uh..." I nodded at her chest. "The twins kinda give it away, babycakes."

Kiera lowered her gaze to her own chest. "Hear that, girls? This bitch is talking smack about'cha." She cupped her breasts and bounced them in time with her words. "Let's get him!"

"Uh, could your tits shut up for a moment, you think?" I tapped an idle rhythm on the counter. "So, are we likely to have any trouble from those wolves?"

"Which wolves?"

"The ones we heard before."

Kiera smiled and placed her hands on top of mine. "Ah, don't worry about those guys. They were just sounding off. Besides, this house is made from bricks. So, y'know... no amount of huffing and puffing will let them in."

"Ha, ha."

"Although, I'm sure my big, brutish cousin will come save you if you need it. Then we might all hear some huffing and puffing. Eh?" She broke into an evil cackle at her own lame humor.

"You're all class, babe." Before I even finished speaking, an enormous yawn overtook me.

Kiera reached across and ruffled my hair. "Tell you what, why don't we talk more about it in the morning?"

"Fine by me." I crossed my arms on the surface of the bench and leaned my forehead on them. "Nightie-night."

"Come on, you pain. You can't sleep here. Go to bed."

"Carry me?"

"How 'bout I drag you by the dick, cave woman style?" She snickered for a moment. "Or I could call Ethan and get him to do it."

"Mmm..." Suddenly, I came fully awake and sat bolt upright. "I mean, um... the opposite of mmm."

"Sorry, honey, mmm is a palindrome. I guess you could say it upside down and it'd be www."

"You're not helping, you know?"

"True. But then, I wasn't trying to."

I eased my butt off the bar stool and stretched. "Okay, then. I saw a couple of dust bunnies under my bed. I might get some better conversation from them."

"Good luck. Those two are skanky bitches."

I smiled back over my shoulder as I walked down the hall. "Then they must fit right in."

"Cow."

"Moo."

CHAPTER ELEVEN

Ethan

IT WAS IMPOSSIBLE to tell if I was awake, dreaming, or undergoing some kind of astral traveling. Every inch of my body was drenched in sweat, and something soft filled my fists.

A glance downward showed me I had a vicious hold on my sheets, which helped me rule out the astral traveling option. Dreaming also seemed unlikely, though my brain certainly wasn't firing on all cylinders. It was almost as if the damn thing had grown a thick covering of hair.

I sat up, rivulets of perspiration coursing down my back and chest. My skin and my core were ablaze as if I'd run a marathon. And I couldn't recall feeling this strong, this vital, since...

Since my first ever shift.

"Damn you," I muttered to my wolf. "You have no place here, anymore."

Clearly, my beast disagreed, the internal snarl growing louder and stronger, and then metamorphosing into a long, fiery howl.

The vibration of the sound, and the spirit of the action, shocked through my body, and I turned my own face to the ceiling, my back arched and my arms spread. It took the act of greatest self-control to keep my voice damped. To hold the roar inside myself.

I should have gone to a motel. Or just headed straight home to Chicago. Instead, I'd stubbornly believed I had my wolf under control. That staying in Kiera's family home—with that hot-blooded, fiery sex-bomb under the same roof—would somehow be manageable. Hell, I'd been so arrogant about my own discipline, I'd even believed it'd be easy.

I might be across the hall and several

rooms away from him, but that meant nothing. Not to wolf senses. And his scent was playing hardball.

I rolled out of bed and opened my door. I was so wired that I could almost see the trail of Gabriel's fresh scent. It hooked into me, piercing right through my nose and ears and even straight into my skin. Dragging me toward his room.

It was only the memory of my failings that kept me from descending into the hell of shifting. Even as the beast strove for control, forcing me to fire my hand out toward Gabriel's door, I stubbornly stayed in charge of my feet. I stepped aside, and kept on moving down the hall, away from the temptation.

Every step I took toward the front door had my wolf barking, scratching at me. Its hackles rose beneath my skin, searching for my weakness, desperate to find a way through.

"No," I ground out through clenched teeth. "You are not in charge."

I flung the front door open, letting the cool night air coat me, and suck the furious heat from my body.

Still, that delicious scent reached for me. Long nails of desire scratched down my back, slicing away my resolve. After so long dormant, the creature was full of vigor, but thankfully, unfocused.

I knew I had next to no time. I had to put real distance between myself and my prey.

No, not prey.

Mate.

Clad in only boxers, I leapt from the entrance stairs and sprinted down the driveway, my thoughts focused only on what I was escaping. Nothing about where I was heading.

I kept running through the darkened streets of town, and on out the other side, into the forest. For a few seconds, I paused, caught between anger at the past and fear for the future. In the end, my choices were hacked away from me by pure need, and I charged on into the trees.

As if in defiance of my natural surroundings, every pace took me farther from my wolf, and closer to the man I needed to be.

Still, it appeared my beast had nudged me a little, taking me in good time to Siren Falls.

All I needed was a way to cool the

beast inside, and without the slightest pause at the pool's edge, I simply dived straight in and let the icy fingers of the water dig into my flesh.

Below the surface, everything felt beautifully dulled. The pressure of the water both held me in place and insulated me from the world. All I could hear was the white noise of the falls slamming into the pool. It was enough even to subdue my wolf.

I broke the surface and swam for the cascade, soaking up the heavy lances of water that drove into my body as I passed beneath it. I climbed onto the rocks and let the liquid curtain shield me from the rest of the world, while I took the time to control my breath.

And my beast.

CHAPTER TWELVE

Gabriel

DESPITE THE TRAVEL, my performance, and my general fatigue, I couldn't quite tumble over the cliff and into sleep. And I knew it was all the fault of Kiera's big, stupid, sexy lump of a cousin.

Every time I closed my eyes, I saw his. Whenever I touched my face, I remembered how exhilarating—and terrifying—it was when he touched me there.

How was it possible to feel so damn tingly about a guy who could run for

President of the United States of Assholia?

When sleep finally did come, my dreams were all messed up, too; full of dark forests and dangerous men. Tall men with tousled hair and broad shoulders. With vise-like hands and shiny white teeth. Ridiculously handsome man-beasts with glowing silver eyes, and who all looked exactly like Ethan.

I came partly awake, my skin wet and my mouth dry. It was like I had a fever, only there were no other symptoms. Just hot blood and hotter dreams that spilled over into consciousness.

Had I gone to bed wearing pajamas?

It was too hard to recall. The only thing certain was that I was naked now.

Within my belly a sparkling pressure rolled and pulsed, as if there was a whole other life inside me.

Was this something like what a woman felt when she was pregnant?

If anything, it felt to me like I had a dormant baby twin I'd shared the womb with, but who'd never fully formed. And now, after twenty-five years, he was suddenly coming to life.

I rolled onto my front and fisted the sheet, burying my face into the pillow. Whatever was happening did kind of hurt... in the same way as a strong fist in my hair during sex would hurt.

Or a perfectly placed swat on my ass.

Soon, the pain grew even sharper, and rose from my core to the center of my chest. I rolled out of bed and onto the floor, landing on hands and knees and letting my head hang low. The closest thing I could compare this sensation to was muscle cramps, only this time it covered every single inch of my body. Even my hair and nails screamed with the pain.

And yet, it wasn't actually an unbearable sensation. Just unexpected and huge. Like getting into a hot bath too quickly.

Or taking a sweet, thick cock you hadn't quite warmed up enough for.

I raised my head and glanced around myself. The near dawn light filtered in around the drapes and gave my eyes enough to work with.

My rapid breath fired in and out, and I gritted my teeth around it, sensing the need to get my damn self under control.

EVIE RILEY

A moment later, I heard a series of light thuds in the hallway, and my heart punched me in perfect time with the rhythm. I scrambled to my feet and opened my door, staying as silent as humanly possible.

It wasn't clear in my mind what I'd expected to see. But one thing I'd never anticipated was Ethan, nearly naked and soaking wet, prowling up the hall away from me.

I'd meant to stay silent, but seeing his hard, muscular body, wearing nothing but boxer shorts made translucent by water, hauled a sinful, needful, desperate moan straight from my throat.

The big, beastly man halted instantly, and I froze, unsure if it was fear, desire, or some otherworldly force that held me immobile.

Ethan turned on the spot and fired that glowing silver gaze of his like a crossbow, impaling my heart and my senses instantly.

Only then did I remember I was completely naked.

To my shock—and delight—Ethan curled his lip and made a deep, gravelly sound as he took a step toward me. I could have sworn it was a growl.

An honest-to-goodness animal sound.

As he prowled my way, the fluid sway of his mighty shoulders made me dizzy, and as he picked up his pace, I widened my eyes in genuine fear.

A moment before he would have reached me—maybe even attacked me—I slammed the door and locked it, diving onto my bed and pulling the covers over my head. The way I used to do when I was six, and hiding from the big, bad wolf.

And other monsters.

To my surprise, there was no heavy slam against my door. No angry pounding of fists, or yelling of demands. It was as if the man had never been there at all.

And as I fought to bring my heart and breathing back under control, I was left wondering if I'd simply dreamed it all and had only just now woken.

CHAPTER THIRTEEN

Gabriel

WHEN I NEXT opened my eyes, bright sunlight had created a warm glow in the room, creeping in around the outsides of the drapes.

I slipped out of bed and crept to the door, putting my ear against it as if the big, sexy beast who'd scared the life out of me last night might still be there. Resting on the other side, listening for me. His hot breath rasping in and out, as he desperately clawed at the thick wood.

If he'd actually been real.

But of course, I heard nothing of the sort. Just the general clink and clatter of people fiddling around in the kitchen.

I threw on my light cotton robe and nervously headed out, still trying to unravel the maze of experiences from the night before. And still unable to decide how much of it—if any—was real.

Kiera sat at the breakfast table, but to my dismay, she wasn't alone. And of course, it had to be *him* sitting beside her. The two of them were obviously talking to each other, but so low that I couldn't hear them, even from only a dozen feet away.

Thankfully, it was Kiera who spotted me first.

"Hey, Gabes. Sleep well?"

My boss had a slightly crooked grin, and not for the first time, I grew suspicious of the woman. She might be my bestie, but Kiera never missed an opportunity to poke fun. And here in Stoke Ridge, the girl constantly looked as if she was the keeper of a hundred different secrets.

Combining that with the fact she'd just been whispering to that man, and I was ready to scuttle back into the guest room and stay there until I could ease the heatwave inside me. Which, if Ethan stayed around, could take weeks.

Months.

"Gabes?" Kiera's repeated question finally cut through my thick jungle of confusion.

"Um, yeah. I think so. I had a... a weird dream." It had to be a dream. Because if it was real, I didn't know how to process all the feels I'd be having.

I took a seat at the counter and leaned my face on my forearms. "Any plans for the day?"

"I don't, but you do."

"I do?"

"Uh-huh." Kiera flicked Ethan's ear, the way he'd done to her the night before. "This lump said he promised you a tour of the town."

The big man smiled and focused those twin silver weapons on me. "So that'll be the first hour taken care of."

Kiera bumped him with her shoulder. "Be nice. Stoke Ridge has plenty to see and do. Especially now we're a part of Gray Vale and all. Why, you could make that tour last as long as ninety minutes."

I desperately needed to change the

subject, and especially the itinerary. Being alone with that man, even for an hour, would be the most heavenly torture. Despite the rocky start to our meeting, Ethan was growing more and more impossible to resist.

The worst part was, my desires were interfering with my natural thoughts. It was hard to be snarky and rude when your damn mind was in your balls all day long.

Whether the night before had been a dream, a reality, or something in between, shouldn't matter at all. I definitely could not let the man get to me.

"Is that coffee I smell?"

"Allow me." Ethan stood, the simple movement seeming to fill the room. "How do you take it?"

"Orally."

Ethan paused for a few seconds, before continuing over to the coffee maker. "Good choice. Shall I give you a shot of cream?"

"Dammit. I should've seen that one coming."

Ethan had his mouth halfway around a smart-ass reply when Kiera interrupted. "Quit it, you two, or I'll hurl right now." She looked over at Ethan. "He takes it with one long squirt, and two sweet lumps."

I struggled to suppress my laughter. "Speaking of hurling."

Ethan prepared my coffee and placed it in front of me.

"Thanks, butt-face."

"You know, you can call me Ethan, if you want."

"Noted."

I wasn't striving to be rude, but I also didn't want to let my ridiculous desires show. More than anything, I desperately wanted to ask about the night before. Whether I'd been dreaming, or if Ethan had actually been prowling around, soaked to the skin, in just a pair of boxers.

Boxers that clung to his ass like a jealous lover.

The way I'd do, if I ever got the chance.

Oh, god.

I definitely needed to push those thoughts way, way down into the background. The memory of that liquid sheen on his skin, and the smooth rubble of his abs. The hard V that ran inward and down from his hips. All of it mixed in my mind and the cocktail of lust had my balls simmering. And my cock pulsing with want.

At the same instant, Ethan and Kiera both hummed, as if they'd simultaneously come up with a good idea.

"What's going on, you guys?"

Kiera was the first to move. "I, uh... have to take some, um... things to, uh..."

"To that place," Ethan finished. "That place with the stuff."

"That's the place," Kiera said as she scurried out of the kitchen. "The place with the stuff. That's where I have to take my things."

And just like that, I was marooned. Trapped in the kitchen with the sexiest man I'd ever seen, heard, or touched.

Or dreamed, for that matter.

CHAPTER FOURTEEN

Ethan

THE THUD OF Gabriel's heart was part heaven and part hell. It pounded into my ears like a drum, and fired straight into my brain. The fact I could hear it straight from the source, and also sense the way it had his cock dancing, only made it harder to ignore.

The trouble was, it bypassed my human side and latched onto my wolf, tugging him by the tail, by the teeth, and by the nose. Jealously and relentlessly dragging that beast toward the surface.

Clearly, I hadn't imagined it, either.

The moment I'd detected Gabriel's cock hardening, Kiera had obviously noticed it as well. Thankfully, my cousin had removed herself from the situation in a heartbeat.

"So," I continued, struggling to form thoughts, let alone actual words. "I'm still available for that tour, if you want. Don't feel pressured or anything."

Gabriel licked his sensual lips, holding my attention with nothing more than that tiny gesture. "I suppose it might be nice."

Even in plain speech, his voice held me rigid. Though it just might have been the slight wavering in his tone, as much as the honey-smoked warmth, that had me ensnared in his being. The sexy spark in his eyes, the sass in his words, the hard planes of his sexy body showing clearly through that thin robe... every moment I spent near him, ground away at my resolve. If I simply released my darker self, abandoned my years of discipline, then all I could envision was a complete mess.

Emotional chaos, lustful indulgence, sensual overload.

So why did that particular kind of

mess have my mouth watering and my breath shallowing... and my wolf snarling like hell?

It had taken all my will, plus a long run and a cold swim, to force the animal down last night. And even after all that, it took no more than a fleeting glimpse of him, a soupçon of his scent, to get the beast pushing through my skin again. Sinking its teeth into my mind.

The smart thing truly would be to turn tail—metaphorically speaking—and flee back to Chicago. Disappear and keep him thinking I'm an asshole, rather than sticking around and leaving him in no doubt.

I'd finally managed to convince myself to do exactly that—leave town in a hurry—when he raised his arms and stretched out the kinks of sleep. Baring his most vulnerable pulse points to me, as if daring me—begging me—to sink my teeth into him.

The hackles rose on the back of my neck as I studied his hard-bodied magnificence through his robe. The tender, stubbled skin of his throat, his blood visibly pumping within, called to me like a feast.

I knew instantly I was utterly lost in him. That even though I could never allow myself to take him as my mate, he was burned into my brain forever.

With that knowledge came a surprising sense of freedom. I had planned to scamper home to escape the pull of Gabriel's pure essence. But, since he'd immediately and permanently spoiled me for all other men, then things really couldn't get any worse.

What would be the harm in staying a day or two longer?

"All right, Gabriel. How about I start the tour with breakfast in town?"

As soon as I mentioned food, his belly set about growling in earnest. Somehow, it even sounded as if it was singing a harmony to the wolf in my heart.

"Um... that might be nice."

CHAPTER FIFTEEN

Ethan

IF I'D HAD any doubt over how perfect Gabriel was, watching the way he savored every bite of his food would have blown those doubts out of the water. Bacon, sausage, eggs, tomato. Toast with butter, coffee with cream. And with that voice straight from heaven, every noise of appreciation he made seized me simultaneously by the heart, and by the cock.

He seemed to realize suddenly that he was the main attraction. At least, to me he was.

"Am I amusing you, butt-face?"

"Ethan."

"I know. Is this some kind of cabaret for you, big guy?"

I used a sip of coffee to suppress my grin.

Hot-blooded little fireball, this one.

When I spoke, I kept my voice low—in pitch as well as volume.

"There's simply nothing quite like a man who appreciates his food." I paused for a moment as I weighed up my two sides—wolf and man—and tried to understand which part held the most sway. And it was impossible for me to know at that moment.

"I have a singer's ego to feed. So sue me."

Barely even thinking of what it meant, I slid my hand down on top of his. Only when the electrifying jolt ran from his body and into mine was I reminded just who we were to each other.

"I know you're making a joke at your own expense. And maybe it's to deflect some of the doubts you won't admit you have." I leaned closer, dropping my voice to a raspy whisper. "But I see you,

Gabriel. More than you'd like to admit."

The rich tan color of his face reddened as the heat of my words registered. He pulled his hand free of mine and glanced down at the plate. When he looked up again, the fire in his eyes nearly cooked me on the spot. I still couldn't be sure if it was anger, arousal, or the perfect blend of both.

"Was that real last night?"

"Which part?" I asked, feeling certain I knew what he was talking about.

"In the hallway. You, prowling around in your undies like a perv."

"What do you mean, *like* a perv?" I gave him a tiny wink, and my heart leapt when the corner of his mouth curled up.

He stabbed his fork into a sausage and pointed it at me. "You still didn't answer me, butt-face."

I nodded, and placed my coffee on the table. "Honestly, I wasn't entirely sure myself. For all I knew, I'd dreamed the whole thing, but the fact you asked me that tells me it must have been real."

"So what were you doing?"

"How much do you know about Stoke Ridge, Gabriel?"

He narrowed his eyes and pointedly

bit through the sausage on his fork. "Don't change the subject."

"I'm not. Not exactly. But if you don't know the secrets of this place—of the people here—then it's almost impossible to explain."

Gabriel frowned, a perfect, kissable kink forming between his eyebrows. "Is this a cult, or something?"

"It's an or something." I put two twenties on the table and stood. "You ready for the tour?"

Gabriel gulped the last of his coffee and stood. "Fine. But we're not finished discussing this, pervy-man."

"Well, we'll see. Things might become clearer as we explore the town."

CHAPTER SIXTEEN

Gabriel

WALKING WASN'T REALLY one of my chosen activities. There was so little need for it in the city, with taxis, ride shares and—ew—buses. Hell, sometimes I was surprised I even had a pair of sneakers.

And yet, the hot spots and aches that had sprung up across both my feet somehow weren't enough to make me call time on this little diversion. As long as I had Ethan's delicious body beside me, and the heat of his voice filling my ears, I felt as if I could keep ambling along all day and night.

What the hell was up with that?

And why was it that every time that gorgeous man made the slightest contact with my skin, it felt as if my legs had turned to liquid?

The tour itself had been pretty uneventful, just as he'd promised. Or maybe *warned* was a more appropriate word. We'd barely run across anyone else, and Ethan had been coldly dismissive of those we had met. I desperately wanted to ask him what his problem was, but after the party last night, I couldn't be sure it was truly *his* problem.

I'd only briefly encountered the man's parents, but already I didn't like them. I got a real strong feeling they were pretty cold about me, as well. Every other person I'd met, apart from Kiera's family, had seemed somehow cut from the same cloth. As if they felt Ethan had to somehow prove his worth to them.

"So, that's that." His deep voice cut through my thoughts. "Unless you feel like heading down to the old Gray Vale area."

I glanced around myself. We'd

apparently gone through every part of this small town. I looked across at the thick forest on the other side of the street.

"What about in there?"

"It's not safe in there. Not for a city boy."

"Oh, please. You haven't seen the back alleys around my apartment building."

I started crossing the street, but before I'd taken more than a few steps, Ethan grasped my shoulders in his big, strong hands.

"No, Gabriel. I mean it. There are dangers in there that I... I can't describe to you."

"How dangerous can it be when there's a damn candy store across the road from it?"

He frowned as he clearly tried to sort through his thoughts. Eventually, he sighed and released me. "People here are... well, we're used to the dangers these woods present. It's like, if you grow up here, you're kind of inoculated."

"Doesn't look any different to any other forest I've seen."

"That's the danger."

I crossed the street, stopping at the edge of the woods. I reached out and combed my fingers through the leaves on the closest branch. A cool breeze ran through the treetops, sounding for all the world like a whispering voice.

I sensed Ethan's bulk behind me, and I closed my eyes to block out sight, and call on all my other senses. Rather than danger, I sensed a warmth before me. Somewhere between a log fire and a thick quilt.

At that moment, a group of children came running out of the underbrush, dressed in nothing but swimsuits. They paid no attention to either of us, simply scampering up the streets and into various homes.

I glanced back at Ethan.

"Dangerous, huh? So dangerous that little kids run around in there. Without any kind of protective wear."

"Just proves what I said. You grow up here, you understand it."

"Will you take me in there? A big, bad man like you would surely be able to protect a soft city boy?"

Immediately, Ethan's face closed down. As if he'd built a brick wall in front of it and pasted on a picture of his frowniest face.

"No, Gabriel. I won't." He took my hand and gently steered me back toward the center of town. "I'm not making this up. There are things in there you can't understand."

I reached up and knocked lightly on the side of his head. "There's plenty in there I don't understand either, big man."

"That's probably for the best."

Though he'd clearly meant it as a joke, there was a coldness in his voice that had my entire body tensing up again.

I cast one more glance back at the forest before Ethan steered me around a corner and I lost sight of it.

***

Sleep proved just as elusive as it had the night before. And for the same reasons.

Every time I closed my eyes, those two silver bullets of Ethan's pierced my mind. My whole body thrummed with an electricity that apparently couldn't be switched off.

The sheen of perspiration was back,

too, along with the volcanic heat inside me. Every inch of my skin was awash, and my cock stood tall like a fucking main mast on a ship.

What the hell was happening?

Was it something in the water?

In the woods?

Or was it that damn man and his ridiculously sexy everything?

I kicked away my sheets and blankets, seeking relief. This time around, the sensations were much more like genuine pain, as if the previous night had been nothing more than an undress rehearsal. Or maybe my soul was bruised all over from the pummeling this experience had given me. It felt as if the slightest touch would ignite every part of me—mind, body, and soul.

I curled into a ball and then rolled over onto my belly. Still the pain gripped me like a gigantic fist. I squeezed my thighs together and pulled my knees forward, propping my ass high, arching my back downward in a deep stretch. The cool night air kissed my puckered ass hole like a lover, and somehow, the combination of cool air and stretching eased the hurt.

The sound of my bedroom door opening sang to me like music, and the musky scent that filled my nose was heaven. Two parts nature, three parts man. Water and forest and the spicy tang of maleness. A low growl escaped his body and it coated my back like it was licking me.

The weight of him as he mounted the bed behind me sent my balance swaying. He curled his hand out to my hip and rested it there, velvet soft and blazing hot. It was a nothing touch, a place he'd easily put his hand if we were clothed and dancing. Yet it drove deep, long roots of want through my entire body.

When he put his other hand up around my shoulder, I lost any pretense of being a big, strong man. I basically mewed like a kitten. He tightened his grip, as if he thought I might flee.

Truth be told, I'd already thought of doing so a thousand times. But running only gets a guy chased, and there was no chance in hell I could ever outrun this man. Not with those long, hard legs, and that cold fire burning inside him. Nor could I escape my own white-hot desire to have him.

Right then and there.

If this was even real.

My mind was a ball of fuzz, and it was just as impossible this time around to tell if I was living a dream. My mind had always had the knack of revealing my wildest desires when I slept.

Ethan—if it truly was Ethan—slicked his hand down from my shoulder and through the indent of my spine. He brought a pool of sweat down and it washed over my willing little pucker.

When he jammed his thumb against me, I gasped, amazed at how soft and open I already was. Like my body had been waiting for him since the moment I'd arrived in Stoke Ridge.

He glided his thumb inside me, and I moaned with the sweet pleasure, tempered with only a minor sting of pain. I even bounced back at him, trying to take him deeper. Readying myself for the beast I knew he was packing.

If it really was Ethan.

A moment passed, and then he slipped his thumb out and gripped my shoulder again as he notched the blunt head of his cock against me. I took a long breath in, holding it. When he drove forward, filling me so fucking easily with his heat and terrifying me with his howl, I let the breath slice its way out of me.

As big as I was, this man effortlessly bumped me around like I was no more than a puppy. He glided that perfect, thick cock of his in and out, squeezing my flesh with those powerful hands. His deep voice rolled out in bitten off growls, like it had taken a physical form and begun chasing me through a thick forest, stepping around every obstacle between us, until it could bury its fangs into me.

His weight pushing down on my back, thumping into my ass, was fiercely erotic. I tightened around him with a whimper and his voice evaporated into nothing more than a steamy hiss. The sheen of sweat over my body made his hand slip, and he released my shoulder, taking a fistful of my short, thick hair instead.

As he slammed himself home inside me, he dragged on my head, pulling hard, blessing me with the sweetest pain across my scalp. I lifted my body from the bed, and he drew me up and back until my shoulders slammed into his chest. I still hadn't so much as looked at him, but when he took my neck between his teeth and squeezed, I couldn't even think about opening my eyes.

He slid his hand around my hip and gripped my steely cock, all the while licking and sucking at the flesh of my throat. If it was still a dream, then I needed more than anything not to wake up.

Like, ever.

Every pump of his hand up and down my raging boner simply detonated within me, driving pleasure up my spine and turning into fireworks inside my head. The wet glide of his cock filling me fired bullets of ecstasy into my blood, and in seconds my entire body tingled in anticipation.

And when his voice returned, a deep, rasping growl, it filled my head, wiping out thoughts of everything but this man... this beast.

With one final punching drive, he slammed home inside me, so hard he lifted my knees from the bed and balanced me on top of his hips. His grip on my hair tightened, sending blissful spikes of sensation down to meet the flames of orgasm erupting from below. The two forces came together in my chest and I swore I was about to burst.

The heat of his fluid cascaded deep inside me, just as he hauled my own release from within me. I fired off like a cannon, painting my sheets and pillow with my juice as I had the biggest climax I'd ever experienced.

As his climax gradually eased, he let me slide back down to the bed. I was nothing more than a lump of pastry, rounded and pounded, kneaded and folded. And I'd need to rest a looong time before I'd be ready to rise.

Without a word, he slid down behind me, his skin still deliciously, blisteringly hot. The last thing I remembered before unconsciousness overtook me was his big, strong arm curling around my body.

CHAPTER SEVENTEEN

Gabriel

I WOKE WITH a start, looking around the room. Though I was alone, it was hard to figure out if that was surprising or not. Sunlight streamed through the cracks in the blinds, landing on the smooth, carefully made blankets covering me. The blankets I swore I'd practically torn to shreds the night before in my desperation to ease the fever inside me.

I ran my hand across my face and scrubbed, trying to sort dreams from memories, reality from fantasy.

Was that mystery man real, or a figment of my horny imagination?

And more importantly, was it Ethan?

I'd felt that weird feverish heat all through my body before he came to me, just as I had the night before. But maybe even that had been just part of a dream.

There was only one thing I was certain of; if I'd only imagined that wild sex, then that would turn out to be the biggest disappointment of my life. But I was alone now, and there was not a single sign around me that anything had happened. Even the bed covers were still mostly in place.

It was only as I tried to get up that my questions found some kind of answer. My arms and legs ached, which surely was a sign I'd been fucked relentlessly. Although, I guess it could easily be from the walking tour.

I finally managed to lift my weary body from the sheets, and sure enough, I found the remnants of my release, smeared into the sheets by my body as I slept.

But still nothing that made it clear anyone else had been with me. Fuck, maybe they just pumped hallucinogens into the guest rooms here, for fun. Just to see how city folk freak out when they come out to the sticks.

The delicious, keening pang in my ass, though, had to be proof enough that everything I'd felt last night had been real.

But with that knowledge came the memory that I'd never even looked at him. Never challenged him. Just let him prowl into my room and take me from behind. I'd been a man-whore before, but at least I made the guys work for it back in the city. Last night, I'd given it up like I owed it to him.

And it had been so fucking perfect it hurt.

From the moment I'd felt the heat, from the moment that man had busted into my room, I'd assumed it was Ethan. But after all, this was Kiera's family home.

What if it had been Mr Larson?

Celebrating his anniversary by switching teams and banging his daughter's plus one?

"Oh, god..."

As embarrassing as that might be, would it really be any better if that was

Ethan's incredible body grinding into mine?

He was arrogant, aloof, and clearly had a roll of razor wire strung around his mind and his heart. Not to mention he was cockier than a rooster farm, and lived in a whole other city, in a whole other state. Nothing could ever happen between us.

I slowly rolled out of bed, dragging a robe on and stumbling to the kitchen. Kiera was already up and far chirpier than anyone had the right to be so early in the afternoon.

"Here you go, honey." Kiera handed over a fresh-brewed coffee. "Wanna talk about it?"

"About what?"

"Last night, of course. You and Ethan. I think we're gonna have to replace a couple windows."

"W–what are you talking about?" So, it had really been Ethan. Trouble was, that meant it had really been Ethan.

Leaning across the counter, Kiera cupped my face in her hands. "Honey, honey, honey. You're in wolf country. Ears don't lie, especially..." She paused for a moment, as if weighing up whether to continue. "Especially ears like ours. But seriously, regular folk two counties away would have heard you guys."

"Oh, god." I pulled out of Kiera's grip and covered my eyes. "It was bizarre. I couldn't even tell if it really happened or not. It felt like a dream all the way through."

"That's normal, Gabes."

"Not for me. When did I become such a trollop?"

"Trollop, schmollop."

"I mean, I just don't do that."

"You don't do it? Why ever not?"

"Sex? Sure. I do it every chance I get. It's just that lately, every chance has pretty much been zero." I took another fortifying gulp of coffee. "But this wasn't even like sex on the first date. I mean, sure, he showed me around town, but then we came back here and I didn't see him again. I think he went back out."

"Still kind of like a date. If that makes you feel better?"

"No. I mean, I was trying to sleep, but it was too hot. He busted into my room. There was no talking. No foreplay. Just..."

"Just glorious, mind-scorching,

sheet-ripping jiggy-jiggy?"

"Exactly. It's embarrassing."

"Why? I told you, wolf country. Sex is as natural as eating around here. And sometimes, it's hard to tell where one ends and the other begins."

"What the hell are you talking about, Kiera? You keep bringing up wolves and talking like... I don't know. Like you're completely deranged."

Kiera frowned as she poured herself a cup of coffee. "I know. I've been dancing around it, but I guess it's time to 'fess up. It's clear Ethan hasn't told you yet."

"Told me what?"

Kiera placed her cup on the counter and leaned forward on her crossed forearms. "This entire town, including me and even my knucklehead cousin... we're all wolf shifters."

"You're what?"

"Wolf shifters. You've heard of us, right?"

I sipped at the blissfully hot liquid in my cup. "Is that like a moving company? The Wolf family and their fleet of lorries?"

"No, honey. Humans who become wolves."

For a moment, I screwed my mouth up to the side. "You mean role playing? I had an uncle who, like, dressed up in costume to go watch Harry Potter."

"And what a fabulous uncle he must have been. But no, not role-playing. I mean we literally turn into wolves."

I glanced around. "Okay, where's the camera?"

"There isn't one."

"We've been having a busy time at work. Maybe your brain snapped?"

Kiera chuckled and wrapped her hands around her cup, leaning forward on the bench. "Nope. I'm as sane as you are."

"Not sure that's exactly a glowing endorsement, you know?" I took a longer slug of the coffee and gave Kiera a double shot of side-eye. "So, what... you're trying to tell me shapeshifters are real?" I couldn't keep the grin off my face.

"Absolutely. It's not exactly a huge secret. But on the other hand, we don't go around blabbing it to everyone we meet, either."

"So, you just, kinda, turn into wolves and go off to play with Bigfoot?" I chuckled at my own joke. "Oh, do you have, like, changing rooms? So you can get into your wolf suit in private?"

Kiera rolled her eyes and smiled. "Now you're being silly."

"Oh, yeah. I'm the one being silly. When you're the one claiming to be a vixen."

Kiera sucked in a quick breath and flared her eyes. "Vixens are female foxes."

"Yeah, yeah."

"No." Kiera stood right in front of me, hands on hips. "Not yeah, yeah. I'm a wolf, not a fox. What you just did... well, it's like telling a Trekkie to use the force."

"Calm your tits, babe. What's wrong with foxes?"

Kiera sighed out so hard it sounded like she was deflating. "Nothing. It's just that I'm not one."

"I know." I put my hands around my mouth in a mock yell. "Because you're a human."

Kiera remained still for a moment, one eyebrow cocked. "All right. I guess there's only one thing for it." She pulled her T-shirt off and started unbuttoning her jeans.

"Hey, look, I love you, Kiera, but only as a friend. You understand?"

"Pfft. I'm not getting naked, I'm just taking off all my clothes."

"Because there's a difference, of course. But the real question is, why?"

Kiera was down to just underwear by that stage. "You ever tried to unclip a bra without your hands?"

"You, uh... remember who you're talking to, right?" I fist-pumped the air. "Gold star gay boy here."

With Kiera now stark naked in front of me, I wasn't sure where to look. Okay, so the girl was curvy and gorgeous, but even in college I'd never tried swinging with the straights.

"Are you ready, Gabes?"

"Ready? For what?" If she said sex...

"Watch."

I kept my gaze locked on Kiera's, mainly because that was a little bit less uncomfortable than looking any lower. The comfort was short-lived, though. After a moment, something freaky started going on with the girl's body.

"Told you... it was truuue..."

As I watched, Kiera's face bent out of

shape, elongating in front as her ears migrated up her head. She dropped to her hands and knees and grunted, as weird popping noises and horrible cracking sounds erupted from all over her body. Before I could truly comprehend what was happening, there was a gray and ginger wolf standing in the kitchen of Kiera's family home.

For a moment, I sat still, gaping at what had happened. Then wolf-Kiera nuzzled at my hand, like a pet dog might, and the spell was broken.

"You gotta be fucking kidding me. How did I not know this about you? About anyone?"

The sound of a door opening down the hallway set wolf-Kiera into alert mode. She raised her ears and turned, stalking toward where the sound came from. Kiera's mom called out, sounding even more tired than I had earlier.

"Morning, you two."

A moment later the sound of the shower running seemed to put wolf-Kiera at ease. With her tail still pointing at me, and with the same disgusting noises, she morphed back into human form, finishing up on all fours.

"Um…" I studied my fingernails. "Uh, Kiera?"

"Wh–what?" She panted heavily, like she'd been running.

"Well, I know you're a wolf and all, and you guys are really keen on the moon… but, uh…"

Kiera glanced over her shoulder with a smile, then wiggled her ass. "Aw, mister Gabes is all confronted."

"Hell yes, I am. My best friend just flashed me everything she has. Oh, and did I mention she turned into a goddamn wolf?"

Kiera stood up and shrugged her clothes back on. "Yeah. I should have told you before we made the trip. My bad."

"Yeah, you should've. Wait… you said Ethan is a wolf, too?"

Kiera paused for thought. "He's more of a lapsed wolf, really. It's not something he talks about. Not even with us."

"Yeah, I noticed he has a select few topics to talk about. And a bunch of no-go zones." Of course, after his performance in my bed last night—all action, no words—I could argue that talk was hella overrated.

The fact I was ranking mindless sex above a meaningful relationship had me feeling like I needed to add yet another point to my whore score.

"All right, so what the hell is with him, anyway?"

"It's a long story. I can tell you some, but not everything."

"Spill! If he can do that, what you just did, why the hell doesn't he do it all the time? Why don't all of you?"

Kiera screwed up her mouth as she shrugged. "What, aside from the effort it takes? Well, there are times it's just better to be in human form. Job interviews, meeting people's parents, BDSM clubs. You know."

"What the hell?"

"It is so damn hard to get a good swing with a riding crop when you have to hold it in your mouth." She caught my expression and held up her hands. "I'm kidding. Sorry."

"You better be."

Kiera shook her head with a smile and continued. "But Ethan? Man, you could barely stop him shifting when he was a kid."

"I don't believe that."

"It's true. He was a wolf more often than—"

"No, I don't believe that guy was ever a kid."

Kiera smiled and stood up. "Come on, this kind of story needs to be served with a side of food and booze. Go get dressed."

"Don't wanna."

"Well, if I'm gonna spill about your bed-buddy, then I want to do it somewhere he isn't."

I felt my guts ice up. "Oh, god. I forgot he was staying here."

"Uh-huh. Suuure you did. Just like you forgot what you and he did last night?"

"Oh, yeah. I was totally thinking with my brain last night, for sure. Duh."

"Yeah, well, not that it would have mattered."

"What are you talking about?"

"I'm saying it wouldn't have mattered if he'd been staying on the other side of town. He still would have found you, whether he tried to or not. And nothing—not even our heavy, locked doors—would have stopped him."

EVIE RILEY

468

CHAPTER EIGHTEEN

Ethan

I WAITED IN my room until I heard them leave. I could just about kill Kiera for revealing our secrets after I'd worked so damn hard to keep it from Gabriel. The last thing I wanted was to scare the guy away, even though I knew I couldn't have a future with him.

Who'd ever want a man who has to constantly battle with himself?

To fight the despicable duality that nature forced on him?

Nobody started a relationship with *that* guy. They might stick around if it developed long after they got together, but equally they might not.

How could I ever expect Gabriel to take on a relationship with a wolf shifter?

Especially so soon after learning we even exist.

After I'd shown him around town, I truly had wanted to escape from him. The man was a drug, and any time spent in his presence got my blood racing. Though he made my body strong and my cock hard as hell, all I felt when I was around him was utterly weak.

Even repeating the previous night's run had done me no good. As hard as I fought against it, the wolf inside had been starved for five long years. Ravenous didn't even begin to describe him.

As with the night before, I'd arrived back to a dark house. When I'd come in, skin soaked and pulse racing, I'd been utterly determined to head straight to bed.

I hadn't even made it as far as my room before the intoxicating musk of Gabriel called out and seized me by the balls.

And the fevered fuzz that had filled my head was unlike anything I'd felt with Clinton, or with any of my casual dalliances back in Chicago. The fire Gabe awoke within me utterly consumed my entire being. My heart, my soul, my lupine lunacy.

And it meant that in the light of day, memories were almost impossible to isolate. Last night was nothing more than a cavalcade of carnal imagery. Hard muscle and slick skin, the aroma of perfection and the breathy song of ecstasy.

All I could recall for certain was that I'd gone in naked, had poured myself into that gorgeous human, body and soul... and then awoken with his delectable body tucked against me in the most heavenly embrace.

But it was fear, pure and simple, that drove me to leave before he woke. And to do my damnedest to hide any trace I'd been there.

Had I stayed, I knew I'd dive headlong into that man, time and again, until I lost any sense of myself. Now that he knew my true nature, our dynamic would be challenging enough. But him being my fated mate would likely be more than his human body and mind could ever handle.

As I stood and dragged my clothes on, I glanced in the mirror and sneered at my reflection.

Be honest with yourself, asshole.

I sighed, resigning myself to a life of torture, either way. The smart thing to do would be to leave right now, put hundreds of miles between us. Live a life empty of emotion, filled with loneliness. Anything, so I could simply be human.

Because more than anything, Gabriel's hold on me left me in abject terror; that he would drag my wolf back from beyond the grave.

And that I'd let him, thereby undoing all these years of effort.

All the best moments in my youth had been as a wolf, yet they were shrouded—suffocated—by that one day of hell.

I knew without a doubt that Gabriel would fill me like nobody else could. He would complete me. But for him to have that chance meant I'd have to complete myself first.

To be wolf again.

I had to break it off with him, before someone ended up hurt.
Or worse.

CHAPTER NINETEEN

Gabriel

AS I SAVAGED my steak, I listened to my bestie relate the story of Ethan's life, as much as it could be told. It was the weirdest thing how I'd barely even met the guy—you really couldn't count the sex—yet, I had an insatiable hunger to know everything about him.

"So, you're telling me he was a little furry monster all the time?"

Kiera nodded. "Pretty much. Any time he didn't have to be human, he shifted. He was a loner for the most part, but not so much by choice."

"What do you mean?"

Kiera shrugged, but her expression turned dark. "Wolves have what you might call poor color vision. A lot of them only ever see things in black and white. Ethan didn't fit in the way most wolves do."

"Because he's gay?"

She screwed up her mouth and crinkled her nose, as animated as ever. "A little bit. Stoke Ridge was a pretty backward place back then. It's only now that we're all part of Gray Vale that things are catching up with the rest of the world."

My heart raced in my chest. I'd kinda known the same struggle, of course. My parents had been cool with my sexuality. I think they knew long before I did. But most of my extended family were assholes about it.

"Also," Kiera continued. "You wouldn't believe it, but he was small. For a long time. A real late bloomer, that one."

"You're right. I don't believe it."

"Not to mention he's scary smart, too, obviously. The other kids gave him hell any time he used so much as a three-syllable word. And he had no interest in team sports, which of course meant, in their words, that he was some kind of fag."

"Well, hurtful words aside, it's not like they were wrong."

"Yeah, but it's like they got the right answer with all the wrong working out. They didn't realize he was gay, because he wasn't even sure. They just tossed what they thought of as the worst insult in the world at him. The fucking dicks."

She looked off into the middle distance. "God, he loved to run, though. Not to hunt, really, though he did his fair share. And when he was older, there was some, uh... chasing of tails, shall we say?"

I got the distinct impression my friend was sounding me out. Testing me for jealousy. Hell, Latino blood was hotter than most, and the thought of anyone else even looking at my man usually got my claws out at the speed of light. Somehow, none of it seemed to matter this time around.

Because he is not your man, doofus.

He's just a guy you fucked, first with your eyes, and then with your body.

"Hey, I never expected him to be a virgin. He might be a total prick, but uh... he's, like, not super-ugly or anything." That was the understatement of the millennium.

"This is true."

"So why isn't he still going wild? Living life, y'know... off the leash."

"Har-de-har. Well, there was one thing. He always had a little trouble shifting back."

I took a sip of my wine. "Really? You made it look so easy."

With a shrug, Kiera glanced around the restaurant. "Mostly it is. For some, it can be a struggle. Kind of like insomnia. You know, when you absolutely have to sleep, and that makes you stress yourself out so hard that you can't? It's like that. The more you know you have to shift, the farther away it seems to move."

"And Ethan has that?"

"As a kid, it didn't seem to matter. He was happier as a wolf. It was just..."

"What? Come on, you can't dangle a *just* in front of me and then pull it away."

Kiera sighed and nodded. "Okay.

You're right. See, it became a thing. He was already an outsider, like I said. Once the other kids found out, they used to pick on him about it. Like it somehow made him less of a wolf."

"So that's it? That's what made him turn away from it?"

"No, not just that. It's a long story." Kiera took another sip of her wine and then screwed up her nose. "Okay, it's not all that long, it just doesn't feel right me telling it. It has to come from Ethan. But one thing you really need to know is, he was mated before."

"Like, married? Yeah, you said something about it before."

Kiera shrugged and moved her head side to side. "It's a little bit like that. But it's a wolf thing."

"You keep saying that like it could mean anything to me."

Kiera suddenly turned serious. "Gabes, you gotta understand... I keep saying it because this is wolf country. There are bear shifters, too, and some other creatures that'd really stew your mind. But here, in both the Ridge and the Vale, it's all about the wolves. So, yeah, everything around here pretty much is a wolf thing." She rested her hands on top of mine. "And if you want to know Ethan, you're gonna have to allow for that."

With a sigh, I turned my hands over and squeezed my friend's. "What was his name? Ethan's mate."

Kiera paused as if it was a hard question. Finally, she seemed to resign herself to answering.

"Clinton."

"And he was like you guys? A wolf shifter?"

"Yeah, of course. But please, don't ask me to explain it all, okay? I'll just mess it all up. I know the facts but not the truth."

"Okay. I get it."

And I did get it. I had no chance with the guy. It really was as simple as that. It didn't make me jealous in the slightest that he'd been married, or mated, or whatever. Nor the fact that, no matter how he felt about this Clinton guy now, once upon a time he'd have to have been crazy for him.

Feelings change.

People change.

Hearts change.

No, for me, it boiled down to one annoyingly uncomplicated fact: he'd found pure happiness with a fellow wolf. There was no way I could compete with that. I could learn every last piece of truth and trivia about Ethan and his kind. But I couldn't ever belong.

Kiera squeezed my hands back. "Aw. Why so glum?"

"I guess I'm scared. Actually, it's more like terrified."

"Of what?"

"Of how stupidly hard I'm crushing on Ethan. And, oh, my god, how quickly. It's so new to me, and so weird, and I know it can't ever work. I'll never fit in around here."

"And why should you? Ethan doesn't."

"In his life, then. Okay, he doesn't love being a wolf, but it's still there. I'll never have that in common with him. And maybe he's not with Clinton anymore, but he clearly holds a strong place in Ethan's heart. I don't... I'm not strong enough to carry that kind of baggage for him."

Kiera looked as if someone had kicked her puppy. She leaned back, taking her hands with her. "Gabes, please don't push me for details. Let me just say Ethan and Clinton were happy, but they were not in love."

"How the hell does that even work?"

"Wolves, remember?"

"Latino, remember? Nosy as hell with habanero blood. Explain!"

Kiera made a point of taking a long, slow sip of her wine, keeping her gaze locked on mine as she did so, apparently taking great pleasure in milking the moment for all it was worth.

"There's a process. I won't bore you with the details, but it's quite common to have couples who mate for life as wolves without ever feeling the same way as humans do. You know, that overpowering charge that you get when you're with the one?"

"The one?"

"Your fated mate."

For a moment, all I could think of was Ethan.

The fierce blades of his eyes.

The frightening heat of his cock.

Overpowering charge might very well be the exact way to describe how it felt when I first saw him.

And whenever he touched me.

Oh, and when he'd come into my room and taken me to heaven as easily as spilling a drink.

But it sounded so much like a fairy tale, I was prepared to write it all off as exactly that. Or at least scratch at the idea to find out its weaknesses. "How do you really know if you've found them, though? This so-called fated mate?"

The smile that crossed Kiera's face was fleeting, but so genuine it lit her up. "If they're wolves, then both partners know it right away. And pretty much every wolf around them can scent it." She reached across again and tapped me on the end of the nose. "Like I did at the party, the moment you and Ethan saw each other."

I could feel my cheeks heating up. "Oh." I put my hands up to cover the blush, but it was too late.

About two days too late.

If what Kiera said was true, then everyone at the party must have known how I felt. Everyone including Ethan, which must have been why he'd come into my room and fucked me so hard and so well.

And why I'd let him without even a moment's fight.

"So, if it's true, and I'm meant to be with him, then why he is being so hard to get along with? Half the time he's an arrogant jerk, the rest of the time he's shutting me out. Was Clinton so important to him he can't move on?"

Kiera pursed her lips. "Gabes, I'll say it one more time, and that's it. It's not my tale to tell. I mean, your average guy is a closed book most of the time anyway. Present company excepted, of course. But dear cousin Ethan is all sealed up, and wrapped in duct tape. In a locked safe. At the bottom of the ocean."

"Ugh, I get it."

"Seriously, though. You're gonna have to get it straight from him, or else not at all."

"Huh. Not at all is not an option."

"Gabes? Tread carefully, okay?"

CHAPTER TWENTY

Gabriel

I COULD BARELY remember the rest of the meal, or our walk back to the house. My mind had been on Ethan, and what his secret—or secrets—might be. Though Kiera had tried to keep the conversation flowing at first, in the end she'd given up.

At the front door to the house, Kiera softly held my arm, making me wait.

"Gabes, remember what I said, huh?" Kiera squeezed my arm before turning and walking toward her car.

"Hey, you sure you don't want to be

here, too, Kiera? Protect me from the big bad wolf?"

Slipping into her car, Kiera smiled while she shook her head. "I'm not even sure you want to be here for this. But I know you have a rock-hard head and you won't let this thing go, so..." She shrugged and closed the door, starting her car on the second attempt.

I crept inside, taking off my shoes as I made my way up the hall. At my bedroom door, I looked inside and paused, thinking on all of Kiera's warnings. It sure would be simpler to just pretend nothing had happened, and go back to my old life of singing to nobody. But that also meant having nobody.

Yep, it sure would be simple. But it would be anything but easy.

Instead, I turned to look back up the hall. And almost jumped out of my skin, seeing Ethan standing there, with a cold fire lighting his eyes and a wild cast to his smile.

"Why don't you ever shift?" I blurted it out before I even thought about it. "You're a wolf, too, right? Like Kiera?"

His nod was so small and quick it

was almost impossible to see. "She's my cousin. It's a family curse."

"Curse? Apparently, everyone else loves it."

He prowled forward, the steel in his eyes flashing a warning at me. "Everyone but me, city boy. I mean, it's ridiculous. Such primitive behavior; howling at the moon, chasing bunnies, sniffing each other all over." He curled his top lip as he stopped right before me. "Be thankful you're only human."

"Hey! Watch what you say about my kind, mister."

"I meant in the sense that human is the only creature you are. You don't need to process the world through two sets of senses. You don't need to reconcile the animal within. Suppress that mindless beast." A small shudder ran through him.

"You, sir, don't get to speak for me. Yeah, okay, I'm human and nothing else. But that doesn't mean it's all simple and clean for me, either."

His laughter dug into my skin like a bee sting. "Please, Gabe."

I grabbed his shirt and pulled down, standing on my tiptoes as I did, just to get closer to his face. "You ever been human? I mean *only* human?"

"Unfortunately not."

"Then you don't know, do you?"

Gradually, the anger in his eyes cooled, and he quirked his lips into what looked like a genuine smile.

"All right. You have me there, Gabe." He worked his shirt out of my grip, straightening it when he'd freed it.

"So?"

Raising one eyebrow, he fired a fresh smirk at me. "So?"

"So why are you the only wolf ever to hate being a wolf?"

"I'm sorry, I don't know where you got the idea that would be any of your business."

I grabbed a hearty handful of Ethan's cock, through his pants, noting it was fully hard. "Maybe it was when you got this business all up in my business."

There was no mistaking the look of surprised pleasure that washed across his face. I made the most of it, seeking out the thick head of him with my thumb and rubbing just below it. The low hum that oozed from his throat made my cock all thick and pulsing with need yet again.

"So tell me, big guy. Why do you hate being a shifter?"

His breath grew shallower with every pass of my thumb. With his eyes closed, he reached across and curled his hand around the back of my neck. It seemed as much about holding himself upright as holding me close. When he finally spoke it was ragged, more gravel than hum.

"I... can't..."

"Can't? Or won't?"

Ethan shuddered all over, as if his legs were going to give out on him. Finally, he growled—a full-throated grumble of sound—and grasped my hand, wrenching it away from his package.

"Does it matter? I know you don't have the senses of a wolf, but surely even your pitiful human ones can tell this is beyond painful for me."

I couldn't help but recoil from his anger, though I didn't feel the slightest physical threat from him. I even managed to let his scornful words about human senses fall by the wayside. Because what I could tell without question was that, no matter what his words said, he clearly did want to tell me.

To unburden himself.

With tiny steps, I closed the gap between us, reaching for him as I moved. His eyes flashed at me with some kind of heat. It could have been anger, but I was willing to bet—my life, maybe—that it was arousal.

When I slid my hands up his arms, he jumped at my touch, like he wasn't even aware I'd moved.

"Ethan, you can trust me."

He pressed his lips together so hard they formed a white line. Eventually, he relaxed them enough to squeeze out a few words. "I know I can, Gabe. It's myself I can't trust."

I figured if I wanted him to bare his soul to me, I had to offer up something to entice him. So I worked my shirt open and shrugged it off, my heart leaping with pleasure at the hunger that lit in his beautiful hard eyes.

Going for broke, I kicked off my shoes, opened my jeans and let them drop. I stood before this beautiful demigod wearing nothing but my tighty whities.

I hooked my fingers into his thick hair and pulled. "Open up to me, Ethan." I used all my weight to pull his mouth down to mine for a soft kiss.

For a moment, he held firm. Then, with a sweet and scary growl, he took my request literally, parting his lips and devouring my mouth. I'd wanted truth and honesty from him. I'd expected it to come in the form of words, but it was there in every moan he uttered, and every caress he blessed me with. And I would never turn my back on it.

Except to let him take me from behind again.

Ethan slid his mouth down to my throat and the entire heat of his body seemed concentrated in that one spot. I threw my arms around his neck for fear of either flying away or simply melting. His breath coursed down over my chest like a waterfall of lust.

"Yesss." I'd meant to yell it but it came out more as a whisper, with a moan chaser. I fisted his thick hair and sliced a speedy hiss from deep inside his chest. He returned the favor by spearing his fingers into my hair and tightening, right at the top of my neck. With a rapid tug, he brought my scalp to life, kinking my head right back until I could feel his eyes and his mouth and his breath over every pore of my throat.

I leapt up into his arms, needing to wrap my legs around him. Not for safety, and not for balance. Simply to pull him closer, grind his body against mine, exactly where I needed him. The bristling, needy heat of my cock needed some strong treatment.

Like, right fucking now.

I locked my ankles around his ass and ground my raging boner up against the huge hardness of his cock.

"Come on, big guy. Let go."

I could have simply thought the words and he'd probably have heard them with those crazy wolf senses. But the moment I spoke, he tightened up again.

"Ethan, please. I'm so hard. I need you inside me."

"No, no... I can't."

"Don't you fucking dare, you asshole. We're fated mates, whatever the hell that means. I think it means you have to fuck me whenever I say."

He sank his teeth so deep into my neck I wasn't sure if he'd meant to turn me to jelly or turn me away. But when he tried to pull my legs apart and drop me to the floor, I found a little of the wild animal inside myself, taking the back of his shirt in my fists and holding on like it was the last enchilada in the world.

"If you turn me down now, mister, they will be finding parts of you in the woods for decades."

"Gabriel, I'm warning you. You don't know what you're asking." He tried again to detach my thighs from around his waist. When that failed, he moved his hands up to my shoulders and pushed me into the wall, trying to get me off him.

I released my hold on Ethan's shirt and instead drove my short, sharp nails hard into his back, dragging them like claws over his shoulders, really digging in through the fabric. The big man stiffened and hauled in the sharpest breath I'd ever heard, even turning his face to the ceiling as if he was about to howl.

Everything slowed, at least in my head. Ethan brought his face back down to mine, the silver of his eyes nudging that little bit closer to blue. But it was his mouth that had me mesmerized... and terrified.

He had his top lip curled up as if it were a creature in its own right, the brilliant white of his teeth glinting through like a predator stalking me.

The room seemed to tilt, and tingles of sensation ran through my body, focused on every point of contact between us. It was as if Ethan was vibrating at a speed the human eye couldn't see.

And for the first time, I wondered if maybe—just maybe—I should have listened to him and backed off.

There was something, like another presence in the room. A sound I could feel more than hear. And it was all over my body, from my neck down to my desperate aching cock. It was a sound too low for my standard old human ears to hear.

It took a moment before I realized what it was.

Ethan was growling.

Oh, god.

It was like a diesel engine vibrating

against me. I still couldn't make out any sound, but where his thick cock pressed against mine, the sensation was unbelievable. And that was through layers of fabric.

I ran my fingers over his shoulders and beneath his arms, bringing them together again around his waist. Whether he was losing control or just desperate to get closer to me, I couldn't tell, but he ground his chest against mine, forcing my backbone into the cold wall behind me.

I knew it was a heavy moment. One that could tip the scales either way.

Intense erotic pleasure, or utter rejection.

But I wasn't about to back down just because Ethan literally had the strength to tear me apart.

I ran my clawed fingers gently up his back and hooked them around his shoulders, lifting myself to where my hard shaft could press on the tip of his cock. If only we were naked, the moment would be just about perfect.

As I lowered myself against him, I ran my hands back down. Without warning, I dug them deep into his back again, harder than before. I couldn't be sure, but it felt as if I'd managed to draw a little blood, even through his shirt.

Ethan's inaudible growl became a snarl of pain. The whole world spun like a carousel on cocaine as he dragged me away from the wall. He dug deep into the flesh of my thighs with his long fingers, gliding his hands higher with every rushed step he took.

By the time we arrived at the sofa, he had my underwear in his grip. And when he'd finished tossing me unceremoniously onto the cool leather cushions, he still had them in his grip.

Only now it was just shredded fabric.

I barely had time to even contemplate the shock and pleasure of being stripped bare in under five seconds.

And so brutishly.

"I fucking warned you, little one..."

Barely had he bitten out the words than he landed on his knees.

Between mine.

For a moment he drew in short, punching breaths through his nose, making random movements with his head.

Oh, god... he was scenting me.

Like prey.

He seemed to lose control of his eyes for a second before he curled his top lip up in that weird sexy scary grin he had. I held my breath, completely unsure if I was in any danger.

Ethan hauled my leg up to his mouth and bit into the soft skin on the inside of my knee, pulling a hot moan from my throat. He salved that little sore spot with his tongue and worked his way up my leg, biting and sucking, drawing closer to my raging hard cock with every kiss he planted.

I expected a tease. A little hover, maybe a cool breath, or even the classic move of switching to my other leg and repeating his actions. What I never expected was for him to open his mouth so damn wide, and to drive his mouth all the way down me with a power and a hunger like I'd never felt before.

I yelped—an actual high-pitched yelp—as he closed his mouth around me and hummed, scratching his hands up the length of my thighs. Every sensation my body could conjure, he pulled them inward, centering them on my most sensitive flesh, as if he'd given my balls some kind of internal gravity.

My hands seemed to be affected as well. I could have sworn I never told them to move, yet there they were, clamped around the back of Ethan's head, fisting his hair, holding on for dear life as he pumped his hot mouth up and down my length. I squeezed harder every time he sucked hard on my tip, and I released only when he did.

The swabbing of Ethan's velvet tongue around my fat head hit me like tequila, and his tight grip around my balls burned like lime and salt. His attention forced me to feel everything around me—everything in the world, it seemed—so strongly and so sharply I wondered if my body might not have room to hold the sensations. And when he slid one hand beneath my ass and bent me upward, pulling me as close to his mouth as he could get me, I almost lost myself completely.

The first tingles of climax crept through me, but before they'd even begun to gather properly, a new sound came into being. Two parts chainsaw, three parts dinosaur. If not for the nirvana of Ethan's mouth on my cock, I might just have fled for my life.

I knew right away it was his predatory growl again, only this time I could actually hear it. Soft and throaty, as old as time itself. The wolf within him was jostling for prime position. Even the flesh beneath his skin seemed to ripple, a tsunami of lust trying to find an exit.

I locked my gaze on Ethan's. The sheer depth of need shining from within him was beyond perfection. I'd felt wanted before, but only ever for brief moments, and only for parts of myself. Nobody had ever wanted everything I had... everything I was.

Never once had I felt so desired.

So integral.

Ethan turned his head and swabbed my shaft with his mouth, covering every single point of pleasure. Every pore, every vein, every tender millimeter. Even from my viewpoint I could see the glistening of his hunger all over my length, and even out to my thighs.

When he curled his top lip up even further and dug his teeth into my sac, I whimpered with want.

But when he shoved my knees up and slid lower, roughly pulling my cheeks apart, I swore I was about to have an out-of-body experience. He fired his tongue in against my puckered back door and tickled with the tip of it, making me quiver all the way through my body.

I gripped my own knees to free up Ethan's hands, and he snarled in appreciation. At least, I guessed that was it, because he swept those big paws of his straight down and gripped my ass cheeks, lifting me higher and spreading me wider.

The wet heat of his tongue gushed against my ass hole, wetting me completely. My balls trembled and my cock tingled with ecstasy as my wild man devoured me.

Stroke after stroke, he heated my hole, going deeper with every long lash of his tongue. I swore his tongue grew wider, fatter, with every passing second, and couldn't help but wonder if he was partway shifted.

Only thing I knew for sure was, I didn't care. Nobody had ever ignited such pleasure inside me.

When Ethan took my cock in his fist, and drove two fingers up inside my ass, I dragged in a deep, sharp breath from the pure surprising bliss and cried out in need. He pumped his hands in harmony and then hauled my balls into his mouth, rolling his tongue over and around each one, suckling even as my balls pulled up tight.

Suddenly, an enormous firework of ecstasy erupted inside me, sparking out through every nerve ending and racing up my spine. My voice seemed to take on a life of its own, pouring out of me in a keening moan of pleasure, and it seemed destined not to end until I'd emptied my lungs, and my soul.

Ethan let my balls slip out of his mouth with the most delicious wet smacking sound. As my climax crested, he opened up and embraced my cock in his savage mouth, growling with hunger as I filled it.

As the rich aftershocks of orgasm sent my body jittering, Ethan bounced his head up and down as he drained every drop from me.

When I'd finished, he came up off the end of me and narrowed his eyes, the silver orbs radiating pure ravenous desire.

Then he stood, tearing his shirt from his body like it was made from tissues. His sensual grace shone through in every movement as I studied the hard lines of his body.

The shriek of his zipper sent a fresh mix of fear and desire through me. It was like a clawed hand being dragged down my spine, hard enough to hurt in that way I loved so fucking much.

The rustle of his jeans falling to the floor brought a fresh ripple of nervousness to my skin, but the fierce strength of his hands had a settling effect.

He let some of my juice drizzle from his lips and onto his fingers, then coated my ass with it, gliding two digits inside me again with a smooth, erotic grace. I closed my eyes and arched my back as he made me slick and ready.

He let the rest of my come fall into his palm and stroked himself with a tight fist, coating his ferocious hard-on.

When he nudged that broad head in against my open, willing ass, I held my breath. I knew it was gonna hurt as he stretched me, but I looked forward to that burn in the most pleasurable way.

Ethan's voice had shifted away from human and toward wolf, coming out in a low snarl that had me simultaneously more scared and more aroused than any one man should be allowed.

He captured me in the glowing silver heat of his eyes for a moment, and I nodded, following up by pretty much begging him to fuck me.

With a quick driving jab of his hips, he plunged half his gorgeous manhood up inside me, and I cried out like fresh-struck prey. Ethan drew back and bunched up his muscles, punching forward once more and this time his hips slammed into me. I had all of him inside, felt so stretched and full, and it hurt so beautifully I thought I might pass out.

My big, ravenous lover swooped his arms around me, lifting me like a damn puppy and carrying me in his embrace, and on the stake of his cock, through to the guest room. At the bed, he placed me down gently, slanted his mouth over mine, and kissed me hard.

He kept his momentum going, rolling over me and onto his back. Effortlessly, he pulled me up on top of him and gripped me at my hip and my neck.

I pressed myself down on the thick heat of his cock as I fought against the beautiful tears in my eyes. It was more than the intense, burning ecstasy of agony. It was the fierce, relentless connection that fired between us, that eschewed words or definition.

With his fat brute deep inside me, I hissed in pleasured pain as he squeezed my flesh, dragging all my thoughts and feelings down to where it counted. The bliss of his cock fired off salutes of ecstasy inside me, and the hardness of his chest gave me a perfect surface to press on while I bounced myself on him.

I dared not look him in the eyes anymore, knowing what power they already held over me. And the easiest way to avoid seeing them was to dive down on him and suck his tongue back into my mouth.

The man was everything, and everywhere. With his big hands on my hips, and his thick cock inside me. With his hot mouth on mine and his fiery skin beneath me. Not for the first time, I wondered if I truly was a big enough man to take this ride.

But when he started growling again,

even more beastly than before, I suddenly had no doubt. He raised his hips from the bed, leaving me feeling weightless for a second, and hooked his clawed fingers over my shoulders. I shrugged, trying to wrestle control back, but he was too fucking strong.

He found my nipple with his teeth and bit hard into the stiff nub. He pulled down on my shoulders, driving my ass against his hard thighs and filling me so sweetly it was like a thousand desserts at once.

What an idiot I'd been to think I could have any control where Ethan was concerned. My mind barely completed that thought before the forked bolts of sheer ecstasy fired through my body again, driven on by the passionate roar of the climaxing man beneath me as he painted my walls with his scorching essence and I clamped down around his length, welcoming the heat of his release.

The pulsing of Ethan's hips eased, and I drifted down to him like a dropped feather, landing softly, my mouth covering his. The heat of his skin toasted mine, and the shared sheen of sweat-

slicked bodies made it so easy for me to
glide down beside him.

CHAPTER TWENTY-ONE

Ethan

AFTERSHOCKS OF PURE pleasure kept firing through my mind and body. Bursts of sensation, mild spasms, tiny cramps... it was so similar to the onset of a shift that it only increased my belief that this man was some kind of home for me. Not that I could afford to entertain such fanciful notions as home.

Or even happiness.

Damn this sexy singer and his undiluted desirability. Damn his tan brown skin, his expressive eyes, his sensual mouth. Most of all, damn the way his lean, hard body called to my wolf.

I simply couldn't get enough of Gabriel. He was already an addiction. And to stay with him, to keep this whatever-it-was alive, would be nothing less than substance abuse.

"You okay, Ethan?"

His voice was syrupy with fatigue. All that did was make him even more desirable.

"I'm okay."

"Can't sleep?" He nuzzled at my chest, which only served to work him deeper into my heart, into my blood.

I already knew he was my fated mate.

Did he have to keep getting more and more desirable?

Fucking adorable, even?

"I rarely find sleep easily."

Gabriel ran his fingers through the hair on my chest and raised his head. "You think maybe it's because you have a whole other being inside you, howling to come out?"

"No." I found Gabriel's deep dark eyes with my own, and sighed. "Probably."

"Then why won't you free him? It won't scare me."

"You can't know that, Gabe."

He kissed my chest and worked his way up to my throat. "You're right, butt-face. I can't. But I believe it. And I trust you... Ethan."

It wasn't the first time he'd used my name. But it was the first time he'd said it like that. Like it was worth saying.

I closed my eyes, hoping it would stem the tears I felt forming. I'd worked long and hard to keep any man from trusting me like that. Only to find now it was the one thing I'd always needed.

Gabriel laid his head back down on my chest, and glided his warm thigh up over my waist. He was a delightful solid weight on me, hardness coated in silk. He held me in place, taking on my heat, and molding to my form. Grounding me like nothing and no one ever had.

And then he sang.

Soft and smoky, as smooth as bourbon. Some lullaby or folk song. The words were nowhere near as potent as the sound, or the fact the song was for me alone.

In the beauty of his voice, I understood I truly had found a home. A solace I'd never believed in. The woman who'd spawned me had never been one for lullabies. By the time Abigail Larson filled the maternal role, I'd been too old and too jaded for kids' songs.

But in that moment, Gabriel enveloped me. In body, in scent, and in sound. He was in my heart already. And with his song, suddenly he bloomed in my mind, in parts I'd considered long dead.

I kissed his forehead lightly. Before I'd even finished, the sound of Gabe's voice faded.

And I slept.

***

I had my teeth in the throat of a lost black sheep. Tearing, choking, savaging. The rich delicacy of blood. Heat, scent, taste. Somehow the poor creature managed to bleat, even with its neck mostly severed.

A second passed and the bleating morphed into the ring of my cell phone, pulling me from the first lupine dream I'd had in ages.

The fresh and spicy scent of Gabriel coursed through my body as I eased his delicious weight off my chest. As he stirred, a soft, sleepy moan escaped him and I considered crushing the phone in my fist just so I could taste him again.

When I checked the number, I almost went through with that thought.

"Hello, mother."

"Son, we need you. Your father's heart... please, come over at once."

"You're at home?"

"Yes."

"I'll be right there."

I gazed down at the hottie beside me, wishing more than anything I could stay. My craving was bone deep, and even knowing my father was in danger couldn't completely push aside the hunger. My cock was hard again, just from the heat of his skin, the scent of his hair. My guts ached, exactly the way they used to in puberty when I went too long without coming. Only this time, I knew, it wasn't my balls calling for release. It was my wolf desperately trying to chew through. To take control of me, for just as long as it took.

"No."

That was the danger I'd faced before, and I simply could not afford to go through it again. As much as I'd tried to deny it, my wolf was more than just part of me. We weren't merely two sides of the same coin. We ran in each other's veins. And if I let the wolf out now, it would never truly release me again.

Addicts who quit and then relapsed always felt it the hardest.

I had to end it with Gabriel. Though it would sap every iota of joy from my life, the mere fact I was still sitting there, captive to his body and the sensations he awoke within me, was proof my wolf could not be trusted. I was supposed to be rushing to my father's aid.

It was as painful as ripping out hairs, but I slid myself away from Gabriel and started dressing. Though I worked quietly, the newly formed bond between us struck again, and he stirred.

"Hey, handsome. What's happening?"

"Medical emergency. My father."

"Oh, no." He pushed the blankets off his naked body and my damn wolf howled within. Gabriel awoke a protective instinct in me that no man ever had. He was not a small man, nor even soft. It was the softness and care in the man's eyes that had me struggling to breathe. And every passing second made me more desperate to dive back into him.

I turned away before my wolf could betray my human side. "So I, uh... have to go."

"I'm coming with you."

"Please, Gabriel. Don't push it."

"Hey, someone needs to have your back. And so what if they don't like me?"

I turned back, needing to ram my next point home like a nail. "They don't like me. They hate you."

The shock and pain on Gabriel's face was a scar I feared I'd never heal from. To know my words had cut him so badly was simply the worst feeling I'd ever had. Bar none.

"How could they? And how could you just blurt that out?"

"Honestly, it's not personal, Gabe. They hate almost everyone. The reason they only dislike me is that I'm their legacy."

"Well, nobody tells me what to do. I'm still coming with you."

I struggled for breath. My heart seemed to swell three sizes with the depth of my feelings for Gabriel. His courage, his determination and his sheer bloody-minded tenacity.

God, he'd be the perfect wolf.

While I was lost in his beauty, he slipped off the bed and pulled some clothes on. "All right, butt-face. Let's go."

"No."

"A straight out no? You're actually trying that on a diva like me?"

"I actually am. This is wolf business, little one."

Though he hadn't seemed to mind that pet name before, it had him bristling before me, narrowing his eyes and loading his pointing finger to shoot me in the face. "Don't you shut me out, dog-breath. If we're supposed to be fated mates and all that shit, then your damn parents need to get with the program."

I made a show of crossing my arms, of shielding my heart from him. My wolf whined at me to take him, while my human strove desperately not to be cowed. "Listen. You don't get to come into my life one day and then tell me how to run it the next. Understand?"

My heightened senses told me the slap was coming, but I let it land. His instinct clearly was to punch me, but something—love?—made him hold back.

I knew I deserved it, and a thousand more. Gabe landed another from the other side, his eyes brimming with tears.

"Bastard!"

The pain in his heart was an agony in my soul, but there was nothing else I could do. If I enslaved myself to emotion, I'd be entirely useless as a surgeon. All those years of education and training would amount to no more. I had to rely on all that clinical calm now. To excise this relationship before it took me over.

"Better you know that now than later, Gabriel." I blocked the next blow, which was far closer to a closed-fist one, and Gabe deflated before me, falling to his knees.

It wasn't until I'd walked out of the room that I heard him start swearing. And it took the greatest strength I'd ever known to stop from turning back and begging forgiveness.

CHAPTER TWENTY-TWO

Ethan

IT WOULD HAVE been quicker to drive to my parents' house, but without a car I had little choice. Besides, I didn't trust myself behind the wheel at that moment. The way my vision kept blurring was more than a nuisance. It would make me a hazard to everyone on the road. I tried to convince myself the tears were due to nothing more than haze in the air from the not-so-distant brush fires.

So, instead of driving, I ran, drawing on the stamina of the beast within, while striving to keep the wolf itself at bay. Oh, how my mother would be pleased to see me arrive on four legs instead of two.

Once again, I was faced with the quandary of my own duality. Shift into wolf form and I'd make it there in no time, but always with the risk I'd be stuck that way. So, I stayed with human form, even knowing it would take a few minutes more.

I arrived barely out of breath, and stormed inside. My mother greeted me in the hallway.

"You're here. Thank goodness."

"Where's father?"

Hugh called out from the living room. "In here, son."

I raced up the hall and through the wide doorway. To find my father sitting in his favorite chair, a tumbler of gin and tonic in his hand and a pretty blonde standing beside him.

And I realized instantly what a fool I'd been. This was Clinton all over again.

Only worse.

Olga spoke from behind. "Now, son. Don't be angry."

The moment she said that, anger was the only emotion I could feel.

How could I have let them manipulate

me so easily?

"Son," said Hugh. "This is Anthea. She's from quite good stock. The Milford Grove Pack. You know them? They're a few counties away, but still worth knowing."

Anthea herself smiled thinly at me. She showed no reaction to being talked about like a prize breeding sow. Nor did she appear to have any feelings for me at all. What was undeniable, though, was the way her scent simply drifted past me, without any effect.

I turned away from her to face my mother. "It's bad enough you don't trust me with anything. Now you think you can fucking convert me? You morons."

Olga caught her breath as though she'd never been so insulted in her life. A detail I knew only too well to be false, since I'd called them far worse before I left town last time.

Hugh stood, his own anger vibrating through his body. "Ethan. You will not speak to us that way. Especially in front of guests."

"I will, actually. You do understand that just because you are wolf doesn't mean you're obligated to cry it, right?"

"We had to get you away from that... human."

My anger instantly turned cold, and sat heavily in my chest. As it drizzled lower I could feel my other half inside me. The first tingles of a shift crept along the length of my bones, feeding on my rage. It was clear my parents could sense it as well, given the avarice in their eyes.

"Good, son," Hugh said, with a smile. "At least use your anger for something. Find your wolf."

It took all my strength simply to hold the shift in check. I couldn't completely suppress it, but at least for the moment I could stop it going any further. The truth was, I desperately wanted to give it free reign, and doubted my ability to resist.

My mother stepped around in front of me again. "Release your true self, son. You don't really have to mate with Anthea. We can find you an even better one. Come home."

The horror show of my own family hit me like a slap. I couldn't imagine how Anthea must be feeling at that moment. But if she was wolf, she'd surely have picked up from my scent and my bearing that she was not... my type.

I realized suddenly that she'd only ever been a pawn. The fact she was female was not a desperate attempt to convert me. It was only ever intended to enrage me, by making me think that.

Suddenly, the image of Gabriel flashed into my mind. The irresistible splendor of his naked body, and the ragged ache I felt knowing I'd likely just thrown away any chance I had to be with him.

But then I recalled the way he'd stood, and dressed, more than ready to come with me. Despite being outnumbered and outgunned, he'd been prepared to confront these fools on their home turf. These people I could barely believe I shared blood with.

He'd been ready to put his head almost literally in the wolf's jaws.

Just for me.

All my life, my parents had sung the praises of our kind. Espousing their belief that wolves were superior to all other beings. That humans were weak, feckless and foolish.

In a matter of seconds, Gabriel had

proved them utterly wrong. He, a mere human, had displayed far greater strength of character than either of my parents ever had.

He was only human... but I knew now for certain; in his heart, he was wolf.

The more I thought about him, the more it eased my tension. Oh, my beast was still prowling down there, hungry for blood. But where I'd usually force him down, compress him, this time I didn't need to.

Gabriel had brought me balance like I'd never felt. In only a matter of days, he'd crashed through barriers I'd imposed on myself. He'd coaxed the darkness up into the light, and somehow, it worked.

Fuck, it bloomed.

Having my mate in my life would mean I wouldn't have to fear the wolf. More than that, though, I just might be able to embrace him.

I closed my eyes and let Gabriel's strength wash through me. If I was the luckiest man on Earth then I might have a chance to win back his heart. But I had to leave right away.

Slowly, I opened my eyes again.

"Anthea, it's very nice to have almost met you, and I'm sorry you were lured here on false premises. Please, let your pack know this was the work of Olga and Hugh Roddick, and nobody else. My leaving now is nothing to do with you."

Before the girl could even get a word out, I spun on the spot and marched out. My mother followed, yapping her displeasure all the way, but I barely even registered a syllable of it. My one focus was getting back to Gabriel.

Before I lost him forever.

CHAPTER TWENTY-THREE

Gabriel

I'D TRIED MY damnedest to follow him. When Ethan ran out, I'd scrambled to my feet and followed as closely as I could. With those stupidly long legs of his, and his... I don't know, wolf cardio classes, I'd had no chance. And I ended up barefoot, shaking, and coming down with an anxiety attack, in the middle of a town I didn't know at all.

"Mister Mendoza?"

I tried to calm my breathing as I turned, finding Abigail and Bernard Larson standing before me, arm in arm.

"What's happened, darling?" Abigail reached out and took my hand in both of hers.

"Your nephew is a..." I wanted to call him all kinds of names, but I'd fallen so damn hard for him the words just wouldn't come. All I wanted was for him to come back. Just because I wasn't a wolf didn't mean I had no instincts, and the world had never felt more right than when I was in that man's embrace.

"Oh, Ethan. Well, that's not so bad." Abigail let a sigh escape her. "Kiera tells us she's brought you up to speed on the town, and its people. Is that right?"

"Uh-huh."

"Then I can tell you, we've been hearing reports of rogues. I thought you might have encountered one."

"Rogues?"

"Rogue shifters. Possibly bears. It's probably nothing, darling."

Bernard lightly touched my shoulder. "Come with us, please? Tell us everything over a coffee. Our treat."

It was a short walk to the café, and we took a table on the sidewalk.

"So, Gabriel," Abigail began. "What seems to be the trouble?"

"Ethan. It's always Ethan. My life was perfect and then he came along and turned it inside out."

Bernard patted the back of my hand, the same way my own father used to. "I know it's not directly our business, but the way our daughter tells it, your life seemed a long way from perfect."

"You're right. It's not your business." I suddenly realized what I'd said. To the people who'd been kind enough to let me stay with them for the weekend. "Oh. I'm so sorry. I didn't mean to be rude. I'm just messed up."

"It's all right, Gabriel," said Abigail. "You must understand, Ethan is the son we never had. I'm sure you're aware by now that you are, without a doubt, his fated mate. Yes?"

"That's what they tell me. Fat lot of good that does."

Their coffees arrived, breaking through the conversation for a moment. Bernard took a sip of his and then turned to me again.

"Now, I don't know the detail here. But let me tell you what I do know. Ethan is a man who's still in pain. I take it you don't yet know the details, but I assure you, he's holding on to something very dark. And a lot of that is inextricably tied to my damn sister and her husband."

"Yeah, well, that's where he is right now. I mean, I get it. His father's sick or something, and Ethan's a doctor. I get that he had to rush over there. But what he didn't have to do was treat me like a piece of shit on his shoe."

Bernard and his wife exchanged a look, and then Abigail spoke.

"Darling, we've just come from their place. Hugh is not sick in the slightest. Nor in need of any medical attention. In fact, he was busy lecturing that live-in student... oh, no."

Bernard bounced his fist on the table. "Those assholes. They're at it again."

My head spun at the rapid change in their mood. "What? What's happened?"

"It seems my sister and her husband are playing their old games with Ethan's life. Trying to mate him with a wolf."

"What? And he just ran off to do it?"

Abigail shook her head. "Never, darling. You said he was called over to tend to his father?"

"That's what he said. I was asleep

when he took the call. If there even was a call."

"Ethan is the most honest man we know, darling. And even if he were capable of lying, you're the last person on earth he'd try it with."

I felt like flipping the table in frustration. "Then what the hell is going on? What happened to him and Clinton?"

Bernard sat back and shook his head. "I'm sorry, Gabriel. I'm sure you've heard this plenty of times already but it's not our story to tell. You're really going to have to get that from Ethan himself. Just promise me you won't make any permanent decision until he opens up. Okay?"

"He never will."

"He will, Gabriel, if you ask him. He'll open up completely. At least, if he knows what's good for him, he will."

"Yeah? Well, he ran from me to be with his parents, so he clearly doesn't know what's good for him."

Abigail smiled, though there were a few icicles hanging from it. "You're technically an orphan, darling? Kiera told us."

"Yes. My parents were killed in a plane crash when I was seventeen."

"And you'd give anything to see them again?"

"What does this have to—"

"Why do you think it should be any different for Ethan? He's lived the last five years of his life as though his parents were gone. If they've tricked him into believing his father truly is at death's door, it's no wonder he ran over there. Medicine is his calling in life, and those two have never supported it, let alone embraced it. He finally had the chance to show them he's not the waste they've always told him he was."

I glanced across the street, only to see the man himself, running back toward the Larsons' house. If anything, he was moving faster than when he'd left.

I made to yell out to him, but Abigail grabbed my arm. "Not here, Gabriel. It needs to be done in private. Pin him down and get the truth. His truth."

I hesitated for a few seconds. No way could I risk tossing my heart to that man. Not if he couldn't break the shackles of his destructive family. The pressure would tear us apart and I'd be left shredded on the floor somewhere.

Maybe literally.

Bernard rested his hand on my shoulder. "Go to him, Gabriel. But remember what I said. Hear him out, and then decide. Please."

The short walk back over to the Larsons' place did nothing to clear my head.

Why the hell couldn't this man be open with me?

He wanted me as much as I wanted him. I didn't need any of those stupid wolf senses to know that. It had hung thick in the air like humidity every time we were within a hundred feet of each other. Yet there was no denying how hard he'd tried to push me away.

More than once.

The house's front door bore the brunt of my seething mood. I slammed it so forcefully behind me it probably deafened any wolves in the area.

I charged up the hall to Ethan's door and thumped everything I could against it—hands, feet, elbows, knees—demanding he open up.

First the door, then his heart.

"Hey, you big tool. Let me in."

Ethan had clearly moved in silence, like a damn wolf. The door came open just as I'd lined up a swift shoulder charge, and I ended up landing on the floor right in front of him.

"Gabriel. I thought I'd lost you."

I looked up, ready to rip him a new one, when I was silenced by the one thing I never expected.

Tears on his cheeks.

As I regained my feet, I pointed up into his face. "Yeah well, who says you haven't, butt-face? I need to know everything. About Clinton and your parents and... and just everything." I'd been warned to tread carefully, but this was too important.

And too close to my heart.

Ethan put his hands over his face. "I've tried so hard to put it in the past, Gabriel."

"Well, you've sucked at that. Whatever the problem is, you carry it around your neck in everything you do." I pushed him backward, hoping to get him all riled up. That seemed to be the surest way to get him speaking honestly. "I know what your stupid parents were up to. Don't ask me how, I just know."

Ethan sighed and hooked his hands around the back of his neck. "I didn't think I could despise them any more than I already did. And then they prove me wrong."

I resisted the urge to snuggle up against him. As much as we both might need it, I needed the truth even more. "I'm not going to stand between you and your family. And I'm not going to force you to make a choice. Your folks can't stand that I'm human, so screw them. But I promise you, I am not going to be with half a man. A man who won't be true to himself."

"Take care, little one. Take great care."

"Ha. I'm not about to start now, butt-face. This is it. Your last chance. I can see it's burning a hole through you. I know you need to tell me everything. And I need you to open up to me, or I swear I'm gonna—"

Ethan moved like the perfect predator, taking my mouth with his and subduing me in an instant. Cutting off my air, and the flow of blood to my brain. As his tongue swept across my lips, my head grew light and fluffy, while my body turned to hot fudge. He had his palm against my throat, his other hand cradling my head as he mashed his lips against mine, suckling at me like I was nectar.

I'd been so determined to draw his pain out of him so I could heal it. To truly know this man, in every way.

Now, with the taste of his mouth, the smell of his hair, the touch of his skin, suddenly, I only existed through him, through the ways he filled my senses. Gravity failed me as he swept me up into his arms and slammed me back against the wall, driving from me the last iota of breath I'd managed to hold.

It took more strength than I'd ever known, but I broke the kiss and forced my way out of his embrace. "No, Ethan. I can't... it's not fair."

"What's not fair?"

"I can't help myself here. I am this close to sinking myself completely into you. One hundred percent. But you're holding something back from me. And it might be small, but it's clearly heavy. If we fall into bed again now, I'll never be able to get over you."

"I don't want you to ever get over me. I need you like water."

I pressed my hands in against his heart, but my only intention was to keep him from swallowing me whole. I dredged my voice up from the molasses of lust inside myself.

"Then you know what to do."

CHAPTER TWENTY-FOUR

Ethan

I LOOKED OUT of my bedroom window. The fires over the hill were kicking out a lot of smoke, but so far there hadn't been any call to evacuate. Not that I'd mind a whole hell of a lot if that were to happen. It was hard enough to be back in Stoke Ridge with all the memories it held for me. But to be surrounded by all these shifters as well was doing my head in.

And now this guy, this perfect temptation, was cutting at me like a fellow surgeon. Asking me to eviscerate myself of all my feelings and my faults.

And God help me, he was right.

I did want to.

I needed to, in fact. I'd kept it pressed down so hard it had fermented. If anyone deserved to know my full story, it was Gabriel. For us to have our future, he needed to know my past.

Fated mates were so damn inconvenient.

I turned back to him, where he sat on the bed, his eyes awash with love and his body trembling in anticipation. He looked so much like prey it awoke my wolf once again, and it took me an enormous effort to push that feeling back down.

Every time I was in his presence, he tugged at my beastly side without apparently doing anything at all.

The sexy bastard.

I took a seat on the floor, lowering myself before him in adoration. "This is not an easy truth."

"I know that much. Kiera and her parents all warned me. But I really need to know you."

I nodded and studied my hands a moment. "All right, then."

And as I spoke, I closed my eyes, traveling back in time. Revisiting the scents and the sounds much more than the sights.

The rumble of thunder came closer as Clinton stripped off, racing ahead of me. The damp earth and humus filled my nostrils when that cute smile lit up his face; the smile that only came when he was about to shift. I fell to the ground, feet tangled in my jeans, the scents of a thousand prey animals firing into my brain.

Then the momentary pain and exquisite pleasure of shifting.

Clinton ran ahead of me, his tail dancing and beckoning. I nipped at him, mock hunting until a prey animal might cross our paths.

Rain was coming. The smell was everywhere. Lighting and thunder filled the night, making everything more urgent. More fun.

A deer startled off to the right, and we turned in pursuit. These were the times we were at our best. Most compatible.

Clint flushed a doe from the bushes and we paced it, one on either side. Hunting for fun, not for food. Wolf time was everything.

Heaven.

Our hearts trilled as we ran. I felt his pulse as clearly as my own.

The rain hit so hard. Got harder. The world was nothing but scents.

Rich soil, dead leaves, rabbits, water.

Rain hitting us harder.

Harder still.

Lightning.

Clint took cover under a tree and I came in behind, pressing against him to take the rain. To shield my mate.

The wind blew faster, the storm grew fiercer. A bright flash as lightning hit the tree above, thunder sounding at the same time. A branch fell, and before we could run, it landed.

Clint yelped, and even through my layers of wolf, I knew right away he was hurt badly.

I pulled at the thick branch, but even wolf jaws couldn't move it, couldn't break it. Clint shifted, his whimpers becoming screams. He should have stayed wolf. All the shift did was tear his belly to pieces as wolf turned to human.

Blood.

Clint's blood.

All my world ran red.

He needed my mind. He needed my hands. I had to shift.

Shift.

Must shift.

There, it was almost in reach.

Shift.

Shift!

Clint's breath slowed as his eyes drifted closed. I slowed my breathing, searching inside myself for the answer. For the man I had to be.

I came back to the present, to the house. To the man before me.

My fated mate.

Gabriel's face glistened with shed tears. "What happened?"

I stared at my hands, studying them. Burning their form and their function into my mind. How I could have used those hands back then, to lift the branch. To staunch the blood, to carry him to safety.

I pressed my fingers to my mouth. The mouth I could have used back then to form the words. To tell Clint not to shift. To let his wolf take the pain. To let the branch block the flow of blood, rather than have it gouge away at his morphing body.

And finally, I admitted my pain. The pain I'd never put into words before. Not for Kiera, not for Clinton's family. Not for anyone.

Until now.

"He died. With my head on his chest, his gaze holding mine until he closed his eyes forever. His hand squeezing my paw, and me unable to squeeze back. Unable to shift back."

Gabriel slipped off the bed and knelt before me, resting his head on my thigh.

I sighed as I stroked his beautiful hair. "That day, I lost my love."

"He must have been amazing."

"He was, but that's not what I mean. Clinton was a wonderful man, and an amazing friend. We were mated, true enough; but we never once felt anything for each other like what is right here..." I put my hand to my chest. "Between you and me."

I screwed up my face, but couldn't stop tears from rising into my eyes. "My best friend died. But I lost so much more. He took with him all the love I'd ever had for my wolf. I knew then I couldn't trust the beast."

"But he's part of you. Half of you."

"And what happens the next time I'm stranded without hands, without words? Whose life will be ended then? Because it could be yours, Gabriel, and I will never stand for that."

"Oh, baby."

I tensed beneath him, unsure if I was truly ready for the weight of all this. For understanding and sympathy and—dare I believe it—*love*.

Gabriel curled his arms around my calf and looked up into my eyes. "I'm so sorry, Ethan. I didn't know." As if he could sense the turmoil inside me, he released his grip and stood. "I shouldn't have pushed. I should have listened to everyone."

Before I registered what was happening, he'd turned and walked away. But he didn't even make it halfway across the room before I'd caught up, seized his arm and spun him back to face me.

"Where do you think you're going?"

"Baby, I'm sorry. I didn't mean to hurt you. The way people talked, it was like you had a messy divorce or something." He swallowed heavily before speaking again. "You have so much to deal with. I... I was thinking about myself, and what I want." He tried to drag his arm away, but I wouldn't release him.

"And what about what I want, Gabriel?" I grasped his other arm and pulled him against my hard chest.

"W–what do you want, Ethan?"

I ran my hand up the side of his face, combing it through his hair on the way back down. Though I followed the movement with my gaze, I quickly turned my focus back to his. "A week ago, there was only one answer to that. Right now, there is still only one answer." I kissed his forehead lightly. "But those two answers could not be any more different. Before, I wanted solitude. Now... I want everything."

"Oh, everything. Is that all?" The little kink in the corner of his mouth awoke that ancient hunger. The one that relied on senses, not words. The hunger I was already learning to embrace again.

I could never truly be mated to this man, in the purest sense, without my wolf. And I struggled to believe I could live another day in the world without being mated to him.

I cradled his head, and bent to him, caressing his lips with mine. Soaking up every scent of his sexy body, every tiny sound of his voice.

By kissing him like that, by taking his essence into my blood, I'd finally set my wolf free. Though I could sense its caution, feel it waiting to be chased back into the darkness, I knew without a trace of a doubt I needed my beast as much as my human form. The two were one, and could never be divided.

"What do I want, Gabriel? I want you. Forever. And I... I want my wolf back."

The scent of tears all over his cheeks was both a rich temptation and a sharp knife. As I carried him to my bed, I kept my gaze locked on his.

I knew I was lost in him. He was my life now. And through him, my wolf had re-awoken.

CHAPTER TWENTY-FIVE

Gabriel

ETHAN TOSSED ME bodily onto the bed, as if I weighed no more than a pillow. In seconds, he'd torn every shred of clothing from my body, his hunger becoming a physical force. He stripped his own clothes off just as quickly, and filled the room with a low, fierce growl.

He leapt over me and held me down in that way I'd never grow tired of. The way that made me feel secure, rather than trapped.

His beautiful eyes darkened for a moment as he scanned my naked body.

Every freckle, every pore, every scar.

I'd never been so proud of my own body, because I'd never had anyone look at it the way he did. Not like I was perfect, but like I was *everything.*

"You're mine, Gabriel. I can't even try to deny it anymore. I knew it—and my wolf knew it—the moment I caught your scent."

He wasn't saying anything new, but there was a sense of ceremony about it. As if it was a spell and he had to say the words just the right way.

"I am yours, Ethan. But only if you're mine."

"I am only yours, little one." He curled his top lip up to reveal his teeth. And the way they'd grown just that little bit longer and sharper. The wolf staking its claim on him.

And very soon, on me.

I nodded. Words simply wouldn't work at that moment.

He closed his eyes and simply breathed. "You will be my mate for all time." His voice was barely a whisper, yet it reached me like a roar.

Ethan dipped his head and seized my mouth in a kiss that was as much hunger as lust. He slid his mouth across and took my earlobe between his teeth, working his way slowly south down the hot skin of my neck.

The lower he moved, the more ferocious he became. By the time he was at my hip, the man had given way to the beast. Not so much in form as in nature.

And somehow, it was as exhilarating as it was terrifying. Just to know I could inspire such passion in this man.

Ethan drove his mouth down my cock, snarling with ravenous desire as he worked me higher and higher. In what felt like only a few seconds, his blistering attack had my consciousness swaying, and my climax boiling up.

I found the strength to push him backward. I curled my legs up and swung them past Ethan's face, rolling onto my belly, raising my ass from the bed and presenting myself to my conqueror.

Every hot-blooded, sweat-slicked, desperate inch of myself.

Ethan's moan grew deeper and rougher, until it was his wolf growling through his human throat. He fell upon me, driving his tongue against my hole with all the power and barbarity of the wolf inside him. He worked me so hard, so fast, and I'd never been more open to another person. I gripped my ass and opened myself up to him, willing him to take me any and every way he wanted.

Ethan sank his teeth into my skin, and all I could do was whimper with the twinned pleasures of fear and arousal. He snarled, his deep voice vibrating through me and making my balls physically tingle.

My big brute released me for a moment and fled to the bathroom, coming back with a bottle of lube. He snapped it open and poured the cold oil onto my puckered hole, and I swore the stuff must have turned to steam. I was that hot.

The slick sound of him lubing up his own thick cock only made me more ready for him. I wasn't fully warmed up, I wasn't sure I could take him again so soon... but I wasn't prepared to wait.

When he snared my hips with his hands, the sharpness of his nails was obvious, like they'd shifted a little closer to claws. Everything about his presence thrilled me, and even more so when I could sense his beast just below the surface.

He nudged his broad head in against my ass, and paused. I couldn't read his mind, exactly, but I knew why he'd stopped. Making sure I was okay.

"Do it, Ethan. Set your wolf free." I glanced back up over my shoulder. "Go wild."

He drove forward and filled me in a heartbeat, stretching me so hard, so quickly, that it was the most perfect blend of pain and pleasure.

"Your skin is immaculate, little one." Ethan sounded trapped between man and beast. As if he was striving to keep the civilized human in control, while inevitably the wolf gnawed its way out. It was the hottest thing I'd ever heard.

And when he snared my hair in his fist and pulled my top half up off the bed, it brought my skin to life. I tingled from scalp to toes, not just from his touch, but from the way I sensed his eyes scouring every pore of my body.

With every drive of his hips, he sent wild sensations clawing their way up my spine, until my head was a bird's nest of pleasure. I was losing myself already, becoming, in my mind, nothing more than an extension of Ethan. I was more at home here, in his bed, in his embrace, than I'd been anywhere else in the world.

He released my hair and clawed both hands around me. One over my heart, the other over my cock, manhandling me so beautifully as his nails dug in to my skin and created a whole new burn. I lost control of my spine and fell forward out of his grip, landing face down on the bed. Only the strength of my lover kept my ass in the air.

"Little one..." Ethan rasped out the words. And then there was nothing but heavy panting and thick growling as he leaned down on me, angling that magnificent cock so it filled me in the most perfect way, nailing my sweet spot with every thrust.

The weight of his body rested on his hands, flat on my shoulder blades, and my breathing became both the ultimate luxury, and totally meaningless. Surely, while he ignited my body like that, I needed nothing else to live. No food, no water, no breath.

Just Ethan's goddamn perfect cock.

The spiraling fingers of bliss within

my balls picked up speed until they became a maelstrom, and as Ethan punched his hips against my ass, I saw a white light behind my eyes. His weight grew too much and it forced my knees apart. I came down, flat on my belly. He stayed inside me as his body slammed down on my back.

His beautiful deep voice cracked as he roared with ultimate pleasure, and a bloom of piercing heat ignited my shoulder blade.

My whole world suddenly exploded in ecstasy and I cried out. Pleasure that seemed to form in my bones, and pierce my skin drew uncontrollable sobs from my body. This was a climax from another world, and bizarrely, it seemed to flow down from my shoulder to my balls and then race like fire back up my spine only to make the same fierce cycle once again.

Then, as Ethan reached his own climax deep inside me, my ass drank the heat from him and I tightened around his thickness with a long, loud scream as I let loose once more, my release coating the mattress beneath me. Only then did I realize he had his teeth embedded in the flesh of my shoulder, deep and hard, sharp as hell. The pain was pleasure and that pleasure was the world.

I was absolutely, unquestionably, his.

Forever.

CHAPTER TWENTY-SIX

Ethan

AS MY ORGASM subsided, I felt my mind struggling to return to my body. My last conscious memory was of Gabriel urging me on. Insisting I get as beastly as I could.

I caught my breath, the wolf side of my nature unwilling to step back from the brink. Though I'd already come, the uneasy balance between my two sides felt for all the world like the struggle to hold back an orgasm.

Beneath me, Gabriel's sweat-slicked body quivered with the aftershocks of his own climax. My senses whirled, my beast and human sides intertwined in a way I'd almost forgotten could happen.

I teetered on the edge of shifting, for the first time in years, reluctant to turn away from it too quickly. It wasn't unlike the sensation of dozing.

As my mind finally processed the sweet and salty tang of blood, I sighed against my tender mouthful of flesh.

And my humanity returned in a flash, like an icicle slicing through my heart. My teeth and nails, both slightly elongated, tucked back into their human form immediately, and I released Gabriel's shoulder from my bite.

"Oh, fuck," I said, my voice a harsh whisper in the near silence of the room.

"Mm. My sentiments exactly."

Oh, hell.

I shook my head, and licked over the open wound on Gabriel's back, speeding up the healing process.

"Hey, butt-face," he hummed, his voice quivering with pleasure at the touch of my tongue on his brand new wound. "That's enough of that. I couldn't possibly go again."

In seconds, the bleeding stopped, and

his skin closed over, leaving behind only a scar.

My mark.

He didn't know.

How could he know?

Until this weekend, he hadn't even known shifters existed. But what was done was done.

I screwed my eyes closed and came down beside him, holding him tight against my body as he drifted inevitably to sleep.

And in the morning, I'd have to tell him the truth. That my mark was much more than just a scar, and held more weight than a wedding ring or a contract. With that mark, he'd be just like me.

Wolf.

***

Even though I was highly experienced, in life and in lust, I had never felt anything like the beautiful ache of having Gabriel fall asleep in my embrace. And the potent surrender of waking up beside him.

As a surgeon, I'd grown used to implicit trust. People who neither knew me nor liked me would routinely submit to my strengths, and place their lives in my care. It was the coldest and most clinical kind of trust I could imagine. And that suited me just fine, professionally.

I'd literally held dozens of hearts in my hands, yet not one of them had affected me like this. It was only a metaphor, but the way I now held Gabriel's heart meant everything.

He was my life.

My completion.

And I had absolutely no doubt how lucky I was to have found him. Not all wolf mates were in love. Hell, it was only through finding Gabriel that I realized how shallow my connection to Clinton had been. Mates in function only. Our wolves had been compatible enough not to kill each other.

Gabriel, though, filled my world and my senses like nothing ever had. My bond to him felt stronger than the immutable tie to my own wolf, if that were even possible.

But above all else, Gabriel had shown me the majesty of embracing my wolf again. And the folly of trying to deny such an essential part of my own being for so damn long.

Which turned my mind, jarringly, back to my mistake last night. I might be highly intelligent, but I was a fucking idiot. To think I could simply open my wolf's cage and expect him to play nice. That he might sit, beg, and roll over just because I said so.

After long years in the dark, in the wilderness, of course he had turned feral. And the moment I gave him a glimpse of freedom, he had taken me over.

I ran my fingers over my mark on Gabriel's shoulder and he stirred, sighing lushly in his sleep. I pressed into it and his sigh caught a little friction and turned into a throaty moan.

As always, the sound of his voice, especially when expressing pleasure, spoke straight to my cock and I was rock hard in seconds.

"Damn you," I muttered, as if my erection would listen. Now was not the time. As much as I'd love to take him, yet again, he had to know the truth before anything else could happen.

There was a process, a ceremony to

turning humans, not unlike a marriage. A tradition, that I'd unintentionally pushed aside.

In the throes of unstoppable passion, I'd lost control, and I'd turned the man I loved. I could only hope he'd understand, and forgive me. But I had to face facts; it just might have cost me any chance of a future with him.

CHAPTER TWENTY-SEVEN

Gabriel

IT FELT UTTERLY self-indulgent to be awoken by sunlight streaming through the window, instead of by an alarm. I couldn't remember when I'd felt more alive. Like I'd been plugged into a charger overnight and was ready to devour the day.

The feel of Ethan's hard body snuggling in against mine was even more luxurious. The man was a human furnace. Wait... a half-human furnace.

I turned in his embrace, searching for those incredible silver eyes of his.

But when I found him, his expression was anything but happy.

"What's wrong, Ethan? Is it your parents?"

He shook his head, closing his eyes and somehow closing his face off to me as well. "I have to tell you something. I hope you won't hate me."

"Impossible. Unless you tell me you're married."

He flinched at that, and my belly tightened up. I slammed my hand into his shoulder and sat up. "Oh, for fuck's sake! You are married?"

"No, Gabriel."

I allowed my breathing to return to normal as I relaxed a little inside.

"Well, thank fuck for that. I really didn't feel like killing you today."

"I mean, I'm technically not. Not exactly. It's... it's us. You and me. We're mated."

"Well, we sure have done it enough times."

Ethan sat up, and I couldn't stop myself from admiring every damn inch of his perfect, hard body. I had to bite down on the desire rising within me, which was pretty damn weird, considering I was still pissed at him for scaring me like that.

"That's not quite what I mean."

What the hell was wrong with him?

So far, he'd been pretty clear with his communication. At least, once he'd opened up.

But now he couldn't find the words to tell me what was going on?

Surely we were past that by now.

"Look, Ethan. Whatever it is, we'll get through it. I can't believe I'm saying this so soon but... I'm stupidly in love with you, and I can see you feel the same way."

He finally opened his eyes again, and pressed his big, hot palm against my cheek.

"God, you're beautiful, Gabriel." He came forward, capturing my mouth with his and forcing me down onto my back. He kissed his way to my hard belly licking and nipping at my flesh, tracing every freckle and mark with his fingers. "Every damn inch of you."

The break in Ethan's voice as he praised me was even more magical than the words themselves.

Ethan's ravenous hunger for me went

beyond everyone and everything I'd ever known. And as wonderful as that felt, it was also a little bit scary.

When he gripped my thighs and wrenched them apart, bowing as if to take my balls in his mouth again, I let out a long moan, which somehow rolled over itself until it became a growling sound.

What the hell?

Where did that come from?

The moment that beastly noise escaped me, it was as if someone had thrown cold water over Ethan. He sat bolt upright, shaking his head and turning his face toward the ceiling.

He let out a long, hard breath, and then relaxed back onto his knees.

"Gabriel... I fucked up."

"We all do. Even brilliant surgeons. Cut yourself a break, Ethan."

"But it affects us. You."

"Now you're scaring me. What did you do?"

He looked down at his hands, and sighed heavily. "I lost control last night."

"And how. It was amazing."

"I gave you my mark. On your shoulder."

I frowned, and raised my hand, reaching over to the exact spot he'd sunk his teeth in. "Oh... yeah. I thought I might've dreamed that. Boy, you really went to town."

"You don't understand, Gabe. That's what I meant when I said we're mated. It's something I would've hoped to do sometime. Eventually. With your permission." He ran his hand back through his lush hair. "I didn't mean to, but I'm so out of practice with my wolf, and I... I couldn't stop him."

I closed my eyes as I glided my fingertips over the mark. It gave me little thrills, almost like squeezing my cock, though not as concentrated. A harder press sent pain signals that were still rich with pleasure racing through me.

"So," I moaned. "We're mated. I was already sold on you, in case you couldn't tell, you big galoot."

"It's so much more than that, little one."

"Why the hell can't you just come out and say it?"

He grimaced and slid off the bed, standing tall, but turned away from me as if in shame. "That mark? It's because

I bit you. And it means... it means I've changed you."

"Is this some weird wolf crap?"

"Yes."

I grinned and slid my legs over the edge of the bed. "You and your damn kind are loco."

"Our kind."

"No, *your* kind. Wolves. You're barking mad, every one of you."

"That's what I'm telling you, Gabriel. That bite—my mark—means I've turned you. You're like me, now."

"I'm... I'm a wolf shifter, now?"

He turned back to me, eyes closed, defeat written all over his face... and nodded.

For a few moments, I stared at the wall. I stood, and stumbled around the room. "You're serious. Aren't you?"

"I am." He dropped to his knees and gazed up at me. "I don't have any excuse. Only reasons. And it doesn't change the way I feel about you, except to make it stronger."

So, just like that, he'd ripped my life to shreds. Nothing would ever be the same. I let out a sharp, howling scream and stepped past him, running down the hallway to my own room.

I yanked my suitcase open and disemboweled it, searching for something—anything—to wear. I finally settled on a pair of jeans and a loose old t-shirt.

Ethan appeared in my doorway, clearly trying to block my way.

"Please, Gabe. Talk to me."

I turned and punched at his shoulder like a drunken washed up boxer. "Most guys can't keep it in their pants. You just couldn't keep it in your mouth, could you? Now you expect me to believe I'll grow fur and howl at the moon?"

"You will. You'll be magnificent. And it will be the most liberating and exciting experience of your—"

"This is the same shifting thing that you said was ridiculous, and primitive, and a curse on your life?"

His sigh was clearly disappointment more than frustration. "Okay, yes, I said all that, and more. But you know now why I felt that way."

"Yeah, I do. But I now also know you're a lunatic with no grounding in reality, otherwise you wouldn't be spinning me this crazy line of bullshit." I elbowed past him and headed for the front door.

"Gabriel, wait."

I spun quickly and put my hand into his face. "Talk to the paw, asshole."

***

I ran out of the Larsons' house, slamming the door so hard I expected the window to break. I had no idea where I was going, nor why. There was simply a wordless voice firing through my head that impelled me to run. And a ridiculous strength and stamina flooding my body, unlike anything I'd ever known.

With no exact destination in mind, I let instinct take over, and it led me to Ethan's family home. I'd never been there, yet something—scent, inherited memory, psychosis—told me exactly who lived there. The bizarre voice inside became a beastly growl, telling me I should kick their door in, and confront the man's parents.

Instead, I simply stopped outside and clenched my fists, letting the anger well up. They'd treated me like dirt, of course, but that was hardly the point. I was far angrier at the way they'd treated my man all through his life.

Wait... was he *my* man?

After that stunt he'd pulled last night with those fangs of his, it was so hard to tell what was what.

I barely understood this new force inside me. It was as if I'd developed a split personality, but one that had a physical presence rather than a mental one.

What was more frightening was that it was composed almost purely of appetites.

Hunger and need and rage and power.

My humanity cracked and fell away beneath the swelling of the wolf inside me, and I let it escape the only way I knew how.

Through the power of my voice.

It started as a low hum, but quickly gained strength. Within seconds it turned into a growl, and then a mighty scream of rage, directed at the Roddicks' house.

The drapes parted, and Olga's stony face showed, a cell phone held to her ear. The only words I could make out were *he's here.*

The beast within took more control of my body. I crouched, ready to pounce at Ethan's mom. Nothing could stop me— not the twenty feet of space between us, nor the double-glazed windows.

"Gabriel!"

Fuck.

Ethan.

Only that could stop me.

I turned to see him running up the street toward me, and I let out a howl of frustration, turning on the spot and sprinting away.

As I reached the corner, I glanced back, fearing Ethan would be right behind me. Thankfully, he was trapped with his mother, who'd come outside to stop him.

I followed the streets of Stoke Ridge for a while, and found myself at the candy store where Ethan had ended our tour before. Without a second thought, I simply ran on into the forest across the road.

The moment I entered the semi-darkness of the thick, lush vegetation, all the tension inside my mind simply eased. It was as though I'd come home, suddenly. And that had to be the wolf within me.

I hadn't planned any of this, of course. And even though the whole situation was overwhelming, I still didn't plan to run too far. This would have to be a bargain-basement pout. That life-altering jerk would just have to come running after me and apologize again immediately, rather than in an hour's time like most guys.

I slowed to a jog, and let myself adjust to the new force inside me. It wasn't all that different to having sex, in a way. This thing—this wolf—was so big, and I just had to ease myself around it. Find peace with it.

In all honesty, it wasn't like I was actually against the idea of being a shifter. It just would've been nice to have been asked.

Or to even be aware it was something that could happen, for fuck's sake.

My wolf senses elbowed the human ones aside. The forest was absolutely filled with scents, though most of them were muted by smoke from the distant brush fires.

Those fires weren't a danger, but the

wind had brought both the smell and haze across to Stoke Ridge. I couldn't see clearly for more than fifty feet in any direction, and despite my anger, I still managed a thin vein of sensible thought.

I rounded a thick tree and leaned back on it, listening for Ethan's footsteps. Every man knew, whether he was gay or straight, human or shifter, it was his duty to follow and to apologize. Except those times he wasn't supposed to, of course.

Any second now I'd hear him.

Any.

Second.

Finally, the crack of a twig beneath a heavy foot sounded from the other side of the tree and I swung myself around, hands on hips. "Well, it's about time... ohh."

I had, of course, expected Ethan, maybe on his knees and looking forlorn. Maybe even with big fat tears in his steely-silver puppy dog eyes. What I hadn't expected, was the man mountain who was actually standing there, hands at his sides like a gunfighter, completely naked, and glaring at me like I was a fresh morsel, ready for the taking.

Close to seven feet tall, and with arms as thick as my legs, he was a giant of a creature. But it was the cold, predatory light in his eyes that gave me real pause.

In an instant, I knew he must be one of the rogue shifters folks had been yapping about. If size meant anything, then he unquestionably had to be a bear.

At least he was only one man, though. With the fresh feeling of strength pulsing through my veins, I was oddly confident I could get away from him.

Hell, he didn't have shoes on.

Or pants.

No way he'd be able to chase me through the thick underbrush without cutting up his feet. Or maybe dislocating his hip when that monster cock of his started swaying.

"Well now," he said, his voice deep and gravelly, with a strong redneck lilt to it. Even over the smoke of the distant fires, I could smell the harsh chemical tang of bourbon. "Lookie what we got here, Mike."

"Mm-mmm." Another voice, with the same raspy hint of danger in it, sounded from behind me, sending my heart into overdrive. "A li'l ol' lone wolf. What you doin' all the way out here on your lonesome, little man? Everyone knows wolves are pack animals. Why, one wolf on they own is 'bout as useful as a paper umbrella."

I dared not turn around, but the way the second man's heat washed over my back told me there was every chance he, too, was naked. I closed my eyes as that guy flicked at my ears and ruffled my hair, like a cat playing with a mouse. "So? Why you out here all on your lonesome, fur-ball?"

"Don't call me a fur-ball." Instinct told me I should keep my strengths secret. "I'm no wolf."

The big guy in front of me scratched at his head, the movement echoed in the jiggling of his thick, somehow threatening, penis. He moved his head around, sniffing and sneering. I could hear the other one, Mike, doing the same. He spoke first, again making me jump.

"What you got, Walt?"

"Fuck, I can't tell. Damn smoke. Can't smell anything else."

"Well, maybe you shoulda been more careful with them joints you were smokin' back there, dickwad. Half the fires are your fuckin' fault."

"Screw you." Captain Cockwobble stepped right up to me, so tall my vision was filled with just belly and chest. Until he ducked and sniffed again. "Yeah, I can't tell. You sure you ain't wolf?"

"I'm human, and proud of it."

The big one in front of me—Walt—stepped back, his eyes wide and his hands up as if I'd pulled out a gun. "Woah... you're human?"

"Uh-huh."

"Damn. Hear that, Mike?"

"Yeah."

Clint scratched his chin. "You know what scares us about humans, boy?"

"N–no."

Mike snaked his arm around my neck from behind, almost cutting off my air. "Not one single fuckin' thing."

Walt bent his face right down to mine, his hot, wet breath coating my skin. "Well now, if you're human, then you must be the one we're here lookin' for. Ain't ya? Roddick's little bitch boy."

"Screw you. I'm a fucking diva. You're

the bitch boys.”

“Yeah. You’re the one, for sure. They said you’d be here in the forest.”

“What the fuck? Who said? Who are you assholes?”

Mike tightened his arm around my throat, completely blocking my airway. He released it a moment later but the message was pretty clear. It was a demonstration of what he could do, if he wanted.

At first, panic overtook my brain. I tightened up, my pulse raced, and adrenaline had its way with me. It wouldn’t have mattered if these guys were regular old humans; I’d still stand no chance against their strength.

Physical power was not my answer.

Maybe talk would do it.

“What did you mean, you were looking for me? I’m nobody.”

“Shut it. A mouth like yours is only good for one thing.”

Walt guffawed right into my face. “One thing at a time, anyways.”

Mike dug his thumb into the center of my back. “And don’t go thinkin’ we won’t just ’cause you’re a guy.”

Walt gave me a light slap on the face.

"I ain't had any pussy in months. I'll take ass instead. Ain't too proud to fuckin' wreck you, bitch boy."

Okay, so clearly talk was useless, and against two men this huge, I didn't have the muscle to back up any fight I might start. So, I closed my eyes and centered myself as quickly as I could. All I really had was the possibility of surprise. These guys were strong as fuck but dulled by alcohol and weed.

I threw my arms upward and wrapped my hands around the back of Mike's neck. A split-second later, I hauled my feet off the ground.

The speedy shift of my weight worked beautifully, pulling Mike down and forward. As I headed for the ground, I kicked my feet out, catching that big, flopping dick of Walt's right in its heart. As he bent double in pain, his head slammed into Mike's, and the two of them roared with pain.

Mike's grip around my throat loosened, and as I hit the ground, I rolled to the side, breaking free from the grip of that mighty arm, and scrambling to my feet.

"Ethan!"

I'd barely finished yelling his name when one of the bears clipped my foot, tripping me over. Knowing I was too far gone to save myself, I spun so I could land on my back and be ready for whatever came.

What came was a huge man I didn't recognize. Had to be Mike. I curled my legs back against my chest, ready to lash out. The big guy lumbered straight at me, like he knew for sure I couldn't hurt him that way. As he towered over my prone form I kicked at him, but he simply caught my feet and rolled me over onto my belly.

The impact knocked most of the breath from my lungs. The big asshole drove the rest of it out when he landed on my back.

His stinking breath poured over my shoulder, but rather than recoil, I spun my head toward the source of it, bringing my elbow up at the same time and slamming it into the side of his head, hard enough that he groaned and rolled off to the side.

Still fighting to fill my lungs, I clambered back to my feet. I couldn't call Ethan again until I had air to use, but I thought his name as hard as I possibly could.

Before I could run back toward the road, a massive hand grabbed me from behind, the thick fingers latching onto my t-shirt and yanking back, tearing it from my body.

"Little fuckin' bitch boy." It was Walt again. He got his fist in my hair and pulled so hard my feet slid out from under me, and I landed on my ass for the third time. I stared up into the ice of his eyes. He was bent over, still with his fist in my hair. "You fuckin' see how this is going down? Two of us, both bears. And you, just a lowly little human—"

"Wait, Walt." Mike had come up behind me. He seized me by the neck and bent me forward over my own legs. "Look at that."

He dug an elbow-sized finger into my shoulder. The one Ethan had marked.

Walt hissed. "You lyin' little queen. You said you was human. Fuck, they told us you was."

"I am." I swallowed my fear. "Wait, who told you?"

"It was—"

"Hey!" Walt cut right across his

buddy. "It was Father fuckin' Christmas. Asked us to check you were still a naughty boy."

Damn.

Mike had been about to tell me.

"But why? What's in it for you?"

Walt pulled me up by the hair. "A thousand bucks buys a lot of hooch. And a lot of cooch. I'd rat on my own mother for half that."

I winced through the pain in my scalp. "Who the hell would pay you so little, just to attack me? What the hell have I done?"

"Bitch boy, I don't know and I don't care. 'Cause now it turns out you're a wolf, and the price just doubled."

"I keep telling you, I'm not a wolf." I couldn't tell anymore if I was trying to convince them... or myself.

"Then what the fuck is this? Huh?" As Mike barked out the words he twisted his fat finger in Ethan's bite mark, the bear shifter's rough skin and sharp nail biting into me. "That's the mark of a wolf."

"No, it's the mark of a psycho idiot who thinks stupid stuff happens."

Mike looked over at Walt. "It's still

fresh. He's wolf, but he ain't never shifted."

"I keep telling you. I'm not a wolf. I just happened to fuck a guy who turns into one. He got a little toothy, that's all."

Mike roared with laughter. "You simple little turd. Don't you understand what that bite means? Like it or not, you're a fuckin' wolf now. Which is just gonna make this more fun."

"Yeah. I like prey what fights back." Walt rolled me onto my front and pulled my ass into the air. "They squeeze so fuckin' tight when they struggle."

I tried to lift myself off the ground, but Mike pushed down on my shoulders with all his hefty weight. As much as I wanted to fight, to escape, it was all I could do just to tug tiny breaths into my lungs.

The moment Walt's huge paws hooked into my jeans, I tightened up across my whole body. I tried to call out, in frustration, in fear, just a call for help, but there was barely enough air in my lungs to make a whimper.

No! No!

It sounded so loud in my head, but it wasn't even a whisper in my throat. The only sound was the shriek of stitches parting as Walt tore the denim of my jeans, ripping everything away and baring my ass.

Before I could make sense of the moment, Mike's weight suddenly shifted off my shoulders, and Walt swore loudly. When I raised my head, I saw the reason.

A huge, gray wolf.

And without ever having seen him in this form, I knew immediately who it was.

Ethan!

CHAPTER TWENTY-EIGHT

Ethan

I'D ALMOST HAD him, outside my parents' house. The link between my mate and me was ridiculously strong, despite being so new. It had called to me like a beacon.

And when Gabriel—my mate—turned and ran, I was ready to follow. As strong as he would be with his new wolf abilities, I knew I was stronger and, more importantly, faster.

But as always, my mother had other ideas.

"Ethan, stop."

As she came down the front steps, I swore I could see a jaunty little skip in her step. She grabbed my arm before I could avoid her.

"Let me go, Olga." There was no way I'd ever call her mother again.

"Son, you're being completely irrational. Can't you see it's over?"

"Oh, it is, is it?" I flipped my arm out of her grip and rounded on her so quickly she stumbled backward. "So, how do you explain the fact he has my mark?"

"H–he what?"

"That's right, Olga. Last night, I made things official. He has my mark... because he's my mate." Somehow, the truth of it all became much more potent in that moment, and I simply couldn't wait any longer to chase Gabriel down and claim him back.

"Oh, no." Olga lifted her cell phone and hit redial, her hand shaking worse than I'd had ever seen it before. "This can't be."

More than anything, I wanted to let my wolf loose, and direct him straight at this woman before me. Instead, I let loose my disgust and rage on her cell phone, slapping it out of her grip and smashing it with my foot. "It is. And you can just get the fuck over it."

The momentary catharsis of inflicting damage was enough to satisfy my wolf's bloodlust, at least for the moment. My only focus now was to get to Gabriel, and do everything I could to make things right with him.

With all the smoke haze filling the forest, I couldn't track him, either with human eyes or wolf nose. So, I simply opened my mind and let it lead me.

In seconds, I had a good feel for my mate's presence. He wasn't far... but somehow, I knew he wasn't safe, either.

The moment I heard him call out my name, I leapt into action and sprinted toward the sound. My wolf growled within, but until I knew what I was up against, I resisted the urge to shift. I'd grown rusty with it after years of suppression and I already knew the worst thing in the world was to be stuck with paws when only hands would do.

I could really use the extra senses, though. The fires were nowhere near us, but the smell of smoke hung heavy in the air. It was possible Gabriel had simply sprained his ankle. But until I had him in my arms again, I couldn't trust that he'd ever be safe.

A deep ursine howl of pain off to my left gave me both a direction to head, and an urgent reason to sprint.

He was not alone.

He was not safe.

My mate needed me.

And though I fought it with every rushed breath, the memories that thought conjured were impossible to ignore.

I tore away my shirt as I ran, knowing my jeans would come loose by themselves. Lupine hips were far more slender than human.

I found him just as the huge guy flipped him over. The fact those two had even got him onto the ground sent a bolt of incendiary anger through my core.

They think they can touch my mate?

Hurt him?

Rusty be damned. That fiery rage fed my wolf and in seconds, I'd shifted. Just in time to see the big bear rip his clothing away.

For a moment, the world was stuck in molasses. Every second seemed to take a minute. I pushed my human into sleep mode and thrust my wolf right into the driver's seat. And it reminded me exactly what was so wonderful about the animal kingdom.

No reasoning.

No bargaining.

No fucking mercy.

The one with his filthy hands on Gabriel's shoulders was closer. I ran noiselessly and leapt straight at the bastard, taking him around the neck in a vise grip. There were no words strong enough to describe my anger, and no wolf would understand the language anyway.

I snarled as I speared my teeth into the tender skin. The guy bugged his eyes, clearly expecting death any second.

But despite my unhinged rage, I couldn't completely push my human side down. Especially that damn oath I'd taken about preserving life.

"Ethan!"

The dread in Gabriel's voice was everything. I released my mouthful and turned, just in time to duck away from the enormous hairy paw the other guy had swung at me.

Bear shifters.

With the smoke and my mate's peril, the scent had escaped me. And if these two were typical of their kind then I could, for once, sympathize with his parents' disgust.

With only a moment to spare, I raised my head and howled. We were a good distance from town, but there was always a chance someone would have their ears on. I at least had to try calling for help. When I finished, I locked my eyes on my mate's.

Run, Gabriel.

I thought it as hard as I could, even glancing off to the side, in the direction of the town. Hoping he'd get the hint. I knew I could buy him enough time so he could at least get to the road, but one wolf against two bears was never going to end in my favor. As long as I could save my mate, though, it would be more than worth it.

I ran straight at the big bear, ducking another wild swing and diving between the guy's hind legs. As I slid to a halt, I turned and drove my fangs into the back of my foe's thigh.

Already fighting for balance, the bear

swiped at me, succeeding only in falling onto his side. By that time, the other one had shifted. He wasn't as big, but he was still plenty big enough. He dropped to all fours and ran at me, teeth bared and tongue flailing.

In desperation, I released the fallen guy's leg and ran forward again, right up the big, hairy back. I leapt over the top of the approaching bear, catching him by surprise. As I landed, the bear overbalanced and slammed heavily on his back, giving me a chance to get a little distance.

I'd made sure to move the action farther away from where Gabriel had been, so he could make his escape even better. What I hadn't expected was to see him still standing there, naked, a thick branch in his hands. He held it like a baseball bat and cocked it, ready to swing, every time one of the bears moved.

For a moment, I lost myself in the vision. My perfect mate, my hard-bodied, soulful singer, ready to take a losing fight all the way to its conclusion. And for the first time, I could admit to myself that this was beyond any kind of love I'd felt before. That this transcended simple compatibility of mind and deliciousness of scent. This was the kind of love that everyone assumed was lust. Because it hit fast, and it hit hard, and it was fucking eternal.

I was pulled from my reverie by a different kind of hard hit. The boss bear had fought his way back to his feet and slammed his huge paw into my neck, knocking me half way across the clearing. When I struggled back upright, my guts clenched, seeing the massive beast charging straight at Gabriel. To my terror, I saw the other bear coming in from the side.

I snarled with pure venom, shooting forward, hoping to grab the big one before he could get his teeth or claws into my mate, but the blow to my neck made movement hard.

Like I'd been sedated.

My heart froze as both beasts stood, ready to fall onto Gabriel. And as hard as I ran, as desperate as I felt, I was powerless to stop it.

I expected the next sound to be Gabriel's flesh tearing, and his beautiful voice screaming. Instead, there was a thick sounding clunk, like a golf club striking a ball, only played at one-quarter speed. And when the big beast fell, it was not on top of Gabriel, but off to the side, taking out the other bear in a moment of sweet serendipity.

My heart filled with love and pride as I saw my sexy fighter still standing there, the branch in his hands now only a stub, the rest of it broken away from the powerful blow he'd delivered to the big bear's head.

It was only a moment of peace, though. That impact would have killed a man, but all it did was slow the bears down for a few seconds. I leapt forward and placed myself between the danger and my mate.

There was no chance I could beat them.

There was no way I'd give in.

I took a second to turn to Gabriel and whine at him, desperate for him to run back to town, to save himself. But either he didn't understand, or he was as stubborn as a tired bull. With all that hot Latin blood, I was more willing to believe the second.

"It's okay, Ethan."

I yapped sharply in reply.

No. Go.

"We got this, butt-face."

I could hear the fatigue in his voice, and took an extra second to lick his leg. He responded with a lightning fast scratch behind the ears.

And then he was falling to the side, a sharp yell of pain firing from his throat. I nuzzled in at his side, suddenly scenting fresh blood.

Gabriel had his hands pressed to his belly, where deep crimson fluid was gushing out.

No!

I turned and bared my fangs, but before I could even snarl, the smaller bear had his mouth on the back of my neck, and sank his teeth in. For all my strength, I was suddenly powerless. The bear stood, clenching his prize, as I writhed and fought to no avail.

The next sensation was a pile-driver punch to the belly, mixed with the cold agony of long claws spearing into my flesh. I yelped and froze, a tiny part of my human consciousness telling me not to make the damage worse by struggling.

Or shifting, like Clinton had.

The bear took the chance to pull his teeth from my neck, securing me instead with both front paws.

From the moment I'd heard Gabriel's first desperate cry, I had been prepared to give my life to save his. My own death, though, would mean nothing if he lost his life, too.

The bear grunted and shook, as though the earth was quaking beneath his feet. I bent my head back, hoping I could at least land a couple of bites and go down swinging.

But what I saw filled me with surprise and pride. There, on the bear's back, fisting its fur, was Gabriel. The bear shrugged as if trying to dislodge him, but he held on and clambered higher. A moment later, he had the bear's ear grasped in one hand, and with the other he raised a foot-long stick.

Not even the slightest hesitation showed in his face as he speared that stick into the bear's other ear, driving it deep into the canal and causing him to scream with agony and fling me away.

The moment of triumph ended almost as soon as it began. When I landed I looked back, only to see the bigger bear swipe at Gabriel, tearing deep lacerations into the flesh of his thigh and sending him thudding to the ground again.

His scream hurt me worse than any of the blows or puncture wounds. I clambered to my feet and limped across to my mate, standing over his traumatized form and growling up into the faces of both bears. I snapped at one, then the other, as they moved in for the kill.

CHAPTER TWENTY-NINE

Gabriel

I'D NEVER KNOWN pain like this. And not the physical damage I'd suffered. None of the ragged tears in my skin mattered at all. It was the agony of having found Ethan—found the man who ticked every damn box—only to immediately be facing death, lying on the floor of the forest, bleeding out. That hurt me more than every other heartbreak in my life combined.

The past few days had been a torture of emotions. The ones I hadn't wanted to feel, and the ones I'd never known I could.

Like a spicy meal, where the pain is pleasure.

My head was a helium balloon, and I could barely squeeze my hand closed over the deep wounds in my belly. The gashes on my legs were seeping blood, and I knew it was over. Ethan's belly ran with blood, too, yet he stood over me, fighting to his last breath.

I plowed my fingers into the fur on his back, my final desire to be skin-to-skin with my mate when my life ended.

As my vision dimmed, I lay back on the undergrowth and sighed. My face was wet, and I couldn't tell if it was blood or tears.

From one side at first, then seemingly all around me, I heard the light crackling of leaves underfoot. Then, in what felt like an explosion of sound, suddenly there were wolves standing beside me, over me. I opened my eyes and counted at least six of them, including Ethan. A pure black one, a pure white one, and a few combinations of the two. Their snarling became a roar, like machine gun fire, and it had the bears backing away rapidly.

I recognized Kiera in the mix, and then smiled as I let my head fall back to the ground. The bears were backed up against a couple of trees, and the six wolves—even the badly wounded Ethan—closed in for what I assumed would be the kill.

The bigger bear stood, looking around himself, and then slipped around the wide tree trunk. The smaller bear went the other way, and the two of them loped off into the forest, each with three wolves on their stubby tails.

A moment passed while I lay still, waiting for the bliss of sleep, knowing I'd never wake from it. I looked up into the beautiful blue of the sky, and the patterning of green from the trees. The bears and wolves had moved far away, and my senses were dulled enough, that I felt nothing but peace.

Then my wolf filled my vision. Ethan lapped at my cheek, and fell beside me, partly on me, and whined at me like a lost puppy would. I scratched him behind the ears again and smiled, hoping he could see me.

I had a blue sky on a warm day. I had a soft place to lie. I had the man-wolf I loved more than life itself wrapped around me.

With nothing left to do, I opened my mouth.

And I sang.

CHAPTER THIRTY

Ethan

I SOAKED UP the perfection of his scent. His skin filled my senses, his breath was beauty. I licked at his neck and he laughed, a sound made weak from trauma.

Then the rich copper scent of his blood hit me anew. The blood I'd only ever scented through his skin before, now leaking from his wounded body.

The seed of my human mind was buried deep under the skin of wolf senses. Gabe's wounds were severe, but unless I could shift, I couldn't tell how bad. And I certainly couldn't do anything for him without my hands.

If I licked his wounds I could help them close, but I could do nothing for the damage inside them. That would only make things worse.

I closed my eyes and pictured how I looked as a man. Tried to hold the image of myself from looking in the mirror. But just like when I tried to order myself to sleep, the harder I searched for my humanity, the deeper it hid.

Gabriel ran his fingers into my fur and scratched at me. A ball of anger filled my belly and chest, which only drove the man inside me further into the darkness.

Rage fed only my wolf; it starved my human.

My only solace was that there was every chance we'd die together. To lose my companion once had been hard enough. But if that bitch they called Fate killed my true mate, then I knew I'd die soon after. I would have no will to live.

Gabriel held me close, and to my surprise, he started singing. Just a light crooning, a sweet little melody made irresistible by the sexy rasping of his voice. It was so soft I doubted a regular human would hear it, but it was a symphony to my wolf ears.

I closed my eyes and lay my head on his chest, letting the music of his song and his body fill me. My rage at the unfairness of life eased away from me, and I slowed my breathing, ready for whatever came after.

I took comfort from the sensation of Gabriel still moving beneath me. The cool of the ground against my skin. The soft feel of my mate's nails, scratching against the smooth skin of my back.

I sat bolt upright as the truth hit me. Gabriel's voice had worked its magic again.

I'd shifted without even realizing.

"Gabe!" I patted his face and he stirred, looking up at me through half-closed eyes.

"Hey there, butt-face. Thought I'd never see you again."

"Wait here a second."

"Please?" The edge of panic in his voice nearly sliced me in two. "Don't leave me."

"If I don't, you'll die."

"And if you do?"

"You might not."

He swallowed, and a fresh stream of tears ran from his eyes. "Then stay. Let me die in your arms."

"No!" I didn't mean to scare him, but he had to understand how vital it was. "I will be back in ten seconds."

I pried his hand loose from my hair and ran as quickly as my wounds allowed, back to where his cast-off jeans had landed. Wadding them up as I ran, I made it back to his side and pressed the bundle to his belly.

"I'm so sorry, Gabe. This is going to hurt like hell."

I hooked my arms under his frame and lifted him, pressing the wadded jeans into the lacerations on my own belly, and held him hard against myself, trying to staunch both wounds in one hit.

Gabriel winced, but didn't cry out, filling me with a fresh burst of pride for my sexy warrior.

My wounds were almost as bad as his, but there was no thought of rest or recovery. My only stop on the journey back to town was to gather up my shirt and tie it across Gabriel's thigh wound.

I kept walking, one foot after the other, maintaining only a vague sense of time passing. My consciousness threatened to fade time and time again. It was only when I wandered onto the road in front of a passing car that I realized I'd reached the town.

I was too dazed to even register the identity of the driver, but thankfully, whoever it was had no problem helping out. Together, we bundled Gabriel across the back seat. The driver grabbed her cell phone and called ahead to the hospital.

I slid in beside my mate, cradling his head as I grasped his hand. "Hold on, Gabe. This will be a rough ride."

CHAPTER THIRTY-ONE

Gabriel

HE WAS RIGHT. It was a hell of a drive back to town. I kept drifting lower, toward the blackness of sleep, only to be pulled back into some form of consciousness by Ethan asking me questions.

"Gabe, what's your blood type?"

"Uh..."

"Please, baby."

My mouth felt like socks. Not the cute little toe socks in the pretty colors. More kind of, like, the ones where you had a little bobble thing up around the heel. I maybe still had a pair of those back home for when I felt like being whimsical and more of a diva than usual. Something like a canary yellow, or a peach. But no, actually, my mouth didn't feel like those socks. More like a basketball player with athlete's—

"Gabriel. Stay with me."

"Hunh?"

"Your blood type?"

"Uh... A positive?"

"Are you asking me or telling me?"

"Sweet. Thanks."

A minute later, or maybe an hour, we came to a screeching halt. I heard his voice, and a couple of others, but they were speaking in some weird language, and it was all buzzing and hissing. Maybe I'd been kidnapped by aliens.

Hell, if there were shifters, why couldn't there be aliens?

The car door opened and a hundred hands grabbed me, hauling me from the back seat. I seemed to be flying for a moment before landing on a skinny little bed. A bed that rolled. The sky was falling. Or maybe just moving. Then lights and darkness and lights and darkness and...

Nothing.

CHAPTER THIRTY-TWO

Ethan

I CAME OUT of my anesthesia haze, looking around the hospital ward. I prodded weakly at the thick bandaging on my belly, satisfied everything was up to my standard.

It took me a moment to realize Kiera was there, sitting beside my bed. She smiled when she noticed I was awake.

"Hey, you big lump."

"Killa."

She stood and kissed my forehead. "We thought we might lose you."

Suddenly, my memory cleared.

Watching my mate being taken into surgery, and being unable to control any part of it, had been an absolute torture. I recalled how my rage had threatened to overtake me again, and if not for my own urgent need for medical attention, I might have shifted. Just to process the fierceness of my anger.

"Gabriel!"

"Shh. It's all good. He's a strong one, our boy."

My heart soared at the confirmation he was still alive. "When can I see him?"

"Soon. He's asleep."

"I didn't ask when he could see me."

"Hey, doofus. Don't bite my head off. I have orders to keep you here in your bed."

I closed my eyes and let a wry smile run over my lips for a second. "Well, I'm afraid to tell you, but I'm not a pet dog." I sat up and narrowed my eyes, feeling the ecstatic lupine rush I remembered from so long ago. "I'm a damn wolf."

"Well, Mister Wolf, we have doctors here, too, you know. Not the high-falutin' fancy-pants Chicago surgeon kind, but they know their stuff."

I struggled to slide my damaged body

off the bed, but Kiera pushed me back down. With far more ease than I'd have liked.

"You're killing me, here, cuz."

"Look, you're much better to stay here. My parents are in the waiting room, but the bad news is, so are yours."

"I can handle them."

"Ethan, there's more. Those guys?"

"The bears?"

"Uh-huh. We ran 'em down real quick. You shoulda seen my mom in full flight. Anyway, turns out those big idiots were nothing more than mercenary bullies. Took my dad all of ten seconds to get them talking once they shifted back." She chuckled without any humor. "One of them was real sorry. He had a stick in his ear when he shifted. Poor bastard will never hear on that side again."

I squeezed the blankets in my fists. "Nothing they said is of any interest to me. They touched my mate. And they were about to..." I swallowed my mounting fury as I remembered the scene.

Gabriel, naked and wounded.

That big fucking brute with his meaty

hands on his tight, scrumptious ass.

"Those opportunistic pricks."

"See, that's the thing." Kiera walked over to the door of the ward, as if getting out of my reach. And maybe blocking my exit. "Like I said, they were mercenaries. It wasn't random. They were hired."

***

The Larsons and the Roddicks all looked up in shock as I limped into the waiting room, fresh blood seeping from the puncture wounds of the IV line I'd torn out.

"You two." I lined my parents up in my sights. "You tell me now. The truth."

Hugh stood and folded his arms. "The truth about what, son?"

"You're behind this? You tried to have my mate killed?"

Olga Roddick scoffed and turned back to the magazine on her lap. "Please, son. You're being so dramatic." She flipped a couple of pages.

Hugh stepped in again. "We only told them to scare him off."

"So, the rape and murder which I only just managed to prevent? What, that was their bonus?"

Olga sighed. "That's what happens when you send a bear to do a wolf's job..." She stood, finally, and walked toward me, arms outspread. "We only want what's best. Now, let's just put this all behind us, son."

In my peripheral vision, Ethan saw Kiera walk over to the waiting room entrance to intercept the two men who were about to enter.

"Oh, I agree on one count, you cold-hearted bitch. This is all behind us now. You have your world, and I have mine. Let's make sure the two never mix again. I know how you feel about keeping things pure, after all."

"Son, you don't mean that. Come meet with Anthea. Properly this time."

I spat my voice out through gritted teeth. "My final reminder, Mrs Roddick. You do not get to call me son. Not now. Not ever. Now, rather than having me meet Anthea, I think you should turn around and meet these two gentlemen."

She spun instantly, almost running into the uniformed police officers who'd crept up behind her as only shifters can.

Olga turned back to face me. For a moment, she stood before me, unmoving. The whole waiting room fell silent. Then, for the first time I could recall, I saw tears in my mother's eyes.

"This is so typical of you, you stupid human-lover. We had a new mate for you. The right kind. Wolf."

"My mate is waiting for me down that corridor."

"He'll never be wolf."

I crossed my arms, and let my mouth curl up into a satisfied smile. "Oh, but I told you before... he already is." I snapped my teeth together to ram home the truth.

Olga's face drained of color as she processed that little reminder. She narrowed her eyes in rage for a moment, and then brought herself back under control.

"Well, I knew it would end badly with you, Ethan. I always wanted a daughter, anyway."

"Hey, I fuck men. Isn't that close enough?" The rush I got from being so damn dismissive was almost as heady as anything I felt with Gabriel.

Almost.

Olga spun away, as if in shame. Whether it was over her own actions, or over the actions of her flesh and blood, wasn't clear. And to me, it mattered less than a dead mosquito.

With my parents gone, my anger fell away, too. All I felt was weak. I turned as freely as I could and reached out for Kiera. Bernard Larson stepped in on the other side and together they supported me.

"Take me to him, please?"

Bernard shook his head. "Son, you need medical attention."

"Just for a minute. I know he's alive. Even if Kiera hadn't told me, I'd know. I can feel it. But I need to see him for myself."

CHAPTER THIRTY-THREE

Gabriel

TWO DAYS HAD passed since the attack. At least, that's what they'd told me. And I hadn't seen Ethan once in that time. When I'd first awoken, my immediate thought was that maybe he didn't make it, but before that idea could even gather speed, my wolf stepped in. I could feel the truth, without being told. Ethan was alive. And even more importantly, he was close.

My consciousness was still as random as hell. I faded in and out for another day or so.

When the darkness inside my head finally cleared, I struggled to sit up, to look around me. Before I could even open my eyes, strong hands gripped mine. At the moment of skin-to-skin contact, I knew for certain it was Ethan.

"Hey, butt-face."

"Little one. Welcome back."

Gradually, I managed to focus on those silver eyes of his, and a fresh burst of heat ran through my body. "Shouldn't you be in bed, too?"

"Hey, at least buy me a drink first."

My laughter soon turned to coughing. "Don't do that to me, asshole. You know what I meant." I pointed at the bandaging on his belly.

"I know, but by your side is the only place I want to be, lover." He pushed his point home by raising my hand to his lips for the softest of kisses.

I vaguely remembered being pissed at him. I even remembered what caused it. None of that mattered anymore.

I pressed my hand gently to his cheek, and soaked up the look of peace that crossed his face. "They tell me I probably would've died if... if I'd still been human."

Ethan bowed his head, as if picturing exactly that. "Probably."

"So, do I get to know what it was all for? Why we were almost killed?"

Ethan sighed heavily. "You won't like it."

"Hey, fangs and claws may break my jaws, but words will never hurt me." I caught the look in Ethan's eyes and felt my insides ice up. "What? Who were those guys?"

Ethan shook his head. "They were just guys. A couple of rogues, doing what they were paid for. They're locked up now and probably will be for a while."

Clear thinking was still difficult, and I rubbed my fingers on the back of Ethan's hand while I formed the words. "You know, butt-face, I'm gonna get the rest of the info out of you one way or another. I always do. You might as well just tell me."

He lowered his gaze, studying my fingers, my arm. Apparently, anything other than looking me in the face.

"It was my parents. You didn't fit into their planning." He zeroed back in on my eyes. "But I think you probably knew that already."

I did, but even so, it still cut like crazy. To think anyone could be so cold, and so out of touch with their own child, went against every instinct I had ever felt. If we were ever lucky enough to adopt kids, I'd just have to follow the lessons of my own family. Except the part about being killed when they were young.

Before they died, my parents had been hard when it came to discipline, but they'd never once turned me away from any of my dreams. All they ever demanded was that I make it count, or else give it up. I realized only now that I'd failed at that before Ethan came into my life.

And that he was exactly what I needed to live my life completely fulfilled.

Ethan sounded close to tears when he spoke again. "I mean, they claim it was a scare tactic. That the bears simply didn't know when to stop." He swallowed before continuing. "But to think my own flesh and blood would go so far to get you out of my life is beyond contemptible. I'm so sorry, little one."

"Hey. You don't apologize for what anyone else did." I fought against the pain and fatigue, getting myself upright and wrapping my arms around Ethan's neck. "Don't forget. You saved me, butt-face."

"God, you saved me so much more, Gabe. And not just from the bears." He kissed my shoulder and grasped my hand, placing it to the center of his chest. "You made me whole, little one. And I can't wait to spend the rest of my life with you."

My belly tingled at the thought, and I knew it was more than simple excitement. "And there's someone else who can't wait to sink his teeth into you, too."

He released me and looked deep into my eyes. "You can feel your wolf?"

"Uh-huh."

Ethan placed his hand on my chest, mirroring what he'd done with my own hand. "I can't wait to meet him."

"You're not scared? You know, that you'll get stuck with four legs instead of two?"

His smile bloomed inside me. "Nothing scares me when I'm with you, little one." He cupped my head in his hands and kissed me on the nose.

"Except the thought of losing you."

"As soon as we're out of here, we're taking this thing to the next level, Ethan."

"Oh? And what level is that?"

"The rest of our lives. As man and... wolf."

THE END

Thank you for reading the Gray Vale Pack series. I hope you enjoyed these romantic shifter tales, and who knows, perhaps in the future we will see more of the growly men of Gray Vale and Stoke Ridge in the other delicious paranormal romance stories my mind is sure to deliver.

In the meantime, if you enjoyed this book, please do me a favor and leave me a review. I do read them, and even a few positive words will help me in crafting more of the books my readers love.
Thank you!
~Evie Riley

For a Preview of Shattered, From The
Edge, Book One, all you need to do is
turn the page...

PREVIEW

Jimmy

The sound of the final bell going off had never sounded sweeter to me than right this moment. I had a love for school, but that last class in the day, political science, could really drag on for centuries. Some days, like today, it took all of my strength just to keep my eyes physically open. I quickly got the hell out of there and made my way toward my locker. Being eighteen and a senior in high school came with a good batch of mixed feelings. Sadness, because the school you had spent the past four years in, growing up in, was no longer going to be in your life. All of the teachers and friends you had made along the way weren't going to be sitting next to you at lunch or making you laugh in the library just to upset the world's crankiest librarian. It was a piece of your life that was finishing and it was bittersweet because your future was waiting for you right around the corner. For me, my future was waiting for me six blocks from here, at my part-time job.

I hastily said goodbye to the people I knew in the hallway as I made my way out of the building. I had to get to my work so I wouldn't be late. I had made a habit of never being late for work and I was not about to start now.

Working at the diner wasn't fascinating, and it didn't help me with my art, but it paid me every two weeks and that money went toward art supplies and my savings for when I went off to college in the fall. Plus, working at the diner was not that bad. There were certainly worse part-time jobs I could be doing. In a city like Gaithersburg, Maryland you still had that small town feel, even though there was a decent size population, just under sixty thousand. Most would find that small, but when you think about how some cities only have a couple thousand people, I would say Gaithersburg was a decent size.

With that small town feel, though, you still had people with small town beliefs, like religion, politics, and sexual orientation. Two out of the three you could easily hide, but the sexual orientation part was a bit harder. Eventually, someone would notice you holding the hand of someone that was the same gender as you. Don't get me wrong, there were a lot of forward thinking people. A lot of accepting people who didn't care who you loved as long as you were happy. It was those people that got someone like me, a gay teenager, through the harder days.

My parents are some of those people. They are truly amazing. I'd been such a nervous wreck when I'd decided to come out to them when I was fourteen. I'd been terrified with how they would react. They'd always been supportive of me where my art was concerned, but I also knew it was one thing to accept that your son was never going to be a football player and another that he was gay. They had taken it like a dream.

I was all prepared for a big showdown. I'd practiced what I was going to say to them and I was prepared for any argument they were going to throw my way. All of my hard work was wasted when my mom just simply said they knew and asked what I wanted for dinner. I had gone in fully prepared that my parents were going to be shocked. Only for the tables to be turned, leaving me the one that was stunned stupid in the living room.

All of my stress and worrying had been for nothing, absolutely nothing. I was so shocked and ecstatic that I went to school the very next day and told my friend Danny all about it. He had wanted to tell his parents about being gay, but he was really worried with how religious they were. He finally told them earlier this year. Only it didn't go over so well.

He'd called me that night crying his eyes out because his parents had kicked him out. All he had left was his backpack and a single duffle bag with his clothes and personal belongings. They completely threw him out without even a second thought about where he would go. I had immediately told him to come to my house and my parents both agreed that he could stay with us if he couldn't stay with his older brother who had his own apartment in town.

Thankfully, Danny's brother was not a jerk and had been pissed at his parents for kicking out his kid brother. Danny moved in with him and never had to hide who he was again. Neither of them have spoken to their parents since that night and I doubted they ever would.

That night, though, gave me a whole new level of respect for Danny. He had shown some true courage to tell his parents and then when they forced him to leave, he didn't try and put the genie back into the bottle. He held his head up high and became a proud gay kid. It was only proof to how strong he was and I couldn't have been more proud of him.

The aroma of the diner welcomed me as I stepped through the door for my shift. Most would find it gross, I suppose, but to me it smelled like the fifties. I can't explain it, but the odor from the grill with the eggs, the sweet sugar smell of waffles, the rich scent of brewed coffee, it always reminded me of poodle skirts and really bad hairstyles. I

t didn't look like the fifties, but the Main Street Diner had been here since then. The one wall to the left of the diner was covered in photos from the past eight decades. They weren't organized at all, either, just thrown up where there was a spot. The owner, Anthony Blackstone, had taken over the diner from his father. It had been in their generation since the very first day. They were a pillar in the community and everyone still came here, even with some of the National chain restaurants just down the street. You just couldn't beat the food here, especially for breakfast.

"Hey, Sal, how are you?" I called to one of my regulars.

He was a very sweet seventy-year-old man who used to come here with his wife. They had been married for forty years before he lost her to cancer two years ago. They used to come here every Thursday night to have date night. They had their first date right here in the diner almost fifty years ago. Every Thursday, they would come in and sit in the same booth every single time. We would make sure no one sat in it before they had the chance to get here.

Sal had been coming here after her death, still. He would sit in the same spot and place her framed photograph across from him. It sounded really sad, I know, but to him it was his way of still having their date night together.

He once told me that there were many days where he missed her so much it hurt, but when he came to the diner for their date night, he felt connected to her. The pain didn't hurt so much and he truly believed that she was sitting in that booth seat right across from him. It was the sweetest thing I had ever heard, still to this day.

I didn't know if I believed in spirits or not, but what I did know is that I hoped it was true. I hoped that Martha was sitting right there in that booth with Sal, spending time together until they could be reunited again.

"I'm still moving, Jim," Sal said, flashing a toothless grin.

"I'm happy to hear that. This place wouldn't be the same without you, Sal."

I made my way toward the back room so I could drop my coat and bag off. I was hoping it might be a little dead tonight so I could get a jump start on my homework. Dead was never good for tips, but it did allow me to get my homework done before getting home, allowing me the time to relax and watch a couple episodes of my favorite show before I would have to go to sleep.

After clocking in, I made my way behind the counter and gave Stella a big smile. "Hey good looking, how's it been?" I asked.

In her thirties now, Stella had been working here for ten years. She'd dropped out of high school at sixteen when she got pregnant. Her boyfriend at the time was a high school senior and he took off right after graduation before their daughter was even born. She came from a single mother, who kicked her out once she discovered that she was pregnant. Stella didn't let it get to her, though. She persevered and she created a life for her daughter. She had been working odd jobs for the first four years before she was given the opportunity to work here full-time. Mr. Blackstone was really good with her and even gave her health benefits for her daughter after she had worked here for six months. Stella had been eternally grateful to Mr. Blackstone and as a result, she always came into work and even worked extra shifts if they had no one to cover. She was a hard and loyal worker and I loved her from the first day we met.

"Not too bad, Jimmy. You know how Thursdays are. How was school?"

"It was uneventful, which is exactly how I like it. I have some homework, but if it's dead in here later I can always work on it."

"You must be getting excited with graduation creeping up," Stella said flashing a warm smile.

"I guess I am. I don't know, it doesn't feel real yet. Maybe it would be different if I was going to travel the world or move to a completely different State. But to me, it just feels like I'm going to school in the fall. Only this one will be like a boarding school that I get to come home for on weekends," I said with a shrug.

"Don't worry about that too much. It will feel more real once you are living in the dorms. Then, in your second year, you'll be getting your own place. It'll sink in once you're there and taking classes."

That sounded about right. I wasn't the type of person who got excited to begin with, really. Of course, I was looking forward to it, but I wasn't jumping up and down with excitement.

Before anymore could be said, the little bell above the door chimed and we both looked up, expecting to be greeting a customer. Instead, we saw our new manager walking in.

We had been told a few days ago that we would be getting a new night manager. Stella had been offered the job, but she liked being a server. She liked the lack of responsibility more than anything. She said she had enough going on with raising a teenager; she didn't need more of a headache. She was open to the idea at a later time, though, when her daughter was off to College herself.

I had been prepared for the new manager to be someone like the old manager, Mr. Wilson, older and not really attractive. This man, though, he was nothing like I was expecting.

He had short brown hair; much like myself only mine was blonde. He had a clear five o'clock shadow that he had no interest in trying to get rid of, which was fine by me. I liked a man that looked a bit rough. He was well built, like he spent some time working out at the gym in his day, but he wasn't so muscular that it was the only thing he did in the day. He walked with his head held up high and his back straight.

He didn't appear to be nervous at all for someone starting a new job. He glanced over at us and I felt a quick, warm shot of arousal at seeing his emerald green eyes. It was only for a moment before he was heading into the back, but I could have sworn he had mesmerized me with them. I couldn't take my eyes off of him, even after he had disappeared into the kitchen area. My gaze lingered on the door, hoping he would come back out.

"Earth to Jimmy, come back, you're drooling," Stella teased.

"I don't drool," I said, feeling my cheeks warm as I forced myself to look back over to her.

That granted me a chuckle. "Man, if I knew the new manager was going to look like that, I would have worn tighter pants." Stella winked.

"I think I should have worn looser ones," I joked back. But in all honesty, getting a hard-on at work was not a good idea. Thankfully, I had a server's apron on that would hide any issues should something get out of control. And by something, I mean my imagination. Hey, I was an artist; I had a remarkable imagination.

One that had gotten me through many lonely nights.

"You're so bad. What do you think, straight or gay?"

"You know, most people worry if their new boss is going to be a dick or not. Not what team they play for," I said with a playful smirk as I leaned my left side against the counter. I was not going to admit out loud that I was wondering the exact same thing.

And praying it was the latter.

"I doubt he's a dick. He doesn't look old enough to be a dick. He's like twenty, maybe twenty-one. And I'm allowed to wonder all I want. I'm just not allowed to ask. I'm going with straight, though. He's got that straight boy look."

"Can't argue with that. He's very pretty, though."

He was most likely straight. Odds were in his favor for being straight, but that didn't mean I couldn't window shop to my heart's content. I didn't have much time to ponder my new boss, because a table of four teenagers walked through the door. I went back to focusing on my work. Whatever was going to happen with our new manager would happen regardless of what I wanted. For now, I would wait until I would get to be introduced.

***

It was a good two hours later when I had a moment to catch my breath. The dinner rush had come through and it was always busy for a few hours before everyone started to head out for home. Then only a few stragglers would come in for a late dessert or a coffee before they got back on the road. While I was in the middle of filling the napkin dispensers once again, Mr. Wilson made his way out of the kitchen with the new manager.

"Jimmy, meet our new night manager, Zane Hamilton," Mr. Wilson said.

Zane.

The name suited him. Strong, masculine, but unique. It wasn't a name you heard every day in your life. Seeing Zane up close like this only allowed me to realize that he looked even more sexy up close and personal than he did from a distance.

His eyes were to die for. I had never seen eyes this green before. He had a strong jaw and chiseled facial features that gave him a model like look. He was truly breath-stealing to look at up close. This man was a heartbreaker and I had no doubt that he would have a trail of hopeful lovers behind him.

I sighed inwardly, knowing working for this sexy-as-sin man would be a challenge of the worst kind on my active imagination.

"Hi, it's nice to meet you, Sir," I said, trying to remember that this was my boss and I needed to be polite and friendly. I was leaving for College come the fall, but I needed this job to make sure I could have enough saved up until I found a job up there.

"Call me Zane, please." His voice held a slight gravelly tone to it, but it wasn't from something like smoking. It was completely natural and it sent a shiver right down my spine.

"Well, it's nice to meet you, Zane. I'm sure you will love working here, the customers are great and the other employees are really friendly. If you have any questions, don't be afraid to ask."

God, yes, please ask me anything you want.

I would love to talk with him for my whole shift. Anything that would allow me to get close to him. I bet he smelled amazing.

"Thank you, I appreciate that. I'm sure I will love working here."

I knew *I* was going to love him working here. This job just got so much better. I couldn't stand around and talk, though, because I had a new table come in and the last thing I wanted to do was leave a bad impression on my new boss.

I sighed, made my excuses, and quickly headed back to work, waving goodbye to Mr. Wilson as he headed out. I did my best to focus on my work, but I could feel eyes on me. Zane's eyes. I knew it without even having to look at him.

I didn't have a problem being watched. I mean, it's common when you get a new boss. A good manager would always look around, check out how you work and what habits you had, or even what routine there already was in place. So Zane watching me throughout my shift wasn't that out of the norm.

The thing was, though, he wasn't looking at me like he was evaluating my skills. He was just following me around with his eyes. It was a little awkward and it left me feeling a bit weirded out by it. That was, until I saw just the slightest glimmer of what could only be described as lust in his eyes when I bent over the table to wipe the far end of it. I looked up just in time for him to snap his eyes away and look over at another customer.

Oh my god!

Is he checking me out?

That couldn't be right, right?

There was no way that he would be checking me out. Even if he was interested in guys, why would he be interested in someone like me? I couldn't be his type. As badly as I wished I was his type. Guys like him wouldn't go for the artistic type like me. I had enough experience in my dating life to know that.

Still, though, the thought of him checking me out didn't leave me feeling awkward or creeped out. It left me feeling a tingle of excitement. I knew nothing could come from it and I was perfectly okay with that.

One thing I did know, work was going to be so much more enjoyable.

For more of Shattered, From The Edge, Book One, check out your favorite online retailer!

OTHER BOOKS BY EVIE

Federal Protection Agency
Mason
Rafe
Ryzen
Cooper
Noah
Damien
Sebastian
Gabe
Logan

Ruthless Empire
Courting Danger
Chasing Danger
Kissing Danger

Smokejumpers
Hawke
Cyrus
Jase
Gage
Jackson
Xavier

Jasper Springs
Cade
Dawson
Drew
Grayson
Riley
Mitch

From The Edge
Shattered
Runaway
Jaded
Rescue
Hidden
Tormented

Gray Vale Pack
His Fated Mate
His Wounded Warrior
His Healing Heart

ABOUT THE AUTHOR

Evie Riley is a prolific, neurodivergent author known for her captivating MM romance novels. She has gained a significant following and topped the LGBT+ action and adventure bestseller charts with her series.

Evie's writing style often explores dark and gritty themes where her men must overcome difficult obstacles in their search for love, but she has also ventured into sweeter small-town romances, incorporating tropes like enemies-to-lovers, friends-to-lovers, age-gap, and forced proximity. She is known for crafting engaging romantic suspense novels and has a knack for creating interconnected series worlds that keep readers invested.

Interestingly, Ms. Riley has hinted at exploring new genres, such as Alien Omegaverse Romance, in the future.

Outside of writing, she enjoys spending time at the beach and has a quirky personality, described by her partner as ranging from cute to deadly, depending on her blood-chocolate levels.

Evie spends her nights writing bad boys in love, and her days wrangling the sweet boys she loves.